A PORTION
PRAIS.

"**Similarities in artistic styles to** that of author **Dan Brown and American film director Quentin Tarantino**"

— *READER VIEWS* BRONZE AWARD

"Notwithstanding the apparent **comparisons to (Stephen) King, (Dan) Brown , and yes, even Dante**, Lloyd Jeffries' *A Portion of Malice* is a **must-read...masterfully written**."

— LEX A., *READERS' FAVORITE* 5 STAR

"**Startling**...will leave readers **stunned**...robust, **provocative**, and soulful...a great read. It's **fresh, bold, and entertaining**."

— *LITERARY TITAN* GOLD AWARD

"Author Lloyd Jeffries offers **beautiful** and **painful descriptions**...making a **fascinating cast** of villains."

"**Excellent** plot that holds the reader's attention on every page. **I can't wait for the next in the series**."

"This **devastating** novel **confronts and provokes** readers... pace is **riveting**...touches a chord and produces a **palpable**, chilling effect."

"Looking for **action-packed** scenes that are surprisingly **thought-provoking** in the outcomes will find *A Portion of Malice* **simply outstanding**."

"**The perfect story**...**had me biting my nails and holding my breath**...pace was addictive...finished this story in a single sitting...**I cannot recommend it enough**."

"Jeffries has a **masterful prose** style...an alluring blend of fantasy, mystery, and history...deeply philosophical...**freshly entertaining**."

A Portion of Malice

Ages of Malice, Book I

Lloyd Jeffries

Library of Congress Control Number: 2022904712
ISBN 979-8-9855269-1-2 (Print)
ISBN 979-8-9855269-0-5 (eBook)
ISBN 979-8-9855269-2-9 (Hardcover)

Cover design and illustration by Jerry Todd
Inkslinger Editing
For permissions, contact
Buckminster Publishing
Info@lloydjeffries.com

This is a work of fiction. Names, characters, places, and incidents either are the
product of the author's imagination or are used fictitiously. Any resemblance to actual
persons, living or dead, events, or locales is entirely coincidental.

For Dana

Thoughts from the Verge

By: Emery Merrick

Consider this backstory. The first volume in a multi-volume epic spanning time, history, Heaven, Hell, and the apocalypse.

This is the story of a simple man mixed up in things about which he should never know.

And I never dreamed I'd be writing this, shouldn't be alive to write this.

Alas, though, fate is a tortured mistress.

I've tried to capture everything as it truly happened and although religion plays a central role, this isn't a story about religion.

No one will try to save your soul. There are no heart-warming points about a loving God who shepherds humanity to a waiting paradise.

In fact, I could write volumes that debunk that myth once and for all.

Ah, but what's the point?

Believe what you want, live how you want, open your mind to the universe, and consider this volume the first steps down a road both twisted and complex.

In the end, you'll find we've just begun.

But we'll get to that.

To all, be well and happy, blessed by whichever God you choose and in whatever way He or She doles those boons. May my story be a warning—a subtle nudge, a singular wink—about all we take for granted, and the very small pond in which we swim.

Regards,
Emery

PROLOGUE

Jerusalem, Time of Christ

B ribes paid, Cain kneels before the bleeding Messiah.

Blood drips from His nose, trickles down His face. Skin, bruised; cheeks, bloated; lips cracked and dry. His eyes are swollen shut.

Cain prostrates himself, lies flat on the sand, squeezes the cool earth.

Tears start as memories invade.

Castaway.

Heretic.

Murderer.

"I beg Thee, Lord, forgive my sins and make me whole. I've labored through all these lives paying penance, seeking only Your embrace. Heal me. Take me in. I beg Thee."

Jesus raises his head, those ghastly eyes glued closed with dried blood. He tries to stand, but rough twine holds him to a thick plank. He strains at His bonds. "Have I not been once tested by you?" His voice is parched, cracks like dry leaves ripe with flame. "Hast thou come to mock me in my time?"

"Nay Lord. I seek redemption. I seek forgiveness."

"You are dark to me."

Cain presses his head to the sand, stretches his arms in penance.

A hushed breeze rustles the trees; flowers brighten the courtyard—lively blue, bitter orange, buttered yellow.

"A vagabond and wanderer are you," Jesus rasps, strains for breath. "Condemned. A fugitive and vagabond, so sayeth the Father."

Cain lifts his head, spreads sand with each syllable. "Nay, Lord, Nay! I wish only to walk with You once more. To flee this miserable existence and be again welcome in Your arms."

The breeze shifts, stifles, comes from the arid south instead of the sea.

Sunlight burns his skin, bakes the bushes.

Sweat appears, mixes with sand to clump on Cain's forehead. "My Lord, I beg thee. My works are pure. My intent, honest. Please release me so I might serve."

The Savior's head droops like a parched flower. A gash beneath his eye reopens, blood trickles to drip in a pool at his feet.

He whispers, voice crackling, blood oozing through His beard, over His lips, drop by drop. "*You* shall endure."

Cain's head drops to the sand, salty tears drip. "Please, Lord. Please. I beg only mercy. Only release."

Jesus' voice rises. A whistling wind through mountain caverns, a raging tempest like millions of insects, swarming, devouring. The Messiah's breath is ragged and wet. He inhales, then heaves His rage.

"You! Endure!"

Cain shudders, stretched hands curl to fists.

It can't be, not after all these centuries.

His mind fills with fields plowed; with enemies thrown down. With all the lives he's lived; all the lives *yet* to live.

Redemption flows away, disappears into the barren desert so precious to God.

He trembles, rises on shaky legs, stares at the Messiah.

Beyond, the sky turns ominous, looms like a spiteful God shaking His fist. Tree and flower become a dizzy array of color and leaf.

Visions enter.

Fiery pillars rend, consume, melting earth, boiling oceans.

Azure skies turn fetid, drip mucous from black clouds and scorched wind.

Humanity screams, pleads, begs God's mercy.

Then an angry God, chuckling in thunder, defiant, even joyous.

God prefers blood.

Cain turns as both tree and flower wither and wilt.

Rain starts, wind rushes.

He blinks into the gale, glances at his hand to find a whip with nine tails, iron shards sewn into its braids.

His voice is calm, even. "What price for salvation?"

The Messiah lolls, says nothing.

"What price?" he asks again.

The whip cracks, leaps for the Messiah's back.

Jesus wails as the nine make purchase, shred flesh like silk.

Rage fills, consumes.

This is freedom.

This is redemption.

Bloody plumes rise, become a hovering, ghostly cloud as nine tails fly forward.

The Messiah shrieks like a crimson ghost, rages against biting bonds, eyes squeezed, blood dripping.

"What price for salvation?" Cain asks with each lash. "What price! WHAT PRICE!"

Blood spatters shy flowers, stone walls.

Trees tremble.

The sky belches thunderous applause.

His arm becomes a blur, whip chasing, starved for blood, famished for flesh.

He twists his hips with each blow, soul raging, overflowing.

Hope turns to vapor.

Redemption to rage.

3

Despair bubbles to blistering animus as he tries to inflict maximum damage, tries to shred the most flesh.

"WHAT PRICE FOR SALVATION!"

Tears pour down his face, mix with blood and sand to drift away on harsh winds.

Spit dangles in thick ropes, eyes fill with fire.

The endless voice of God mutes to feral agony. He bucks, shrieks, blood flowing from head and torso, the plank clatters, trembles.

Trees bend, then snap.

Flowers cower, quake, hide from bloody mist as petals turn brown and die.

Then, with the harshness of a slap, a sharp sting on his face.

One of the nine has sliced his cheek.

Salty tears sting him to reason.

He stands panting, arms aching, whip dripping.

He trembles in place, stares at the bleeding God, watches a bloody torso rise and fall with each breath.

Thunder runs away.

Wind dies.

Rain ceases.

Silence invades.

Then, barely audible, comes the Savior's rasped voice.

Cain leans in, listens to wheezed words, endlessly repeated:

"You shall endure. You shall endure. You shall endure."

Tears stop, centuries of guilt drain from his soul.

The world feels sinister and beyond redemption.

He closes his eyes; hypnotized, breathless, dripping sweat and blood.

"You shall endure. You shall endure. You shall endure."

His portion of malice grows.

He raises the nine-tail whip and starts anew.

CHAPTER 1

DUBAI, UNITED ARAB EMIRATES

I hit the record button on my iPhone, then stare at him. I sit in a comfortable, high-back chair of red leather, coffee mug steaming next to me. I write in a small notebook as my mind fills with questions. In the end, I say only, "Well, that's a bunch of bullshit."

This coaxes him from his thoughts, and he focuses all at once onto me. Long seconds pass until he speaks. "Yes," he says, "quite unbelievable, but every word true."

"So, *you*, personally, whipped Jesus Christ with a cat of nine tails?"

"Yes."

"Because He wouldn't forgive you?"

"Yes."

I lean forward, elbows on my knees. "You do know that Jesus is kind of known for His forgiveness—i.e. *Forgive them Father they know not what they do.*"

"I do. I actually heard Him say those very words."

"So, you're the one guy in recorded history whose sins are so vast they can't be forgiven?"

He shakes his head, strokes his temple with a gloved hand. "Oh no, there are others."

"You mean Hitler and the like?"

"No, I mean a few of us who are completely forsaken by God. I know only of four; the Roman, the Jew, the Apostle, and myself. If there were others, I'm certain I'd know because I can see them."

"You mean like ghosts or vampires?"

"Don't be a fool," he laughs. "I mean living breathing immortals. Forsaken by God. Doomed to endure. They emit a green aura only I can see. They appear quite normal to mortals such as yourself."

I shake my head. "Doesn't make sense, immortals forsaken by God? For what reason?"

Drake, now with pencil in hand, doodles on a yellow legal pad on the right side of his desk. "Some think for our crimes, but I don't see it that way. I believe God plans for us to take control of this realm."

I pull the mug to my lips and consider this. *The Dove's a nut job,* I write. *Great, just what I deserve.*

"God's retiring?" I ask.

A flare of anger crosses his face.

I push on. Many times, if you can get a subject angry you can get them to reveal much more than intended. "So, the heavenly retirement plan is a few thousand years, then God finds a suitable substitute and moves to Tampa?"

Drake drops the pen, stands, adjusts his tie. Then, placing his hands on the desk, leans over it and smiles. I'm surprised by the gleaming crease, for in it I feel comforted, feel as if this man couldn't *possibly* lie to me. I feel—no, I *know*—in my heart of hearts this man has my best interest in mind. Questions vanish, my doubt floats away. My expression must change because I see the realization of something on Drake's face.

"You've put me under a spell," I say. Then I peer inside my mug for signs of chemical additives. "I feel subdued and content, a little euphoric." It's been a long time since I've felt any one of those sensations, and they strike me as glaring now, a definite departure from the norm.

"One of my gifts," Drake says. "You see, I received the gifts of charisma and diplomacy from a source I shall not mention at this point. These gifts have served me well and afforded me certain advantages throughout my long existence. For now, though, suffice it to say all I tell you is true and that, yes, one can say I lost my cool a little when the Messiah rebuffed me—"

"About two-thousand years ago?"

He's unperturbed at the interruption. "Yes."

"To control Earth?"

"In a way, yes."

"What way?"

He resumes his seat. "We'll get to that. It's a long story and I'll tell you all of it. But for now, let's say that we immortals will rule Earth and all who live here."

"Nonsense. How could anyone possibly do that?"

"You'll see. It's the reason I hired you."

I roll my eyes. "Okay, but maybe you can tell me why you and your immortals are the chosen ones?"

He doesn't miss a beat. "I murdered my brother."

I consider this for a moment, can't hide my skepticism. I picture the next words in my mind as if writing them and take an extra beat of pause for each comma and period: "With over four hundred thousand murders per year, with many killing a family member, you've been singled out, by God, for murdering your brother. More than two thousand years ago." I look him right in the eye, shake my head. "Sounds like bullshit."

Drake crosses the room. Past pedestals with marble busts of Beethoven and Caesar set beneath well-aged paintings, certainly priceless, both busts and tableaux. Around exquisite couch and chairs pilfered from a Louis XIV living room, maybe *the* Louis XIV. To finally a view from enormous windows that overlook the expanse of Dubai. He stares for a long time as I sip my coffee. Silence hangs between us and I consider stopping my phone recording to save the battery.

I empty the mug and stand to leave.

"My name is Cain," he says. "I'm cast out for killing my brother Abel."

I freeze, almost drop my phone. Drake turns from the view and looks surprised at my expression. My thoughts go back to the Sunday school lessons forced on me as a child. Cain. Killer of Abel. Cast out by God. The world's first murderer. Then it hits me.

Wearer of the mark.

I speak a little too loud when I say, "Where's your mark, Cain?"

He takes a step toward me and stops. Maybe it's the light or the contrast between Dubai's bright sun and the darkness of the room, but, in that haze, he looks like a kicked puppy. He raises his right hand, trademark gloves in place as they always are with this man. Then, in a single motion, removes the glove.

I'm engulfed with red light.

My skin tingles, then pins and needles erupt—even my eyebrows stand on end. I feel depressed, repressed, feel like dropping to my knees from the effort of standing. Sight deserts me, enveloped and encased by this all-consuming crimson. I feel like I'm having a panic attack. My breath runs from me and is hard to catch. My limbs crackle with small currents of electricity. I can't tell my position in space: standing, sitting, spinning? Time itself dematerializes and I float, terrified and breathless, awash in this malicious light.

Then it vanishes.

He stands by the window, glove now back on his right hand, small tendrils of white smoke rising to the ceiling.

Startled, I check my surroundings. The same chair now holds me, on the table next to me the mug sits on its side. My phone's untouched. The busts, all in place. No art hangs askew on the wall. Dubai's bright sun streams through the window.

I stifle nausea, lean forward, try to collect my senses.

"Wha…What in…the hell…was that?" I'm reeling. My chest feels heavy. My limbs, wired to an electrical grid, charged and tingling. I stop, will myself to breathe. After a few seconds, I manage to raise my head, see Drake by the window standing impassive like a Greek statue.

"You wanted to see my mark," he says. "More coffee?"

CHAPTER 2

DUBAI, UNITED ARAB EMIRATES

I've never been in the Burj Khalifa. Never even set foot in Dubai, or the Middle East for that matter. My journey to this place is pretty run of the mill. An American dream gone bad.

I won my first Pulitzer at the age of thirty and then another at thirty-five-ish. I say -*ish* because I'm not sure what year it was when I won that. I'd been on a bender of drugs and alcohol and didn't care much about anything, least of all time or prizes. My life should've been easy after that second Pulitzer, coasting on reputation. But my darker side had other plans. In short, I bought off on my own legend— that I was gifted and everything I wrote, a masterpiece.

I found the bottle, and it became medicine. The drugs followed and became medicine, too. The wife left, and I was eventually invited to leave my post at the *Times*. Money dried up. Friends faded, and in short order I was the guy at the bar with all the stories and none of the money. Then came the shabby apartment at two-fifty a month in a crappy little town in upstate New York, Ramen noodles most nights, I'm sure you know the rest. It's not that uncommon of a tale.

On to the night I press a pistol to my temple. I remember chuckling, high as Heaven, as I push its bluntness against my skin.

Relief. My time was over and nothing that lay ahead could be worse. Rock bottom, they call it. I squeezed the trigger by increments, savored the release, not afraid at all. Then a knock at the door, ill-timed to say the least, and I remember thinking: Might be *Publisher's Clearing House.*

Flash forward a couple days and here I am, across from one of the most revered and influential men in history. *The Dove,* the press calls him, a reference to his astonishing skill at making peace in war-torn regions.

My research before choosing to come—as if *that* had been a choice —had yielded almost one hundred percent positive results. Thaddeus Drake, international peacemaker. A well-heeled gentleman by all accounts who lives a life of casual luxury. For some decades now, Drake has been a central figure on the world stage, appearing in areas wracked by war and somehow creating peace from chaos. In fact, he's so talented in this aspect, his name has become synonymous with the word *peace.*

It's also well-known Drake holds the ear of numerous world leaders, and I find considerable documentation and photos of him with some of the most famous people of our generation. It's odd, but Drake never goes in for political dogma, offering his services to dictators and presidents, communists and religious icons alike. He seems to put little thought into who he's helping, but his results are always extraordinary.

One thing though, my research reveals no reason for the gloves or why he always wears them. There are, of course, many theories: a childhood accident, a skin condition, even an article about how his hands are actually alien and not human. Drake's silence and refusal to answer the question eventually wins the day, and mentions of the gloves gradually fade until all the world just accepts the fact that the Dove will always appear with his gloves securely in place.

When this gloved man showed me his mark, his hand appeared normal. And by that, I mean, not disfigured or alien. The mark itself is certainly abnormal, but perhaps that's the answer, Drake hides his mark, the mark of Cain, so unbelievable and distinctive that if a journalist ever sees it, it would become an instant sensation. And if that's fact, then what Drake says must also be true. Thaddeus Drake, formerly Cain, killer of Abel, now a peacemaker among mortals.

So here I sit, staring at the gloved hero beloved of all, stricken with a feeling of dread and fear. He's lit a cigarette and smoke rings his head in lazy coils like a demon's halo. I press the mug to my lips and remember it's empty. I wonder if I've been drugged. This hasn't been a typical morning.

I check my phone. RECORDING. I wait for Drake to speak.

The smoke-plumed king adjusts some papers on the desk he's returned to. Slides some pencils to his left and arranges them in a neat line of three. He looks at me under his eyebrows, adjusts his cufflinks.

"Now, shall we begin?" he says. "Where to start?" Exhaled smoke punctuates his speech. "Have you a pad?"

"Yes, and I also record," I say, nodding at my iPhone.

"Very well, then let's begin. Or I guess we have begun." He straightens as if rising, though he hasn't yet sat, and moves toward the bar, a dark mahogany slab with a few bottles of liquor. Ice clinks into a glass and I hear the liquid mix with it.

"I'm not a very good storyteller, I'm afraid," he says, turns toward me. "But now you know where the tale starts. Amended, of course. There are centuries of tales prior to that, but the day I whipped Christ was a singular turning point. Caesar's Rubicon, yes? I suppose in my rage I knew that even then."

"Then why'd you do it?" I ask. "Why not walk away?"

"Have you ever had truly nothing to lose and only a single speck of light on the horizon?"

"I have nothing to lose now." The words pierce like the crimson light. I feel the stab of my ultimate loss. With considerable will, I force the pain inward and out of my mind.

"Indeed, dear Emery. So you can relate. Longinus tells me he found you with a pistol pressed to your head. Was that your solution?"

I stifle my reaction. When the giant man knocked on my door, I'd stuffed the Sig under a couch cushion before answering. There's no way he could've known I was a finger twitch from oblivion. My mind tries to grasp it, how could they know? Unless…

"You guys were watching me?"

Drake sits, leans back and chuckles. "Of course, dear Emery. Your task is far too important to leave to just anyone. Did you not think it odd Longinus appeared at exactly the right moment?"

"Now that you mention it." God, I've been naïve. The Dove's a little more sordid than I imagined. "I was making a tape when he interrupted. Where is it?"

He drags on his cigarette. "It's safe," he says, "and available if you should like to have it."

The thought hits me again, my heart swells, bleeds in my chest. "Not right now," I say quickly. The idea of listening to my suicide note holds no temptation. "Too fresh. I need some time."

He holds my eyes for a few seconds, and I hope they don't betray my emotions. "Of course, dear Emery. As expected." His glance is a mixture of joy and pity. Striking because it's so misplaced. "Shall we go on?" he asks. I nod.

He snuffs the cigarette in a silver, ancient-looking ashtray. "I was in the same place as you when Christ refused my redemption. Lost. Adrift." He stares into the air. "Angry. Hopeless. When I was denied, I…well…snapped, as the kids say." He's smiling now, beaming even. "It was then I became free. *Everything* changed. I was born again, you might say. After centuries of solitude, centuries of wanting only to be with God once again, centuries of trying to make amends, seeking redemption, doing everything I could to gain His approval, it became crystal clear I was chasing the wrong thing. Know this, my dear Emery, God is not a redeemer. He's a butcher."

Standing now—when did he stand?—he places his hands on his hips. "My freedom came with that realization. God prefers blood. Never, ever forget that."

I digest the words, scribble them as reinforcement, as Drake thumbs a button on the small black phone on his desk. The line rings once then a female answers.

"My usual table, please," he says.

"Of course, Mr. Drake."

He pokes another button and the line dies. He looks at me. "Hungry?"

CHAPTER 3

DUBAI, UNITED ARAB EMIRATES

"I suppose a start would be to introduce the cast."

"Nice place," I say, a bit nonplussed at the room's display of luxury.

Drake glances around, eyes widen a fraction as if noticing for the first time. "Ah yes. It is nice, isn't it? A private little club for me and my associates."

We sit at a round table draped with an unblemished white tablecloth. Tall crystal glasses stand in formation before us as our food is presented on white plates. Fish for him, a marvelous steak for me. When mine arrives, I notice Drake grimace and suppress a gag.

"Is this not good?" I ask, nod at the meat.

"Excuse me, dear Emery, it's a personal matter. Please, enjoy."

He picks a gleaming silver fork from beside his plate and shaves off a bite of fish.

This man is a fashion model. A relic of style and class. His hair is perfect, perfect salt and pepper. Perfect as if someone has taken great pains to make it just the right blend of salt and pepper. His features are sharp—no, strike that—chiseled. Like a statue at a Roman bathhouse. Olive skin contrasts with dazzling teeth. The dark suit, the sublime white pinstripes, the necktie in gray with flecks of ice blue. All of this atop dazzling, brown monk-straps polished to a high gloss. The man reeks of wealth, yet no one can pinpoint from where the money comes.

The waiter fills his glass with Chataeuneuf-de-Pape.

He swirls the white liquid, then ventures a sip. He nods and the waiter tilts to fill our glasses. I cover mine with my hand. I'm trying to lay off the sauce. Trying to stay sober for just a few days. It's what she would've wanted. The waiter picks the glass from the table and disappears into the restaurant.

"Recovery," I say, a bit embarrassed.

"Of course," Drake says, dabs the corners of his mouth with his napkin. He sizes me up for a few seconds, then places the napkin on his lap.

"I will show you wonders, dear Emery. My tale is quite unbelievable, especially in these days of instant news and universal sharing." He smooths his suit, looks out the windows at Dubai's expanse. From the 128th floor, the view is spectacular. The Burj, easily the tallest building around, presides over a tapestry of steel and concrete and glass. A blue sky stretches over the limitless cobalt of the Persian Gulf. Dubai gleams like the Earth's crown jewel.

"You must know a few things before we start." He nips another bite, then cuts a French green bean with his fork. "First, everything I tell you is completely true. These events actually happened, as unbelievable as they'll sound."

I nod and sip my water, try not to stare at the wine.

"Do you have sources?" I ask.

Drake laughs. "Hardly," he says. "Anyone that could be a source is dead already."

"Already?" I ask. "As in they'd still be alive if it wasn't for you?"

Drake smiles again. "Come now," he says. "I can't be responsible for millions of deaths already done and the millions more to come." Dark eyes hold my gaze as if waiting for a reaction.

"Millions?" I say. "I'm afraid I'm going to need a source. I mean, can you...are we talking about murder here? Hitler shit?" My eyes shift to the wine again. "Genocide?"

Drake pulls a cigarette. A waiter appears from nowhere to light it.

He draws, then emits a stream of smoke. "In some cases, I suppose genocide is an apt term. In others, I'd say God made His play and *He* actually committed the atrocity. As for Hitler, I admit at having something to do with that, but I assure you it was all for a greater plan." Steepled fingers press against his lips as he chooses his next words. "A more noble intent, let's say."

Oh, yes, let's say. I start to write in my notebook as I exhale the words, "Genocide as noble."

Drake laughs at the pantomime. "Yes, I understand." He shakes his head. "Genocide as noble. Dear Emery, I believe you'll understand more as I tell the tale. I believe you'll see things from my perspective after all is revealed."

I sigh. "Okay, what else?"

"Second, any attempt by you to interfere, intervene, change details, alert authorities, etcetera, will be taken as an act of aggression and instead of being paid the vast sum agreed on, you will inherit misery and death."

I can't stifle my laugh. "You're threatening me?" I say the words as I write them: "This Dove has fangs!"

Drake glances at the Omega on his wrist, adjusts the glove on each hand as he stares at me.

It becomes unsettling after a bit. His face is expressionless, his dark eyes seem to hold a deeper knowledge. The look someone gives when trying to impart a great gift on another, only to realize the other person has no idea the gift's value or the great service they've been done.

I close the notebook and clear my expression. This may be *my* personal shot at redemption, at getting some semblance of my life back. I can't help but hope past the pain and the near-death experience of the Sig pushed to my temple. "Um…okay…," I say. "Well, a good journalist never becomes the story." I search his features for approval.

He regards me for a few seconds more. "Established." He goes on. "Third, you shall be granted access to wondrous things. My people will be available for interviews as well."

"But what about—"

He silences me with a raised finger. "Fourth," he says. "You will record everything exactly as it happens. Without spin or opinion or commentary. Leave nothing out and record accurately."

I'm put off by his stare. Dark eyes now glisten with malice and, somehow, loss. I open my mouth, but the stare stops me. I glance at the wine, then take a long draft of my water.

"And if I want out?" I ask.

His expression becomes one of pity, like watching a poor sap on the street.

"Be careful what you wish for."

I stare for a long moment, then slide a bite of steak in my mouth. It's amazing and melts away, leaves only buttery flavors and tenderness.

I haven't had a decent meal in a while, certainly not a great steak and certainly not in a lavish environment. My reaction is gauged by Drake, whose grin tells me he finds it amusing. I rein myself in, tempted to tear the meat apart in seconds. Drake allows me to finish in silence, watching as I savor every single bite.

Soon I relax against the back of my chair, sated. The table's cleared by the staff with attention given to every crumb. Then, white porcelain cups appear and are filled with coffee. I raise it to my nose, savor the smell.

"Shall we start with the cast?"

"Alright," I say.

"Fine, let's see, I suppose the Jew should be the first."

"Jew?"

"Yes, Igneus. A mousy, little man with a frail heart and weak constitution. What he lacks physically, he makes up for in other ways. He's been vital to my plans."

"Which are?"

Drake sips his wine. "In good time." He pauses to allow the ever-present waiter to light another cigarette for him. "As with the others, I first met Igneus around the time of Jesus' crucifixion. He was quite put off by the whole affair, and I only saw him from a distance. It was then I first heard the voice."

He pauses, his eyes lose intensity, become unfocused as if reaching through time for some memory. He reaches for his wine as a waiter appears with a dessert tray. He waves it away without a glance.

"A voice? Who?"

"All in good time," he says.

My inner skeptic speaks. "Again, I must call bullshit. You're telling me you witnessed an immortal being born? During the crucifixion? And some magical voice was speaking to you? And all that happened centuries ago, based solely on the biblical timeline, which would make you about six thousand years old?"

"You should believe the biblical timeline, and yes, I am."

"Doesn't add up."

Drake chuckles. "I'm certain." His smile causes me to squirm a bit. "Please be patient and know I remain cast out, even after all these events."

I shake my head and stare at the vista before us. The Persian Gulf blooms beneath a burning sun. Past the horizon is the Levant Landscape. The land of prophets. The land of God. With a sigh, I relent. "Okay then, we'll come back to that. It'll give me some time to think it over. Back to the Jew, if you don't mind."

"As you wish," the Dove says. "I bore witness as Jesus carried his cross…"

CHAPTER 4

JERUSALEM, DURING THE CRUCIFIXION

B ent trees rise, crooked and parched, even as probing roots sniff precious moisture from barren land. New growth, long since scorched away, leaves the harsh sun to sear mankind's stench and greed and jealousy into the Earth's core.

Cain pushes through the heated, stinking bodies, marvels at their bloodlust, at buildings that appear vacant and merciless. Compassion does not dwell here. Indeed, has a compassionate man ever tread this soil?

As the macabre pageant begins, the Earth is subdued. No birds soar in the beauty of the blue sky. No creatures rustle on thick branch, no sound emanates from the fields. The day is windless, hot, covered by a palpable, if sheer, haze.

They know not what they do.

Venomous cries fill the air to combine with the reek of the human herd. They stare wild eyed, lips trembling, laughing, mocking. Today they'll murder their salvation. Today they'll assure their barbarity lasts the age and defines mankind's very existence. They are joyless, petty, know neither loyalty nor love. Creatures that withhold mercy and mete out sacrifice. Who overflow with self and are bereft of goodness.

He will die for them.

The Man struggles the cross through Jerusalem's stone streets. Those in the crowd abuse and mock. At this moment, as the Man limps and struggles, Cain feels only sadness. Some small part of him remains that mourns the loss of man's redemption; a part that suffers with mankind even as they lead the Messiah to His slaughter. What price shall they pay for these sins? What penalty for this crime? He feels powerful, as if he's brought all this to pass by murdering his brother. He shakes his head like a dog sloughing off drenching rain. No time for these thoughts. God has His plan and so do I. And I am satisfied.

When the nine-tailed cat laid the Messiah's back bare, he found his redemption. His freedom. His own personal turn of mercy. Emotions of self are gone: remorse, pity, joy, anger, grace. Replaced by profound hatred and an immense feeling of relief. Like a man exhausted after having born a heavy burden for far too long, the relief of being unbridled, of biting chains cast off. He feels free and, even as he pities the actions of man today, he relishes the thought of God's death.

"I will go on." He knows that certainty now, but it inspires neither fear nor hope. His punishment is nothing more than existence, and if he must go on, he will endure. He will not, however, beg. Never again will he prostrate himself before his creator. Never again will he ask forgiveness, nor bear witness to a Messiah or a heavenly God.

The slashes delivered have cleansed him, relieved him from the worry of goodness, each lash slicing another bond. Not forgiven, not redeemed, but somehow free and eternal.

So sayeth the Father.

The Man carries His cross. The timber is heavy, the Man exhausted. Every step brings some new barbarity, yet the Man moves forward blood flowing from open wounds.

Cain doesn't admire Him and watches only with curiosity. Will these stinking, stupid people actually murder their Messiah? Have they the capacity to condemn themselves for all eternity? Are they so blinded by their need for blood they can't see the truth? They, savages, their stench equaled only by their viciousness, made in God's image, preferring blood.

Cain fights nausea, looks over the gathered mass steaming like excrement beneath a burning sun. They deserve all they get from a vengeful God; deserve it more than any crime Cain ever committed.

The crowd moves forward, laughs and mocks. Cain moves with them, staying to the periphery, watching. The Messiah drops the timber and looks to the sky. Sweat and blood mix to watery red lines on His face. He wipes His forehead, lowers His head, shoulders slumped, chest heaving, mouth open.

A man steps from the crowd. Fine silk robes hang from an emaciated frame. He squints at the Messiah through sallow features, face without expression, eyes locked.

A thin hand rises and he slaps Jesus' face, sends a shower of fresh blood into the crowd.

The crowd wails with glee as Cain spews a laugh despite his detachment. The skinny Jew stands defiant before the Messiah. His bald scalp glimmers above a pointed nose. He stares at his blood-stained hand. His lower lip trembles, his body quivers beneath the lush fabric of his robes. He looks shocked, repulsed, eyes darting from Jesus to the crowd to the ground.

Jesus leans close, whispers something.

The frail man leaps as if struck with a whistling, birch switch. Legs flailing, he high steps away from the Messiah. Cain laughs as the dancing stick figure attempts to flee, wide-eyed, pushes into the crowd, then, rebuffed, sprints across the street. The effect is comic.

Then, an emerald aura surrounds his shadowed figure. Laughter clogs in Cain's throat.

Something there.

"Remember this," a voice says.

Cain jumps at the intrusion.

The voice continues: "Why would Jesus hurt this man but make no move to defend from your whip?"

The skinny man presses through the gathered throng. No one pays any heed. They've returned their attention to the bleeding criminal. Cain, however, watches the glowing figure, heeds the voice's words.

The frail man finally stops outside an alley. He jolts forward at the waist, then vomits in a single, chunky burst. He stands utterly still, sways a bit, then sprints between the buildings and is lost to Cain's sight.

Sweat runs over Cain's brow. He's thirsty, parched even. He scans the area for water, then takes in those around him. How odd no one noticed the spectacle of the glowing, green man.

Jesus plods toward the place of execution, leaves bloody footprints behind.

Cain looks over the crowd, is again assaulted by their congealed odors. He stifles a gag and moves with them to the Hill of the Skull, Golgotha.

My mouth hangs open like a Venus Flytrap and I can't close it. My mind fills with questions and, worst of all, I'm starting to believe this tale.

I force myself serious. Despite everything I'm still a journalist.

"So, the Jew steps up and gives Jesus a smack in the mouth?" I say. "Seems like that might've pissed Him off."

"Yes, unfortunately for poor Igneus, that was and is the case."

"And then he turned green?"

"Yes. An emerald aura. The first one I'd seen. I almost dismissed it as a trick of light."

"Will he be green for me?"

Drake shakes his head. "I'm afraid not. I'm the only one who can see this."

"You know that sounds incredibly Joseph Smith, right?"

"I'm not familiar…"

"Joseph Smith, the guy who received some magic plates from an angel that only he could read. He hid them in a hat and read them to someone who transcribed them. No one ever saw those things and he was like, *Just take my word for it or you'll piss off the angel and he'll come and kick all our butts.* Then he founded Mormonism."

"I have heard that, now that you mention it."

"And your thoughts?"

The check arrives in a fine, leather bifold.

"I have no thoughts on that," Drake says. "It is well beneath me."

He opens the bifold, and I can't help but lean forward to try and see what this meal cost. I can't make out the number or even most of the writing as it's in Arabic. But what strikes me is how the Dove signs it. Instead of a scrawled signature, he draws a neat X then superimposes a P over it. He snaps the bifold shut and places it on the table.

I sit back, a little disappointed but also curious as to the symbol.

"Religion is beneath you, or just Mormonism?" I ask.

"Religion, I suppose." He leans close. "Religion is a construct of man and therefore flawed. I have little time or patience for such foolishness. I have known, spoken to, and walked with the singular God. After that, *nothing* comes close. I can't enunciate it, and you, my friend, could never imagine it."

"The Dove isn't religious? Interesting."

"On the contrary, dear Emery, I am very religious. I use it to attain my goals."

"And how do you do that?"

He stands, nods at the waiter. We move past walls of shiny wood, beneath a grand and elegant chandelier, toward the exit.

"This is an epic story, Emery," he says. "All in good time."

CHAPTER 5

DUBAI, UNITED ARAB EMIRATES

The next morning, I meet Drake for breakfast, my skepticism unabated. Ah, how the mind of a mere mortal can't possibly fathom the timeline of which Drake speaks.

He appears in a fine gray suit. Ever the model, he gleams like his surroundings at the Burj. I take my first, glorious sip of coffee, anxious for the caffeine, for a jolt of energy to chase off the prior night's sleeplessness. Thoughts of *her* plague and consume, devour my heart in bits and nibbles.

"I apologize, dear Emery, but something's come up and I must leave immediately." He flashes that world-famous smile. "In the meantime, I'd like you to attend a meeting in Jerusalem. I've arranged your press credentials." He hands me a manilla envelope, large, perfectly clean. "It's of tantamount importance you attend as part of the press corps." Inside I find my press pass and airline tickets.

"*The Guard's Journal*," I say. "Never heard of it."

His teeth flash in glorious perfection. "Of course you haven't, dear Emery. It doesn't exist. It's just a name we use when we need press access." I upend the envelope to assure it's empty. "You see," he continues, "the persons attending the meeting are there for peace talks, and as you know, peace is my profession."

27

I giggle, remember a line scribbled on a wall outside a military base. "So, war is just a hobby?"

Drake's laugh is loud and long. "That's wonderful," he gives a single clap of gloved hands. "And apropos. Those attending are high level and will be discussing ways to find an amicable solution to the Arab-Israeli conflict. I'd like you to report on events. Mr. Slabav is the Prime Minister of Israel and probably the most reasonable and well-meaning of the bunch." He hands me a white envelope with EMERY scrawled across its front. "For expenses."

The envelope isn't sealed, and I peer inside. A stack of one-hundred-dollar bills. I purse my lips in a soundless whistle. "Should be ample."

"I believe you'll find your travels..." he pauses, searches for the right words, "slightly more comfortable than those to which you are accustomed. After the press meeting, please go to London. Longinus will collect you, and I'll join you both shortly after."

I nod, raise the coffee to my mouth. "Great. Longinus," I say, remembering the giant who'd knocked on my door.

"He's a tad, let's say, overpowering at first. He'll take good care of you. Finish your breakfast on my tab." He grasps my shoulder. "See you soon." Then turns and glides from the room.

Drake didn't lie, my accommodations are indeed more than those to which I'd become accustomed. The taxi arrives at the airport, then I'm ushered to a dark, SUV-type limousine, which carries me to a long, sleek Lear jet. I'm received by a gorgeous stewardess who's accommodating and professional. With every request comes a warm smile as she acquiesces to my every need.

I can't believe my good fortune. The terms of my contract, once completed, will assure my swift departure from the shitty apartment in Carter's Glen, New York. Indeed, the contract guarantees all future comforts and will ensure I spend the rest of my days in the luxury of my choosing. A bottle—or syringe, for that matter— soft sheets, big houses. I'll have few worries from a financial perspective. After all that's transpired, a dose of luxury sounds pretty good.

Now, as to Drake, or Cain, I'm still not entirely sure what he wants, but I'm excited to join the press again as a member, even if from a made-up news journal. A nice break from endless evenings full of liquor and venipuncture— nights spent with my old friends, depression and despair.

I'd spent the night prior babysitting my demons while researching the legend of Cain. The biblical version shows Cain as a cast out, marked by God, cursed such that nothing he tries to farm will flourish. Various commentaries by so-called experts state Cain was a farmer; his brother, Abel, a herdsman; and that Cain killed his brother in a fit of jealousy because God preferred Abel's sacrifice of flesh over Cain's sacrifice of harvest.

This strikes me as peculiar. First, we're talking about God, *The* God, the honcho, the big kahuna, the magic man with all the answers. Can God have human emotions like jealousy, anger or envy? Does God hunger? Does He mete out punishment? If so, am I being punished? The Gospel is rife with stories about God's anger, His wrath, His miracles, but assigning human flaws rings hollow.

Drake's words come back to me: *Never, ever forget, God prefers blood.*

Could this be a simple case of bruised ego for a slight that goes back centuries? An assumption by Cain that because God rejected his sacrifice, His preference runs to blood?

History is bloody, as I recall, an everlasting saga of human savagery. All available evidence supports a conclusion that God does, indeed, prefer blood. But perhaps Drake missed something. Perhaps God, if He exists, just doesn't care; He is completely and utterly detached. Plenty of evidence to back that, as well.

I watch the sky trail lazy clouds and contemplate such concepts as omnipotence and omniscience. If God knows everything, past, present and future, doesn't it stand to reason Drake stands zero chance of ever having his day of reckoning? That God will always be a step ahead?

Wouldn't Drake know these things if he'd actually walked and talked with God?

This is bullshit, I think, reliving the same sense I've had since the start. *Complete, Grade-A, undiluted bullshit, straight from the farm.*

But what of Cain's mark? I can't deny its existence, the staggering effect it had on me, washed in its horrible crimson. Had it been a trick? Had I been drugged? Something more elaborate? I mean, I was so overwhelmed I barely managed to keep my eyes open.

A chill runs through me. I never want to see the mark again, never want to feel that way again. The thing, whatever it is, is utter hopelessness, pure evil in growling scarlet.

The pretty stewardess appears with a pillow and blanket. I recline my seat.

Primary job, I think, *don't fuck it up. Write the biography, get paid. One-two-bee-boo.*

CHAPTER 6

JERUSALEM, ISRAEL

Laslo Slabav, Israel's Prime Minister, is in his early fifties with gray temples and a powerful jaw. He slides his hands under the table like a man determined to spare the rod, and thus, spoil the child. He burns to let loose, allows himself, perhaps a fit of arrogance, an exhale in a long, singular breath.

I sit on the room's periphery, watch the men at the table exchange pleasantries. All the Middle East's power players are here today, seated at a long conference table in the Israeli Prime Minister's office building.

I regard each of them, try to feel what it's like to sit across from one's oldest enemies. The room we occupy is large, well lit. A thick wooden table dominates. To Slabav's right, a single, framed landscape depicts hostile, ragged trees and shifting desert dunes. I stare at the vibrant golds and unfortunate browns, notice a single set of footprints that flow to the horizon. Cigars, body odor, and expensive cologne mingle with the salty sting of caviar and the aromatic pique of French champagne. Fluorescent lights cut a sterile glare over the whole arrangement. I adjust my notepad and ready my pen. My iPhone has been confiscated, so I've no way to record.

Leaders from the Muslim Brotherhood, the Palestinian Liberation

Organization, along with other, smaller contingents, sit with each other as Slabav sits alone on the table's far side.

Peace talks, I think, mulling the words. Slabav displays irritated fatigue, as if he's about to endure another tiresome dialogue that makes the West happy but, in reality, accomplishes less than nothing.

Joining me around the room's perimeter are numerous advisors, clerics, councilors and assistants. We parked, forgotten, in dark office chairs, keffiyeh and yarmulke equally dispersed upon watching heads. Arab and Jew trade hateful stares, cloaks of strained tolerance. I stare ahead in silence.

"Gentlemen," Slabav begins, "your intifada has become tiresome." He looks at his nails, takes his time as if contemplating a manicure. "Stones to statehood," his upper lip curls, "laughable, really. How many more?"

Nearest him, directly across the table and out of arms reach in what can only be a gesture of mistrust, sits Pavel Sundamir, the leader of the Palestine Liberation Organization. *"A bloated Arab with a smooth tongue and feline patience."* I remember the quote from my research. The fat man's robes bulge with the effort of holding his huge belly, and he listens with dispassionate, creased eyes over cheeks stretched tight with corpulence.

To Sundamir's left is Oshi Khalifa, leader of the Muslim Brotherhood's more violent branch, Hamas. I try to hide my disdain as I think of the deaths for which the man is responsible. *Be objective,* I think. *Report. Nothing more.*

Khalifa is a stark contrast to Sundamir, as thin as the other is fat, with a face formed to an expression of permanent strain—as if to make sure the world never forgets how he carries the full weight of his people's cares on his slim shoulders. His desert khakis are faded and well-worn, as seedy as his thin, rough beard. Research has born him to be a heartless killer whose violence is matched only by his ambition.

Slabav holds their eyes. "In 1985, after what is called the Six Day War, you declared intifada. To what end?"

Sundamir looks bored; Khalifa's cheeks grow more taut across his thin face.

"More bloodshed. More terror," Slabav says. "More graves. Certainly, less peace. You failed to achieve your aims and have succeeded only in widening an already impassable chasm."

He leans forward, suppresses a scowl, looks at Sundamir. "You did, however, force us to the table, and if that was your aim then you have my praise. For the first time, Jew and Muslim, Israeli and Arab, sat together in Oslo to discuss the issues."

I remember these, the Oslo Accords, the first peace talks designed to finally satisfy all parties and bring peace to the region.

Slabav fingers his necktie, trades glances between the two. "The world expected great things," he says. "We were poised to *do* great things. To barter an agreement that would echo through the centuries and finally undo the knots of hatred between us."

He looks up at the ceiling's fiberglass, tiles flecked with gray and brown. Another sigh. "Then your bombs." He says this as an afterthought. "An end to negotiations. Another intifada declared." He looks at Sundamir. "I believe you were instrumental in bringing that about, yes, Pavel?"

Sundamir takes a long moment, then speaks with the confidence of familiar power. "I don't need a history lesson, Laslo." A thick accent causes each word to sound like it originates in his nostrils. "I'm aware of my actions—and yours—over the past decades." He waves a hand, shoots a glance to Khalifa. "This meeting is pretentious, the terms preposterous. *Peace accords* are what western politicians bray about like lazy camels." He touches the side of his nose, ever the nomadic-clan leader, then winks. "We are sons of the desert," he whispers. "We seek atonement."

Slabav's eyebrows rise. "You've abandoned peace?"

"I've abandoned nothing, only accepted the reality of our times." Jowls flutter with each syllable as lips strain beneath the burden. "There can be no peace with thieves. There *can be no* sharing of land." *Can be no* is lyrical, high-pitched. "These talks are cloaked wastes of time, a pantomime of the stupid. The answer is simple. When Israel gives up its claims to our lands, only then can we sow seeds that grow fruit." Sundamir sits back, adjusts his keffiyeh, itches his enormous belly. Beside him Khalifa wears a broad smile.

Slabav scans the others in the room. A few scribble in small notepads, record sound bites to increase Sundamir's already outrageous fame.

The PM sighs. Fists appear above the table, seem to gouge crescent divots in his palms. "Does anyone have anything to say that might save these proceedings?" He glances around, holds my eyes for a second. I shake my head.

Smothered hatred fills the space with grudging silence.

Standing, Slabav adjusts his suit with both hands. "Gentlemen, until we meet again, safe journeys." He offers his hand to Sundamir, who shakes it twice. Khalifa looks at it, then moves past without a word, face strained against invisible burdens. With the sound of shuffling feet and ruffled papers, the room empties, and I'm left alone staring at a picture of a twisted desert, wondering why in the hell I was sent here.

CHAPTER 7

JERUSALEM, ISRAEL

I stand outside the PM's office building, wondering where I can find a bed for the night. With the task of attending the meeting accomplished, a meal and fully stocked bar are in order. Perhaps I'll even sleep.

Day gives way to evening as I pick a direction and start. Then, rethinking the whole thing, I turn back and re-enter the PM's building. I'd seen a receptionist there. Maybe she'll be kind enough to point me to the best nearby hotel.

She smiles as I approach; her words, however, are foreign.

"English?" I say. She shakes her head.

"Perhaps I can help?"

I turn to see the smiling face and square jaw of Laslo Slabav, the Israeli PM.

I mumble something at first, then manage, "Yes sir. It seems I've failed to make accommodations for the evening. Could you recommend a hotel close by?"

Slabav glances at two security men who stand a step behind.

"Of course, my friend," he says. "And you are?"

I shake my head. "How rude of me," I say, clearly out of my element. Only days ago I'd hit rock bottom, now I'm talking to the head of the Israeli government. "Emery Merrick," I say. "Reporter with *The Guard's Journal.*"

His handshake is warm and firm. "A pleasure, Mr. Merrick. I noticed you in the meeting and realized we haven't been introduced. Seems I've never heard of your paper but am aware of your exemplary work at the *Times*. Marvelous reporting, Mr. Merrick. What's the name of your paper again?"

"*The Guard's Journal.* It's a regional paper with an interest in Mideast affairs." I don't feel quite right lying to the man. I'll come up with a better story later—after a goodnight's sleep, after curling both arms around the hotel's minibar. "Recently Thaddeus Drake joined the advisory board and wishes us to have a larger footprint."

His eyes light up. "Ah, Mr. Drake. The Dove. And you're in his employ?"

I nod. "I am. Recently hired and told to come here by Mr. Drake himself."

"I've often wondered why Drake avoids our conflict," he says. "We could use his help. His results are remarkable in every way."

I nod again, decide to keep quiet. Too many lies may expose the fraud I am.

Slabav looks me over, seems to contemplate something. "Mr. Merrick, perhaps I can help your little paper. Why don't you join me for dinner, off the record, of course, and I'll see to it my staff finds you a room tonight."

I smile, realize the ploy. The man is smart. He knows a personal connection will help him get good press as the fictional journal grows. Generosity gives easy marks in the campaign for personal loyalty.

One of the security men whispers something in his ear. Slabav waves a hand. "I know," he says. "I'm not worried about it."

The security man steps back, continues his scan of the space.

I wonder what Drake will say if I arrive in London too late to meet him.

"Well?" Slabav says.

"An offer I can't refuse," I say. "It will be my honor."

Three hours later, the limousine stops at a gate both massive and impressive. The entrance to Slabav's private estate, thick black bars rising to point at twinkling stars. An armed security man steps forward as windows lower with a whir of servos. Slabav glances up from the papers scattered across his lap and nods at the guard.

Along the vehicle's opposite side, another guard inspects the limo's undercarriage for concealed explosives. Beyond him, masked by manicured bushes, are two more armed men. A great black Doberman sits beside them, looks bored by the whole affair.

The guard eyes me, eyes a clipboard, then nods and moves away.

"The price of being Prime Minister," Slabav says. "Extra security, especially after a friendly meeting with one's oldest enemies."

I'm amazed at the setup, the number of guards, the dogs, helicopters spinning overhead. "I can't believe you're doing this," I say. "Heads of state aren't usually so lax in their invitations. Is all this security for me? Have you made these guys crazy because I'm an unknown?"

Slabav chuckles. "Mr. Merrick, you're hardly an unknown. Your reporting for the *Times* precedes you. If they're starting a new paper, and they had the foresight to bring you on, it's the least I can do." He winks. "May pay me some benefits when your paper is the next big thing. Besides, my staff spoke to Drake while we dined. He verified your credentials and identity. So, you've checked out to security's satisfaction, and, in the end, it's the least I can do. I enjoy talking to people, specifically Americans. Our dinner was delightful and the conversation stimulating. It's a pleasure to get a break from all that other nonsense from time to time."

"That's very gracious, Mr. Slabav."

He waves a hand. "It's nothing, and completely self-serving. Perhaps you can persuade Mr. Drake to visit sometime. I'd welcome his counsel on our situation."

"Perhaps," I say, acting like I have some sway with the Dove. "He does seem interested."

"I've been looking forward to these few days of vacation," he says, switching to non-diplomat. The guard motions and the car drifts forward, moves up the curved driveway through manicured grounds. "My son's already here, and of all the things with which I'm forced to deal, nothing is more important than him."

Slabav stares out the window. "Such a beautiful place, shame I can't be here more."

It seems an odd moment of reverie from the PM, but it's hard to fault his sentiment.

As we weave toward the residence, I'm stilled by the sudden lushness of thick grass and fragrant trees. Topiaries perch on stands of polished marble, seem to blend the evening's pale orange and creamy yellow with a hint of spice. I'm awed by the verdancy of the grounds, such a stark contrast between oasis and desert. A jolting flip from dry and barren to fertile and groomed.

Then, the estate's beauty pales as our advance up the half-mile drive is punctuated by guards with alert eyes and automatic weapons. Stern faces peer at us, dressed fully in black, wearing combat boots shined to a high gloss. Seems there's nowhere to escape the threats this desert country offers.

Slabav sighs. "For the first time today, I feel safe," he says. "It's always a trial meeting with such men, the Arabs. Stubborn and rough, like chewing gum too long under a desk." He shows a smile that's kind and genuine. "There's no doubt of our safety here, though. All these men were specially selected from an elite Israeli Commando unit."

We stop in front of a large, stone house. Broad spotlights expose every shadow of the house's three gabled sections. I notice the center section is recessed and flanked by the other two. A path of river stones leads to an oversized double entryway centered between the two outer sections.

A guard opens the limo's door. Slabav stuffs his papers into a briefcase and exits as I follow. A helicopter buzzes overhead, its rotors a blurred silhouette against the cloudy dusk of night.

"Are we expecting an attack?" Slabav asks the guard.

"No sir," the guard's speech is firm and quick. "Something tripped the alarm earlier. Probably wildlife, but we're being extra cautious."

Slabav nods, shakes his head a single time. A nervousness grips his usual stoicism as we move toward the house.

When we enter, we're greeted by a boy of about sixteen. Slabav grasps him up in a huge, lingering bear hug. "Israel, my boy, I've missed you!"

"You look tired, Papa." Dark hair frames his good looks and partially conceals his acne.

"I am," Slabav says. "Meetings all day. By the way, this is Mr. Merrick, a reporter."

Israel steps forward, shakes my hand like a seasoned politician. "Mr. Merrick," he says, then turns to his father, a broad smile forming. "Another stray, I see."

Slabav laughs, turns to me. "My boy's sold me out," he says. "You're not the first reporter I've invited to the estate." He holds up his hands. "Full disclosure, I find it a handsome way to assure doubt's benefit."

I grin, marvel at the man's guile.

He turns to his boy. "Israel, why are you still up? It's so late."

The boy points at the ceiling. "Helicopters."

Slabav places a hand on his shoulder. "C'mon. To bed," he says. "You need your sleep if you're to excel in your studies."

"But you said we're on vacation."

Slabav grins, eyes shining with the love he holds for his son. "We are, but the tutor will be here for a few hours tomorrow."

The boy shuffles his feet, looks disappointed.

"It won't kill you," Slabav says. "A few extra hours can put you at the top of your class."

Israel nods, but discontent lingers on his features.

Slabav gives him a playful nudge toward a staircase so grand it appears as a waterfall in white marble.

Slabav follows the boy, motions me to come along.

At the top of the stairs, Israel embraces his father. "Good night."

Slabav tussles his hair. "Sleep well, little one."

The boy moves toward a door at the end of the hall.

"Well, then," Slabav says, "let's get you settled for the night, shall we?" We move along the landing, down a hall bearing photos of family and friends, of fish caught and boats sailed.

"Here we go," he says. "You'll find everything you need in there. If you require anything else, pick up the phone and one of my staff will see to it. I'm not sure I'll see you in the morning, but a car will be waiting for you outside so you can depart at your leisure. I'd hate to have you miss your flight."

"Thank you for dinner and such a pleasant evening," I say. "I can't say enough about your graciousness. You're a true gentleman."

Slabav takes the compliment with stoic grace. "Good night, Mr. Merrick. Sleep well."

She comes to me at night. Certainly, I have thoughts of her during waking hours, but the night is where she shines. Walking in rainbows, drifting, speaking in lilting tones, saying our lives will never end, that death cannot rend us.

Her hair is exquisite, her aroma divine. She comes and sits, memories drifting across an expanse of sky. Ice cream, strips of moonlight, jazz men playing as we nourish ourselves on each other's sight.

I awake wet, sweat drips from my chin, my hair is moist like a hound too long in the surf. At these moments I always look for Rhyme, but she's never there. Her smell lingers, though, unmistakable, as if she's just risen from our bed for a drink of water, surrounded by light that embraces in haloed rings of mist and memory.

I rise, sit on the end of the bed, then move to the sink and splash water on my face. Her smell fades by degrees; her form, in increments.

I'm surrounded by shadow and dream. I long for her, wish things would've been different. Wish I could've been the man she loved, but without vices, without a nose for the story. But I've come too late and

Pulitzers be damned. I should've known, should've cast off the plague of societal dreams; of money, houses, fame, or chemicals.

I move to the door, perhaps I can stroll. The guards know I'm here, know I pose no threat. It's worth a try, worth the fuss if the night air can cleanse the unreasonable dreams of failure and folly.

The hallway is dark like a tunnel. I see things in shadow. I look to the landing at the top of the stairs, see a square of dim light fall from Laslo's room. I'm surprised he's awake at three in the morning, but then, I know nothing of Israel's gracious leader other than he's a man who's taken me in and with whom I've enjoyed talking.

As I approach, I hear voices. I don't want to eavesdrop, although my reporter's nature makes it all but a certainty. I think to fight the urge, but instead creep forward like a master thief.

The voice is rough, deep, throaty. It has an accent, and I can barely suppress the urge to peek around the door jamb. Then I hear it.

"Ye may as well enter, Merrick."

I freeze, press against the wall, consider how silently I can return to my room. What a terrible house guest I am.

Then Laslo's voice: "Emery, please come in."

The aroma hits me, chases away what lingers of my wife's lilac and vanilla. It's a unique and pungent odor, something familiar, something I should recognize.

I step into the light and see something wholly astonishing.

Slabav sits in an armchair in front of a regal desk, an executive's desk. Upon it sits an open humidor in dark walnut. He wears just a towel around his waist. A loose robe hangs from his shoulders. Behind him, a huge bed occupies the room's left side. Light shines in a cone from a slender lamp. I place the aroma, Cuban cigars.

I squint at the shadow on the desk's other side.

My mouth falls open.

Behind the desk is the largest man I've ever seen. A man I know. The same giant who'd visited me on the night I meant to change everything forever. This is Longinus, a man singular in appearance and speech. A mythical Golem from Jewish fairy tales.

Beside him, Slabav's son kneels, his face a picture of pure terror.

Slabav looks at me as eyes plead and dart.

The hulk motions me in, and I take a tentative step, wondering if I'm fast enough to sprint away and alert the guards.

"A pleasure to be seein' ye agin," the giant says.

Slabav's shocked face is frozen, but his eyes shift, like a mechanical doll, between me and the monster, until falling on Israel where they settle in impotence.

I cross the room, stand next to Slabav. "Look—" I start, but the giant interrupts me.

"Ye'd be wise to hold ye tongue." His eyes are dark, lifeless even as they hold mine. I feel a chill, an instinctual warning to obey.

"I'been waitin' to meet ye, Mr. Slabav."

The hulk smiles through a face dark and hard. It's completely inexplicable that this man can be sitting here with such nonchalance. I'd seen the security myself, seen the guards and guns and razor wire. There's no way anyone could enter this room without being seen.

Yet here he is, a scowl on his face, muscles rippling like a stallion on anabolic steroids. He's the definition of a boogey man, looming even as he sits with feet propped on the desk, cigar hanging from his lips and glowing like a wolf's eye.

"You two know each other?" Slabav says with a shake of his head as if his trust has been misplaced.

I nod. "We met once."

"Non a mate to be sure," the hulk chimes in. "I'd jus' as be killin' him, as I would ye."

My blood runs cold. I scramble for the words to tell Laslo all of this has nothing to do with me.

"I do non mean ye harm," the giant says. "I wish only to be makin' ye an offer of peace."

Laslo collects himself, gives me a skeptical glance. His fingers stop twitching, and he fully focuses on the giant. He speaks in a voice devoid of emotion. "Your methods do not inspire trust, Mister—?"

The man ignores the question. "Would ye rather I sit 'cross from ye in a conference room and offer empty words?"

Slabav glances at Israel. "I can take nothing you say at face value when you threaten my son."

The man smiles through enormous lips, puffs smoke into the air. "He is non threatened. I do non have a weapon. The lad sits here of his own."

"So, he can leave?" Slabav asks.

The man nods his giant head. "Aye. He may leave me side, but non the room."

Israel leaps into his father's embrace.

Slabav squeezes hard as a tear drops from his eye.

He holds the boy at arm's length. "Go sit on the bed, Israel," he says. "You too, Emery. This will all be fine."

The boy hesitates, then follows his father's instruction. I sit next to him, feel his hand slide into mine and squeeze hard. I give him a nod I hope is reassuring despite the fact I'm scared to death.

"If ye try to rise an alarm, ye will die, he will die, and many of ye soldiers will die."

"And of course, you will die," Slabav says.

The giant sniffs the air with an expression that welcomes the thought. The wolf's eye glows as he exhales another tower of smoke. "Anon and agin," he says, "perhaps. But I assure ye, that will non be necessary. Ye have a reputation for listenin', so let me be on with it and we will part in peace."

"I'll listen, but know that when you leave, you'll be arrested within three steps of my door."

Another smile from the giant; Laslo's threat is comical. "Anon and agin, perhaps," he says, taking two quick puffs of the cigar. "Lest be on with it. Me organization is in a position to offer ye lifetime's desire."

"And that is?"

"The rebuildin' of the Temple on its original site."

Slabav's laugh splits the room, divides us into those soaked in fear and those in charge. "The very idea is ludicrous," he says, "the cause hopeless."

The man draws on the cigar, unphased by Slabav's reaction. "Ashtray?"

The Golem is imperturbable. "Top drawer."

The drawer slides open. "I see only a pistol."

Slabav tenses. "Other side," he mutters, a tremor slipping into his words.

A thick, stone ashtray appears, and the giant flicks his ash into it.

"A rebuilt Temple is more than a lifetime desire for me," Slabav says. He speaks like a master orator lapsing fully into speech politico. "It represents the hopes of all of God's people. It is the pinnacle of our entire belief."

Longinus nods. "Aye."

Slabav studies the man's broad features. "For centuries, this has been the hope and promise of my people. Do you not think we've tried every conceivable way to make this happen?"

"Anon and agin, perhaps." He puffs the cigar two more times, then lays it in the ashtray.

"It's an impossible task," Slabav says. "But in the interest of courtesy, I'll indulge you." The politician is in full force now, rending control of the conversation. "How do you intend to do this for my people? The Arabs have a mighty grip on the site."

"They'll be cooperatin' once they see 'tis in their best interest."

Slabav laughs and I'm impressed by his boldness, giggling in the face of a hurricane. "And *you* are going to convince them?"

"Anon and agin…"

"Perhaps," Slabav finishes the sentence. Beside me, Israel crawls deeper into the bed, even yawns and sprawls out. At his age everything is either over-the-top exciting or boring as hell. Slabav glances at his son, then back at the giant. "You realize we've tried this many times— a sharing of the site, so to speak. They've always flatly rejected us, always refused compromise."

"Aye."

"And you know this is the supreme holy landmark for multiple peoples?"

Now the giant suppresses a yawn.

"And how do you propose to gain their cooperation?" Slabav asks.

"Me organization is influential. We believe it can non be folly."

Slabav stares, takes a few seconds to consider all the possibilities.

If what the giant says is true, Slabav will be the prime minister who delivered the impossible. His fame will be outrageous, revered for all-time on a level with Gandhi and Mother Teresa.

"My father used to say, 'Beware the bearer of gifts, for a dagger they may conceal.' What is it you expect from me?"

"We expect ye to build the Temple, Mr. Slabav. We be expectin' crowd control. We be expectin' the cooperation of ye government in transportin' Jews from all over the world to Israel."

Slabav looks slack jawed. The man talks as if it's already a done deal. As if all he has to do is thumb a few buttons on a cell phone and the rebuilding of the Temple will start.

Longinus glances at his watch.

"Excuse my ignorance Mr.—?"

"Longinus." He pronounces the word with an A in the middle. *Long-a-nis.*

My memory races back to the day the man knocked on my door, the day I'd pressed the pistol to my skull, my surprise at the giant's presence and his subsequent offer of work with Thaddeus Drake. That both I and Longinus the Giant find ourselves in the same room inside a heavily guarded compound in the dead middle of the night is beyond happenstance. My stomach churns as I wonder at Drake's reach, consider his tale of immortality, measure it against truth and reason.

"Mr. Longinus," Laslo says, "many organizations work toward a rebuilt Temple. For which organization do you work?"

The giant's head shakes. "I'm non at liberty to say."

Slabav leans back, tries to look confident despite the fact he's clad only in a towel and a robe. Israel stands and moves behind his father. Longinus stares with coal-black eyes. "That does affect my level of trust," Slabav says.

Longinus rises, his shadow covers the entire wall behind the desk in sinister ebony.

"We do non expect ye trust, Slabav. We be only expectin' ye cooperation."

"And what agreement has been made?"

Longinus shifts his weight, leans forward. It's like watching a landslide. "We be makin' the Arab's play nice. Ye rebuild the Temple."

"Of course," Slabav says. "But you promise the impossible."

"So we be havin' a deal?"

Slabav stares at the man, his fear forgotten. I try to will my thoughts into his head. The giant's on the verge of leaving. Once gone, he can be identified and taken into custody—*if* he even makes it off the grounds alive. We'll all be safe, and the Golem will be gone.

Seconds tick exhausting as I watch the PM.

Finally, he nods.

"Excellent," Longinus says. "Ye'll be contact'd when arrangements be final. I'll be seein' meself out."

The robe droops from Laslo's shoulders as he stands. Israel clutches his father's hand with trembling fingers.

Longinus exits without a glance.

Slabav flies to the desk, tears open the drawer and retrieves the pistol. He glances at me, flashes the gun, then points it at the door. Israel moves as far from the door as possible. Slabav slides his fingers along the desk's edge, pistol shaking as he tries to maintain his aim.

The alarm is shrill and deafening. The entire mansion, suddenly and entirely filled with blinding light.

I look at the door.

Longinus, I think. *The guy I'm to meet in London tomorrow. That should be a hoot.*

Chapter 8

London, England

Longinus's face is swollen, his breathing harsh and labored. He struggles to his feet, is struck behind the right knee and goes sprawling. Air and blood spew from his lungs.

A large man stands over him, arms raised above his head, fists pumping the air.

Stale, yellow cigarette smoke wafts over me. The elite here, dressed in their furs and tuxedos, sipping cognac and smoking cigars. I see more than one notable person and wonder how they can come here and avoid the press. They circle the arena in tiered seats rising one hundred feet or more, separated from the combatants by industrial plexi-glass. Fat fists clutch wads of cash and pound against the plexi-partition.

Longinus rolls to his left just as the man's foot stomps down, misses his head by a fraction.

Then another man, a masked Asian, delivers a kick to his ribs. He flips over the Roman and disappears with astounding speed.

Longinus wears a tuxedo that's no longer recognizable. A blood-soaked shirt hangs in tatters beneath a gash on his left cheek. This man is huge. *And immortal,* I think. If what Drake says is true, I'm watching a living member of the Roman Legion. A true gladiator in battle.

Drake warned me Longinus was a bit overpowering, and I thought last night proof enough. But nothing prepares me for what I see tonight.

Longinus stands on shaky legs as the Asian streaks past on his right. The large man, still smaller than the Roman, wears a smirk, circles left, cocks back a giant fist.

Their plan is obvious; use the Asian to distract, while the large man lands a brain-scrambler.

Longinus must see it coming, because he spins into the blow and smashes an elbow into the large man's throat.

As his elbow hits home, the Asian switches direction, flies through the air, foot leveled at the base of Longinus's neck. Either their timing is off, or the Roman anticipates this too, because he ducks at the last second.

The Asian's foot misses by what looks like a single centimeter, then connects with his teammate's nose. The man howls, falls to his knees; blood spews over his mouth and onto the concrete floor.

Longinus moves with surprising speed for such a goliath, spins behind the downed man and grasps his neck between two massive arms. The man's eyes bulge as the Roman twists.

I'm riveted. *Is he actually going to kill this guy?*

I'm struck by where I am. I'd seen no adverts as I entered; no vendors move through the crowd, selling peanuts and stadium fare.

I'd been collected at the airport then dropped in front of this non-descript, gray building. No neon flashed tonight's bout; no crowd mills outside, no scalpers, not even a ticket box. A shiver runs through me as I watch the Roman's muscles constrict, twisting the man's head.

The crowd wants death. Their howls mount to a deafening crescendo.

Then the deep bass of a foghorn fills the arena, rolls over glass and steel to fill the space with glaring noise.

I hold my ears until the blast echoes away. Then, startled, I look around to see what's going on. The people roar, exchange money and high-fives, eyes gleeful and bloodthirsty. The man next to me is tall with gray hair and black eyes. He slaps me on the back. "Give me ten thousand on the Roman?" The woman with him, elegant and half his age, adorned with diamonds, leans in. "Make that fifty," she yells through lips glossed ruby red.

I stammer something, wave my hands side-to-side to let them know I can't take the bet. I feel ashamed because at present I have about twenty American dollars in my pocket, the entire sum of my net worth. Any other money has been provided by Drake, and I doubt he meant *expenses* in the way of betting on illegal fights. The couple pause in unison, look me up and down, raise their noses at my Men's Wearhouse attire. She shoves her middle finger in my face as they both turn away.

I step aside and look toward the arena floor. Longinus limps toward the wall at one end, while the other two move toward the opposite. On the Roman's side, a small door opens and a stool slides in. Longinus flops on it as the door slams shut.

His jacket hangs in shreds. The shirt beneath is tattered, blood covered. The air clotted with the scent of flesh and money, of blood and perfume, of cigar and cognac. Longinus snorts and bloody sputum rockets from his nose to the spackled concrete.

Across from him, his opponents wipe their faces, talk in low tones. The large one's chest heaves, a great bruise of purple and black appears over his throat. He looks scared.

The Asian, however, glances at Longinus with eyes calm and focused. He leans close to his compatriot, the creases of his mask moving as he talks.

"*Wheel, wheel, wheel*," the crowd begins to chant.

Their fists hammer the plexi in time with the words.

"*Wheel, wheel, wheel*."

Longinus rips the jacket and shirt from his body and throws them to the floor. The crowd roars. He's muscled like a stallion, like Schwarzenegger in his prime, but much hairier. Long, puckered scars crease striated flesh as the crowd's momentum grows—banging the glass, stomping the floor, chanting in a fever pitch.

"Wheel! Wheel! Wheel!"

Gleaming steel walls surround the fighting area, and I'm surprised when they come to life and start to sparkle. Behind each of the combatants a section of the wall becomes translucent, then changes to colorful, cartoonish pictures.

The crowd erupts with renewed vigor, voices mingle with yellow haze to create a deafening buzz in both eye and ear. I move closer to the plexi.

Is this the wheel?

The pictures start to spin: A pickaxe, a gun, a short staff, a broad sword, a taser, an axe, a whip, a trident, a spear. Gaining speed, they congeal and blur in long colored arcs.

Longinus smiles, spits more blood.

"Wheel! Wheel! Wheel!"

The place shakes. The noise ravages steel rafters and sound proofed walls.

Images whirl like a Vegas slot machine.

I feel dizzy, watch the tumult of spinning color over bloody concrete.

The wheel slows.

Then stops.

The crowd wails.

Two pictures flash behind the Roman's opponents: For the Asian, a cartoon pistol. For the large man, a cartoon Bo staff.

I look towards Longinus. Neon blue flashes from the wall. The legs of his stool cast long shadows over rough concrete.

Above him, the crowd is wild with glee.

He places a thick hand on his knee and turns.

Eyebrows lower as blue neon flashes from sparkling teeth.

The cartoon: a sword of gold and silver.

I stretch to the length of my tiptoes, press close to the plexi. In a moment, I'll witness a warrior from the Roman Legion do battle with a weapon the Legion made famous. I can't hide my excitement. My heart races. Anticipation sizzles as sweat drips off my nose.

Three cables descend from the ceiling, each holds the selected weapons.

Longinus hefts the sword in his hand, tests its balance and weight.

Across the circle, the other two exchange glances, then switch weapons. The Asian spins the Bo in a blinding, blurred buzz saw; around his back, over his shoulder, then still and vertical. He assumes a pose like a scorpion, Bo over his head, weight on his back foot.

The large man chambers a round with a confident grin as silver light gleams from the pistol. He aims at Longinus.

I press closer, realize I'm holding my breath and exhale in a whoosh that fogs the plexi. Frantic, I wipe it with my hand, hoping not to miss anything.

The foghorn blares its deafening boom.

Fat fists and red faces impact the plexi. Savage screams rise into the air and congeal to a mounting crescendo.

The pistol spits flame, and a bloody hole appears in the Roman's left abdomen.

In the same instant, Longinus moves, muscles flowing through a centuries-old motion.

The sword flies from his fingers, spins a single, lazy rotation, then impales the large man's chest.

A harsh whoosh escapes as the pistol rattles to the concrete.

Bloodlust takes the crowd, and they howl like branded banshees.

The large man takes a step, eyes bulging toward the sword.

He collapses face first.

My mouth is bone dry.

The Asian moves with a speed born of practice and confidence, Bo spinning like a writhing serpent.

Longinus circles toward his sword.

The Asian blocks his path.

Now, both gun and sword are out of Longinus's reach. Blood pours from his abdominal wound, spills onto the concrete.

The Asian feints right, then spins the Bo over his head and into Longinus's shoulder. A fleshy crack mingles with the crowd's screams.

Longinus launches himself at the Asian.

The Bo strikes three times: shin, hip and forearm.

The Asian thrusts the Bo at Longinus's forehead.

Longinus drops, leaves a layer of skin as he slides on his knees.

The Bo hisses past, misses by a fraction.

Then Longinus has him.

The Asian strains amid the Roman's hug, back arched, neck veins popping.

The arena shakes.

The crowd hammers the plexi, kicks at the seats, crushes against the transparent wall. Eyes pop, lips wide and red, cheeks flushed and elated. I scream with them.

White teeth glare from Longinus's mouth as he opens wide, then chomps down on the Asian's throat. The man flails for a few moments, then goes limp.

The Roman lifts the body over his head, blood runs down his chin and naked torso. His teeth glimmer red as he spits the remnants of the Asian's throat into the air.

The crowd goes ape shit. Louder than the foghorn by far. They stomp and cheer and high-five, crazed faced and wild eyed.

He heaves the body across the arena. The Asian slides until stopped by the corpse of his dead partner.

Longinus limps to them, retrieves his sword from the large man's chest, props the blade against his shoulder. Then walks to the door and is gone.

I flop into a seat. My limbs tingle; I can't quite control my breathing. I lean forward and vomit into the aisle, then I sit holding my sweaty head in trembling hands. *Two men died,* I think. *No one gave a shit,* I think. I glance at the bodies, watch as they're dragged from the arena leaving long smears on the concrete.

A team appears and starts to hose the floor.

I try to stand, but my legs betray me. I feel confused, anxious, panicked, overwhelmed. I'm hyperventilating. *Two men, murdered. Alive one second, dead the next.* My fingers and lips tingle, my throat feels constricted. I try to stand but only collapse in my seat. Sweat pours over my scalp, down my back, into my socks. My head spins, my chest feels heavy.

I close my eyes.

CHAPTER 9

LONDON, ENGLAND

Thaddeus Drake assumes a chair in the posh locker room, waits for the bout to end. He hears the crowd, the new Romans in their neo-colosseum, a tsunami of bloodlust crashing against the building's glass and steel. He has no interest in the outcome. The fools who battle Longinus have no idea they died before the first blow ever fell.

He reaches in his pocket and produces a small recorder. He grins at the relic, ancient by modern standards, and he wonders if Emery has any special attachment to it.

He presses PLAY and the recording starts.

Emery's voice fills the space in tinny hues.

<cough>

Okay…well…I should start with my name…it's Emery Merrick. And let this recording serve as my suicide note. I've named it, 'And now it comes to this,' after a great Rush lyric.

First, I'll set the scene. The pistol I'm holding, I call him Sig, is a last, surprising token of Rhyme found in a Skecher's box in the back of the closet. Who knew she owned a gun anyway?

<sigh>

I suppose in one's last moments; one should be completely honest if they wish to leave a record of their exploits. I should start with the

*standards, name, age, address, occupation. But that feels insignificant.
I mean, insignificant on a level we all ignore because facing our
insignificance would mean we are small, meaningless and...well...
insignificant. No matter how grand our exploits, we're still only
microns piled atop a universal scale.*

<liquid pours into a glass>

*Yet here I sit in my insignificance; feeling the pain, soaked in
alcohol, full of regret. And yes, I can say it, I mean to end my life.*

*Perhaps this is nothing more than an exercise in self-indulgence,
you know, to record my last thoughts, make me feel like I'm worth a
damn. I guess it feels like the last thing I should do. No...said that
wrong...um... it feels like my dearth of morals, courage, and heart
can't be completely glorified without a record, and I'd be remiss to end
it all without first blabbing into this thing.*

So, give the man his dying wish. Right, Sig?

<deep breath, sigh>

Jesus H, you people are harsh.

<rustling paper>

Okay, here goes.

<cough>

I'll start where I think my life started and I'll end with a bang.
That's a pun, for those listening at home, the bang being the gun that...
You know what? You'll figure it out. Here goes.

I first saw her at the party for my first Pulitzer. She had ice
cream, a small bowl like the one's girls get when they're in public,
with those little rainbow flakes on top. She approached and our eyes
met. I nodded, smiled like a rogue because I think girls like that kind
of thing, then she surprises me by asking, "Aren't you Emery
Merrick?"

It's funny, thinking about it now, but my breath stopped. I mean I'd
been in disaster zones, in back alleys skulking like a mangy cat, in
third world countries, in the deepest, darkest shitholes on the planet,

but with that single question I feel my heart quicken, my blood warm like a simmering teapot. Then her perfume reaches me.

<long inhale>

Vanilla and something like lilac. Her eyes dance a playful green. No…too plain, and plain she was not… more like a deep emerald, like Atlantis' lost jewels popping up to float on a tropical surf. A timeless, epic treasure. And me, the scoundrel-slash-treasure hunter that, while drawing his last breath, falls to the sand from pure exhaustion and sees his long-sought fortune lying wet before his eyes.

And that was true with her. She was a jackpot, staring at me, holding that ice cream, emerald's shining above a tight black dress with a plunging neckline.

"Your ice cream's gonna melt."

Then she smiles, and I know my fate is sealed. Her eyes hold me under a crinkled brow, her laugh comes as a crystal echo that tickles my ears, hypnotic. Perfect lips glisten as she speaks.

"Well, someone's gonna have to help me before it gets all drippy."

"Like my heart?" I say, trying to smile like a rogue.

I can tell this throws her. She looks at me as if she'd read me wrong, an inner dialogue that adjusts the corners of her mouth and subdues the emerald gaze.

I panic a bit. You know what they say about love at first sight? Yes, yes, I know you think it's all nonsense and so did I. Even now I must think that, but somehow, standing there, heart hammering and dry mouthed, thinking I was somebody, knowing I wasn't, I knew I was on the verge of blowing it.

How old was I then? Jesus, probably thirty-two or so, and I know, even through the burn of testosterone and longing, if I blow it, I'll never again be so fortunate as to stand in the presence of such magnificence.

You see, and it's stupid even as I say it, but the universe was talking to me, telling me this is my one chance.

<liquid pours, slurp>

I'm hooked like a fish. And not lust, mind you, although her auburn hair is tantalizing and her skin flawless, carnal thoughts never cross my mind. I only stare, a deer in the headlights. No…wait…I can do better. Let me have a little sip here.

<slurp>

Okay. Um. I stare as if all the lights in every city have just clicked on and woke me from total, and complete darkness. I'm surprised as a beggar with a winning scratch-off ticket and realize, through the shock and emeralds and melting ice cream, that the universe has tossed me a turning point. A singular encounter with which to make the most.

The feeling demanded my attention, and somewhere deep in my little hidden patch of soul, you know, the one that everyone protects and never lets out? The one that we keep hidden until it raises its head to appreciate a moment, or something breathtaking? Make sense? I suppose it's conscience or something, but whatever it is, it tells me this is not to be missed. That this woman, with the dripping bowl and goddess grin, is someone I must know. An imperative, like breathing, like getting hit by a bus to save a baby. Yes! A cosmic imperative. Something beyond humanity, past the confines of body or Earth or galaxy…even universe. Something timeless and innate. Lying at the center of not just ourselves, but of all things, everywhere. This was universal. Couldn't be ignored. My life beginning, plain and simple. And as the ice cream melts, and as I stare dumbly at those emeralds, I know I'm fucked, know as certainly as I've ever known anything else, maybe even more than anything I've ever known, completely and permanently fucked.

This woman is my destiny.

And just like that, nothing matters. Just like that, I'm relieved of any choices regarding my partner in life. The universe chose for me, placed her in front of me and demanded I take notice. And why was I fucked? Ha! Isn't it obvious? Because I'm no longer safe. My emotions sprouted tendrils that bloomed through the little patch of insignificance that was my soul, then reached out and wrapped themselves around her.

I'm fucked because now I love someone. Yes, just like that. And that, as the universe so boldly points out, is trouble. I no longer have the luxury of thinking only of myself and whoever she is, good or bad, naughty or nice, I know she'll be by my side through all the rest.

Next thing I know, my mouth's open and she's sliding ice cream in. Ha! So bold of her! I realize I have tunnel vision. That everything in the room, all movement, sound, sight, has disappeared and that I see only her.

Ah, well, let me wipe my eyes for a moment. You see, this was a singular event in my life and when I relive it, it makes me a little blubbery.

<tissues pulled from a box>

Yes, that's hard. Pardon me won't you while I take a little sippie-poo of this here Macallan. I aim to end this bottle before my time is up.

<slurp, sigh, slurp>

So, okay, um, I say to her, "Let's get out of here," and take the bowl and set it on a table. Then we walk into the cool New York night to end up at a little jazz club where Jin works the door.

Now Jin is a small Asian with a knack for being in the right place. He'd been a good source through the years and greets us warmly as we enter. I can't tell you at this point who's playing or even how many folks are in the room because I never take my eyes off Rhyme.

Jesus, have I even mentioned her name yet? Just seems like everyone should already know it. But then everyone here is me right now, unless one counts the Sig Sauer or the Macallan, both giants in their own right, and a tip of the cap to them.

<slurp>

Anyway, yes, her name is Rhyme. Rhyme Carter. And I never saw her coming.

<sniff, tissues pulled>

And so, as we sit sipping our drinks; a scotch rocks for me and an Old Fashioned for her; she never takes her eyes off me. We talk and laugh, and nothing goes unnoticed, her every nuance recorded in my mind, and I have to impress her. Have to bind her to me as surely as I'm bound to her.

The jazz men play, and we sit there in our own little world. Then she leans back and yawns, lifting her arms, hands clenched in tiny fists, mouth stretched and curled, eyes squeezed tight, maybe the cutest thing I've ever seen.

"Let's get out of here," she says, and twenty minutes later we're in a studio off Greenwich Square.

<sigh, slurp>

And now I'm standing full in the tricky part.

Do we fall in bed and make love like savages? Do I have a drink and thank her, then move on in such a way that I maintain a gentlemanly facade? Do I wait and see if she makes a move? I refuse to think she's a barfly and that I'm tonight's chosen entertainment. No, no, the universe ordained this. So, there I stand, holding the drink she's given me, staring like a dumb ass, waiting for the universe to give me some clue.

Then she empties her glass and crosses the small apartment to her room, motions me to follow. I don't hesitate. I stand beside her bed, and she undresses me down to my Tommy John's, then giggles when she sees my obvious erection.

Then she strips, taking me in as she does, slowly removing her dress like a corn husk. How her skin glowed. And those emeralds, glistening like a prowling feline. Sensuous hands, the contours of her body in the room's dim light. Intoxicating. All I can do is stare, feeling like a cave man suddenly in the modern world. Everything is new here. She, like a Christmas present you don't want to unwrap, and as badly as I want to make love to her, I hope we don't. It's too soon, and I'm certain the universe doesn't have that in mind.

She slides into bed and spoons close, her back against my chest. I caress her arm, feel like a cat in a patch of sun, drifting to those places cats go when they're halfway between sleep and the ethereal.

Then she speaks, whispers.

"I found you. I knew I would."

I don't respond but know exactly what she means. I kiss her ear, take in her hypnotic fragrance. Her body relaxes against mine. Then she's asleep, her face shadowed in a dim light that darkens and enhances, and if I'd had any doubt about it before, I have no doubt now. This is the most perfect woman I've ever seen.

Her breathing is deep, cleansing, and the thought never crosses my mind of: *Well, I guess I'm not going to get laid.* This is so much more than that. Those feelings seem so base and primitive. No, this is something poignant, and I kiss her shoulder and caress her hair, savor her scent, the softness of her skin, the easy rhythm of her breath. I do that for hours, completely lost, fully consumed with a passion different than anything before. A passion of souls who resonate on the same frequency, then find, in those harmonics, complete and total peace.

I push myself close, gently pull her hips to mine. Not in a sexual way, but because I can't possibly get close enough to this woman.

Rhyme. My universal gift, my chance at significance.

<sigh>

I whisper her name again and again, lying on her tiny bed, covered in thin strips of moonlight, enjoying the taste as it slides off my tongue.

<slurp, sigh>

Rhyme, my love, how I wish things ended differently.

"Who's that?"

Drake looks up to see Longinus. "You look horrible. Trouble in the subway?"

The giant glances at himself and moves to the sink. A bloodied reflection shines back from a long, clean mirror.

"Ye should see the other lads."

CHAPTER 10

LONDON, ENGLAND

"Did you find my cow?"

    "Non exactly."

"Disappointing."

I awake on a long, hard bench in a well-appointed locker room. I try to sit up, but my throbbing head stops me.

"Alas, my dear Emery, how are we feeling?" It's Drake.

I rub my temples then my eyes.

"Seems the lad's seen better." The giant Roman sits on the bench across from me. He looks like a mountain from this close, except with more clefts. A shiver runs through me. Who could possibly stand against such a foe? His mere presence spawns fear. An unstoppable force, towel hanging from his neck, dangling from massive shoulders, a granite face crusted with dried blood and a few days stubble.

I remember the gunshot and look to his abdomen. Blood falls like a metronome...drip, drip, drip. I'm swept up by nausea. I feel flush, stifle a gag. I can't look, but somehow can't look away. The wound is circular with jagged edges and a dark center. I peer closer, watch it swirl like a mini black hole then disappear.

"Just...What in the fuck," I stammer.

Drake moves toward me. "Do try to sit up, dear Emery." He holds a glass with one hand as he helps me to seated with the other. The room spins and I grasp the bench to steady myself.

My body runs on its own, runs from the trauma, from seeing enough to say I've seen too much.

"I'm non takin' this one as a fighter, eh?" Longinus says, eyeing me.

I sit with my hands propping me up, then take the offered glass and down the liquid. It's Scotch whisky and it tastes amazing, my first drink of liquor in a day or two. Its warmth soothes my body and eases my mind.

Drake sits on a long, pale-wood bench. His dress is meticulous: pinstriped, dark suit, necktie in bold stripes of gray, silver cufflinks, hair perfect.

He dips in his pocket and retrieves a silver cigarette case. "We must double our efforts to find the cow," he says to the Roman.

"I don't think you can smoke in here."

An emaciated man in a too-big suit enters. What Longinus is to largeness this man is to frailty. A pointed nose pokes over shallow, sullen cheeks. He's balding, maybe five-foot-nine if he stretches for it. He's dressed in gray, and I'm astonished to think how forgettable the man is. He slides his scarecrow body in an over-stuffed leather chair, then crosses one leg over the other. This must be Igneus, the Jew from Christ's crucifixion.

"Great," Longinus says, "ye brought Mr. Happy."

Igneus runs a hand over his bald head, betraying his ire.

"We need to talk," Drake says, ignoring Igneus and lighting the Treasurer.

Longinus moves to a sink, its gold-plated surface reflecting his blood-smeared face. Turning away, he splashes it with water, then lets his trousers drop to the floor. Boxers follow and soon he's nude. A massive, shaggy mountain.

Turning from the sink, he stares down Igneus, who wiggles in his chair and averts his eyes. Longinus looks to Drake.

"Talk about what?"

"X'chasei."

"There is non to discuss. There is non left to conquer."

Igneus interrupts. "Can we discuss this in the club? *After* he showers?"

Drake looks at Igneus, glances at Longinus. "Capital idea, Mr. Igneus. Longinus, do clean up, then meet us in the private room. Do you feel up to joining us, dear Emery?"

I get the feeling if I refuse, my employment will be short-lived. I also get the feeling my life may be short-lived. I stand, unsure if I'll fall or not. "I'd be happy to."

Igneus rises and moves toward the door. Longinus spins the towel in a tight spiral and pops him on the backside with a crack that echoes through the room.

Igneus wheels and levels a silver pistol at the grinning giant.

Longinus is unphased. "Care to join me?" he says with a wink. "I'll show you a real gun, eh? It may non hurt you to live a little."

Igneus holds the barrel steady, crinkles his nose in disgust. "Oaf."

Longinus flips the towel over his neck. "Anon and agin, it may hurt a little...at first."

The Roman's booming laugh chases Igneus out of the room.

"Who gave him a gun?" Longinus asks.

Drake stands. "Thirty minutes."

"But I'll miss me massage."

In a single motion, Drake rockets the cigarette into Longinus's chest. A shower of embers and ash explode in the air and fall on the room's thick carpet. Longinus flaps his arms, slaps at the sparks, appears comical overreacting to such a small thing.

"Then miss it."

CHAPTER 11

LONDON, ENGLAND

O ur footsteps echo as we wind our way through shadowed halls. Each corridor, lit with ancient metal sconces. Each sconce, polished to a high gloss. Silver light shines on walls covered with art.

Drake becomes tour guide.

"You may remember some of these, dear Emery," he says, motions to the art, "thought lost to the modern world."

The place smells moldy. I stop and stare at the first one. Instead of canvas, it's painted on a round wooden panel. The image: a woman's severed head, mouth agape, frozen in surprise. Snakes form her hair, appear to writhe as I watch.

"DaVinci's *Medusa Shield*," he says. "One of his earliest works."

"Wow," I say. "Those snakes look surprisingly real."

"DaVinci, my boy," he says and moves along, flicking his finger this way and that. I follow as he describes others.

"Here's Michelangelo's *Leda and the Swan,* a gift from the King of France in the fifteen hundreds. Rafael's *Portrait of a Young Man,* thought to be a self-portrait…"

I'm amazed. These works hang lonely in a musty, moldy, humid corridor when they should be behind an inch of climate-controlled glass at the Louvre. Yet, they're incredibly well-preserved, as if painted yesterday. I try to reason this out as we walk.

Before I find an answer, we turn a corner, and the corridor ends. I stare up at a huge painting, at least seven feet tall and five feet wide, depicting a scene of judgment and victory. Outlined in blue, it shows what I think to be God sitting on His throne with an arch of the hosts of Heaven above Him. Winged bodies span from one side of the painting to the other. He holds a book on His lap, flanked by angels bent over their own writing. Beneath Him on the right, angels carry the Just to Heaven. On His left, the wicked are cast into Hell. In the bottom center, an angel subdues Satan while a battle rages all around.

"*A Vision of the Last Judgment,*" Drake says. "Robert Blake painted this around 1808. It's my absolute favorite."

I lean close, then stand on tiptoes. A busy painting. Angels and demons everywhere. The wicked condemned; the Just rewarded; Satan subdued. I follow each line, become lost in the contours, the details, imagining where I'll end up on such a day of judgment.

"You'd better be on the right side of right when this day comes," I say.

"Indeed," Drake says. He presses his hand on the stone to the painting's right. A seal breaks with a whoosh then the wall pivots inward on hidden hinges.

"After you," Drake says, motioning me along. I move forward as instructed, but he stops me with a raised hand. His expression turns serious. I glance away, put off by the stare.

"Emery," he says. "I need to tell you, once you enter this room, there's no turning back. You'll be bound to us with your next step."

I return his stare. I think about the money. I think about his words. I think about her. I consider what it means to be *bound to us*.

Drake continues. "You can still turn back, cancel the contract, and agree to speak of this to no one under penalty of death. This next step is *your* Rubicon, dear Emery, for in this room you'll hear what you can't unhear and see what you can't unsee. You'll be fully involved in this project as per our contract." He adjusts his tie, glances down. Then his dark eyes hold mine, and again I feel dazed and euphoric.

"I've seen two men murdered tonight for sport," I say, suddenly emboldened, thinking of the Roman's bout, thinking about the fact I can't *unsee* what I've already seen. "Now I'm hanging out with immortal billionaires who hang priceless works of art in musty corridors."

Drake nods.

"Then you give me some mysterious choice between *us*—" I make air quotes for the last word— "or leaving now under *penalty of death.*" More air quotes. "As funny as this sounds, you're my last light on a dark horizon. I need the money. If you hadn't intervened when you did, I'd be dead already. At least with all of this..." I wave my hand around. "I'll have some small purpose. Right now, I have nothing."

Drake's chiseled expression gives away nothing. I glance at Blake's *Vision,* then peer into the room's darkness.

"I'm in," I say. "It can't be any worse than what I've already seen."

Drake wastes no time. "Marvelous!" he says, punctuates with a muffled clap of gloved hands. He moves inside and I follow.

It takes a second for my eyes to adjust. The room is dim and obscured by shadow. Slowly details come into focus. Six plush chairs surround a long mahogany table. Metal sconces hang on the walls about every six feet. A huge vase bursts with flowers of all colors and types from the table's center. The room fills with a subtle, but pleasant, aroma. A gift after the haughty odors of the arena.

An elegant chandelier hangs above the table in three tiers, each drips cascades of crystal. Drake speaks a command, and its lights brighten to further reveal the space. Thick Turkish carpets cover floors of stone block. Tapestries fall from the walls in swirling colors. I step forward. Igneus is already seated on the table's right side. He glances up, then back at his phone.

The table is meticulous, set with silver for a sumptuous meal. White plates bounce the chandelier's brilliance onto crystal stemware. The crystal further refracts the light, and diamonds splay onto the table's dark wood. It's charming, otherworldly. A mise-en-scène of sfumato worthy of DaVinci.

My eyes fall on the room's far end. Pressed into the wall, in gold, is the same symbol I'd seen Drake use to sign his check in the Burj Khalifa.

I move to examine it. "What's this?" I say, run my fingers over smooth lines.

Drake assumes a chair at the table's head. "That's our symbol," he says. "The Labarum. The symbol of X'chasei."

I repeat the word. "X'chasei. What's it mean?"

Drake pauses to light a cigarette then exhales a cloud of smoke that hovers like a storm cloud. "It means God shouldn't have forgotten us."

Thirty minutes later, Longinus appears. His hair is wet, its blackness shimmering in the room's crystal. He, too, dresses in a designer suit: gray pants and matching coat, silk shirt with a blue collar, a necktie dotted pink and red.

The giant moves to the table's other end.

Drake watches him. "Sometimes I marvel this is the same man I first encountered on Golgotha," he says. "Where that man was a slob and hooligan, this man exudes sophistication."

Longinus's teeth are perfect, his nails clean and manicured. His face, clean shaven, reveals a strong, square jaw. Wounds shatter the image, though: a fat, purpled left eye; cheeks deeply gouged. The bottom lip swells through a dark blue bruise. I wonder why these haven't healed as the bullet hole did. That's if it did at all. I remember my skepticism. This could still all be theatrics, although to what end I can't imagine.

Staying somewhere between ruffian and fashion model, Longinus grabs a napkin from a crystal plate. With a harsh look at Igneus, he snaps it and places it in his lap.

I hit record on my phone.

"X'chasei has met here since before World War One," Drake says.

"And who exactly makes up X'chasei?" I ask.

Drake motions to those present. Longinus smiles. "This is X'chasei's membership in total. This small party has directed much of what goes on in the world for centuries." He draws from the cigarette, exhales as Igneus waves an irritated hand at the smoke.

"Of course, there are more," Drake says. "Thousands more among our ranks, but they're not X'chasei members, per se, just, um, *associates*."

I'm surprised to hear the interjection from Drake, generally not one to hesitate while speaking. My thoughts are interrupted by an abrupt opening of the door, and a line of servants stream in. Dressed in black pants and red vests over white shirts, each carries a tray. The room fills with savory aromas, and my stomach leaps. They arrange the food on the table beneath the large vase of flowers. Our glasses are filled with wine, and the staff vanishes. A man, wearing a silver vest leans forward to make some quick adjustments, then stands with his hands clasped in front of him.

Drake snuffs his cigarette, takes a sip of the wine.

"Very nice, Nigel," he says. "Do give my thanks to the staff." Nigel returns a quick nod and exits the room.

Down the length of the ten-foot table is an assortment of meat: roast beef and chicken, bison and ostrich, caviar and shark. Steaming loaves of bread complement the courses, intermingled with bowls of rice, potatoes of every sort, and roasted yams. Tomatoes and olives mingle with selections of Mahi Mahi and Sea Bass. My mouth waters, but I contain myself.

Longinus hefts a large chicken leg and takes a giant bite. Grease runs down his chin and he chews with his mouth open, looks at Igneus the whole time, even as he dabs his face like a princess.

Igneus grimaces. "I hate you fuckers."

"What?" Drake says.

"I hate this place, I hate this time, I hate this life, I hate this Earth and I hate this goddamned immortal shell." He punctuates his comment with a rapid downward shake of his hands.

Drake sighs. "My dear Igneus, our time is soon, our plan moves forward."

"Nonsense!" Igneus spits. "You've been saying that for centuries." His voice changes to a kind of playground mockery. "Our time is nigh. We're almost there. Redemption is ours." The thin man looks into Drake's face. "It's all nonsense."

Drake looks surprised. Longinus leans back in his chair, arms folded across his massive chest. A grin stretches over broad lips. "Seems our lad is growin' some marbles."

"Dear Igneus, I admit some mistakes but now we're poised for victory," Drake says. "A little longer and we'll succeed."

Igneus's lips quiver, his cheeks draw tight over high bones. "Like you succeeded in wiping out Christianity?"

Longinus laughs out loud. Drake's face betrays a wave of anger.

Igneus stares at the Roman, returns to the mocking playground voice. "We'll watch and see what happens. We'll keep an eye on them." He turns to Drake. "Fantastic idea! Flash forward a few centuries and they're the biggest religion on the flippin' planet—the Bible, the best-selling book in history. I suppose you didn't see that coming in your Constantine days?"

Drake sips from a crystal glass and regards the Jew. "Not only did I see it coming, I nurtured it."

Igneus's expression changes, surprised. His lips move without words, his eyes dart to Longinus, then back to Drake. A thin hand smooths his bald scalp. "Then what," he says. "What secret do you keep from us?"

Longinus leans forward, elbows on the table, dark eyes cold and riveting.

Drake places his chalice on the table and retrieves a pear from his plate. "There are no secrets. You both know what I did as Constantine and you both know the reasons. *But,* if I must restate them..." He looks at both men, holds each one's eyes for a couple of seconds. Then at me with a look that says *no going back now.*

"I have acted—and continue to act—with the best interest of X'chasei in mind. Which is to say *our* interests. I agree it's taken longer than expected, but God has the advantage of omniscience, whereas I have only you two idiots and my hatred for God."

Longinus's brow furrows, lips draw tight around his teeth. Igneus presses his fists on the table and stares at Drake. I trade glances between them all. The tension is thick and may lead to violence. I keep my lips together and watch.

"You've both read the Apostle's Revelation and know what is to come."

Igneus's eyes grow-wide, his clenched fingers tremble.

"Relax," Drake says, lowering his voice. "We won't be here for any of that. In the meantime, I don't believe either of you is living harshly. If we must bide our time, I don't see a source for complaint. Every possible luxury is afforded you. Name it and it's yours."

Drake slides from his chair, hands on the table. He leans forward. "I grow tired of this impatience—from both of you. And more tired of your impudence." He looks at Igneus. "I've been patient with you. I've suffered your whining diatribes, even as I wait for you to finish your directives. Tasks only you can accomplish. Please do not try me."

Igneus leans back, gaze shifting from Drake to the floor.

Drake turns to Longinus. "Have you found my cow?"

Longinus lowers his head and mutters, "Non."

"And how long has it been since the search began?"

Longinus crinkles his lips. "I'm non sure."

"At least a century. And I find myself sitting at a table, inhaling the repulsive smells of cooked flesh, listening to the two of you accuse me of secrets." His voice lowers. "Consider your allegiances and what part you play in our combined fate. Then perform your tasks, and I'll show you the way out of this prison."

Silence permeates as Drake returns to his seat, elbows on the chair's arms, fingers steepled in front of him.

"I'll leave tomorrow," Longinus says.

Drake nods, then looks at Igneus.

The man stares ahead, eyes dart like reading some document only he can see. Drake waits, Longinus returns to his meat.

"It seems my choices are the same as they were centuries ago," Igneus says. "I'll do my part, if only to be away from you."

Drake claps his gloved hands a single time. "It's a deal," he says. "Longinus will find my cow, and Igneus will unify the currency."

"And you?" Igneus says.

Drake flashes a sizzling smile. Igneus averts his gaze as if the look might hypnotize.

"As for me," he says, "I'll bring peace to the world."

CHAPTER 12

GOLGOTHA, DURING THE CRUCIFIXION

He stands in front of the cross fighting his sickness. The place is a breathing cesspool, but he wants Jesus to see him, to look upon his face as He slowly dies.

"He knows you're here," the voice whispers. Cain's certain this is true, knows the Man can feel his presence, his face in the crowd, enjoying the sights and sounds of such Godly amusement.

Cain watches, becomes more disinterested as Jesus suffers. The day is hot, each breath a new assault of corpulent waste, of sticky-fat flesh exhaling their toxins. With a force of will he masters his senses and stands for hours, not tiring.

Will God let this happen?

"Yes," the voice responds.

They wait and watch. The hours drag on. The sun does not relent. The only entertainment comes from a large, well-muscled soldier who acts as the lord of this hill. He spits commands at his underlings, offers amusement to the crowd as he beats a young soldier unconscious after he doesn't obey fast enough. He's boisterous, loud. His body scarred from previous battles. He is the face of the Roman Legion.

He speaks to the Messiah, who struggles for breath, hasn't the strength to answer. "How ye doin' up there? Do non go dyin' on me now lad, I've some coin ridin' on ye?"

The Messiah lifts His head, looks toward the sky. Blood pours over His forehead, over His face and naked body. "Father! Why hast thou forsaken me?"

"Shud'up!" the Roman yells. "Ye da's non here. Save ye strength lad! Good advice to be sure."

The Messiah's head lolls, and He says no more.

Today, three crosses occupy the Skull. Today, three will die. The massive soldier moves to the cross to the left of Jesus. He examines the criminal then sends up a barrage of curses. A young soldier appears beside the centurion and a huge fist sends him sprawling. "Ye let'm die!" the centurion bellows. The soldier spits blood, shakes his head. The big Roman glares up, raises his spear, and impales the criminal's thigh. The man on the cross makes no move. Dead, indeed.

The centurion kicks the kneeling soldier in the ribs, then bends to his gasping face. "M'be next time ye'll be keepin' a better eye?"

The soldier crumples, gasps, nods.

The Roman plods toward the next criminal. This man's abdomen flutters as he gasps for air. The Roman grins, then speaks to the soldier at this cross's base. "The wife?" he asks.

The soldier motions to the site's myriad caves and catacombs. "Waiting for you," he says. "Same deal as before, her pleasures for his quick death."

The Roman shows yellow teeth through a bristly, black beard. "Aye? Ye've done well lad."

The soldier beams.

The Roman plods off, stops to cast lots in a wager for all the criminal's collected clothing. He whoops in thunderous bass when he wins, then orders another soldier to collect his bounty. He moves off toward the catacombs, toward the dying criminal's waiting wife.

Toward evening, the centurion returns, a grand smile on his face. A lady follows, speaks fast, her tones pleading. The Roman ignores her as he trudges up the hill. He has a peculiar gait, as if he's been marching since the day he was born. The woman's face is bruised and lined with tears. She grabs the centurion's arm.

"Finish him," she begs.

The Roman looks toward the criminal, points a thick finger. "Can ye non see, he's already gone." The woman's mouth falls open. Her eyes blaze with hate.

"Do non be sad, lass. Twas ye whore's ways that did'm in," the Roman grins. "Saves me the trouble."

He barks an order, and his charges move to the cross and lower the body. "There ye go," he says, "ye can be takin' him home now." He cups her breast with a massive hand. "Do non be forgettin' me, tho."

She slaps his hand away, sprints past her dead husband, shrieks trailing behind.

The Roman watches, laughs all the way. When she's gone, he moves to the base of Jesus' cross. "I win again, lads," he bellows. "This one's still alive." The others groan in response.

He raises a gleaming spear and levels it at Jesus' side. Then, he notices a chalice at the cross's base. It's partially filled with blood. "Who's the sick bugger t'be huntin' blood?" He speaks to the crowd. None answer.

He upends the cup and the Messiah's blood pours. "Ye be some sick'uns to be sure." He scrapes his finger along the cup's inner rim, then holds it out. "Wanna lick?"

Those closest step away, horrified. The Roman shrugs, then pops the bloody digit in his mouth as the crowd gasps. Cain almost vomits. The Roman smiles, yellow teeth coated deep red. "Always refreshin'."

He tosses the cup and hefts his spear, pushing it into Jesus' side, speaking as he advances inch by inch. "C'mon, lad," he says, "look at the pretty Roman. Can ye non see me? Look here, lad. C'mon, boy, find me eyes."

Jesus' entire body lifts toward the sky. With a gasp, He cries, "It is finished!" Then He's dead.

The words ring through Cain's head, as if Jesus isn't referring to His ordeal, but to the fate of Humanity. His skin erupts in gooseflesh, breath flutters in his chest. They know not what they do.

With a rush, the wind howls fierce, sudden. Cain spreads his arms, fully faces the gale, unsurprised.

The sky turns black. Murmurs, then panicked screams race over the crowd. Lightning shrieks, slices the air as thunder rolls through angry clouds. Cain stands, open-mouthed and sweating, as the crowd runs in panic. The beasts push past, stink trailing in palpable tendrils and swept away by the rushing wind.

Sadness becomes confused contentment. He smiles, unafraid of God's theatrics. God's been removed, cast aside by His own creation.

The corpse hangs from the oaken cross, and Cain regrets that Jesus never once looked at him. He expects the Messiah's broken form to become whole, to leap from the splintered cross, to rain fire from the heavens. To slay them all with a single word.

Then something catches his eye. He focuses, heart hammering like a tempest on taut canvas. Cold chills fling spiked shards through paralyzed nerves.

The huge Roman glows emerald green.

The voice whispers, "See this."

CHAPTER 13

LONDON, ENGLAND

Igneus quits the room shortly after we dine.

Drake, Longinus, and I remain to enjoy a digestif as I wonder at my surroundings. Wonder at how much my life has changed in only a few days. Then she leaps into my thoughts, and I suppress the grief, take a long drink of wine.

Ever-present questions float through my mind to multiply by the hour. My notepad's been getting a workout.

I open my mouth but then snap it shut, unsure if I can speak freely in front of Longinus.

Drake reads my mind. "I'm sure you have many questions."

Longinus pushes himself from the table, is stilled by Drake's gloved hand. "Do stay, Longinus," he says. "You and Emery should become better acquainted."

Longinus retains his seat; Nigel appears with cigars and brandy on a polished silver tray.

Drake looks at me, waiting. I adjust myself in my chair and move the brandy a bit closer.

"I must apologize, dear Emery, it seems I'm a bad influence."

He reads my confused expression and then nods at the snifter in front of me. "Recovery? You told me you were in recovery."

I stare at the liquid, the glass of demons. *Sipping tea in hell*, I think.

"It's not every day you see two men murdered for sport by a member of the Roman Legion," I say. Drake watches; he knows there's more to the story.

Longinus perks up at the mention of the Legion.

"How about Constantine the Great?" I continue. "Tell me about that. And about unifying some currency, looking for cows, bringing peace to the world."

"And is this *the* Longinus of legend?" I add.

The giant wraps thick lips around his cigar and sizes me up.

"*The* Longinus who wields the Spear of Destiny? The pike that killed Christ?"

I look the giant right in the eyes as I speak. Perhaps the brandy has made me bold. Perhaps I feel Drake can protect me. Either way, the Roman doesn't react a bit, only stares with eyes as dark as a murderer's soul.

"May I see this spear?"

Longinus glances at Drake. "Non," he says.

"Well, is it true? Are you, he?" I ask.

"Aye," he says, emitting a steam-engine's worth of smoke.

I sip the brandy and return Longinus's stare. "You see, this is what I call ABnormal," I spell the first two letters aloud. "Or better put, complete and utter horse shit. Excuse my skepticism, but all I can say for a fact is that you guys have plenty of money and too much time. I should be in awe, eh? Sitting here with the actual man who finished off Christ *and* the actual man who was like the third or fourth human ever on the planet. I mean, Jesus Christ…" I trail off, struck by the vulgarity of using God's name as a cuss in this specific context.

I hear a chortle from the end of the table.

Then Longinus's laugh fills the room. I'm struck by the giant's expression, teeth bared, head back, laughing without care. Drake has a huge smile, too.

I laugh until my eyes water. "Jesus Christ," I say and laugh harder. My old pal booze has chased the demons off for a bit. It feels good to laugh; and foreign; and I'm struck by the sensation, the pleasure.

Longinus refills my brandy, then clips a cigar and hands it to me. I hold it in my mouth waiting for him to light it. The laughter dries up, the Roman's eyes are sinister as he grasps a candle and slides it toward me, keeping his distance from the flickering flame.

His actions are odd, and at first I can't quite account for them, but then I remember his reaction in the locker room when Drake flipped the cigarette into his chest.

"Why are you scared of fire?" I ask.

The Roman is halfway to his seat. He stops cold, turns to me. Sweat beads on his brow, his lips turn down at the corners as dark eyes wander away.

"You see, dear Emery," Drake says, "Longinus has suffered much through the centuries. Being a Legionnaire had its discomforts, but back then, I had a problem. I'd seen two who were special in some way. The problem: I knew not where to find them. It took a bit of coin to accomplish, and then, once found, they both had the same skepticism as you but showed it in different ways. It wasn't like I could use LinkedIn, but even then, my resources were vast. So, after putting some silver in the right hands, I invited dear Longinus for an audience."

The Roman sits, cigar drooping from his lips, eyes in a faraway place. "I do non care to hear this tale," he says.

Drake looks at him like a father looks at a child. "Do indulge me this once," he says, "for Emery's sake?"

I don't think Longinus relents for my sake, but he offers a small nod, finishes his brandy in a gulp, then refills his glass to the brim. His nod is lost in the darkness of the room's shadows.

CHAPTER 14

JERUSALEM, TWO WEEKS AFTER THE CRUCIFIXION

The desert sends a stirring breeze as Cain descends the spiral staircase and strides into the courtyard. He inhales, thinks about the barren expanse outside these high, stone walls. Dead dunes, constantly shifting, burying deed and memory.

In the courtyard's center, a fig tree grows, healthy branches bent by fat fruit. Beneath, a bench sits on large cobblestones that spread in a circular pattern. Like sprouting roots, they branch wider as they go, like the web of a spider.

Weeds aren't permitted here, and the stone is swept daily. The walls are scrubbed weekly to assure dust has no time to settle. Along the perimeter, flowers bloom in decorative clay pots and emit a sweet fragrance as they splay bright red and purple over weathered stones.

Cain likes the seclusion here, has spent many nights wondering at the stars, asking who will outlive whom. Like the desert, like himself, the stars are immortal, ever-changing, even raging, against forces unseen. Unlike the celestial, humans are nothing more than victims of God's theatrics. Living, breathing, talking bags of His favored fluid.

He settles on the bench, flaps the bottom of shimmering red robes, crosses his left leg over his right.

Sham'beth the Servant and Longinus of Misthli stand before him.

The former seems uneasy, stands a safe distance to the left and behind the hulking Roman.

The soldier wears a scowl behind his coarse beard. He's been made to wait while Cain finished breakfast.

Cain regards the Roman's armor, dull with smeared stains of many types of bodily fluids. The man takes no pride in his appearance. Large, hairy arms cross over his breastplate; thick leather sandals dig into the stone. He returns a steady gaze.

"Where's the money?"

Sham'beth shuffles a few inches away from the Roman, glances between his master and the soldier.

"Sham'beth, you may go. I'll see you this afternoon," Cain says.

Sham'beth doesn't argue, he nods and steps past the soldier, stays well out of arm's reach.

Cain turns to Longinus. "You wish to get right to business?"

"Is that non why I'm here?"

"It is indeed," Cain says, eyeing the blunt hilt of his sword.

"Let's be gettin' on with it," Longinus scowls. "I non have all day."

"Of course, of course," Cain produces a bag of bulging coins. "I'm sure you're busy."

Longinus watches the bag, and his expression softens. It contains more money than he can make in a year up on the Skull, even considering that earned by various creative means.

"I've an interesting proposition and I want you to think it over before giving a response," Cain says. "I'm going to place this money on the bench, and, if you do as I ask, you may have it all."

The Roman steps forward, licks his lips. "I be listenin'."

"I want you to kill me."

The soldier's eyes flash for a half a second. His hand inches close to his sword. His lips twitch, then he bursts into laughter.

"Kill ye? Kill ye! Aye, a cherry deal to be sure, then 'tis me hangin' from a tree up on Golgotha?" Teeth flash from deep inside his beard. The wind rises in a gush to sweep through the fig tree's leaves. "I do non think so, citizen," he says, shakes his head. "I do non think so a'tall."

"Perhaps you should rethink," Cain says. "I've planned everything. You slay me, then simply wait until Sham'beth returns and slay him. I've instructed all others not to return until two days from now, so you'll be quite alone. Take the money and at some point, when our bodies are discovered, everyone will think it was robbery or revenge." He favors the Roman with a smile and a wink. "In any event, I doubt too much attention will be given to this sort of thing. No one will know, and you'll be richly rewarded."

Something stirs in Longinus's eyes, as if more intellect bubbles beneath the Roman's harsh exterior.

"Think about it carefully," Cain says, turns to put the purse on the bench.

He hears the sword slide from its sheath. His lips stretch into a smile as the blade plunges through his back to appear in his midsection.

One never gets used to the pain.

Flowers blur to a wavering, mixed smear as Cain falls to his knees, grips the sword's razor point, amazed at the length of steel protruding from his gut.

The coins drop to the ground with a chink.

Then, the Roman's foot is on his back, and the sword's pulled out with a quick tug.

Slashes appear on Cain's gloves. Blood pours through and onto the stone.

The centurion steps in, retrieves the money bag, then stands smiling, watching Cain die.

Drake looks at Longinus. "I rather think you enjoyed that."

The hint of a smile appears on Longinus's face. "I be sayin' the same about ye."

I tap my cigar into a silver tray. "You killed him?" I say to Longinus.

Longinus shakes his head. His eyes darken. "Non," he says. "I sealed me own fate with me own blade."

Drake sips his brandy, then pops a grape in his mouth.

"I was wondering," I say, "because he looks quite alive at the moment, which causes me to cry bullshit." Certainly, this story affects the Roman in a way even the best Hollywood actor can't pull off, this fear of fire.

Longinus looks at me for a long time, then says, "The tale non be finished."

"And what of Igneus, did you have him kill you too?" I ask Drake.

At that, both men laugh.

"The best part of Igneus non ever entered his ma's womb," Longinus says.

"Our dear Igneus lacks the constitution for such methods," Drake says. "But since you ask, I found him dying in an alley. He'd been robbed and gutted. He died in front of me, so I brought him to my house where he survived. Needless to say, he didn't take the news he was immortal very well. So, while Longinus was busy killing me, Igneus was upstairs recuperating and trying to come to terms with his new circumstances. What happened next certainly didn't help."

I refill our glasses as Drake continues the tale.

———

Cain sputters, leans back on his haunches. Blood dribbles from his mouth, pours from the wound in his mid-section.

Tarnished teeth flash as Longinus wipes the blade clean on Cain's tunic.

"Pleasure doin' b'ness with ye." He proffers a salute and replaces the sword in its sheath. Jingling the coins, he moves away, a spring in his step.

"Stop," Cain says, forces the words. "There's something else."

Longinus stops midstride, faces the man.

"Do ye be wantin' another deal?"

Cain speaks too low for the soldier to hear. Longinus moves close, leans into his face as Cain fumbles with his gloves, pulling with urgency.

The gloves peel from bloody hands as Cain lurches forward. He grabs Longinus's hair with both hands, pulls him close. The mark glows, blinds, as if lava flows through its circles and drips over the vortex of triangles.

Longinus struggles against the grasp, eyes darting around the courtyard as if searching for an unseen army. Cain's blood soaks the Roman's armor, splatters onto his face.

"This is going to hurt," Cain whispers, then releases the Roman with a push.

Longinus skittles across the stone, draws his sword in a well-practiced gesture. His expression becomes rage as he races forward, pike raised to strike.

Cain hears his own laughter far away, feels only the dismay of one who's lost too much blood.

A hoarse cry roars from the giant. Cain imagines the sound raging across the battlefield, flying in the face of vicious enemies and laying them low.

A cry that announces the Roman Legion, announces the warrior Longinus has entered the fray.

Raising his face, Cain offers his head for the final assault.

Longinus's beard starts to tremble. The sword falls to the stone, clangs like a hammer on an anvil. His eyes squeeze shut, massive hands drop to his belly. A questioning invades his features, then his eyes fly open, examining Cain, searching.

He falls to his knees, hoarse groans escape. He's on all fours, crawling in a loose wander, hands clawing the stone beneath.

He spasms, rolls on his back, broad hands scratching his belly, feet and legs pumping as spiked tendrils of flame spark between his fingers. The deep cries of before are replaced by something more guttural, something more agonizing and desperate.

He tries to gain his feet, gets one leg in front before, with a crash of white-hot flame, he's consumed by a conflagration.

The screams are terrifying. Longinus howls, contorts on the stone, his armor melting, dripping molten steel to the ground. Flames shoot yards, sizzle from his open mouth and nostrils, furious reds and yellows that race through his hair and over his wiry beard.

Skin ripples, then peels away in crackling flaps. A scent of burned meat overwhelms the flowers, fills the courtyard with an oily spice that stings the nose and seizes the stomach.

Longinus leaps in the flame, tries to oust the fire with flapping arms. He whirls and stretches as burning fingers reach for Cain's throat, coal-ash eyes filled with rage.

His head tips toward the sky, charred mouth agape, eyes flaming into the day's heat.

All the agonies of all the ages combine in one feral howl. A cry that sends Cain's ears into a high-pitched buzz. A cry so furious, filled with such pure emotion and molten intensity that the courtyard's lone fig tree shivers. It resounds off the surrounding stone like some jungle cat moving deft and enraged. Searching, searching for some point of finality.

Then Longinus collapses.

The fire dies leaving a smoldering, charred pile on the spider's outer web.

The remnant of the soldier draws no breath, makes no move as silence presides like some newly crowned boy-king, exalted and aimless.

Protected by God Himself, Cain thinks. He staggers to his feet, feels weak, steps over the smoldering corpse to collapse on the bench beneath the fig tree.

His wounds begin to heal, his nostrils fill with the ripe pungency of burnt flesh. The mark is raised and rough, shows no light or animation.

The corpse in the courtyard will be hard to explain. Hopefully, the servant's allegiance is strong enough to help dispose of it without asking too many questions.

Then another thought hits him.

The green aura is false. The corpse still emits the color, but its life is completely spent.

All a dream, he thinks, nothing more. Which means Igneus

survived his wounds by sheer luck, not immortality. Cain realizes he's the only immortal. The only person condemned as such.

Disappointment fills him as he looks to the clear sky, revolted by the bloody courtyard.

Then, he hears a shuffling footstep.

Igneus stands at the bottom of the stairs, his chest thin and bony above clean white bandages. Eyes bug above a sharp nose. He trembles, reminds Cain of an oft-beat heel hound. Tears stream from grief-stricken eyes.

"We are condemned," he says. A question and a statement. His face is ashen, his body quakes. Trembling hands grip the sides of his bald head.

He takes two steps, lips quivering.

"*We are condemned!*" he screeches, hands reaching to the heavens, sharp chin leveled toward the sky.

"WE ARE CONDEMNED!"

The thin man expels his emotion with a wavering shriek.

Cain makes no move to comfort him.

Igneus falls, sobs, his body shakes, tears pour.

Between the Jew's sobs, a scratching becomes apparent. The charred corpse struggles to its knees. Empty, smoldering eyes meet his; its mouth opens with a crackle, like dried leather being stretched.

The wail that follows deafens, full of a century's anguish and pain.

Igneus presses his head to the stone, covers his ears, makes only small whimpering sounds.

The scorched man rages. In four thousand years, in all the lives Cain has lived, no cry has ever matched the emotion or intensity of this howl—save the sound the Earth made the day he'd murdered his brother.

Smoldering, Longinus starts to move. Black smoke rises into the cloud-spackled sky. Charred flesh struggles to stand, strains to speak.

Sobbing and hopeless, Igneus kneels, quakes into the courtyard's stone, his frail frame wrapped like a skeleton in a shroud.

This, Cain thinks, is my army.

CHAPTER 15

I awake to darkness, hear the shuffle of feet like sand on a concrete floor. In the distance a steady, faint dripping. The place smells cold.

My head throbs like a warning beacon. *Probably all the booze,* I think; I sense no other pain. My old nemesis the hangover is back like a loud-mouth brother-in-law you can't disinvite to Thanksgiving. I sit on something hard, try to move my hands, realize they're bound together even as my feet are bound to the base of whatever I sit upon.

The first thin fingers of panic move into my throat, and I stifle the urge to yell out. I doubt this is by Drake or Longinus's design; they have no reason to capture and bind me. I tug at the binds, search for a knot or buckle that I might undo.

"Ah, Mr. Merrick," a voice says. "I have many questions for you."

I say nothing, try to discern from where the voice originates. I've seen enough movies to realize that when one finds oneself tied to something with a hood over one's head, it usually doesn't bode good things.

Something heavy screeches across the floor, and I hear the person pulling it exhale with every effort. Then it stops, and he speaks again, this time much closer.

"We mean you no harm," he says. "We merely have some questions and grasped an opportunity to ask them. I apologize for our methods, but discretion is important in our fight."

Those icy fingers return. *Terrorists. I've been kidnapped by terrorists.* I search my last memory, remember leaving Drake and Longinus to walk London's streets. As a young reporter, I'd lived in London and always enjoyed the night air and tapestry of its thoroughfares. It was the middle of the night, and I strolled the silent streets thinking of Rhyme, filled with regret, wondering about these immortals to which I'm now bound. The night air helps to clear my head and London's sights are always welcome to my eyes.

I remember being approached by a clean-shaven young man. He wore an interesting pin on his lapel, two knights riding a horse in tandem. He produced a cigarette and asked me for a light. I remember asking him the meaning of his brooch as I searched my pockets for a lighter. Then he jabbed me with something.

"You assholes tazed me!" I struggle at my bonds, pull with all my might, shake my head against the shroud.

I feel a hand on my shoulder which sets me to a higher gear. I'd seen the videos. *They're going to slit my throat. They're going to exploit me on video for their own savage ends.* I try to scream even as I'm surprised by my will to live.

The hand squeezes hard, then I feel a tingle in my testicles. At first faint, like a lover's touch, then growing until it achieves just the edge of pain. I freeze in terrified silence.

The hand on my shoulder relaxes a bit.

"Mr. Merrick, we mean you no harm. You will be released after we have our answers. If you do not care to answer, then…"

The tingling rises. My testicles sizzle like eggs on a hot plate. I feel them retract inside me, fleeing the pain. I writhe in my chair, wail into the shroud, try anything to move. My penis fills with live current, feels like it will burn right off my body. I shriek, shudder at my bonds.

Then the sizzling stops.

I sit breathless, head pounding, fighting nausea. Vomiting in this shroud will be messy and could compromise my airway. My scrotum feels the last tickling spasms of electricity drift across its area and then disappear. I dry-heave once but manage to keep my stomach at bay.

The voice continues. "Well, that's unpleasant but it does make a point. Let's say we make a deal, you and me? A bargain with one another, eh? Let's afford each other the courtesy of being honest." Here he pauses. His accent sounds Arabian. "If you lie, I'll fry your balls to oblivion."

"Jesus, what could I possibly know about anything?"

The hand gives my shoulder a gentle squeeze. "Do try, Mr. Merrick. You might surprise yourself. And please, do not use the Lord's name as a curse."

"Are you fucking kidding me?" I say. "You have my balls wired to a car battery and you don't want me to curse? I can think of no more perfect time to curse than now—you fucking asshole!"

I will the panic away and swallow hard. "You're fooling no one, jerk off. I was trained for this in the Army. I know the story. No matter what I say, I'm dead. And if you torture me, you'll not know if I've told the truth or just said anything I can think to stop the pain. Either way, I'm fucked. And by extension, so are you."

There's a long pause broken only by the sound of those distant water drops.

"Come now," he says, "we both know you were never in the Army."

I hear the sound of a transformer and my balls reignite. The muscles of my lower abdomen contract, force my chest toward my lap. I seize, my torso tighter and tighter, my vertebrae about to pop like corn kernels; my penis is red hot, my balls wrapped in the coils of a writhing electric python. It feels like flames will shoot out my ass at any moment.

The fire stops.

I sit pitched forward, bound to my seat, heaving my breath as the serpent's slimy fire dissipates from my groin and abdomen. I wonder if I've pissed my pants.

"Remember our deal," the man says.

Rage consumes me. I pull with everything I have; trying to kick my shaky legs, screaming at the top of my voice, straining against the bonds. "When I get free, I'm going to kill you!"

There's a laugh. "Mr. Merrick, we both know you've never killed anyone and wouldn't have the first idea what to do even if I set you free this instant." I hear him shuffle a little farther away. "Why must you make this so hard?"

I open my mouth to scream more expletives, but then some shred of reason stops me. Why *was* I making this so hard? I don't even know what he wants.

"Okay, dipshit," I say. "Ask your questions. Although I'm much more likely to cooperate without electrodes on MY BALLS!" I scream the last two words with every ounce of rage and pain in me. In my mind I'm shrieking in his face, spit flying with each word.

"Mr. Merrick, what is the nature of your employment with Mr. Drake?"

I'm dumbfounded. "Are you kidding? You want to know about Thaddeus Drake? You're cooking my fucking jumblies when you could do a Google search? Fucking seriously?"

I feel the tingle start to grow.

"*Okay*, okay, okay," I say as fast as my mouth can form the words. "Easy with that thing, fucking asshole. Drake hired me to write his authorized biography."

"About?"

"About? What do you think it's about, Einstein? It's about his life. You know, like how biographies are generally about someone's life."

"Yes, thank you for clarifying. But what about his life in particular? What highlights will you focus on?"

I breathe a bit easier. Although I haven't told him a direct lie, I certainly haven't told him anything close to the truth. *Gambling with your balls,* I think. *That's some Bruce Willis—Die Hard shit.*

"Um...Well, I'm starting with his humble beginnings: farm kid, small town, etcetera, and hope to wrap it up after this peace summit he has planned."

I wait, not knowing if the python will find my balls again. I have no idea if I'm lying this time. I don't know and haven't asked Drake about his current backstory. I haven't researched it either, figuring I'll ask during the course of our next interview.

The electric coils don't come, only a void of silence.

"Is that what he told you?"

"What? That he's a farm kid?"

"Yes."

"Well, something to that effect, working in the fields and such," I say.

"And he's planning a peace summit. Is that the one in Jerusalem?"

"Jesus, where are we and who the fuck are you?"

A quick jolt from the electric serpent rattles my testicles. My pain bounces back to me from the surrounding space.

"The Lord's name," he says, "please, don't profane it."

My testicles throb like little dried-up meatballs in a chafing dish. The thought flips my stomach, and I dry-heave again.

"Do you speak of the summit in Jerusalem?" he asks again.

"I'm not sure. We haven't gotten that far. I mean, it's not like I'm the one planning the damn thing."

"Mmhmm," the man says. "And what else does he have planned? What are his minions up to?"

"Is this the goddamn *Avengers*? Is Drake a super villain? Do we need to go sock his thugs in the kisser? Activate the Bat Signal?" I say.

"You use humor as a defense," he says. "I'm impressed because you should be bawling like a newborn. Mr. Merrick, I'm referring to Longinus and Igneus. What are they doing?"

My mind races. A much tougher line of questioning. I'd sat in the meeting and heard the plans. These will be hard to avoid and impossible to lie about.

"I'm not sure," I say.

My balls sizzle, this time for about 30 seconds. I choke back hot bile.

"What are they doing?"

My head throbs. My balls feel like they're weeping. "I…We…" I search for some plausible answer. "Longinus is looking for cows," I say. It sounds like a lie even as it leaves my mouth and I tense for the next jolt.

"Interesting. Do you know why?"

"No, but Longinus said he's been looking for a long time."

I hear feet shuffle. "Centuries," he says in a whisper. "And Igneus?"

"No idea," I say. "Drake's set him on a task, but I don't know what." This is a calculated risk on my part. I know Igneus has been sent to unify some currency, but I also know there are some things this man doesn't know, and I'll be damned if I'll give him the satisfaction.

"Have you ever heard of the Kilal?"

"Yeah, I wrote one once. Wanna hear it?

"My balls are my friends,
"Together forever, we.
"Does that make me nuts?"

I laugh, hysterical, desperate.

"No, Mr. Merrick, that is a Haiku. I speak of an old, iron pot."

"Never heard of it," I say.

"This is important, Mr. Merrick. Does Drake have the Kilal?"

"This is my answer, Mr. Asshole, I don't know."

"Has he showed you his mark?"

I play dumb. "You mean a mole or something?"

The electric serpent comes alive, only a slight tingle. A warning.

"No, Mr. Merrick, I mean the Mark of Cain."

My mind goes blank, all thought suspends. He knows Drake is Cain.

I sigh. "Yes, I've seen it. Terrifying." I say this last almost under my breath, thinking back to the mark's crimson light, filled with hatred, its malice gripping my soul.

"Indeed."

CHAPTER 16

JERUSALEM, AFTER THE CRUCIFIXION

"Go into all the world and teach my gospel."

Light surrounds the Messiah, bleeds through his clothes, changes dark hair to bright white. He levitates, takes in each disciple as He rises. The Temple's roof shimmers, becomes translucent. Then He's beyond the roof and into the sky, leaving the Earth to be overcome by desert sand and lifeless landscape.

John wants to say more, wants to go with Him, wants to embrace death and witness Heaven's expanse first-hand.

His friend is high above him now, blinding bright, moving into a cloud, and up and up until John sees only a speck in the distance.

With a glimmer, the great stone roof becomes solid once more. Others stand near John, some with mouths open, rubbing their eyes, still as stone. All look upward.

Great joy rises as John's laughter surges in great hoarse peals. The others look with strange expressions, then one by one join until they all stand laughing in a loose semi-circle.

Peter embraces. James, tears in his eyes, slaps his back. John hugs the Disciple next to him, joy fills them all as others give and receive, bask in the glory of the moment.

Peter's teeth flash through a red beard as he smiles at the others; his voice rises over the din. "We must tell all as Jesus commanded."

John doesn't know what the future might hold, but he'll start to spread the news today. Jesus has commanded, and he isn't going to waste a single minute before starting his ministry, won't waste a single second before nourishing parched earth.

Time is precious and short.

James embraces him. "Let us go, my brother. We have much to do."

They move through the Temple, cast glances at the pillared ceiling. Others stand immobile, show expressions of awe and disbelief. Some weep, some lie on the floor or lean against the room's vast stone pillars. John moves through the crowd, a broad grin on his face.

The other apostles enter the mass, and soon the Temple fills with emotion as loud prayers rise glorious to the rafters.

John kneels beside an old woman, lays his hands on her shoulders. She sits, legs splayed in front of her, gazing into his face, smiling through sunken cheeks—a toothless smile. Tears leave watery remnants over hard-earned wrinkles.

"In my lifetime the Messiah has come," she says.

"Yes, Jesus awaits you," says John.

Another sob escapes, and she lifts her head. "I wish I could go today." John kisses her forehead, squeezes her hands.

Most of the crowd are now on bended knee as his brothers move among them.

He notices a small group of men who, unlike the others, stand. Two face him—a sickly, bald man, and a jittery-eyed, bearded creature with the look of a servant. They speak with a giant who faces away.

He steps toward them, but Peter grasps his arm. His face is radiant. "There are even more outside. This is our miracle."

John smiles. "I'll join you shortly."

He watches Peter bound across the room, then turns and walks into a chest like granite. It's the giant he's seen only moments before.

"Ye'd do well to watch ye feet rather'n ye boyfriend."

John's face heats with embarrassment. He opens his mouth, but his words are stolen as the man bends so they are eye to eye.

A stench akin to rotten meat comes from the man's throat. His eyes are as dark and lifeless as post holes. John shivers, then surges with confidence. "Did you not witness the miracle, brother?"

"I am non ye brother." He breathes the words into John's face.

John suppresses a grimace. "We're all brothers in Christ." He opens his arms, awaits a hug.

The giant glances at his friends, his expression, confused. His mouth moves beneath a thick beard, as if he chews a distasteful morsel.

Then, a large black globule hits John full in the chest.

"Per'aps ye can hold that fer me. *Brother.*"

A deep bass booms as the man laughs. His companions look abashed. The sick one shudders, as if he'll collapse at any minute. His eyes are large, reflect disgust as he stares at the stain on John's tunic.

The giant slaps the sick one on the shoulder, causes him to stumble into the servant. Laughter resounds as he walks away, crowd parting in front of him.

John wipes the front of his tunic, holds his breath against the stain's stench. Raised voices come to him from the Temple's courtyard.

As he exits, the sun comforts. But it's the sight, from atop the Temple's steps, that solidifies all he's just witnessed, a scene that glorifies the Messiah's majesty and freezes his resolve in place.

People are scattered; some lie, some kneel in the dirt, some with hands lifted toward the sky. A few hundred, each one singing praises. They've all witnessed the event.

They kneel, rise, in small groups, hold hands, sway in unison as someone starts to sing. It sweeps across the square. Voices rise toward the clear sky, young and old embrace. Bodies break away, dance, jump and spin, sing, robes twirling in browns and greens.

People flood the courtyard. The day has cooled, and the crowd rejoices as if a drought has ended. They love, sing, laugh—or weep— baring emotion like a neatly wrapped gift, each accepting and returning in kind.

A new covenant's been struck. They feel it; John feels it. He joins in song as responsibility presses, a feeling of warmth and purpose. Of mission and quest. His chest feels heavy, his head spins, skin erupts in gooseflesh. The extreme weight of all that must be done bears down. There are churches to start, followers to recruit, events to record so the whole world, for generations to come, will know of this new life and the wonderful chance for salvation. It's the task of Jesus' followers to bear witness to the life of Christ and His miracles.

Other disciples spread through the crowd, lay hands on those gathered, speak of the Messiah in loud voices.

The first roots of ministry, the beginning of Earth shaking change.

He notices a lone man staring into the sky, a sharp silhouette against the bright blue horizon. He doesn't worship like the others, but stands, dumbstruck, dark hair ruffling, moving with the breeze as robes swirl around his legs. He wears tan leather gloves balled into fists at his sides.

A peculiar feeling grips John's stomach. *Do I know this man?*

The man averts his gaze, looks ahead, licks his lips, rubs gloved hands together. He shuffles, looks down, rubs his eyes again, then looks to the sky.

John has to tell him what's occurred and allay his confusion. He starts down the stairs, wiping the stain on his tunic.

As he reaches the bottom, he realizes the man now stares at him. His mouth drops open, his eyes become wide, awed. His expression is a combination of contempt and disbelief.

He points a single, gloved finger, snarls as blazing eyes stop John in his tracks.

"No," he says.

John smiles, opens his arms. "The Messiah has come."

The snarl turns from contempt to exasperation—an oddly foreign expression within the midst of the praising throng.

"There's nothing to fear," John says.

The man's eyes soften; the snarl becomes a sardonic smile.

"There will be," he says, and disappears into the crowd.

CHAPTER 17

ROME, ITALY

A young priest approaches, glides across the marble floor without a sound.

"It was that day I met the Cain of legend. The vagabond and wanderer." He takes the chair next to me. "Of course, I didn't know it at the time. I was just too...high? Yes, that seems like a good word, *high* on the events that transpired. I'd witnessed, the murder not only of the Messiah, but of my best friend. Then, I'm there as he's resurrected and raised to Heaven."

Holding my eyes, he hands me a blue ice pack. "For your...injuries."

I've been in this place for three days; a very old, very large room; a basement of some sort, but the vastness of the complex makes me think it isn't some ordinary place.

I push myself up, place the bag under my groin with some care. My testicles throb, add a twinge of nausea. I lower myself with some delicacy. "Thank you."

The priest looks someplace far away. "Do you realize how incredible that is? To know everything you believe is true? To quote scripture: *We wrestle not against flesh and blood, but against principalities, against the rulers of the darkness of this world.* You can't imagine the joy of knowing, for certain, that you're doing the will of God."

I think about it, try and see from his point of view. "I can't imagine," I say. "For us these days, every single thing is in doubt. Media is manipulated, things you see may be a trick of technology or just a ploy so the corporations can get more money. Nothing's real anymore."

The man chuckles. "There's one thing and that's God. He's real."

I regard the man for a few seconds. "So, you're immortal too? The Apostle John in the flesh before me?"

"I am," he says, expressionless. "As for immortality, I sincerely hope that *isn't* the case. I can't imagine the splendors of Heaven, but I'm well-familiar with the horrors of Earth and hope when my task is complete, I can leave this horrid place and join my friends in Heaven."

"And that task is to ruin Drake?"

"Cain, you mean?"

"Of course."

"I'm not sure. I don't know if I should be wasting any time on Cain."

"God hasn't told you what to do?"

"Have you heard the story of the Last Supper?"

I sip my water, adjust my position on the ice pack. "Yes, when Judas betrayed Jesus."

"Of course, but that was all in the design, I think. To accomplish Jesus' martyrdom was the real goal. Of course, I don't know this for sure, but I've had long centuries to ponder these questions. We didn't know it was our last supper with Him. But what no one else knows is that Jesus spoke with me privately. This was before He went to the garden to pray. He told me I needed to perform a task. He didn't say what the task was but told me the path would be hard and I'd know when it was time. He then grasped my hand, and I felt an energy surge through me. Then He was gone, and events played out as God intended."

"And that's when you became immortal?"

"Again, I'm not sure, but I think so. After that, we started preaching, growing the Church as God commanded. There were those who didn't care for this threat to their power. They hunted us; persecution and murder followed. Burning, crucifying; women, children, entire congregations. To them, it mattered not. Eventually, I was cornered in a barn while trying to hide, then run through by a young man receiving encouragement from his soldier father. I was his first kill and heard them congratulate the boy while I faded toward death.

"A great relief washed over me in those last moments. I was going to be at Jesus' side once again." He stares far, as if seeing the ghosts of his comrades.

"And then?"

He pauses a second longer. "And then I woke on the floor of the barn, blood pooled around me. Yet, there was no wound in my flesh. I actually felt energized. I remember thinking that perhaps I'd dreamed it all. That the blood had been from the slaughter of some animal before I'd entered and sought refuge. Perhaps I simply hadn't noticed and then passed out from sheer exhaustion and dreamed the rest."

I sip from the large silver chalice, ease my feet to rest on a small ottoman. My groin throbs, my testicles are swollen, bloated and blue. My abdomen is sore as if I've started Navy Seal training. Another priest enters the room, my doctor as I recover here. I glance at the saline dripping into my right arm.

"More morphine?" he asks.

I nod, relax. The cold seeps through my testicles as the opiate seeps through my mind. Such glorious danger. Such demons, cackling up transparent tubing, rushing through my veins, chasing regret and grief to depths unknown. My mouth waters as the drug soothes my shattered psyche.

"Why am I here?" I say.

The Apostle raises his eyebrows. "I don't quite know. I guess my hope is you'll give me information about Drake. Be a sort of spy for me and the Church."

"So why the torture?"

John frowns, shakes his head. "I apologize for that unpleasantness. When I discovered you'd joined Cain's inner circle, I asked to have an audience with you. The priests collected you in London and brought you here. Through the centuries, I've been forced to learn and employ distasteful methods to get information. Which was all I wanted with you. I thought you knew the location of the Kilal. Then God intervened."

I almost spit my water but manage to swallow it. Some enters my lungs and I break into a coughing fit. My balls throb with each jolt, my stomach seizes. "God intervened on my behalf?" I ask, gaining control of the spasms.

"Yes, He told me to treat you as friend."

"And if He wouldn't have said that, you would've killed me?"

The Apostle's face becomes perplexed astonishment. "That would never happen. It breaks a commandment. I do not kill." He states the last sentence with such finality, as if throughout the entirety of his long life the thought's never entered his mind. As if torture outranks murder on morality's scale.

I adjust my position with a wince that John picks up on. "Again, my apologies," he says. "You are quite safe now."

I clear my throat, take a sip of water. My nausea fades by degrees. "And where am I?"

"You are in Italy, Mr. Merrick. The Vatican, to be exact. You are presently under the protection of the Pope."

The demons cackle, stream through my veins. I've made it, at last. The Pope protects me like the lost lamb I've become. Maybe they'll let me wear his hat.

The room in which we sit is cavernous, certainly a hundred feet or more in depth and breadth. Ancient tapestries hang on the walls, each with a religious theme or tribute to saints. It's filled with comfortable but old furniture. Not old, like purchased at a yard sale, but old as if finely crafted and given to some powerful lord or king. Everything is stone: large stone blocks for the floor and wall, marble tables for stone busts of ancient men, a vast vaulted stone ceiling with painted frescos held aloft on great pillars of white.

"The Pope knows my name? He knows I'm here?"

John laughs. "Oh yes," he says. "For I am the Pope. Or was, anyway. Do you know anything about the Catholic church?"

"Well, I suppose as much as the next person."

"The Church is the direct line to Jesus and his disciples. As we grew, we realized managing such an endeavor required better organization. Peter had been commanded by Jesus to build His church. So, the Disciple Peter was the first Pope. The line has remained largely unbroken to this day. The problem for our church was what to do with a Pope that cannot die."

I nod. "That sounds like a problem."

"Actually, it wasn't hard. I was, and am, given special status as a living disciple. I have served as Pope but under another name. Now my sole job is to guard against X'chasei."

I search his features for deceit but find nothing but kindness. I feel no reason to disbelieve him, although I'd wanted to cry bullshit a few different times during his tale. But somehow, that word doesn't fit this man. I believe him, and if I believe what he says, then the rest of the story must be true. I mean, once you jump in the water, you're wet. Can't get *more* wet, right?

I think of Magritte's *Philosopher's Lamp*. I've become that image, sucking my own brain through an apple pipe. It can't get more surreal than Cain as first murderer, cast out, now going by Thaddeus Drake. John as Apostle, immortal by Jesus' hand with some task yet to accomplish. Longinus and Igneus as Cain's evil henchman. *Add Penguin and the Joker and we've got a real party.* Turns out morphine and surreality are great pals.

"When did you discover your immortality?"

"Ah," John says. "I credit your friend Longinus for that. You see, after the crucifixion and holy ascension, the persecution and eradication of the Christians started. The Legion did all it could to stamp us out of existence.

"It was then I encountered Longinus. I intervened while he was trying to rape a member of my church. He knew me, although I didn't remember him, then he punched me so hard I thought I'd never again catch my breath. I lay struggling to breathe as he murdered and burned my flock. But he didn't kill me or even try. He took me to Cain." John leans forward, plucks a date from a silver dish on the table between us.

I listen with rapt attention, pain subsiding by increments as the morphine does its job. "What did Drake...I mean, Cain, do?"

"He sent me to the island of Patmos. In those days, Cain was known as Solon and had a great gift for convincing people to do as he wished. He was valued by the Legion as a diplomat. I'm certain he was paid well. Looking back, I realize Cain had a better understanding of the oceans of time before us. A true understanding of what could be accomplished by mere persistence. Remember, he'd lived for centuries before I was even born and had built himself a comfortable reality. A word from his mouth, and I was banished to the island, where I was supposed to die of hunger or the elements or whatever. There was no escaping Patmos. Every so often soldiers arrived in boats and dropped supplies, but as time went on those drops became increasingly sparse."

"And you didn't die because you're immortal?"

"I don't think so. I remember thinking I probably wouldn't last much longer, hungry and exposed as I was. I don't know if I was being tested like Job, or if what I believed about completing a task for the Messiah was actually true at all." He adjusts his position in his chair. "I abandoned hope many times on that miserable island. But the worst part was the frustration. God sent me to build up His church, to spread His news, but there I sat unable to do anything of the sort. Every so often Cain or Longinus would come and update me on which of my churches had been burnt or what they'd done to one of my brothers in Christ. They'd be as detailed and graphic as possible, relishing my despair." He looks far off here, as if looking through a window to centuries passed. "That was the height of my despair. Those were the days I questioned God the most."

"How did you escape?"

John surprises me with laughter. "Again, God has His plans, and I was there until He needed me elsewhere. So, I went on and lived my life among the rocks and bent trees. Through heat and rain and solitude and hunger, until God turned His attention to me yet again. Then what

I saw…" His look changes to one of astonishment and pure wonder. "What God…showed me there made everything that came before and everything that came after completely trivial and worthless." He leans forward, stares directly in my eyes. "He showed me His plan for humanity. He showed me everything, Emery."

CHAPTER 18

ISLE OF PATMOS, 94 AD

H e'd been deposited here eighteen months ago. Left for dead. His churches abandoned. His ministry paused. Taken from his cell and herded, bound and gagged, onto a small vessel.

The trip had been long, with John lying on the wooden floor of the vessel, listening to the sound of the boat's oars as they struck the water and to the waves as they lapped against the hull. Just when he'd closed his eyes to sleep, he'd been hefted to his feet and deposited on a white, sandy shore.

"Welcome to Patmos," one of the soldiers said, tossed him a satchel and pushed the boat back into the water. A few deft strokes and they were gone, leaving him standing on the shore.

Opening the satchel, he'd found only a modest supply of stale bread and dried fruit.

Why hadn't they killed him like everyone else?

The Apostle stumbles along the path through sheets of rain, and down the small mountain, searching for the cave he passed on his way up.

He imagines his brother's gentle face as tears slide down his cheeks to mix with the rain. Jesus warned of great persecution, and John imagines his own is just beginning.

He shivers, wills himself to stand and move.

The wind blows strong, rain stings his face. Thorns bite as he struggles for a handhold within gnarled bushes on either side of the path. Trees bend as the wind drives harder.

He stumbles, then falls headlong. Stones tear outstretched palms as he slides down the path to stop in six inches of water.

Teeth chatter, fingers and toes go numb. He crawls through the puddle, breathes a prayer of protection. Lightning streaks the darkness and the cave's entrance appears like the maw of some giant creature.

Caked with mud, brown leaves sticking to matted hair, John scrambles forward on bleeding hands and scraped knees.

The cave is dark, lit only by sporadic flashes of lightning. John scrambles in, collapses against the wall.

Cold grips like the devil's hand, shivers become quakes. He hugs himself, tries to think through the clatter of his own teeth. He has no means to start a fire. His head swims, his lower half feels frozen. Water pours over the cave's entrance, creates an expanding brown puddle.

He starts to nod, catches himself, stands, stamps his feet and rubs his hands together. The cave is dank, its rocks cold. His limbs feel like dead weight. He craves clean water and warmth. Despite being immortal, he can still experience the pain of dying, the misery of the flesh. Hunger, dehydration, and the rigors of the cold numb his thoughts.

He moves under the waterfall and fills his mouth, absorbing the liquid like a crusted sponge. God has provided.

Thirst slaked, he returns to the cave and slumps to the ground. Exhaustion overwhelms, beckons to a place warm and safe. His shivering stops, his heart slows. Breathing becomes measured and deep, eyelids impossible to keep open.

His eyes open. The cave is gone, leaving only angry sky above. He blinks against the driving rain, shields his eyes.

Then, the rain stops.

Above, clouds roll up and up, begin to boil, silver-green and silent. He flexes fingers and toes, stands as the clouds cast off the darkness. At first a faint shade of white, then a touch more vivid. Warmth oozes in, hunger disappears, the clouds brighten.

He squints into dazzling whiteness. A dark speck moves, eons away. It's a man, walking. Clouds billow and roll with his approach.

John shades his eyes, strains to make out the figure.

The man takes no shape—*is it a man?*—meshing with the cloud's brilliance, multiplying it a thousand times.

Sweat runs over his forehead as a pleasant breeze tousles his hair. Then a measured, enunciated thunder rings across the island with the clarity of voice. Echoing, timeless, it commands, "Be cleansed and whole."

Warmth fills him. Garments become dry and clean as if just laundered. He examines his hands; injuries have disappeared.

The being bristles with gold and silver. Beams collide, refract, then leap to the horizon like a million lines from a million nets. Clouds fill to bursting, then rise farther into the atmosphere, spread to the horizon, wash over it brilliant in their opalescence.

The sea reflects their glory in magnificent alabaster. Calm waters magnify sprawling hues, add pale blue and crisp magenta, strawberry red and a radiant, warm yellow.

His head swims, body sways as if on a boat besieged by strong waves. He plops to the ground. The world dazzles, overwhelms. He's filled with a sense of pure joy.

The figure glows fantastic. Shards of gold and blue, yellow, silver, green and deep purple spring from Him in brilliant clarity. His features clear.

Golden flames dance in His eyes, cast a vibrance through a tapestry of shimmering color. Hair flows over a face like mammoth thunderheads. A massive beard descends, dips into the sea, foams in wondrous greens and frothy blues. Dolphins appear, at first a few, then dozens, then hundreds, dancing, flipping and splashing, cackling with delight.

Immense robes flutter—thunder roars long and limitless. He steps forward. Sandals glow orange and black as if reflecting a bed of coals that darken the sky in broad strokes.

John rises, breathing fast, limbs afire. His eyes catch every detail, dilate to their fullest. The figure's glory covers the entire island, the entire Earth. Birds flock—storks and parrots, eagles and gulls—every imaginable type swarming over the sea, through the Man's beard, across the island in massive congregated arcs.

Other fish join the dolphins. Great humped backs split the water, glistening barnacles reflect the cacophony of color and light. Then thousands of fantails pop through the foam to slap with tremendous splashes and add wet applause to the entire scene.

John sees for miles, raises his hand, waves, panting through a broad smile. His feet march and he knows not why. He tries to speak but no words come.

The figure raises its right hand, then all around becomes dark. The dolphins and eagles and whales and colors disappear, leaving John in an orb of blackness. No sky, no earth, no sea or beach or tree—only darkness, rich and deep and endless.

A massive eye appears, leagues high, peering down through eternal darkness and transparent night. It's as huge as John's vision will allow, and he realizes all he's seen, the animals and fish, color and landscape, appear alive and alight within that single eye.

John smiles into the void.

Darkness fades to dim gold as a star blossoms through the blackness. Then another star, and another, and still another, until seven rise to form a perfect circle. They spin as John lifts into their midst, floats through them, past them.

The stars spin on the palm of a giant human hand. Great creases branch its surface, and John realizes he's just come from inside that spinning, golden sphere.

He hangs suspended and without fear, knows only he is safe and warm and filled with joy.

The figure looms, too big by far for John to appreciate His totality.

An impression of speech floods his mind, and, although his ears register no sound, he knows what is said.

"I am the Alpha and Omega. The first and last." The voice rises in perfect pitch and harmony, resounds like a thousand trumpets. "Write the things which thou hast seen, and the things which are, and the things which shall be hereafter."

John's mind fills with a torrent of images as the voice narrates in tones sometimes harsh and loud, and other times whispered and calm. He has a faint idea he's writing but doesn't know what on or what with. He knows only the faintest whisper of a notion that his hands act on their own.

The voice continues, and John gives himself fully, listening, suspended in brilliance, writing, as God reveals in detail the ultimate fate of mankind.

CHAPTER 19

THE VATICAN, ROME, ITALY

"I cried for weeks after that," the Apostle says.

"Why? You make it sound like a glorious experience."

For a long time, he stares at stone walls. "Have you ever been in a war, Mr. Merrick?" I shake my head. "Imagine all the atrocities of every battle ever fought," he says. "Not tame and civilized like today. There were times when thousands were crucified every single day. America has never experienced the savagery of such conflict. These are wars fought centuries before your country was ever founded. Our history here, on this very land, is nothing but war and brutality. Human hatred and greed. What I saw on Patmos was a million times worse than I could've ever imagined." He holds my eyes. "What I saw was humanity's reckoning for turning its face from truth."

"Yes," I say, "when I was a boy, I was forced to go to Sunday school, and I disliked it so because they were always telling these scary stories. Like the religious version of scared straight. I remember they had a contest once; whoever read Revelation got a big candy bar. That was a ploy they often used, candy for dogma. But I remember Revelation being one of the most frightening things I'd ever read: plagues and locusts and horsemen, all intent on killing we sinners."

"You didn't read the original work."

"I read the work from the Bible—St. James version, I think."

John nods. "Yet another trick, another manipulation by the Wanderer."

"Cain?" I say.

John wrings his hands, leans forward. "I wrote Revelation on Patmos, never aware I was writing anything, just lost in the vision. But someone reported it to Cain, and he visited me one day to take the writing away. He knew I was immortal. How? I still don't know, but he knew and told me as much."

"It's because you're green to him," I say. "He told me he can see other immortals because they appear to him as with a green aura."

John leans into the folds of his chair, eyes wandering back and forth. "Isn't that interesting," he says to himself. He sits silent for a long while, contemplating, muttering. "The writings were gone when Cain came looking, and he was very put out by this."

"Where did they go?"

"I don't know," he says. "I'd become friendly with a guard who visited the island, and I gave the writings to him so he could take them away and distribute them to my churches. A portly man with a rusty helmet, I remember him well. I certainly remember the day Cain broke his neck as I watched."

"For taking the writings?"

"Yes. Cain's a formidable opponent and has fought in so many wars that he's very adept in combat. Of course, when one knows they can't die, I'm sure it's a boost."

I laugh. "Seems like a nice bonus."

"In some ways," the Apostle says. "In others, not so much. There are fates worse than death. A downside of immortality is you still feel pain and if applied long enough you realize there's no escape. As your friend Longinus told me once, 'The beatings will continue until morale improves.'"

John pauses, takes a long drink.

"So, you've met Longinus?" I say.

"Ah, yes, Cain began a search for the writings, and when they weren't readily found, he had Longinus try to force me to rewrite them.

The problem was, I couldn't do it. I mean, I had vivid memories, and wrote those, explaining that I actually *wanted* the vision spread through the populous. That this was about more than growing a church, that this was about the fate of every living thing on the planet. It was a warning to be sure, but it was also a road map to salvation. The population simply *had* to know."

"Did he find them?"

"I think so. You see, Cain is a rather exceptional fellow. I mean, besides his immortality, his actions over these centuries have been informed somehow. It's as if he takes direction from God. But that can't be—God cast him out." With this, he shakes his head. "Cain retains his mark and is condemned to wander."

He moves to a large globe mounted on a marble stand. He turns it without purpose, lost somewhere in time. "You see," he says, "the vision you read in the Bible wasn't my vision. Parts are missing or omitted. And that's where Cain's genius lies. At first, he tried to stamp us out but succeeded in only making us stronger. Then he switched tactics, and the persecution slowed as he consolidated power. As the Emperor Constantine, he created the Bible, but I fear he did so with his own ends in mind." He turns to face me. "I'm ashamed to admit it, but I helped. When he was Constantine and converted the kingdom to Christianity, I fell for it. So much so I baptized him in the name of God and the Church. You see, back then I worked for the church under the name of Eusebius of Nicomedia. I was a Bishop. And a fool. But such was my faith in the grace of God."

I consider this as the Apostle speaks. "That's some amazing foresight," I say. "Cain was ahead of the game."

"Yes," John gives the globe another absent spin. "As I said, he always had a gift for the bigger picture. When I realized what he was up to, I immediately alerted my churches of the persecution to come."

"You mean they let you go? Longinus—Cain—they just let you leave?"

"Indeed, sir. One day I'm Longinus's punching bag, the next I'm free to go. I was suspicious to say the least and thought as soon as I returned to my ministry I'd be recaptured. But I wasn't. I mean, certainly we were still persecuted, but things were better. We grew, largely unharassed by Cain and his followers. At the time, I thought God intervened. I thought I was fulfilling the command to grow the church and spread the gospel." He sighs, shakes his head. "I was naïve."

He returns to the chair, refills my cup but leaves his empty. "You see, during this time, Cain was building influence. He'd infiltrated Roman governments, local and national politics, agriculture, trade. He spent his time wisely, consolidated his power. As I helped form the Church, he formed X'chasei. Then suddenly he rises as Constantine. We prepare for war, using our influence to gain allegiances and amass an army. Then, Constantine embraces Christianity throughout the kingdom. We were shocked. Persecution stopped for the most part and our numbers swelled. It was joyous, we could worship freely, join in communion, confess without fear."

"So, Cain did something good?" I say.

"Yes, it appeared that way. I thought perhaps he was trying to get God's attention so he could finally be redeemed." He bites his lower lip, shakes his head again. "Completely naïve. He was up to no such thing. Suddenly we had a printed Bible, blessed by the Emperor and widely circulated. Information was being distributed, but not by us, not sanctioned by the true Church, but by this usurper. This serpent with a marked right hand."

I pull the now-melted ice pack from beneath me and set it on the floor. "To what end?" I ask.

John leans forward, elbows on his knees, looks at the stone floor. "To control? To undermine? To muddle? To divide?" He says these like ticking through a checklist in his mind, shaking his head with each sentence. "We were looking for enemies in the night when we should've been watching the friends in our midst."

He looks sad. Looks as if he's aged thirty years in a couple of sentences. "It was then when the perfect became tainted. It was he who separated us from God."

"How so?"

"By dilution and division. By embracing the church and then

placing those loyal to him in prominent positions. The church splintered; then fractured. The message, now so different depending on the denomination. You see, Mr. Merrick, he managed to obscure any direct path to Heaven by using human weakness against us. He paid. If that didn't work, he murdered, or burned, or invaded. He stoked war and was fueled by its profits. X'chasei's roots are deep and unknown. They can do anything, guarantee any outcome. They've been made rich from the church's coffers. And now he's known as *the Dove*, Thaddeus Drake, peacemaker. He's learned over the centuries, learned from his mistakes. Now he can show up anywhere with instant credibility. If he gets involved, things get fixed, peace reigns. At least as far as anyone can see."

"Why not imprison him?"

"On what charge? He's the Dove, known for bringing peace. He's positioned himself perfectly but to what end I can't tell. Even with the full force of the Vatican at my disposal, he continues to outmaneuver us. To operate at will for his own agenda."

He rises from the chair and stands before me. "Do you know what he's planning, Mr. Merrick?"

I rise too, groan a little. "I'm sorry to say I don't."

The Apostle places his hand on my shoulder and squeezes. "Can we count on your help, Mr. Merrick?"

CHAPTER 20

ROME, ITALY

I 'd been a guest at the Vatican for a couple of weeks when a grumbly, old priest with a face like a worn leather book collects me and bids me to follow. He's accompanied by a young priest with blonde hair whose mouth remains closed. As we walk, I try to remember the route we take, but it takes upwards of sixty minutes through winding chambers and long passages. We arrive at the base of an iron ladder attached with rusty bolts to a water-soaked wall. I'm instructed to push on the ceiling at the ladder's top, and when I do, a hatch opens with a slight squeal.

I climb through and find myself in a library. I look back just in time to see the young priest give a wink and close the hatch. It blends with the library's floor and there's no sign it's even there. I wonder at the construction, fight the urge to examine it for a latch or secret keyhole, anything that allows it to be opened from my side.

I wind my way through tall shelves piled with books. The place smells of cigarettes and ink in the way of a newspaper stand. As I near the building's exit, a short, plump woman stops me. "Mr. Merrick," she says with a thick Italian accent, "for you." She pushes a leather bag toward me, then turns and disappears into the library's depths.

I peek inside and find a note. SAFE TRAVELS. -J, it reads. Beneath the note, I find a complete change of clothes, my iPhone, my notepad, and my wallet, the latter now brimming with thousands of dollars in different currencies and denominations. I find a pair of black oxfords and blue socks, a suit coat with slacks, both dark blue, a dress shirt in light gray, and a silk tie in aqua. There's no doubt about the quality of the items. European men spend vast amounts on wardrobe, unlike American men who carry unbridled pride for their t-shirt collections. Only one set has adopted the correct stance vis-à-vis style or self-respect.

Still, I wish for a New York Yankees ball cap with shorts, t-shirt, and flip-flops. I duck into a bathroom near the library's entrance and change out of my shabby brown coat and the shirt with three holes in the armpit. I stuff them in the trash, then regard myself in the mirror.

"Ciao bella," I say to my reflection, having no idea what the words mean but achieving the international patois for which I'm searching. I regard the bag, consider whether to keep it or leave it. I run my fingers over the bottom and discover a zippered pocket. It contains a cell phone. I press the button and thumb to the contacts section. It holds a single number but no name. I consider trashing this as well. What will Drake do if he finds it? I slide it in the pocket of my new jacket. *Just in case,* I think.

I exit onto a tree lined street, astonished to find I'm staring across the Tiber toward the Vatican. *Secret passage,* I think, feeling and looking more like Fleming's *Bond* than ever before.

I decide to go left. I've no idea what I'm doing or how to get back to Drake. I make it almost to Via san Pio when a long, black sedan pulls up.

The rear window descends, and I'm surprised to see the bald head of Igneus.

"Get in," he says, "we've been worried sick."

I stand in my new duds, staring at the little man. My heart fills with fear. Has Drake sent him to collect and punish me? Should I tell him about the Apostle? I shake the thoughts away. I doubt Drake would send Igneus if I was to be punished or murdered. The Jew doesn't have the stomach for such things. Longinus would probably be the pick for something like that. Besides, I'd been kidnapped, it's not like that's my fault.

I enter the car and we speed off.

"How did you know where to find me?" I ask.

"Drake told me."

"And how—" I'm stopped by Igneus's raised finger, skinny as a skeleton bone.

"And you're going to ask, 'How did he know?'"

I nod.

"There's no way to tell. One thing you need to know about Drake is he just knows everything. You can spend all day trying to figure out how but, in the end, you'll realize it's useless. Much better to go with the flow and save yourself the headache."

I think about this for a second, then I think, *When in Rome…*

"Where are we heading?" I've never been to Rome and find myself staring out the window as houses and shops give way to gradual fields and vineyards.

"We have much to do, Emery. Drake asked me to collect and look after you until we can see him. So, looks like we're travel buddies." Thin lips stretch across an emaciated face. I know he's trying to be welcoming, but the sight is rather ghastly. "To the airport," he says. "We have business in Las Vegas."

"Vegas?" Could any other place be *less* Rome?

Igneus nods. Then my new phone rings.

It's Drake, and I'm surprised he has this number as I've had the phone less than an hour.

"I trust the Apostle treated you well?" he says. I glance at Igneus, who's heard and grins with an I-told-you-so expression.

"Well, not at first," I say. "He wired my balls to a transformer and tortured me."

"Dear Emery!" he says. "How are you feeling?"

"Better now, but let's say it wasn't the most fun I've ever had."

"Tsk, tsk. And he used to be such a nice boy. You were there a long time, what information did you give?"

I sigh as my mind searches for a believable story. Then I say, "Everything he asked, I answered."

These words may seal my fate, but instinct says if I lie, I'll only make a hash of it. I have no idea what Drake knows. X'chasei is incredibly well-informed, and I need no proof other than the fact I'd been picked up from the Vatican minutes after being released. I recount what the Apostle asked and what answers I gave. I tell Drake about John's recollection of events and how he feels as if he's a step behind. "The good news," I say, "is he has no idea what you're planning, but he knows you're planning something. He also knows you changed the Bible. He knows his Revelation is not the same as what's printed now. Although he can't remember what's missing."

Drake laughs long and loud. "Well, dear boy, that should keep him busy for a while."

"I was afraid I'd be...um...punished for getting caught? For divulging information?"

There's a long pause, and my palms start to sweat. "Punished?" he says, finally. "Why on Earth would I do that? Who would record these events if I did such a dastardly thing?"

His words warm me. In fact, I feel joyous, free. I exhale with some theatrics, then glance at Igneus and act as if I'm wiping my brow and shaking off the perspiration. "That *is* a relief," I say.

"Do you think so little of me, dear Emery? I'm not some madman, but rather an ordinary man in unpredictable currents. No one can comprehend the mind of God," he says, "which makes my task all the more difficult and my adversary all the more cunning. The Apostle and his Templars." He spits the words. "I'd done away with them on the famous Friday the 13th. All it took was a whisper in the ear of King Phillip the Fourth and in no time that thorn in my heel was gone. Yet, John persisted with his interference. Just a pest, really. Neither John, his Templars, nor God Himself can stop me. My counsel is one who is beyond the grave. Even God can't read his mind. Thus, they have no idea what I'm planning or doing. At long last, I've completely turned the tables." He chuckles. "They're not a threat to us, dear Emery. Did he leave you a way to contact him?"

Like you don't know, I think. "Yes. I'm talking to you on it."

"Ooh, a secret Vatican phone," he says. "The Pope's Bat phone. The *Popephone.*" He laughs, and I join him. I feel at ease, safe. "Keep it," he continues. "Speak with him as much as you like. Interviewing him will only make my story more grand and complete. I've told you; things are well in hand."

"But what if I divulge too much? What if, by some little detail, I ruin your plan?"

"Dear Emery, I appreciate the concern, but don't worry about the Templar. Just believe in me."

"And about this counselor you mentioned," I say, "care to fill me in?"

"Patience, dear Emery. All will be revealed in time. We have other things that demand our attention. God doesn't sleep, you know."

I like Drake, like his style, his manner of speaking, his confidence and poise. His complete control of every situation. So what if, centuries ago, he'd murdered someone? By today's standards, he's paid for that crime a thousand times yet remains imprisoned. I struggle with the unfairness of it. If Cain has forgiven himself, why can't God do the same?

"Seems to me God's the asshole in this whole situation," I say.

Drake's laugh is nice. "If the Apostle heard you say that, he'd wire up your testicles again."

I feel a tingle where the electrodes were. "Of that, I have no doubt."

We end the call and I look toward Igneus. "Drake says hi," I say. The little man chuckles, glances at my Popephone.

"I see he has the number already."

I nod. "Seems so. Not like you didn't warn me." Igneus shakes his head but doesn't reply. "So, what's in Vegas?" I don't feel much like the flashing strobes and clamor of that city. *Perhaps I can get a nice bath and think about all I've lost.* Even as the thought strikes me, I'm reminded of her, a hollow ache in my gut. The auburn hair, the delicious smile, the right cross she'd given on the day she left.

Igneus gestures out the window and I see we're nearing the airport.

"We're going to see Mr. Ramirez," he says.

"Ramirez?"

Igneus nods. "Let's just say he's a person that needs convincing."

CHAPTER 21

LAS VEGAS, NEVADA

Twelve hours later we stand on a second-floor balcony. Below, the sight is spectacular. Every object screams, whoops, bleeps. Every sound, placed with keen attention, designed to add to the overall chaos. Neon flashes overhead, cascades like a mystical river, over rounded banisters and above screens that spin like movie reels. Twirling slot machines whistle; change *cha-chings*; worn carpets swirl in abrasive patterns and clashing stripes.

The casino roars. The guests move as a mass, wear street clothes that call out their life's station with some subtlety, or with none at all. Each thinks their odds of winning better than average; each is leveraged to spend as much as they can. Probably more.

The ceiling stretches over the cavernous space in broad white tiles. It's made to look like an ancient Roman bath house—thick squares bordering detailed bas-reliefs. What once was splendid is now stained yellow from cigarette smoke exhausted from crinkled mouths and hopeful faces.

"A way to separate hard-working folk from their hard-earned cash," Igneus says and gives a bashful frown. "Even the floor plan is clever, guiding patrons into the casino's bowels, to turn them around and always," he pauses here, re-emphasizes the next word, "*always* present them with another chance to try their luck."

"X'chasei owns this?"

Igneus looks as if I've asked the world's dumbest question. "Many of these," he says.

The games are packed as waitresses in high skirts and low tops ply guests with free drinks and bulging cleavage. Slots whir, ever fed by eager hands. Roulette wheels spin in black and red, a small marble clattering even as it strives to land. People mass at the craps tables, leave no room for even a curious passerby to peak over their shoulders and see if the *bones* are really *smokin'*. The crowd groans and cheers in unison pending the outcome of certain random pips and adding to the general tumult.

"It's quite ridiculous and I never thought it would work. But Drake knew, and here we are. You see, people are hard-wired to always try their luck." Igneus smirks. "You know the old saying about fools and their money?"

"Mr. Igneus?"

We turn to see a man who looks like a teamster. He's just exited the high rollers' room directly behind us.

"Yes, Tommy," Igneus says.

"A guest is trying to make a big bet."

Igneus nods, glances at me. "This is a gambling house, Tommy. Patrons are supposed to do that?"

Tommy shuffles his feet. His nose is red and bulbous with large pores. *A drinker,* I think.

"This bet is *big,*" Tommy says.

Igneus looks to the gambling floor where a fat woman has just hit a jackpot of nickels. She whoops, and her chubby friends, dressed in shades of polyester and spandex, lean from their own machines to examine her good fortune. "Take it to Henry," Igneus says.

Tommy clears his throat. "I did, sir. He said bring it to you. It's Mr. Ramirez."

Igneus's ears perk up. "Mr. Ramirez is the head of Cuban financial policy," he says to me. "The man, and more importantly," he says this with a raised finger, "the country he represents, have been of much interest to us. One of only a few who are not members of the International Monetary Fund." I'm surprised he's talking about this in front of the teamster, but he continues without pause. "There's much debate and ill-will throughout the world directed at the Cubans—at Mr. Ramirez—for numerous failings, numerous jibes, and nose-thumbings."

"Like?" I say, trying to remember these details. My recording app will never pick up his voice within the casino's racket.

"Like low per-capita income, restricted foreign investment, co-operative socialism. They're vital to have on board to create a world currency, and tonight Ramirez is taking the chance we need." Igneus grins like a cartoon villain. *Drake must be rubbing off on him*, I think.

The little man turns to Tommy. "How much?"

"Fifteen million."

"How much is he down now?"

Tommy screws his eyes toward the ceiling, "Pretty much been even all night. He's pretty drunk, though."

"Give me five minutes, then take the bet."

Tommy's eyes grow large. His tongue trips before he blurts, "You're going to guarantee it?"

Igneus places a fragile hand on Tommy's shoulder. "Yes, Tommy, we're going to take it."

Tommy starts to protest but is silenced. "Tommy. Take the bet. Five minutes."

Tommy nods and is gone without a word.

———

Five minutes later, we're stationed in the control room, watching a monitor. The picture shows Mr. Ramirez. A signed voucher rests on the space in front of him. Beside him a middle-aged man wears a tan sport jacket and white cowboy hat. He fiddles with his chips and glances at the voucher.

"Place your bets," the dealer says.

The man in the cowboy hat tosses two five-thousand-dollar chips, then grins at Mr. Ramirez.

Ramirez doesn't notice, staring straight at the voucher. He portrays no sign of nervousness, except an occasional twitch of his left thumb, which is wrapped around a Mai Tai.

The cards slide over the table's green felt, blue diamond backs blur as they exit the chute to spin across the table and skid to a stop in front of Ramirez and the cowboy.

Ramirez looks at a seven and an ace. "Eighteen," Igneus says. "Looks like the cowboy has a three and a seven, which makes ten."

The dealer, who has a card face down, receives an ace.

"Insurance?" the dealer asks.

Ramirez exhales in a rush, buries his face in both hands, rubs his eyes.

Igneus giggles. "This is getting good. Insurance will cost half the amount of Ramirez's bet, seven-point-five million dollars, just to guard against the thirty-one percent chance the dealer has blackjack."

I marvel at the fact he knows the odds off the top of his head.

Igneus continues. "Of course, if he takes insurance and the dealer actually has blackjack, he'll reap two-to-one odds. If the dealer doesn't have blackjack, he'll be out the seven-point-five million and still have the original fifteen million at stake."

"Holy moly," I say. "It's a side bet of seven-point-five million?"

"Yes, if he takes the insurance, which I doubt he will."

We look at the monitor to see Ramirez shake his head, refusing insurance.

The cowboy waves his hand as well.

The dealer peeks at his card. Ramirez's inhale is audible. A blackjack means the hand is over and he's lost.

"No blackjack," the dealer says. "Card?" he asks Ramirez.

Ramirez leans back, exhales, tugs on the short-cropped trusses of his temple. He looks at the dealer, glances at the cowboy, then at his cards. He leans close to the table and turns his ear toward the cards as if they're speaking to him. A broad smile shows teeth like Chiclets as he waves his hand to indicate he doesn't want another card.

The dealer looks at the cowboy. The man adjusts the big ten-gallon on his head, then leans on the table with both elbows. Cheeks flutter as he exhales, then lifts his hat and itches his bald scalp. I marvel that the man is taking ten thousand dollars this seriously when the guy next to him is betting a fortune.

"Card?" the dealer asks.

The cowboy looks at Ramirez, then says to the dealer, "Hold your horses." He crosses his arms over his chest, grabs a beer and has a swig. He holds the bottle close as he thinks.

"I'd like to call Tommy and have this guy slapped in the mouth," Igneus says. "Just for taking so long when he's sitting on ten."

The cowboy slams his beer on the table and says, "Hit me!"

The dealer gives him a ten, adding to his seven and three, for a total of twenty. The cowboy whoops and pumps his fist in the air as sweat trickles down his face.

The dealer reveals his down card, a five. Mr. Ramirez gasps and slaps the table.

"The dealer now has six or sixteen against Ramirez's eighteen," Igneus says. "The house *must* take a card."

The dealer doesn't hesitate.

He slaps down the next card.

Mr. Ramirez stands, mouth open, hands held to the sides of his head.

Igneus sighs and shakes his head.

The cowboy stands and gives a cry.

The dealer's card is a three.

"Nineteen over eighteen," the dealer says. "The house wins."

Ramirez nods, attempts a smile. He stands, proffers his Mai Tai in salute, staggers two steps, then drops to the floor in a dead faint.

Two hours later we enter the presidential suite. The television blares an old *Kung Fu* rerun at loud volume, and the floor is littered with various clothing items and empty liquor bottles. Ramirez sits in a green chair whose enormity makes him appear fragile. Seeing us, he stands. He wears a pair of white boxers and a sleeveless t-shirt. On his feet, black shoes and argyle socks rise to his knees, mirror in the floor's white marble. *Two feet in hell*, I think.

Igneus offers his hand, which the man accepts. Ramirez shakes my hand as well. His palms are cold and sweaty, like grabbing a fish by the tail.

"We have much to discuss," Igneus says.

Ramirez shakes his head. "No habla."

Igneus nods, continues in Spanish. "We have much to discuss."

Ramirez flops in the chair and stares at the ceiling. He's breathing hard, one leg bouncing at high speed. "Go on," he says in perfect English. Again, I marvel at the little man. Not only does he speak Spanish, but he'd been prepared for Ramirez to claim a language barrier as a way to avoid talking about his debt.

Igneus is quiet but definitive. "Counting tonight and other nights, you owe us twenty-one million American dollars." The astonishing number is stated as a matter of flat fact. Ramirez's head shoots up, shaking. "I can't," he stammers, "I can't owe that much." His statement comes as a question.

Igneus gives a gentle smile. "Ah, but you do. You've been our guest before, and unfortunately your luck hasn't been so...lucky."

Ramirez slumps forward, deflated. "If I can return to Cuba, I can secure the money within seven days."

"I'm afraid that won't do," Igneus says. "All guests must settle their debts at the time of departure."

Ramirez places a hand on his heart, lips quivering. "You have my word. I will pay." His leg is now a metronome on high speed.

Igneus moves to a bank of floor-to-ceiling windows. Lights twinkle their adverts to a desensitized town: Penn and Teller, David Copperfield, dollar-ninety-nine buffets. "I'm afraid that won't do," he says.

The sigh tells me Ramirez is cooked. Soon, muffled sobs fill the room. "I've brought disgrace on my station. I can't return, and I don't have the money to pay you. I'm ruined."

Igneus smiles at his reflection, a skeleton's grin in gleaming glass. He waits a minute more. "Perhaps," he says, "there's another way."

"Drink, sir?" The stewardess is lovely with flowing dark hair and a single dimple on her left cheek. Her eyes are a radiant blue.

"Do you have scotch?"

"Yes, sir. We have Macallan, Glenmorangie and—"

"Macallan is fine."

She smiles and moves off.

It's been three hours since we left Ramirez. The man, now broken and, as such, an X'chasei Associate.

"What would you have done if he hadn't agreed to your terms and just refused to pay?"

Igneus raises a snifter to his nose, glances at the passing fog. "Well," he says, "that's what Tommy and the boys are for."

"So, what now?"

"Let me think," Igneus says. "Vegas was a huge success. Mortals are so easily bought and paid for."

"Mortals?"

He grins. "A term I use to allay my guilt for binding humanity so. Seems to depersonalize the business. Like Cuba and North Korea, bought and paid for, but it's not like it will do their people any good. They'll still be exploited." He gives me a no-shit look. "Next is D.C. Drake's there meeting with some senators. I need to tell him the good news."

The brunette returns with my scotch, and Igneus hands her a fifty.

"Oh, I couldn't sir," she says.

"You will," he answers and slides the money in the hip pocket of her tailored blue uniform. She smiles, blushes. "Thank you."

"It's been a wonderful day." He turns to me, glass raised. "To vagabonds, apostles, reporters, and Romans."

I turn to the mist outside the window. The aircraft has entered a cloud, and I wonder at the thick gray vapor and the airframe's buffeting vibrations. I think of Rhyme, my love, how I miss her. I remember every time we encountered turbulence, how she'd squeeze my hand until it turned white. I trace small drops of water as they bead and flow on the thick plastic window. *I wonder what she'd think of this little man.* So frail and unassuming, except where money is concerned, as in the casino. There he's a little Mafia boss.

A plush, gray chair cradles my body like a baby blanket. Its feathery folds comfort as I stare into fluffed clouds and savor the moment when we burst into vibrant blue sky.

Sleep descends like a welcome shade.

Across from me, Igneus's eyes are closed and fluttering.

Must be a hell of a dream, I think.

CHAPTER 22

JERUSALEM, AFTER THE CRUCIFIXION

The Temple's cool against the heat of the day and Igneus's sweat-soaked clothes serve as a device of relief.

Green and blue tiles fill the expansive stone floor. Above, a flat ceiling gilded with thick golden rafters. From the room's corners, seven candles send light into the Temple's darker recesses. Sunlight pours through western windows as dust particles float without pattern or form.

Longinus stands against the room's far wall, arms crossed, biceps bulging, a disinterested look on a face covered in a maze of tattooed lines. Small horns jut from his head. His eyes shimmer blood red as he winks at Igneus and blows a kiss.

Beside the Roman stands Sham'beth the servant. His beard is disheveled, skin ashen gray. Small red dots appear on his chest, then reach to join one another until the whiteness of his tunic is overrun with blood.

Igneus points at the stain. Sham'beth grins. The robe fades to black, then Sham'beth is engulfed in shadow and gone.

Longinus doesn't notice.

Igneus blinks twice, licks dry lips.

Outside the Holy of Holies, Jesus speaks to his followers. The disciples listen with rapt attention; some weep, others nod, frowning through wiry beards.

Igneus watches as if through a fogged window. His mind returns to the day he'd struck Jesus. Why had he done such a thing? He feels an overpowering urge to approach the Master—an urge to plead forgiveness, to beg mercy, to be free from this fate. Surely Jesus can't deny him mercy.

The Messiah turns His head. His gaze is gentle, yet stern and commanding.

The Savior speaks to His followers, but His eyes ensnare Igneus.

There are no words, yet supplication is demanded. Igneus is rooted in place—a minion, frail and weak, arms and legs unresponsive.

He struggles, can hear Jesus' voice in his head, echoing as if over a great distance, gentle as a cooing baby, timeless as the heavens.

"Don't."

He thinks to plead, to fall on his knees and beseech Christ's mercy. Muscles tense as he tries to step.

A blinding pain halts his progress. His head starts to throb.

"Endure."

The word is whispered, a creamy smooth baritone, sticky and sweet.

His fate is sealed.

Warm tears slide down his cheeks. He has to move, has to speak. This is his only chance. The Messiah's eyes tell him that as surely as they bid him to stand fast.

He tries to form a word, then notices movement to his right.

Cain places a hand on Igneus's shoulder and smiles. His fangs drip blood.

"It's well in hand," Cain says. "You're where you need to be."

The gloved hand recedes, and Cain starts to grow. In an instant, as tall as the room itself.

He smiles at Igneus. "You are with us." A question and a statement.

Igneus cranes his head upward, then turns toward Jesus.

The Messiah's eyes demand obedience.

Igneus tries to open his mouth, but no sound escapes. Trembling hands hang useless against his hips.

Cain becomes monstrous as gloves fall away to reveal his mark in blistering fire. He grows to a lumbering dragon, fills the Temple as red eyes pierce the gloom, as scales reflect white pillars and petrified faces. Maroon splotches cover his talons as the mark changes to crystal blue. Igneus stares at the pulsing liquid lines, feels strong and safe.

The Messiah continues to speak to His disciples.

"Obey," His eyes say.

A sword appears in Igneus's hand.

The monstrous figure is totally unaware of his presence. Demons crawl within folds of scale as he squats, belly on the checkered floor marbled in thick layers of impenetrable plating.

Igneus strains his vision through clawing imps and scaled hardness, notices a soft, unprotected area.

He jolts forward, suddenly free of invisible bonds.

"Kill."

The vulnerable area is perhaps six inches, a slat of small silver barely visible on the huge being.

A shudder runs through him. Cain will do unspeakable things if he fails.

Grasping the hilt with both hands, he braces. One good skewer will do it.

He holds Jesus' eyes. The Messiah smiles, His voice loud in Igneus's skull.

"Obey."

"Obey."

Igneus draws back, levels the sword at Cain's belly.

Jesus speaks to His disciples.

His eyes command.

Poised, sword in hand, ready to strike, eyes riveted on Jesus, he awaits a final order.

Jesus' eyes grow dark. He waves His hand, dismissive, irritated.

The air erupts as thick smoke curls around Igneus's frame, fills his lungs, chokes his breath.

Above, Cain shrieks.

The Temple trembles. Huge stones fall from the rafters and crash to the checkered floor.

Igneus cowers, the sword gone. Was it ever there?

Dust and debris rise and choke as more stones thunder from above. The structure shimmers, wavers, then is gone completely.

The beast wails in the distance.

Igneus is pocked with dirt and ash. Dripping sweat, shivering, afraid and alone, he curls into a ball, whimpering.

The symphony of war plays: the canon's rhythmic bass, the crisp tenor of crashing armor, the shrill aria of dying men.

Jesus appears, commands His disciples, voice echoing over the din.

"Go into all the world and preach my Gospel."

The disciples vaporize, leaving only tufts of smoke. Jesus' eyes mirror Igneus's frail image.

Then He's gone.

War machines screech as mechanical minions lumber forth. Great caissons roll on tracked threads and spew death from long, metal snouts. Airplanes, striped in gray and sage, spit fire from silver wings, then streak overhead. Mechanical tripods belch conical spirals to the sky.

The flames rise for miles as cries of innocence split the night, as men race forward, black rifles aloft.

Cain soars in a golden chariot. He's glorious. Face ringed with golden leaves, chest adorned with gleaming, silver armor finely etched with his own mark. His eyes are bright, welcoming as he soars above, rallies his legions, crushes any who dare stand against him.

Igneus leaps, hands waving.

The chariot swerves toward him.

Cain's smile grows.

Igneus races to meet him.

CHAPTER 23

WASHINGTON D.C., UNITED STATES

The Hotel Dupont's penthouse suite is immaculate. The receiving room is adorned with bronzed figures on opulent white pedestals and precise modern artworks hang in thick, gold frames. Our heels click on the marble floor as we cross to one of two facing couches that flank a low marble table framed in bronze. The couches are from the seventeenth century, French, if I remember right. Sitting, Igneus regards Drake, who looks back from a Louis XIV fauteuil.

I move to a chair in the room's far corner and hit my phone's record button.

Drake is dapper as always. His temples, recently grayed, frame spectacles that are thin and smart and dark. I know the gray and the frames are only to keep up appearances of the aging process. Drake leans forward, silk suit shimmering in the room's subdued light.

"How nice to see both of you," Drake says, offers a charming smile.

"You as well," I say.

"I have news," Igneus adds.

Drake's smile beams with invisible light. "Of?"

"Your world currency is complete."

"The Cuban?"

Igneus slides forward, rubs at the fingernail of his index finger. "Partly—a catalyst to be sure. One of many. Lichtenstein. Monaco. Cuba."

Drake nods. "Ah, Lichtenstein," he says, eyes squinting into the upper reaches of the room. He flashes a quick wink, and I laugh.

Igneus laughs too, and I'm surprised.

"Shall I explain?" Igneus says. He's in good spirits despite sitting across from the man for whom he harbors such fear and disdain. Seems Cain's gifts affect the Jew as well.

Drake moves to the bar. "A drink first. You must be parched? I know you prefer Macallan, but I have only Longmorn. Will that do?"

Igneus nods, and Drake fills a glass. He retrieves a bottle of Perrier from the bar's refrigerator, pauses and says, "Emery?" I accept and Drake brings us our drinks.

I dip my nose to the glass. The smell is rich; burnt oak, nutmeg, candied apples and honey.

Igneus holds his glass before him, stares at the liquid. "I remember when I thought this foul. When I could barely choke it down." He takes a long sip. "Now I savor every drop and relish the complexities."

Drake lifts his glass and we all drink.

"You were saying?" Drake says.

Igneus leans into the couch and looks at the ceiling. "Okay," he starts. "So, you remember what befell us in '71, right?"

Drake nods. "Yes, the end of the gold standard."

"The what?" I say.

Igneus turns to me. "The gold standard was a way for all countries to value their currency based on an amount of gold." He squints, looks disgusted. "Then Nixon," he says. "The Nixon Shock, they call it now, and believe me when I say, we were all shocked. Everything I'd worked for, destroyed with a stroke of a pen. The dollar, no longer tied to gold."

The little man looks dazed even thinking about it. "The dollar no longer worth anything but the *promise* of the United States. Ruined everything. No more gold standard meant no more currency based on a single value, which meant zero hope of creating a one-world currency.

Poof, gone in a puff. That single shock obliterated my quest for a world currency." He raises a finger to emphasize his next point. "It's taken me all this time to undo, and all along, the answer was right before my eyes. It just didn't dawn on me until I heard the Russian president call for a supranational reserve. Then it hit me like a thwack on the skull."

"Supranational reserve?" Drake says.

"Yes, sorry, a reserve of currency independent of nations, but that all nations draw from. A new standard, like gold."

I nod, steal a look at Drake, who looks as lost as I am. "Okay?" he says.

"The answer is special drawing rights."

Igneus's tone is expectant, as if his words should have a profound effect on us. He stands triumphant, like a champion chihuahua, takes a long sniff of his dram and looks quite content. Drake shrugs his shoulders. It's obvious he doesn't know what Igneus is talking about, either. I chuckle, even as I'm surprised to hear Igneus giggle. The Jew is consumed by that old Drake-pleasing feeling, and the scotch only feeds the sentiment. He acts carefree, like it's nice to speak with Drake as if they're old friends.

"I don't get it," I say. The Jew stares at me then glances to Drake.

"Okay," he says after a few seconds. "Here's how it works. Remember in 1944 when the International Monetary Fund was created?"

"No." Drake replies. I shake my head.

"Remember after the war when the nations banded together and created the gold standard?"

"Yes." Drake nods. "That I do remember."

"That's when the International Monetary Fund, or IMF, was created. As part of that, there was a system put in place called special drawing rights, SDRs if you will. At the time, SDRs could be used by members of the IMF to draw loans based upon the size of their own economies."

"Okay," Drake says.

Igneus sips his drink, starts to pace. "As the years passed these special drawing rights were nothing spectacular. Something necessary?

Yes. Something important? Yes. But nothing vital. Then, when Nixon ended the gold standard, effectively creating fiat money, the dollar was still the ipso-facto reserve currency but couldn't stand up to the prophesied vision of a one-world currency." He glances at Drake who returns a blank stare.

"What I mean is the entire world wasn't using one currency," Igneus continues.

Drake nods, produces a silver cigarette tin with X'chasei's symbol etched on its front. He pats his pockets as Igneus, still talking, crosses to the bar. "Interesting things have happened since then. First, the dollar is not the only huge currency in the world anymore. There's the euro, the yen, the British pound sterling, and of course the Chinese renminbi." He twirls his fingers in the air as if to say, *And so on.* "When special drawing rights were first established, they were based on the value of the dollar bill." Igneus moves to Drake and flicks the lighter he's retrieved from the bar.

Drake leans the Treasurer's end into the yellow flame. Igneus drops the lighter with a clatter as Drake offers me the silver case. I decline.

"As times changed," Igneus says, "the definition of the special drawing rights had to change with them. As such, these SDRs are now valued based upon a basket of currencies—specifically, the dollar, euro, yen, renminbi, and pound." Igneus pauses, looks at Drake.

"Fascinating," Drake says.

"It really is, and the beauty is that now we have our one-world currency—our standard—by way of special drawing rights. Of course, it wasn't easy—it's taken me the better part of thirty years to get everything in line."

Drake blows smoke in a neat ring. "How's that?"

"Since its inception in 1944, the IMF has been steadily growing. The problem is—was—for one reason or another all nations weren't represented."

I laugh. "The allies were keeping out the commies."

"Not at all," Igneus says, "anyone can join, and politics has little to do with it, even dictatorships are supported by the IMF."

"Then what?" Drake says.

"Internal strife. Complicated economic policy, world leaders being uncooperative and quitting."

"I don't get it," Drake says.

Igneus blinks, takes a long pull of his scotch. "North Korea, Monaco, Lichtenstein, Cuba—all the places I've been visiting are non-members. Their refusal to cooperate in the fund was a barrier to our goal of uniting the world's currency. You see, all nations have to be IMF members to utilize SDRs."

"Okay." Drake's tone still sounds confused.

"What I've managed to do is convince them that it's in the best interest of their countries—or in some cases themselves—to become members of the IMF. There were some big problems there, like the Muslims who have religious rules about usury, or, um, that is to say, paying interest. And not all the leaders could be bought."

Drake opens his mouth, but Igneus continues.

"*And* without killing anyone." He says these words loud and slow. "I've managed to get them all to join. It cost us almost a billion dollars in cars and cash and schools and donations—" he says the last word drawing imaginary quotation marks in the air—"but I'm sure you'll agree it's a bargain."

Drake snuffs out his cigarette. "Money means nothing." I can tell it's a phrase Drake's used before.

Igneus nods. "Perhaps to mortals it means something." He gives me a sheepish grin, and I realize I'm the only *mortal* in the room, present only by the lure of Drake's money.

"So, what's the new money look like?"

Igneus pauses, gives Drake a blank stare. "There's no new money."

"I thought you said we had a world currency?"

"We do," Igneus says, throwing his hands out. "But not like all the doomsayers think, not like the Apostle's revelation has us believe. Modern economics is so convoluted, so complex, that real money means almost nothing. Everything now is computer files. The whole system is based on reserves, meaning whatever you call money has to be backed by something of value. It used to be gold, then the dollar, then nothing except a government's sovereignty, now it's the SDR, which is based on currency, which is based on an equation."

Drake sits with hands clasped in his lap; legs crossed as Igneus continues. "The beauty is no country has to change its current currency. All transactions are standard to SDRs. So, whether you're spending Japanese yen, or British pounds, or Israeli shekels, that currency is valued based on one single system, the SDR."

Drake stands. "That's brilliant." Realization dawns in his eyes. "The Templars will never see it coming."

It's Igneus's turn to look confused. "What do you mean?"

Drake takes Igneus's glass and returns to the bar. "I mean, the problem in trying to do this is Christian nations will regard a one-world currency as a sure sign of the apocalypse. I was afraid this would be a major roadblock, that the idea would be raged against as soon as we tried to roll out a standard currency." He refills the glass, hands it to Igneus. His eyes dance. "But you, my friend, have made that a moot point."

Igneus glows warm and rich like the golden scotch in his glass. A smile stretches across his face. "Now what?"

Drake looks over the city skyline then glances toward the room's plush loft. He motions to the hallway leading to the master suite, and Igneus moves to follow. "Now," he says, "you both need some rest. We're almost there."

"How much more?" Igneus says.

Drake chuckles. "Longinus tells me he's found my cow. It's currently being inspected. So now we just need the Temple and world peace." He hefts the scotch, tosses the liquid down his throat.

Igneus rolls his eyes. "How on Earth are you going to pull that off?"

"The Temple I'll leave to Israel," Drake says. "And you, of course."

Igneus freezes, scotch halfway to his lips. "Me?"

A smile blooms on Drake's face, and I wonder if he's using his gifts.

"Yes, dear Igneus, you are the man for this job. I've taken the liberty of scheduling a meeting between you and Mr. Sundamir three days from now. Take Emery with you, he may find useful things to record."

Igneus stands like a statue, scotch suspended, eyes darting back and forth. "That fat PLO leader?"

"One and the same," Drake says. "The man is vital to our plans and I hope you'll help him see what's in everyone's best interests." He moves down the short hallway and opens the door to the master suite.

Igneus shakes his head. "So, you already have Israel's cooperation?"

"Not exactly," Drake says. "But Longinus has spoken to their Prime Minister."

"What's his name again?"

"Slabav," I say. "He's a nice guy."

"I think he'll be happy to help," Drake adds.

"Of course," the little man says, "they've been so successful to this point."

Drake levels a hard gaze, then a sly grin crosses his face. "My dear Igneus, have you learned nothing? Israel has failed because they haven't yet had our assistance."

Igneus sputters. "And you're going to get this Slabav to join our little organization—our *secret* organization?"

"You fail to see the subtle. I'm going to show him how our organizations can work toward a mutual goal."

Igneus finishes his drink in a single pull. "That should be easy," he scoffs, "because the Muslims just don't *give a shit*—" he elongates these words as he speaks—"about the Temple's proposed site."

Drake's laughter echoes through the room, flutters around like a lost bird. "Dear Igneus," he says, "do you kiss your mother with that mouth?"

CHAPTER 24

BEIRUT, LEBANON

Three days later, Drake sits in a stretch limousine in the middle of the desert. Even with the air conditioner set to high, the interior stays warm. *A few more minutes and I'll go deal with the Arab,* he thinks.

Emery's recorder slides from his pocket and he presses the play button.

The reporter's voice fills the space.

<Ahem, sniff>

"Excuse me, had to take a little break. Now. Where was I? Um, the Pulitzers I think, the next chapter in my treatise on a wasted life.

So, I'd just won the Pulitzer for investigative reporting and, in so doing, secured my entire career. At the age of thirty-something no less, which meant I now had some say about the instincts I followed and what dirt I dug.

It doesn't really matter why I won that first Pulitzer, so I won't bore you with it. But since we're on the record, my official comment is…big fucking deal. Certainly, it meant something at the time, and I was celebrated, but now, well, I can't think of anything that means less…unless it's my entire existence.

<slurp>

Okay, sorry, that last sentence is a little sloppy, even Macallan left the room in disgust, so strike it if you want. I mean, I hope you don't think I'm sitting here feeling sorry for myself—I hope it doesn't sound that way. I want people to hear this record and learn the lessons. Maybe this will help someone. Is there a Pulitzer for self-deprecation? I doubt it, there'd be too many finalists. And for the record, I'm sitting on a shitty old couch in a shitty, little apartment, in a shitty town, drinking splendid scotch—worth the money, even if you have none—and cleaning my gun, or Rhyme's gun, as I think about it. Or rather, I'm wiping it repeatedly with a rag, which I guess would technically be dusting my gun. So, I apologize if I slur my words or lose track of some thoughts, but I'm trying to do this in one take. Ha! A one-take masterpiece, my final byline, the op-ed to end all op-eds.

Oh! I almost forgot. I wrote a poem for the occasion. Now that Macallan has returned, we can recite it. Ahem, here goes:

If, indeed, you find me dead,
leave the bullet in my head.
For on it lies my broken dreams,
my wasted days and memories.
Think about the life I led,
now etched upon this dented lead.
Forget me quick, forget me now,
but leave the bullet where it's found.
–Then plant me in the dirty ground.

Blap! And that deserves a drink!
<glug, sigh>
Am I rambling? Jesus, can't rewind the tape or I ruin my take. Um, was it Jin? I think it was Jin.

Jin was this Asian guy who was a great source. He knew plenty of what was happening in the city and would call me with leads from time to time. So, he calls and wants to meet in Chinatown. Now, by this time, Rhyme and I are married, it's been about three years since we met, and we are happy. I mean, over the moon, in love, happy.

146

So, I meet Jin and he tells me his sister is missing. Tells me about this outfit that's shipping people from China but also from all over the world. Mostly places where there's war, China, Africa, Pakistan, Cambodia, Afghanistan. He tells me if you pay enough, these people will transport your loved one to the country where you live. What Jin didn't know is that they ship them all in the same containers they ship guns or drugs or whatever.

Now, understand, Jin is a family man. He has about six goddamn kids and seems to be related to everyone in Chinatown. A cousin here, aunts and uncles, even a couple of brothers. Jin knows a thing or two about everything that goes on. So, he says he paid a guy named Leslie four thousand dollars to get his sister here from China. Then he tells me she never arrived, and that Leslie disappeared. He asks me to look into it as a personal favor. Now, bear in mind, Jin had done me numerous favors and I can never buy a drink or pay for a meal in Chinatown. By that I mean, every time I went there, everything was comped. Am I rambling again? Sig says stay focused; he's getting impatient.

Okay, long story short, I'm at the docks where Jin says a container is arriving full of people. Of course, I alert the police and they meet me there. Hold on, I need a drink before—

<slurp>

Ahh, that's the stuff.

Jesus, Sig, who knew you could get so shiny? I guess it's time to load you.

Anyway, um, yeah, so we open this container, and it's literally stuffed with bodies and stinks to high heaven. Sixty-four total, most of them women and children, among them Jin's sister. All dead.

<long breath>

I mean, can you get PTSD from such a thing? That haunts me, those people stuffed in a big metal tomb, shipped like a commodity.

I can still smell it. Right now, the decay, the putrid flesh. All I have to do is think about it, and I can smell it. The cops told me they'd been dead for about forty-five days, just festering in that container.

It was too much for me, and way too much for Jin.

He went a little crazy after that, asked me to help him find Leslie and bring those responsible to justice.

He wasn't fooling me, though. As soon as he found whoever was responsible, they were in for torture and death.

<sigh>

So much death.

<glug, slurp>

I guess that's the way these things work. I know only I should've gone to his sister's wake and let it be. But my reporter instincts told me there was something big here. So, I dug.

Dug my own grave, now that I think about it.

It takes me about fifteen months of investigation, and during that time Jin gets himself killed and is found hanging upside down in a Chinatown fireworks warehouse. When the police arrive, the place explodes. Now if that isn't suspicious, I don't know what is. But more than that, Jin's entire family disappears. All those kids, the cousins and aunts and uncles, the extended family, his father, all of them. Just gone. Coroner said Jin was killed by a sword. He was very specific. Not a knife, a sword, as if some samurai had been brought in to perform the execution.

Super weird, right? So, I did what I do, which is to say I started investigating. I like to think when I get a whiff of a good story, I'm tenacious. But for this one, I was a hound with a strong scent. I never let up, worked on it seven days a week about sixteen hours a day. I didn't sleep, hardly ate, lost weight. I realize now I was trying to chase away the memory of the bodies in that container, trying to make amends in my own small way. Anyway, I started using booze as medicine. I couldn't live without it, but long before I realized that simple truth, I was too far gone. I used everything, drugs to wake me up, booze to calm. Drugs to concentrate and stay alert, drugs and alcohol to help me sleep. I was in a tailspin.

Then there's Rhyme. She's about seven months pregnant or so and begs me to stay home. "But I'm at the tail-end of this story," I say. "Hungry for the finish, you know?"

So, we fight and fight, mostly about my drug and alcohol use, which I never tried to hide, and about my long absences in pursuit of the story. I tell her it will all be over soon, that life will go back to normal.

Then she starts having these nightmares. Now, I knew she had a past, something dark she'd never talked about and that I never pressed her on. The one time I'd tried she'd only said, "For some sins you never stop paying." So, I left it alone. I mean, life was good, why would I start pressing buttons and awaken her demons. Back then, for me, I was being a good husband and fake therapist. Now I realize I was ignoring the obvious in order to preserve our happiness. Which, by the way, was gone by that point, but I hadn't noticed.

Happiness is like that, I think. I'm fairly certain it can never last in any form for anyone. Ever. Sig is nodding, he knows. Enjoy happiness while you can because it will end. Has to. Can't sustain itself. Ever. Sig knows.

<sigh, liquid pours>

So anyway, we'd fight, and I'd disappear. And every time I leave our apartment, I glance over my shoulder to see her sitting in front of her favorite window, looking out at the city, both hands clasped over her pregnant belly. She's always silhouetted by either the moon or the sun, and I act like I don't see the tears dropping from her cheeks and onto our unborn child.

Like she said, there are some sins for which you never stop paying.

Her tears never stop me, though. Most of the time I'm heading for my fix. Jesus, what a dumb ass.

<slurp, cough>

So, the investigation leads to this group called Octavio. A corporation who deals in *international acquisitions*. Some corporations hide themselves pretty well, and it took me awhile to understand Octavio's vastness.

These guys were into everything: guns, people, drugs. Anything illicit, they shipped, and always from regions wracked by war.

Flash forward, and I prove they're responsible for the death of Jin and those people in the container, as well as hundreds of others. I prove *acquisitions* means *trafficking*. All I need is a name, you know; the main guy, the kingpin, someone big, icing on the cake.

But I never found him, this kingpin. Octavio was shut down, and I always felt as if I missed something. But that's the breaks, as they say.

Alas though, <*liquid pouring*> I digress.

So, Rhyme is about seven months pregnant, and I come home and tell her all I've uncovered, the entire story. I think it'll cheer her up. I'm almost done, and we can get back to normal. At least, I think I told her everything. I was rarely lucid then, but I'm pretty sure I was soft and sweet with her. Anyway, when I mention Octavio, all the blood drains from her face. I mean, I've seen dead people with more color. She starts to shake and literally begs me to bury the story. Tears flow and she's trembling, on the verge of panic. She tries to leave the apartment and won't talk to me, so I grab her arm and spin her around, and she connects with a right hook that sends me reeling. Thinking back on it, that probably isn't entirely accurate because most days I probably could've been knocked out by a feather due to the amount of drugs and alcohol in my system. Suffice it to say, when I come to, she's gone.

I call and text and call some more, no response, which I guess is fitting based on the number of texts and calls I'd ignored from her in the preceding months. So, I start to go to her favorite haunts. She has no family, but there's a coffee shop she likes to visit, and sometimes she likes to stroll through the park. Fact is, I couldn't find her, which was odd considering all she'd put up with from me, the drinking, the absenteeism, the drugs. She wouldn't have left me for a story and damn sure hadn't punched my lights out on a whim. Something was up. Why had she gone pale? Why had she popped me? Why had she left?

I need another drink. I thought this would be easier. I wonder if the bullet hurts less if I'm completely shit-faced? Sig has been silent on the question. Wonder if I'll feel it at all. Some reporter, can't see what's right in front of me.

<*slurp, exhale*>

Anyway, I spend my time typing up the story, working with the paper's researchers and fact checkers, calling Rhyme twenty to thirty times a day, texting even more, spending my evenings looking for her.

After three days, I file a missing person report. After a week, all I can do is stay pickled. I'm empty without her. She's my anchor, my safe harbor, my proof of unconditional love. Without her, I'm a mess and my use of chemicals increases exponentially.

Then, almost two weeks after she leaves, I get a call from St. Joe's Hospital. Rhyme's been shot and is in critical condition. I rush there, bouncing my BMW off more than one car and some other things on the way. Never drive drunk, kids! That's the moral there. Macallan agrees, by the way. He doesn't say much but when he does, it's wise to listen.

Jesus, this part is hard.

<slurp, ahem>

When I get there, Rhyme's in and out of consciousness. The doctors tell me she may not make it. They say our baby didn't make it. They say she can never have kids due to the uterine damage from the gunshot.

The police say it's probably a robbery because she had nothing of value on her person when she was found. Which makes sense because when she'd left our apartment, she hadn't even taken her purse. I mean, what did she do for two weeks? Wander around? Without money or food? All while pregnant?

"She was somewhere for two weeks?" I tell them. They say she probably got mixed up in drugs or something and paid the price. And so, I sat there, leaving her side only to poke a needle in my vein or to shoot something up my nose. I'm gaunt and exhausted, malnourished and badly in need of real sleep. Then, the day I return to the hospital and she's awake. How the tears poured down my stupid face. I kiss her, and she tries to push away but is so feeble she can barely lift her arms. She tries to speak, so I lean close. She says, "Leave. Never come back." I'm stunned. I mean, even through all the chemicals, the words hit like a nuclear bomb. I shake my head, lean closer.

"What?"

"Leave," she says. "I hate you. Don't ever come back."

Of course, I think this is the Dilaudid talking, so I kind of laugh it off. Then the police are there with a restraining order. They escort me from the premises and tell me I can't come within a hundred yards of her.

Now, how or why she'd obtained a restraining order, I could never surmise. But I was arrested twice for trying to see her. I wrote letters, left messages, paid staff to deliver notes, all for naught. She was done with me. I'd pushed her too far, and she'd decided, even after the death of our baby boy and while fighting for her life, that if she's going to die from her wounds, she won't die while married to me.

A few days later, the divorce papers arrive. A real kick in the beans. I stare at them for hours, then sign and mail them back. I even write a note on the actual papers begging her to return. Saying we can work it out. Nothing.

Meanwhile, my story gets published and puts Octavio in the spotlight. Fifty-seven people indicted domestically and scores more internationally. The organization folds, those responsible either go to jail or kill themselves.

I hardly remember any of it. Fuck them.

I stay in the city and try to report on things, but I'm too far down the tube of my vices to be effective. Then I get the call from my editor saying I'd won my second Pulitzer, this one for international reporting. I had no clue I was even up for it.

I remember going to the ceremony, another junkie on the subway. I stumble to the stage and accept my award and see all the faces waiting on my remarks. Now, in my head, what I said made perfect sense. To those in attendance, it's obvious how high I am. They try to stop me once they realize, but I'm determined to speak. I clock an old man, the chairman of something, and then whip out my dick and piss all over the podium. I'm told it's quite a show. You can probably pull up the vid online if you're curious.

After that, I get fired, get evicted, can't pay the "damages" from all the lawsuits from my drunken drive to the hospital; I'm in legal trouble for driving drunk and ignoring a restraining order—twice. I can't pay my attorneys. I'm divorced and mourning the death of our child. I go bankrupt and end up in this shitty little apartment in the shitty little town of Carter's Glen in upstate New York, the town where Rhyme was born.

<sigh>

I wonder if they've ever had a suicide here.

<slurp>

Something tells me I'm going to be the life of the party once this bullet gets done with my skull. My parting gift, everyone. To liven up the place. Aaaand you're welcome.

<liquid pours, slurp>

<sigh>

I can't believe how fast it went to shit.

<slurp>

I guess I hoped she'd come for me here. That her love wouldn't allow her to desert me. That, despite myself and all I'm not, she'd be true to what we shared and the love we had.

In the end, I suppose it was too much for her.

<sniff>

I regret not being the man she thought she loved.

Maybe I'll see her on the other side.

I love you, Rhyme. I miss you. My head swims with what could've been and what was: of bodies in containers; babies, dead before they're born; urine-soaked podiums and the rush of the needle. But mostly, I'm full of mourning, for you, our son, for our love, for the eternity we planned.

This morning, they called and told me you died.

The shock I felt as I held the phone, tears streaming, speech stolen, stupid knees trembling, vaporized any desire I retained to go on.

<slurp, sigh, slurp>

Pure grief engulfs me. I'm lost. I'm bereft. My only hope is that I see you on the other side and that there, when we meet, you'll know me for the man I truly am.

Until that time, I'll be waiting for you. I *cannot* forget you. I *cannot* let you go.

I'll see you soon, my dearest love.

<sigh, gun racking>

Okay, Sig, I'm ready.
<doorbell>
What?
<loud thumping>

Drake chuckles as Longinus pounds the reporter's door. Exactly on time, and precisely as ordered.

CHAPTER 25

BEIRUT, LEBANON

"We propose a sharing of the Temple Mount," Igneus says.

The bowl hits the floor and shatters. Dates fly everywhere.

Igneus lurches, as if afraid the fat man might lash out. The room is large, vacuous, and we sit on over-stuffed pillows in the PLO leader's private meeting area, a second-floor office of sorts within Sundamir's mansion. Stefani, Sundamir's advisor and assistant, looks on, his face horrified at the rudeness shown by his boss. I keep very, very quiet.

Drake ordered Igneus to make the offer as *delicately as possible,* and for Igneus's part, he's tried to broach the subject with great care. The scattered dates are testament to his failure.

Sundamir moves well for a man his size. The settee creaks as he rises, arms sweeping skyward. "Do not mention such things in my presence!" He shouts, storms around the room.

Servants, young girls in thin white body-veils, press themselves against the room's walls. Stefani moves close to the PLO leader, corners him in a far alcove, speaks in quiet tones. Sundamir's eyes shift above plump cheeks as Stefani whispers. Sundamir nods his head, then shakes it hard. "Never!"

Stefani holds his ground, speaks in hurried tones and hushed gestures. Igneus watches from his low, round cushion. I scan the room and try to remember everything. My phone's been confiscated prior to entrance.

Whispers continue, and Sundamir's eyes blaze. "Enough!" He levels a finger at Stefani. "Get away from me, traitor!" Stefani blinks, takes a rapid step back.

Igneus rises, tugs on the lapels of his gray suit. He appears as a man on the verge of panic. "Mr. Sundamir," he says. "I assure you this arrangement is only temporary. If you'll just hear me out—"

The fat man wheels so fast, Igneus steps back a pace. Saliva flies from the Arab's lips as he shrieks. "You can all go to the devil! Ours is not to barter what remains of our heritage! Do you have any idea what you suggest?"

Igneus tries to look fearless. "We suggest only a final solution. You must have the strength to grasp it."

"Get out!" Sundamir shrieks. "Get out before I have you shot!"

I wonder if the man's powerful enough to make good on such a threat. Then Stefani beckons me with a wave. He grasps Igneus's arm and leads him out of the room. I rush to join them.

"Best to leave him to himself for a while," Stefani whispers once we exit. He speaks excellent English and, even under this pressure, carries himself with a suave confidence.

We find ourselves in Sundamir's anteroom, surrounded by ten men each in traditional white gallabiyah and long, flowing keffiyeh. Whether they're here for business or protection, I can't tell.

Two of them split from the group and flank us.

Sundamir bellows from inside the room. "Send in my wife!"

Stefani snaps at a sallow boy, who leaps to his feet and runs from the room.

"I must apologize," Stefani says to us, "he's been a bit tense lately."

Igneus nods. "Don't give it a second thought, young man." I marvel at Igneus's calm. Distance from the fat Arab must've emboldened him. "Please pass along my thanks to Mr. Sundamir. Perhaps I can visit again when he's in better sorts."

Stefani clasps his hands in a praying motion, bows. "You're very gracious." He nods to the guards, who motion us toward the exit.

We leave the anteroom, pass under a thick arch and onto a wide balcony that surrounds the large oval of the mansion's main living area. A vast chandelier catches the sun's rays and dapples plush carpet and gilded furniture with glittering light.

Illuminated in delicate rays, a grand piano fills the room's eastern side. A slight, fragile girl works the keys, elegant fingers create beautiful music. She plays a sad, lilting song that seems to possess the space with melancholy. Then she ups the tempo, plays a complex piece. I recognize the tune but can't name it. It's fast and complicated, just like this new world in which I've found myself.

"Sundamir's daughter, Sima," Igneus says. "One of the finest pianists in the world." A long divan and three matching chairs stand silent vigil as Sima's fingers stroll across the keys. Numerous cushions sit on the floor close to the furniture. More cushions of every size and texture and color sit in complimentary pairs and trios lining the room's walls. Five windows overlook the living area, immense rectangles framed by abundant curtains of beige and brown and gray.

We move to the right, passing rooms along the upper landing. At each end of the balcony, stairs hug the structure's round walls and descend to the main floor.

Six women pass on the balcony's other side. A tall woman leads at a quick pace, head held high, face covered in a fashionable hijab. Others follow in a loose V, talking and giggling. None cast a glance our direction as they disappear through the arch.

Soon, we're down the stairs and through the mansion's entrance, where our belongings are returned. We stand on a landing atop a wide flight of stairs, the palatial entryway to Sundamir's mansion. Our escorts appear as stone gargoyles as they wait for us to step away. There are four guards here; two who escorted us out, and two who man the entrance. Igneus pockets his belongings: a cell phone, a wallet, some car keys. I thumb my phone to life and examine it for signs of tampering.

Then I hear the noise.

It's funny how some sounds register in your brain and become obvious. Sometimes it's surprising, as it was for me when I heard the sword loosed from its scabbard. Before I can turn my head, the guard to my right falls. I look behind him to the extent my head can turn, and by the time I look to my left, the other guard falls.

Then a mountain moves between us, and I realize Longinus has come. The two other guards reach for their pistols, but long before they even make contact, both of their heads slip neatly from their necks and topple to the ground.

Longinus has taken all four of them with a grace equal parts primal and elegant. I'm frozen, mouth hanging open, trying to make sense of all that just occurred in the span of about three seconds.

Igneus steps toward the giant, speaks in a spitting whisper. "What the *hell* are you doing?"

The corners of the Roman's mouth point down. He tips his keffiyeh like a Hollywood cowboy. "Just followin' orders, Sheriff."

Igneus goes pale. "Oh no."

CHAPTER 26

BEIRUT, LEBANON

I 'd like to say I was bold in the moments that followed. That I was above the fray and all a man should be when confronted with such atrocities. I'd like to say I witnessed these events in a detached manner, as one scanning junk mail or watching an old movie. *And* without being affected.

But the truth is, I'd underestimated these people. I'd applied to them my own feelings of fairness and gentility, even after all evidence to the contrary. I must say, with no small amount of journalistic regret, I became a part of the story in this mansion in the desert. For in this place, I realized all that could not be undone. I realized how over my head I actually was. Here I knew, whatever followed, whether weeks, months or years, my fate was securely tied to these people and that my ruin was assured as certainly as if I'd squeezed the trigger of that Sig Sauer.

I long for Rhyme.

From within the mansion, we hear the screams of the dying, Igneus and I. The booming resonance of Longinus's laughter echoes through the place. There are occasional gun shots, but they're silenced in short order. After that, the place takes on an eerie stillness wherein, if one listens hard enough, one can hear the foundations weep and the walls bleed. In that moment, I know only I don't want to go back inside, ever. I feel grateful I've left the mansion before witnessing the horrors these sounds feed my mind. My feet are rooted in place, my clothes drenched in sweat. Lifeless bodies lie around me, severed heads stare at the blistering sun.

The mind can envision almost anything from the sounds it processes. The screams, the crash of furniture, the Roman's glee; I know only once I enter the mansion, I'll be forever changed. I know I don't want this but can't escape it. I imagine all horrors to the extent of my imagination's limit. Each thought matching the horrific sounds that echo from the depths of the mansion.

Igneus motions, but I stand fast. He pauses, searches my face and, I think, realizes he and I share some of the same qualities. His expression softens as he approaches, tugs on my coat sleeve.

"Come, Emery," he says.

I step back, shake my head. "I can't…don't want to," I stammer. "I think it's going to be bad."

Igneus's eyes are far away. "With these guys," he says, "it's always worse than you think."

When we enter, the luxurious interior has been made into something from a slasher film. Blood streaks the walls, and corpses line the stairs. Glancing across the lower level, I see more of the dead, those who'd tried to run from the scene. Their faces are like masks, some frozen in an eternal wail. Others look serene, as if death has granted some lasting peace.

Igneus tugs my sleeve and we move toward Sundamir's quarters, stepping over the dead, slipping in the unavoidable fluids that seep into the plush carpet. It's hard not to gag, and each time my body revolts I emit an involuntary gurgling sound—*glack*! I feel terror and revulsion in equal parts. I smell death, a thick scent that sticks to my nostrils and penetrates my brain in echoes and howls.

We move under the archway and enter the room in time to see

Longinus's sword move in a tight and effortless arc. Stefani's head pops straight into the air.

My mind records the scene as if it's become a video camera: the sword's lithe motion; the uncaring, orgasmic face of Longinus; the open, surprised eyes of Stefani; the headless body, standing, hands clasped at waist level; the tear-streaked faces of Sundamir's wife and daughters.

Their open mouths must be wailing, but I can't hear them, can't register sound. I can't command my eyes to close or my feet to run. I stare as Stefani's head lands, then rolls across the floor, dribbling blood behind it in curlicues. I realize then the true, psychopathic nature of the Roman Legion. Longinus's eyes are wild, his face, pure glee. The Roman likes to kill. *Needs* to kill.

Sundamir screams, his voice cracks with emotion. He holds his daughters close, eyes brim with disgust and hatred, lips curled to a snarl.

Longinus steps over Stefani's body and faces the fat Arab.

"Who's next?"

Sundamir leaps forward. "You will leave here immediately!" His voice catches for a moment, and he continues, pleading now. "You can take me with you. This does not involve my family. Leave them in peace. You can do what you will with me."

Behind us someone speaks.

"Regrettably your family *is* involved."

Thaddeus Drake stands in the doorway, looking at his gloved fingers. He appears bored, as if contemplating which five-star accommodations will suit him for the evening.

Longinus snickers and moves aside. Drake steps toward Sundamir, kicking Stefani's head as he moves.

"You were offered a deal—more money than one man could spend in a lifetime. More wives, more land, more luxury. But you refused. You have defied us."

"Surely something can be worked out," Sundamir blubbers. "I've seen the error of my ways." Fat jowls bounce his tears onto the carpet.

Drake shakes his head. "My friend," he says, "the time for

negotiation has passed. I'm not here to bargain." Drake speaks the last word as if it tastes sour on his tongue. "I came only to witness the justice of X'chasei."

Sundamir explodes. "You think there will not be repercussions! Do you think my family shall not avenge me? That the world will not cry for the execution of my executioners?" He punctuates his words by pointing at each of us in turn. "You'll be held accountable, Drake!" He sweeps a pudgy arm across the room. "All of you will be held accountable!"

Igneus looks at the floor. Longinus shakes his head, a broad smile on his lips. Hushed sobs come from Sundamir's family. I stand still as stone, paralyzed by horror.

Drake retrieves a silk kerchief from his suit and dabs his forehead. "I fear you're wrong, my friend. We've eliminated all your contacts, and Mr. Khalifa has graciously accepted the offer you turned down. Your cousins, uncles, brothers, and close business associates will die today. Mr. Khalifa was also gracious enough to volunteer to manage all of their assets until such time as an..." He looks toward the ceiling, "An heir, comes forward. Incidentally, he will manage *your* assets as well."

Sundamir looks as if he's been punched in his considerable nose. His eyelids flutter. His fat lips quiver under a bushy moustache. He begins to mumble, incoherent, eyes darting around the room. His wife reaches for him, but before she can make contact, Sundamir launches himself at Drake.

"Die!" He screeches, his body straining to move with the speed of youth and fitness.

Longinus intercepts him, levels a punch to his stomach and then a hard knee to his face as he falls.

Sundamir lurches, cheeks flutter as he gasps for air. Blood runs from his broken nose and over his beard. He falls flat, vomits on the carpet.

Longinus laughs.

I almost puke.

Sundamir's daughters cry out and reach for their father.

Igneus moves to the room's far wall, closest the door.

Sundamir's wife dives toward Longinus. In her hand, the unmistakable silver of a blade. She moves with a graceful speed, calm and fluid, fearless, a Queen of the Desert.

I want to cry out. Want to move to her aid.

I *want* the lady's blade to plunge deep into the Roman's heart.

She lunges, blade leveled, inches from the Roman's broad back.

Then Longinus reacts, turns with a speed both blinding and impressive.

Her blade misses by less than an inch. The good lady, now off-balance, speeds past struggling to stay upright. Longinus moves with her, in pace and a step behind.

I see the shimmer of steel. Then the lady's head simply falls off.

Her body moves another few steps before collapsing sideways.

Longinus turns. Blood streaks his beard, stains his teeth. He looks rapturous.

Sundamir howls.

The daughters wail and tear at their garments.

The camera in my head records, even as I empty my stomach onto the plush carpet.

Drake raises his hands for quiet. Then, speaks over the sobs, a finger pointed at Sundamir. "She was more of a man than you." He says this as a fact that can't be disputed.

Sundamir's eyes stare lasers at Drake. His jowls move, his lips purse, his body shakes from grief as bloody snot hangs from his nostrils.

Drake nods to Longinus. "Let's get on with it."

Longinus steps forward, plucks one of Sundamir's daughters from the clutch of her sisters. It's Sima, the pianist. The girl is frail, fine hands and a round mouth. She's like a porcelain doll in the Roman's grip.

Sundamir doesn't move, only sobs pleas at deaf ears.

Longinus pushes the girl down, sword poised above her. He looks at Drake.

Drake raises a hand, then turns to me.

I almost lose my bowels, almost drop in a dead faint as I think he's going to ask me to kill this girl. To prove my loyalty, to eternally bind myself to him forever with a single act. I can't look in his eyes, my hands tremble, my legs strain to keep me upright. My head buzzes as my stomach turns over and over like a butter churn. There's a pause that takes forever. In the distance, somewhere far off, through the haze and stench and tumult in my head, I hear Drake's voice.

"You may go," he says.

I sprint from the room, head reeling with bloody visions.

CHAPTER 27

BEIRUT, LEBANON

I race through the mansion, legs fully alive now. Leaping corpses, I slip twice in their fluids. I make it out the door and race down the wide arc of the drive. My legs burn with the effort, but I'm spurred on by what I've seen.

Only one thought consumes me: to get as far away as I can. No money is worth this. I race through the large iron gate and down the road. The desert's heat is stifling. The sun burns into my skin, steals my breath and energy.

I press on, terror whipping wild, like a spooked horse chased by a demon.

I hear a sound, manage a look over my shoulder. A large black car approaches. It's Drake, coming to collect me, to calm me with his smile and soothe me with his words. I want no part of him, or this. I double my efforts, sprint into the desert's heat. I think, with luck, I'll fry, die of heat stroke before Drake can catch me. I pass more corpses, outlying guards I suppose. Longinus must've done them in before entering the mansion.

The car draws close and I veer right, running headlong into the desert. My legs can't go much farther, but I suppress the pain and quicken my pace.

The car turns off the road and follows. I can tell it doesn't intend on overtaking me, merely follows at a close distance. Drake knows I can't sustain this. He's a son of the desert, knows full well I'll succumb to the heat. That I'll fall in the dirt, panting, unable to go on. At that point, he'll either finish me or capture me in his spell. Either way, I'm fucked.

I'm numb, can't breathe. My lungs simply can't inhale more air, the demands of my body are too great to support. The heat's an unconquerable foe.

Still, I press, staggering now, stumbling over small stones, feet dragging. I try to turn again but collapse in the sand of the desert floor.

I hope the car will turn away, let me die. Or Drake exits the vehicle and plants two bullets in my brain. I can't accept a different fate. I can't be a brother to these madmen.

I lie coughing, spreading grains of sand with each ragged breath. I hear the car stop but don't attempt to look. I've given up fully. I'll die here, even if that means using my remaining energy to attack Drake. I feel a square stone next to my right hand and squeeze it tight. A plan forms: when he approaches, I'll hit him with the rock and make my escape.

I hear the footsteps, crunchy on the sand. I sense he's close, feel a hand on my shoulder.

I muster all my speed to turn and strike.

It's Igneus, sallow face stretched to a pitiful smile. "Emery," he says, "let's get out of here."

CHAPTER 28

BEIRUT, LEBANON

"If Drake wants to find us, he will," Igneus says as we race through the desert. "But he won't."

I'm exhausted, slumped in the passenger's seat. My legs are so numb, I'm not sure if I can find the will to stand. "He won't find us?" I ask.

"He won't look. He'll call at some point and beckon us to him, but he won't come looking. He knows these horrors take time to process. He's very astute in that regard. He'll give us time, a few weeks maybe."

"Where are we going?"

"Damascus. There's a nice hotel that will treat us well. And they won't ask questions."

"We just hole up there? What's the plan after that?"

Igneus gives me a wry look. "There's no plan after that. We return to Drake."

"Are you serious?" I hear the strain in my voice as I speak.

"What do you propose? We serve at the pleasure of the gloved man. Trust me, there's no escaping him, and once you're in the net, you may as well swim with the other fish."

"I don't think I can," I say. "I'm not cut out for this. I mean, what I saw back there...well...that was...it's murder. We need to report this. When we get to Damascus, we need to find someone who'll listen. You heard him, he's planning to kill all of Sundamir's associates, the rest of his family. Who isn't going to notice that? How does that not raise some eyebrows?"

I search his frail features. A small grin comes to his lips. It strikes all hope from my mind, a grin of acceptance. The realization of hopelessness.

"Any raised eyebrows will be trimmed," Igneus says. "Don't you see, Emery? Haven't you put it together, or is your mortal brain unable to process the vastness of our organization? Everyone serves X'chasei, or at least anyone who matters. The dead will be...processed. Those who think to ask questions will be bought off, replaced, killed. Whatever. Drake does what Drake wants. No one stops him."

My mind races with the possibilities. Is this the deep state that gets so much press? The secret organization that controls every aspect of life while we mortals stumble through our seventy- or eighty years picking crumbs from the trash?

"How is that even possible?" I ask. "How can that happen? There are systems in place. No man is above the law. This cannot stand." I'm speaking without thought. My body aches, but my tongue yet has life.

"Emery, you're thinking like a mortal. I've been here for the whole damn thing. It started with the Legion—"

"The Romans?"

"Yes, that was Cain's first steps into what X'chasei has become. You see, Cain spent centuries persecuting Christians. His aim was to stamp them out for all eternity. He was so angry, he declared war on God."

I laugh despite myself. "War on God? How does one do that?"

"By exterminating his presence. By erasing all memory or thought of him. That was the big change, when Cain realized if he couldn't beat them, then he may as well *direct* them. I was around during the sacking of Herod's Temple. He'd suddenly changed. He told us then we'd become gods ourselves and claim dominion over this Earth. If our punishment was to live forever, then we would live like kings. I remember the words he used—*a peaceable kingdom*. Once established, all war, poverty, hunger, would be banished. All would live under our rule and be well-provided for. Then, hundreds of years later, he embraces the religion. Gives them the power they now have by providing them the very text they use as a road map for salvation."

"Constantine?"

"Precisely. He told them this was a divine book, written by the hand of God. Had his priests do the same. Eventually everyone believed it because the believers became the monsters. Killing in the name of God. And don't get me wrong, God is every bit as malicious as any human, at least that's what the evidence tells me. Have you heard Cain say it? *God prefers blood?* And I can't disagree. By all indicators, whether X'chasei reigns or not, God's preference *is* for blood."

I stare out the window and watch dust fly from our tires. Harsh, bent trees and endless sand flows by undisturbed and uncaring.

"Modern people have no idea of what's occurred throughout history," he says. "Everything now is *civilized* and *convenient*. But before, there was nothing but blood. Do you know the horrors of Hitler?"

"Of course," I say.

"Nothing compared to ancient times, yet the world was shocked. That was another of Cain's attempts to fulfill the prophecies. That war ended but not because of what the history books tell you, but because the gloved man ended it. Do you think Hitler committed suicide in some obscure bunker?"

I nod. "Yes, that's what we were told."

"And who do you think put the story out?" He glances at me, then at the road. "Cain did. He needed the war until something changed his plans. Some prophecy that couldn't be fulfilled messed everything up."

"You mean it didn't end because of the Normandy invasion? Because the Allies stopped Hitler and his cronies?"

Igneus laughs a sort of squeak. "Hardly, and it didn't end because Cain was too horrified by all the death. It ended because it no longer fit the gloved man's plan. Cain killed Hitler himself. I was there. That fucking guy was crazy as shit, let me tell you."

I'm surprised by Igneus's expletives. "So, Cain wants the Jews exterminated?"

"Not at all. Cain cares little for the Jews or anyone else. The extermination plan was all Hitler, made possible by Cain's indifference. Cain has other plans. He doesn't care what happens to any mortals, whether they be Jew, Gentile, animal, vegetable or mineral." He flashes a small grin. "Cain cares only about facing God, and there's no atrocity he won't support to that end."

"So, every war is directed by Drake?"

Igneus shakes his head. "No, but most are at least okayed by him. You see, Cain isn't God, and God is a worthy adversary. No man can comprehend the mind of God, that's scripture right there and probably the truest thing ever said. Imagine if you were a hermit crab living under a rock in the ocean. You have a little bit of sea floor that's your own, and every now and then you poke your head out to grab some food, then dart back under your rock before you get eaten."

"Okay."

"Now imagine the little bit of sea floor is the Earth and everything we can see from the Earth."

"Okay."

"The crab doesn't know the vastness of the ocean in which it swims. It doesn't know there's land and continents, space and galaxies. It knows only its little slice of the sea floor. To the crab, that little space is everything. It's all relative, you see. We're just microbes on a universal level."

"I see where you're going. You're going to tell me God doesn't matter."

"No, I'm going to tell you to try and comprehend the mind of God. God knows about that little crab and every bit of sand in that environment. He knows about the Earth and everything around it, he knows what lies past that, or over that. He knows and manages every single speck of every single thing in every conceivable space, everywhere. We humans," he raises a finger, "even immortals, think because we're intelligent and can build tall things and big things and things that fly, that we can arrange atoms and cure disease. We think we comprehend the mind of God. That we are like gods ourselves. That we're special. But again, if you examine the evidence, we can't even fathom the vastness of our planet's place in our own universe. We are the crab. Do you see how completely insignificant that makes us?"

"Like we don't even matter."

"Yes. But at the same time, not insignificant at all because God can fathom the universe fully and completely, give each of us his undivided attention at the same time, every second of every day. Comprehend that for a second. True omniscience."

I blink at the landscape. This is hard to imagine, and my mind works over the staggering proportions of the Jew's statements.

"Some say Heaven is just the next step of a soul's journey," the little man continues, "but the truth is no one knows because no one can comprehend the mind of God. Our big brains are too small, and we all think ourselves too special." With this, he stops and considers his next words. He reaches under the seat and retrieves a bottle of Oban and passes it to me. "Sorry, I forgot I had this in here," he says.

I pull the cork and take two great gulps, then I close my eyes and wait for the liquid to seep through every cell, to numb the terror.

Igneus continues. "There is one man who has a better idea of it all than anyone else on the planet, and that's Cain. You see, he *actually walked with God.*" Igneus smiles at this. "Can you imagine what that must've been like?"

I think about it and shake my head. "No, I can't."

"Me, neither," he says. "And I've tried really hard to do that. Tried to put myself in Cain's position; I have this incredible life where I hang out with God until I displease Him and suffer the harshest fate ever doled out to a human. But here's the big difference: Cain is convinced it matters. He knows all I've just told you but continues undaunted. Does that mean Cain has some special knowledge of God the rest of us lack? I believe he must. That on some level, his path is informed by having spent time with God. I can tell you if God offered forgiveness tomorrow, Cain would accept without a second's doubt. Even after all these centuries, he longs to walk with Him. I believe this knowledge guides his decisions. Although, no matter how much I've thought it over, I can't come up with an explanation as to why Cain suffers such a fate. It doesn't make sense to me." He trails off at this point, deep in thought.

The desert sun dips toward the horizon as I watch the little man. Frail wrists lead to delicate fingers that grip the steering wheel with white knuckles. He doesn't appear as much, but as I watch, I'm struck by the fact that he's survived, even prospered, while living with these lunatics.

The heart of a lion, I think. I wonder if I can trust him. Perhaps Drake has sent him to pick me up and spy on me. The thought lingers in my mind like a lost word. I'm truly fucked here. Truly trapped by these immortals. If I mention the Apostle, what calamity will that bring? If the Jew rats me out, what horrors await? The setting sun casts a luminous glow on his bald head. I squint at him, try to see the green aura of which Drake speaks. I sigh and pour scotch down my throat, then wipe my mouth with a still-shaking hand. From any perspective, any angle cast through this jagged prism, I'm going to die at the hands of these madmen. Like Ramirez the Cuban, I'm placing a big bet with little chance of winning.

"Fuck it," I say aloud. Igneus glances at me and motions for the scotch.

I sigh again, feel the liquor seep through the holes in my logic. "I may know someone who can help."

Igneus rolls his eyes and takes a long pull from the bottle. "And who might that be?"

"The Apostle John. Do you know about him?"

"The Templar? Yes. He's a continual nuisance to X'chasei's aims, although I think he's as clueless as he is harmless."

"Perhaps we fill him in on the details."

I watch his eyes widen. He turns a deeper shade of pale. "You mean cross Drake? No, no, no, you can count me out. If he finds out, he'll kill you and do even worse to me."

"Not so," I say. "Drake knows I've spoken to the Apostle and has told me I may speak to him as much as I'd like. He said it will make for a more complete history."

Igneus stares forward, bony fingers clutching the wheel as long shadows of dusk stretch toward us. He's silent for a long time, every so often pouring more scotch in his mouth. I say nothing, amazed at the amount of liquor the frail man can ingest. This man has been kind to me, and I don't want to push him.

Igneus takes another long drink, sighs. "Okay," he says, "how do we reach him?"

CHAPTER 29

JERUSALEM, AFTER THE CRUCIFIXION

I t will rain soon.

Igneus sits in a wooden chair in the room's corner. Beside him, an uneaten meal on a sparse table. He hasn't eaten since finding Longinus's burnt flesh rising from the center of a charred courtyard. His expression is blank, numb, as he stares out the window like a skeleton propped in a crypt. Sparse hair gathers in mussed spikes and points in all directions, as haggard as the man's face. His chin quivers like a leaf, catching odd remnants of breeze but holding tight to the branch.

Wilted flowers lie on the table. Removed from the vase but not yet discarded, their hidden secrets beckon from clustered petals as candlelight flickers, revealing, concealing, revealing. Gilded stands lift tallowed candles high and throw sputtering shadows; from the bare scalp of Igneus to the formerly purple—now inert gray—orchids, up bare, cracked walls, then plummeting to the brown-checkered floor.

Cain paces, chewing his lip.

"Care to eat, my friend?"

Muffled sobs reply as Igneus shields his face with trembling hands. His bony frame juts through the contours of his robes.

Cain inhales, then sighs.

Igneus is a mystery, but something says he's vital, that patience must rule, tender assurance, even friendship.

Cain moves close to his perch, a small balcony from which he can see the city. It yawns in the night as Moonies offer their shrill cry to the clouded skies. Patience yields all things.

Yes, patience. But…

The man cries at the slightest provocation.

Perhaps he should've considered that before he slapped the Messiah. What a fool, what a great fool.

His own bad luck, stumbling upon us in the courtyard the way he did. Igneus had related the entire tale: waking, dizzy in a strange room, leaving that room and wandering through the house drawn toward muffled voices, then reaching the top of the staircase just as Longinus plunged his sword into Cain's back.

He'd witnessed all the events that followed, his horror growing until his final, panicked shriek.

We are condemned.

The words ring in Cain's mind.

Cain brought him to this room, his perch high above the jaded, aged city, hoping to ease his pain. Wine and food were offered, but the thin man didn't even look at them, had only perched himself by the window.

"What's he blattin' about?"

Longinus appears in the doorway. A silk sheet polluted with soot circles his waist. His sword pokes from the fabric's left side. Scars run the length of his torso: thick and thin, long and short, linear and angled. Too numerous to count, their raised edges pucker above taut, charred skin. Within the matted confusion of hair and scar and ash, Cain sees what appears to be newly grown, hairless skin, pink and supple, covered with a shiny down like a newborn's scalp. Beneath that, thick wads of muscle.

Igneus startles, a tear-streaked face holds the strains of fear.

"Feeling better?" Cain asks.

Longinus limps in. "Gettin' by," he says, wincing as he moves, then grimacing as he takes a seat at the table across from the frail Jew.

The smell of burnt flesh fills the room like a spitted calf marinated in beech bark and urine. Small bits of ash fall from the Roman to land on the floor with a ticking sound. He leans forward, takes Cain's eyes in his own.

Cain returns the gaze. The eyes are the only still-normal part of Longinus—if indeed those have ever been considered normal. They're dead black, alive with pain and confusion.

Cain sees, too, an ember of something he likes very much—a balled-up, pulsing kernel of pure will. It shines: *Bring what you will, I'll never quit.*

Longinus's lips part; his voice emerges like a blistered croak from a boiling swamp.

"Somebe's gonna tell me what's anon and agin," he says, fingers tapping his sword hilt, dusting ash onto the floor. "Or we be dancin' the jig of spinnin' steel."

After the fire, Cain carried, or rather dragged, Longinus to a spare room and laid him on cool, linen sheets. He'd retrieved the sword from the courtyard as an act of kindness, thinking that, upon waking, the soldier would be comforted by the sight of his trusted weapon.

Cain nods at the tapping fingers, but his face becomes hard as the steel itself. "I wouldn't advise that," he says, looking into the Roman's coal-black eyes.

Silence rules as the two men stare at one another, neither moving.

Seconds tick.

In the distance, a cow bawls its disgust to the moon.

A chair creaks as Igneus adjusts his position.

Then the Roman places his sword hand on the table and leans back in his chair with a subdued groan.

"I'm glad you came to your senses," Cain says, walking away. "I'll be glad to relate everything." He turns back to them. "But you must always remember one thing."

Silent eyes regard him. He can almost see the smoke wafting from the Roman's burnt stubs of hair.

"Any harm you try to inflict upon me will be returned to you sevenfold." He smiles at the half-naked giant. "But you probably know that."

The Roman's face remains expressionless. "I'll be havin' me answers now or anon."

Cain looks at Igneus who stares with the slack-jawed gaze of a punch-drunk pugilist.

He inhales. "This—" he thinks about the word—"gift, let's say, is one of the terms of my imprisonment."

"Imprisonment?" Longinus looks about the room as if expecting a steel cage to drop over them all.

Cain raises a hand, eyes half-closed, nose raised in a curt nod. "I'll explain everything, and you'll have your answers. But first, you must listen. I'll only explain this once and, in the future, will not entertain questions." He trades his glance between the two. "If you have questions, ask them now. Agreed?"

Longinus nods, air whistling like a steeped teapot through ash-crusted nostrils.

The Jew nods.

"Good," Cain says, clapping his hands a single time. "Let's begin."

CHAPTER 30

JERUSALEM, AFTER THE CRUCIFIXION

"That can't be true," Igneus whispers. "Punished by God?"

Cain stands before the two, arms crossed over his chest. Longinus and Igneus sit at the table half-facing each other.

"I observed each of you as you made the transition," Cain says.

"Aye?" A single syllable question from Longinus.

"I've committed no crime," Igneus says, speaking more to himself.

"I've recently developed the ability to tell if someone is as I am," Cain says. "I knew you by your emerald auras. A gift, it seems, that is solely mine. A way to tell immortal from mortal. In all these centuries—"

"I'VE DONE NOTHING!" The room rings with Igneus's voice.

Longinus moves for his sword.

Igneus stands in front of a toppled chair, eyes wide and terror-stricken. His nostrils quiver above stretched, white lips. He looks at Cain, fists clenched in defiance.

"Really?" Cain's voice drips with pity. "What a grave mistake? Punished for innocence alone?"

They stand eye to eye as Cain continues. "Or, perhaps, you did something as stupid as slapping the already bleeding and bruised face of God's Son?"

Igneus's mouth falls open, his eyes focus on nothing. A faint glimmer of remembrance flares inside them.

Excuses fall from his mouth, punctuated with the words *never have, couldn't remember* and *never knew.*

Cain nods as if he cares and waits. Igneus sputters to silence, then stands with panicked eyes, one thin vein bulging from his forehead.

"Be seated, my friend," Cain says. "Your excuses mean nothing to me. I can neither forgive, nor change the past. All I can do is help you bear this load. I'm here to guide you along a path I've worn with my own feet, a path—"

"What did I do?" Longinus asks.

Cain looks at him. "What haven't you done?"

"I damned certain did non as evil as slappin' God." He pronounces evil as ewil.

Cain laughs. "Certainly not! A centurion of the Legion would never resort to violence." He takes in the Roman's blistered face. "But what about when you drank his blood? Remember that?"

Cain watches him closely. He places a hand on Longinus's scorched shoulder, feels the rough patchwork of flesh. The man's face contorts but he doesn't move.

"My dear Longinus," Cain says, "in your line of work, I'm sure they all look the same after a while, but do you remember?"

Longinus nods, looks at the floor. The hint of a smile appears.

"Splendid, you both remember. What a big surprise, eh? Jesus *is* the Son of God, the Messiah of prophecy. And you drank his blood," pointing at Longinus, "and you," whirling toward Igneus, "were so consumed with bloodlust, you couldn't show even the slightest mercy."

Igneus gasps at the accusation, shakes his head as new tears fall. Cain lets the two consider their actions.

"I witnessed your transgressions, watched as your punishment fell upon you. Didn't you feel rather peculiar after those incidents?"

Igneus nods through watery eyes. Longinus continues staring at the floor.

Spreading his hands before him, Cain says, "Welcome to your fate."

The room becomes quiet.

"We must be redeemed," Igneus whispers, "even now it can't be too late."

"Of course," Cain says. "Redemption. That's what we need." He holds his hand to his head, looks stunned. "Now why didn't I think of that?"

His expression becomes serious, his eyes burn into Igneus. "From whom?"

The Jew gives no answer.

"God?" Cain says. "God doesn't forgive when your offense is such as ours."

His voice becomes loud, harried. "God sent his son to be crucified as a man. Don't you see?" He looks at them, waits for an answer. They remain silent.

"A God—" he says with an exaggerated, wavery tone—"that can offer his son—" the same wavery tone—"as a lamb to the wolves does not offer redemption." He turns between both men as he speaks. "Do you think He considers you or your punishment? Hmm? To God, a thousand years is like a single second. Do you think after a thousand years He'll take pity on you?" Cain's face flushes. "Tell Him you're sorry, you fools. Beg His forgiveness. Spend four thousand years seeking salvation through your good deeds." His voice drops to just above a whisper. "Know what you'll find?" His head snaps between them like a door in a gale. "You'll find salvation is futile and you're no longer worthy."

Cain moves to Igneus, grasps his face in a firm embrace, ignores his whimpers. He hisses, "*I've been crucified a thousand times!* I've suffered more than any man—even Jesus!" His voice lowers as Igneus trembles. "Where's God's pity? Eh? Where's His mercy? *Where's His love?*" He holds the Jew's cheeks for a fraction longer, then releases his face with a jerk. The frail man reels, almost falls over.

Cain crosses the room and faces the wall, slides gloved hands over fine robes, takes deep, measured breaths.

He turns to them, his face a normal color. He takes another deep breath, then exhales.

"I apologize, my friends. Please don't be offended."

Igneus stares as if witnessing a nightmare. Longinus sits at the table flaking ashes from his arms.

"Good deeds don't garner rewards," he says, shaking his head. "God doesn't concern himself with us. Our punishment is to endure." He says the last in a voice without emotion, a statement of flat fact.

He circles the room, head lifted, brow crinkled. "But we're not helpless." He looks at Igneus, slowly speaks the next words. "Not *condemned*."

The thin man's eyebrows raise; his upper lip shakes beneath a sharp nose.

"I've played this silly game for centuries. A pawn begging scraps at the king's table. But I've learned. Yes, and I've watched. And what I've discovered is the key to freedom lies within our prison. At *our feet* within our prison." Eyes flash with excitement. "Do you not see? Our punishment presents our salvation. Through simple endurance, a compromise is made."

Silence follows.

"What are ye' suggestin'?" Longinus croaks.

"I do *not* suggest, dear Longinus. This isn't a decision, but rather a single path through a treacherous wood."

Longinus leans back as a thick piece of ash falls from his stubbed scalp onto the mottled skin of his chest. It lands beside a dried grape that used to be his nipple.

"How?" the Roman asks.

"We embrace our confines. Discover how to bend it to our will, how to attain dominion over it. As God watches, or doesn't watch for that matter, we become kings."

He glances to Igneus, who stares but doesn't seem to see.

"We'll rule rulers," Cain says. "We'll judge the judges. We'll grant wisdom to the wise and counsel the counselors. We'll re-create this place in our image and assure it's reshaped by our vision. We'll command the Earth, and it will bow at our feet, tremble at our voice. We'll demand peace and supplication. We'll enforce an ignorance of God and wrest from Him the praises of His own creation. They'll come to us for their needs. They'll seek our blessings in all their endeavors. We will be their kings and rule them justly. We'll take this land from a collection of warring factions to one nation united under our authority. All we desire will be ours, and no one can stand in our way, not even God."

His eyes jump from man to man. "If God decides to grace us with His attention, then we offer Him our kingdom as trade for our heavenly reward."

"And if He does non?" Longinus asks.

"Then we live forever as supreme rulers. Gods on Earth."

Longinus's face becomes a crinkle-lipped smile.

Igneus remains stupefied, looks hopeless and terrified.

Cain continues, "I can do this without you, both of you, and it should be noted I've wasted four thousand years chasing redemption. I'm asking you to join me, to cast your lots with me for all eternity, to usher in a kingdom of our own choosing."

Cain nears Igneus, takes in the man's sallow eyes, searches for sanity. "I know it's been hard, dear Igneus, but I promise it'll get better. This is the only way, I assure you."

Igneus stares like a man in a lion's den.

Cain glances at Longinus, smiles. "Besides, it's not like we're going anywhere."

His words rebound off the room's bare walls, over the dead orchids and into Jerusalem's streets.

Cain takes a step back, gauges their response.

They can refuse, he thinks.

If he's learned anything over the centuries, it's patience—a lesson relearned many, many times over. They'll see it his way. *If they don't, I'll wait.*

A scorched laugh breaks the silence. Longinus stands, ashes fall with a slight scratching sound. Cain marvels at the man's capacity to withstand pain even as his laughter fills the room, chest shaking a tempest of dust, eyes filled with glee. "I do non thin' 'tis goin' to be so bad," he croaks. He turns to Igneus. "What about ye, little man?"

Igneus looks straight ahead, his face haunted, eyes reflecting bewilderment and something else—insanity? Fear? Determination? He rises, candlelight showing welted cheeks from Cain's grip. He steps forward, eyes unfocused, betraying something—hatred? Contempt?

Cain's mind grasps silken webs. Confusion? Injustice?

The thin man turns toward the window. The candles create an eerie silhouette, make his shadow large and sinister as it flickers like a hollow specter.

Igneus takes another step, then launches himself from the third-floor window.

They hear a sound like breaking boards as he hits the street.

Longinus rushes to the window, leaves behind a whirlwind of ash. Cain joins him, both looking at the Jew's rumpled and broken form. Blood oozes from his head to spread across the stone.

Just then the door bursts open. It's Sham'beth the servant. His chest heaves as if he's just run a great distance. "The tomb's empty!"

Longinus chuckles, eyes returning to the form in the street.

Cain says nothing, watching as the frail man dies.

A hard rain begins to fall.

CHAPTER 31

DAMASCUS, SYRIA

John arrives on time. A nondescript man, I think. He doesn't exude power or grace or look the way some others do. I shake his hand and introduce him to Igneus. The frail man greets him with a small bow and a smile.

"You're the Igneus of legend?" the Apostle asks.

Igneus's face turns a slight shade of crimson, which makes him appear healthier by comparison with his usual paleness.

"I am," he says. "And you are the Apostle of the Bible?"

John nods. "Yes. One and the same. I've long wanted to speak with you, my friend." Igneus looks uncomfortable, but his face brightens, even appears, dare I say, hopeful. John enters and assumes a chair, one of two across from a long, low settee with rich blue cushions all around.

Nestled in the Old City, we've been at the Hotel Beit al Mamlouka for a few days. Our accommodations are small in this old hotel, but posh and comfortable. Igneus has been a marvelous tour guide, citing tales of mosques and palaces, taking me to Mount Quassion so I can see the beauty and breadth of Damascus in its entirety. We are guests of X'chasei and as such have been offered every luxury from women to vices.

John sits, crosses his legs, then smooths his tie. "I understand you're in trouble and need the Templar's help."

I start to answer, but Igneus speaks first. "We're not in trouble, as you say, but were hoping you could help us." John leans forward as Igneus continues. "Thaddeus Drake seeks to fulfill the prophecies and usher in the end times."

John's face goes pale. He leans back and props his elbow on the arm of the chair.

"And he knows you're here?" he asks. "Meeting with me?"

I shake my head.

"Of course, he does," Igneus says. "We weren't here two minutes and he knew."

I'm surprised by the information and realize I shouldn't be. Igneus hasn't been silent on the fact the gloved man knows all.

"And he'll suffer you telling me these things?"

I speak up. "Indeed, he will. He encouraged it."

John rubs his smooth face. "Interesting, to what end I wonder."

"He seeks an audience with God, seeks to rebuild Solomon's Temple on the original site."

John chuckles. "Oh, so he's going with the easy stuff first?"

We both laugh.

"I'm not sure anything has ever been easy for him," Igneus says. "Cast out of God's sight, paying an eternal penance with no hope of forgiveness. We all labor with these chains around our necks. Unlike you, John, assured the glory of God and an honored place in His kingdom."

His words hammer home the stakes of things, and I marvel. A broken down, discredited journalist sitting here with two immortals, one of whom happens to be an original disciple of Jesus Christ. Surreal as Dali, I think, and my mind fills with a thousand questions for each to answer, a million details throughout history. I glance at my phone to be sure it's recording.

"I wish I could offer apologies on God's behalf," John says, "but the truth is your punishments were delivered by your own hands."

"And what of you then?" Igneus asks. "What have you done to gain immortality?"

John glances at me. "I'm sure Emery has told you, but in case he hasn't, I believe I'm here to serve some task, although I don't know if that task involves the man I know as the Vagabond, your Cain or Drake, or some other purpose. I spend my time organizing churches and preparing for the day Jesus returns." He fixes a stare on Igneus. "Do you remember the day He left?"

Igneus lowers his head—not for shame or pity, I realize, but for piety. "I do," he says. "It's like looking through a veil at a foggy day. Throughout all these centuries, that memory has never been quite clear. My crime was failing to show mercy to the Man during His passion, but I remember no such slight. That sort of thing is *completely* out of my character. Yet, I suffer on the shoulders of eternity for a crime I can't recall. It's been hell, just a miserable existence."

"So, you're both confused?" I question them. "You both have no knowledge of what you're doing here or why?"

They look at each other for a few seconds and then nod their heads in unison. We all laugh, although the joke isn't really funny.

"Perhaps yours is to stop Cain," I say to John. "And yours is to stop X'chasei," I say to Igneus.

Igneus pours a glass of water from a sweaty pitcher on the table between us. "Stop X'chasei," he says with a snort. "That just isn't going to happen."

"Why not?" John asks.

"For the same reason you're not going to stop Cain. It's too vast, there's too much. He's infiltrated everything. There's truly no government, institution, or boundary he doesn't control. The network is huge and full of intermediaries. Proving ties to X'chasei would—wait, strike that—proving X'chasei even *exists* will be impossible. And then to try to stick the whole thing on Thaddeus Drake, the Dove, beloved by the entire world? Seriously? Cain has been planning this for centuries. Our only hope is if you, Apostle, can beseech God for his forgiveness. Cain would leap at that. It's been his single-minded purpose for millennia."

John looks shocked. "Men are saved by the blood of Christ, not by the pleas of His followers."

"Then why is Cain singled out as the only one who can't ask forgiveness?"

John stares at the floor. "Is he? It seems you and the Roman suffer the same fate."

Igneus reacts as if slapped. He shakes his head. "I guess so," he says in a low voice.

"I know not the answers to your questions. I am but a servant of Jesus and will do my best to fulfill my task, whatever that may be. Until then I'll be vigilant and work for the church in whatever capacity is needed."

Igneus laughs. "You mean by being the head of a secret society?"

John smooths his tie again. "Yes, the powers of darkness are vast." He pauses here, measures his words. "And mostly minions of X'chasei. The Templars have done all in their power to thwart these plans with the belief that working against such a dark and menacing foe is God's work. For our efforts, we've been martyred and betrayed. I can only think that as God gave dominion of the world to Satan until His return, He also lessened our effectiveness against these powers. Church numbers are shrinking as every vice grows, corruption prevails through all societies and governments, avarice is the cornerstone of daily life and God becomes increasingly forgotten in the names of science and human intellect.

"You say Cain wants to usher in the end times by fulfilling the prophecies. I can't say you're wrong because I see parts of my vision come to life almost daily. Watch the news. I'm not sure if the righteous can win on this Earth. In the final tally, I am but a servant of Christ trying to do my best. If Cain wants to bring about humanity's destruction, I can't guarantee the Pope will attempt to stop him. Even now I can't tell friend from enemy, whether in the Vatican or in any church I visit. I've watched the wheel of time turn and remain puzzled by its machinations. The prophecies may not be easy to fulfill, much has changed."

"Be that as it may," Igneus says, "Cain means to see it done. We may require your help to stop this."

John shakes his head. "I'd have to get permission from the Pope."

"You're a living disciple," I say. "You have to get permission from the Holy Father? From a mere mortal?"

John leans forward, elbows on his knees. "Indeed, that is a tenant of the Church and the Templars. The Pope is God's representative on Earth. He has final say in all things. Even I can't undermine him. It is as Peter was directed to make it, and I can assure you it was by God's command, at least then."

I shake my head.

Igneus refills his glass, then another and slides it to me. He offers the pitcher to John, who waves it away. "And if the Pope refuses?"

"Then it won't happen," John says. He moves to the window, parts the blind and looks out over the Old City. "Please, tell me what you know so I can give a full accounting."

We tell our tale, trying to be as thorough as possible and pausing only when John has a question. We finish with the events at Sundamir's mansion and an explanation of Cain's effort to rebuild the Temple.

"He won't have his Temple," the Templar says. "The Dome of the Rock sits there. Islam will not allow such an intrusion; it would cause a world war."

"Drake's working on that," I say. "A sharing of the holy site."

My Popephone rings and startles me. I've forgotten it's even in my pocket. I show it to the Disciple, then answer.

"Dear Emery, how nice to hear your voice." Even over the phone I feel like I'm melting into Drake's words. "I do want to apologize for the, let's say, events at Mr. Sundamir's compound. I realize those were probably off-putting for you."

"To say the least," I say. "I'm not sure I'm the man for this job."

Drake laughs, a soothing and comforting sound. "I can assure you that you *are* the man for this job. I can think of no other. Besides, now you've been through that, had time to deal with it, the rest should be easy." I feel relaxed, Cain's spell at work. He continues without waiting for my response. "Is Igneus with you?"

"Yes."

"Good, I've sent a jet to Damascus to collect you both. Big things are on the horizon, and I need you there to record them."

"Okay," I say, "how long until we leave?" I'm amazed at my acquiescence even as the words leave my mouth. Gone are the feelings of escape and terror.

"It will be there in two hours. I'll see you shortly."

"Okay," I stammer. "Anything else?"

"Yes, please give my regards to the Disciple. I look so forward to meeting him again someday."

I click the button and slide the phone in my pocket. I'm shocked at the fact I said nothing about my distaste, displeasure or guilt over the events at Sundamir's mansion. I look at John and grin. "Drake says hi."

CHAPTER 32

PRAGUE, CZECH REPUBLIC

"Who's the band?" I yell over the music.

"Seventh Sunday," Igneus replies. "The Roman's favorite. He made them famous."

The music is heavy with synthesizers, mixed long with a fluttering drumbeat and harsh guitar riffs. The lyrics are spoken so fast, I can barely follow.

> She likes her, but she wants they.
> 'Me' they think but never say.
> He likes him and never falters, on his knees at the altar.
> Wearing white around his neck, thinking of the
> kiddie sex.
> She wears bobbles on her lobes, longs for fame to make
> her whole.
> He likes football. She likes cats. 'Me', they think and
> slap their backs.
> Them who like the blanket parties, them who eat the
> orange smarties.
> Wear their pants around their toes, wish for love, teem
> with woe.

They who think they're very special, always first with
trusted counsel.
Mother was the one to tell ya, sex and drugs are gonna
kill ya.

Bass thrums into my chest like a jackhammer. The nightclub is cavernous. Twenty massive chandeliers hang from the ceiling, orbited by a myriad of disco balls. Thin lasers slice the room's smoke; careen off the balls and chandeliers to splay over the room's inhabitants. Lines of yellow and green, crimson and azure crease the haze of ecstatic faces and glazed eyes.

I watch the huge man with equal parts jealousy and admiration. The laser lines on his face create a maze of squiggles and jagged edges. The women around him gyrate; short skirts tight on lithe butts, breasts bulging below make-up drenched faces and sweat-soaked hair. Longinus sways with them, the harlots of this era.

Having been collected by a limo in Damascus and set on a Lear jet, I still can't shake my revulsion at the slaughter I'd witnessed five days ago at Sundamir's mansion. I realize I'm wringing my hands together and drop them to my side.

Lush purple carpet ascends four yawning staircases and leads to the club's upper levels. It's a comfortable expanse filled with plush leather couches and settees. Partiers pack multiple gleaming bars and shout their orders at harried barkeepers.

Longinus beams, perfect teeth glowing in electric neon of blue and red.

"Every sort of vice is plied here with no risk of police raid or journalistic inquiry," Igneus yells. "A safe place for the masses to seek their pleasures."

And they do. Grinding, snorting, injecting, and ingesting. They drink deep, inhale smothered gasps, grind inflamed pelvises and explore the objects of their desires.

Perhaps two thousand fill the club as hulking bouncers keep careful watch. Any who get too free, or zealous, or drunk, are removed with extreme prejudice. Dancers and escorts roam like runway models, sleek and sensual. Igneus must see me watching them because he says, "For the right price, they'll give you the time of your life."

We move down a short staircase and approach the dance floor. "These people disgust me," Igneus says. "Children of society, privileged youth of this generation, spending their trust funds."

The music grows more intense, the beat hypnotic, throbbing, as we move through the mass of revelers. Hands reach forward to cup my cheek or slide over my shoulders. Igneus yelps as a strange hand pinches his butt. Laughter follows as he pushes past one of many long metallic bars.

Through the crowd and up a curved staircase, we're on the second floor. I look down and see Longinus. The Roman's face is a picture of ecstasy, eyes closed, head tilted toward the sky, lips parted. One of the new harlots has taken him into her mouth, kneels in front of him as the crowd gyrates. No one notices or cares. Except me, and I stare, amazed at the difference in his expression when compared to the glee he'd shown at Sundamir's mansion. This expression is happy, but not joyful. He looks entranced, where at Sundamir's he looked elated. I suppose nothing compares to the thrill of the kill if you're a legionnaire.

Igneus grabs my arm and turns away. He looks even more appalled. Around us, various other acts are taking place: a boy, face hidden by a mop of black hair, pokes a needle in his arm; two young women explore each other with their tongues, grinding their hips, as a fat, old man watches; a group of six, well-dressed, young men down shots of brown liquor and caress the escorts that sit on their laps.

The music heats up, the words fast and close like a machine gun.

> *She likes they and they want he.*
> *'Me' they quip and go to sleep.*
> *He so vicious, she so tawdry, see you at the after-party.*
> *Cocktail weenies high in hand, furrowed brows on*
>   *empty heads.*
> *They like causes, they like cake. They just like to take*
>   *and take.*

*Eat the profits, eat the flesh, cannibals don't starve to
    death.*
*Them who like the blanket parties, them who eat the
    orange smarties.*
*Wear their pants around their toes, wish for love, teem
    with woe.*
*They who think they're very special, always first with
    trusted counsel.*
*Father was the one who said, sex and drugs'll fry your
    head.*

Igneus moves to the elevator. "This is the way to Drake." The man guarding the metal doors says nothing and presses the wall's only button.

I wonder what the crowd would do if Drake made an appearance. The man's fame stretches across the planet, known for wholesomeness and charity. If word leaked that Drake was at the Devil's Needle, world respect would disappear in a flurry of press releases and special reports. Of course, Drake would never allow that to happen, and even as we wait, I realize X'chasei associates are probably well represented among the club's patrons.

"Howdy, partner."

Longinus smooths his suit. His eyes are glassy, and I wonder if the cause is the girl or the drugs.

Igneus nods, says nothing.

"Still mad?" Longinus says, pokes the little man.

Igneus ignores him.

Longinus leans close. "When are ye goin' to stop bein' such a pussy? Do non ye get it? We do what we must. Anon and agin, these people are cattle. They should be feelin' fortunate ye even notice 'em."

The elevator opens and we step in. Longinus regards the little man for a moment, then steps forward. I'm amazed at the number of drugs the man can do and remain functional.

"Ye need to be gettin' laid," Longinus says. "Alas, when was the last time?"

Igneus looks at his shoes.

"Was there non ever a time?"

Igneus's face goes red. "I was married, you know." He sounds like a little boy defending himself on a playground.

Longinus nods. "Ah, aye, what was that bein', anon fifteen hundred years gone?"

Igneus thumbs the button and the doors close. Seventh Sunday's frantic beat becomes muffles then fades.

He likes her, but she likes she.
'Me' they think, and take their leave.
She so gaudy, him delicious, for their cravings so
*   ambitious.*
Concerned about the cause today. Concerned, but not
*   enough to pay.*
A world of orphans, all are victims. All the people so
*   afflicted.*
Mental scars or acts of God? 'Me' they think and
*   smartly nod.*
Them who like the blanket parties. Them who eat the
*   orange smarties.*
Wear their pants around their toes, wish for love, teem
*   with woe.*
They who think they're very special, always first with
*   trusted counsel.*
Jesus told us long ago, the path to Hell's a golden road.

The upper room is well-appointed in black and steel. Thick, black carpet covers the floor and the walls are framed in slick metallic beams. Twelve crystal glasses line a shelf above a small bar at the room's far end. Within the room stand five wide and elegant leather chairs. They surround a low square table. Drake sits in one, a smile set on his face. He wears a maroon suit and gray tie with a small, smart knot. His left foot props on his right knee, and he balances a glass on the chair's arm.

Across from him sits Mr. Khalifa, the leader of the Muslim Brotherhood. His entire image has changed. Gone are his heavy, desert khakis; in their place, an elegant black suit with creased sleeves and matching silk tie. His face is shaven, and he too smiles.

Drake stands. "How nice of you to join us."

Longinus, nodding, moves to the bar. Igneus doesn't speak at all. We all know he's had no say in the decision to actually join the group. I shake hands with Drake and assume one of the chairs.

Drake motions to the others. "Please have a seat."

Khalifa stares at the Roman with fear and wonder. The Arab most likely knows of Sundamir's fate and I wonder how he feels sitting so close to the man who brought that end about.

"I was just discussing the terms with Mr. Khalifa," Drake says. He looks at Igneus, then Longinus. "Please stop me if I misstate anything."

Longinus nods. Igneus stares at Khalifa. I start to record.

"As I was saying, Mr. Khalifa, the PLO is in disarray, and we've taken the appropriate steps to assure your rise to power will be unopposed. As the leader of both the Brotherhood and PLO, your influence will be unmatched."

Khalifa raises a hand. "And what of Hezbollah?"

Drake smiles. "You and Mr. Longinus shall travel to Lebanon and secure their support. I do not see that as an issue, especially with all the good press you're getting."

I remember the press releases, pouring accolades on Khalifa as if he's the answer to all problems within the Middle East.

"And then?" Khalifa asks.

"Then we act. Mr. Slabav will personally oversee the rebuilding of the Temple and the transport of Jews from all over the world to Israel."

Khalifa doesn't flinch at the mention of rebuilding the Temple. "And my men will be there to assure no Muslim history is destroyed?"

Drake nods. "Yes, and Mr. Longinus will be in charge of site security."

Igneus scoffs, and we all turn toward him.

"Am I forgetting something?" Drake asks.

"I don't see how Slabav is going to cooperate," Igneus says. "What are you going to tell him? *We've arranged some security for you?* It doesn't make sense."

Drake nods. "Very perceptive, Mr. Igneus, and I believe you're right. However, we will not be providing the security. That will be the task of United Nations peacekeepers."

Igneus looks astonished. "You've arranged the UN to provide peacekeepers from our combined organizations."

Drake smiles. "Precisely."

Khalifa's face stretches to a strained grin. "We can keep a watch on things and set up a secure area." He straightens, seems to puff up. "Once the Temple is built and the world's Jews have relocated, we can begin the extermination."

Drake nods, takes a sip of his cocktail.

Longinus grins and drains his glass.

Igneus looks like he's going to vomit.

"You're talking about genocide?" the Jew says, visibly shaken.

Drake waives a hand. "Hardly."

"Killing off all the Jews, have you lost your fucking mind?"

Khalifa laughs, rolls his eyes. "Mr. Igneus, by the time the Temple is constructed, the *peacekeepers* will have infiltrated every possible area of Israel. We will have located every Jew and already have a plan for their neat extermination and disposal."

The man's eyes are dead yet filled with purpose. The plan to kill millions doesn't affect him at all.

Khalifa continues. "While that's occurring, X'chasei will be tracking the rest of the world. By the time it's over, all the Jews on the planet will be eradicated, the Temple destroyed, and the matter settled for all time." He speaks in earnest, even joy. "It's a final solution that, although drastic, is quite necessary."

Igneus slumps in his chair, dejected and defeated. Drake smiles at him, and I wonder if Igneus's rage can overcome Drake's gifts.

Igneus must know how these deals have been bartered. Knows Thaddeus Drake has brought his considerable charm to bear. Knows where Drake's charm failed, Longinus's sword has succeeded.

"I'm too disgusted to speak," Igneus says, glances at me.

My face betrays me. My liquor sits forgotten on the table as I consider Drake's plan. *How deep will I sink?* I wonder. *First, I witness a complete bloodbath at Sundamir's, now I'm party to exterminating a race?* My mind spins, overwhelmed, disgusted with myself, afraid to speak, thinking how disappointed Rhyme would be. My feet feel swollen in my expensive loafers, and I long to tear the fine clothing from my back and return to the run-down little shithole on Mulberry Street in Carter's Glen. My insides feel rotten, like a hole blown through me. I stare at the floor, try to hide my outrage and shock. I glance at Igneus and his expression tells me he feels the same.

"This is what it comes to?" Igneus says. "We welcome bloodthirsty thugs to our inner circle."

Khalifa snarls and starts to rise. Longinus stands as well, but I can't discern if it's to protect the little man or to aid Khalifa in some violence.

Drake raises a hand and both men stop. "Mr. Khalifa, I must apologize for my associate. I had no time to brief him before this meeting. I can assure you he is a valuable asset."

Drake stands, and they shake hands. "Let me see you out," Drake says. "We've arranged a car and some entertainment for the evening. I hope it lives up to your standards."

Khalifa winks. "If she's anything like the last."

Drake laughs and escorts Khalifa to the elevator. They make more small talk until the elevator arrives and Khalifa leaves.

Drake moves a chair close to the Jew, sits and places a hand on Igneus's leg. "Are you okay, my friend?" he says, looking into his eyes.

Igneus looks like a summer grape too long in the sun. "I'm fine."

Drake nods. "That's good, because for a moment I thought you'd lost your mind. How can you argue in front of someone like Khalifa?"

"How can you offer a plan to exterminate the Jews? What is it with you? That's the same shit you let Hitler pull. Do you secretly want them dead?"

Drake's expression is serene, a loving father giving advice. "Dear Igneus, I care little about the fate of Jew, Muslim or Christian; even less for sinner, martyr and heretic. The only way to see the Temple rebuilt is to convince the Muslims it's their idea. I merely provided them a reason. They'll use the Temple as bait and then do what they will. I doubt peace will reign after we're gone, and I don't care if every one of these sheep die, provided we are removed."

My face flushes. I realize I'm one of these *sheep*. Actually, a suckling lamb at a wolf's buffet.

Igneus leaps to his feet and levels a finger at Drake. "You've made a deal with a madman!"

Drake chuckles. "As if he's the first. We're all mad men, dear Igneus." He's unphased by Igneus's contempt. "I'm always amazed at your surprise. If you'd like, I'll warn Slabav before I enter the Temple. Do you not see we're closer than ever?"

"To what?"

Drake stands, sweeps his arms across the room. "To everything. It's all coming together. We have a Jewish state, a world economy, the Children are ready, the Kilal is secure, the red heifer lives, the entire world will be at peace very soon…all we need is a rebuilt Temple and the prophecy is fulfilled."

"Ah yes, the prophecy of the end times." Igneus frowns. "The prophecy that ends the world." He shakes his head. "I apologize, I should be happy."

Longinus chuckles and Drake shoots him a glance. "Listen," he says, "this is what we've been trying to accomplish for an eternity. Virtually from the moment I realized I'd made the Christians stronger. Martyrdom has never been the answer and it's taken me centuries to recover from that mistake." His eyes gleam, his words hang like a silk web. "As Constantine I created the Bible, *my* Bible. I joined their little movement and managed to control it. Now we control everything." He examines Igneus as he speaks. "We have the means to destroy the planet if it takes our fancy."

Igneus glances to Longinus, then down at the floor. "And?"

"And? And all we lack is an audience with God to barter the terms of our release. Don't you see, God will have to choose, the destruction of mankind—on our terms—or forgiveness for our sins."

Igneus sputters a laugh. "I thought you didn't care about forgiveness?"

"I don't, but what more is there to conquer? We live like kings. I've kept my promise to both of you. The only quest that remains is to confront God. As I have used His church, I shall use His creation. From the time of my sin until now I've realized why God has punished me so. It's the only thing that makes sense."

"And that is?"

Drake paces to the bar, gloved hand to his chin. It looks like he's thinking about what to say next, as if he's having an internal struggle. Then he turns, inhales, and regards each of us.

"God has groomed me to replace Him."

The room is silent.

I stare at Drake, try to fully process his words. I feel like a lost penny.

Longinus moves forward, his glass forgotten on the bar, his face a mask of disbelief.

Igneus stares, confusion becomes shock. "God chose *you* as *His* replacement?"

Drake beams. "Yes, dear Igneus, He has."

Igneus scoffs, then whistles. "The centuries have finally gotten to you."

Drake's expression is solemn. "All these centuries I've had an advisor—one whom I trust without question. He provided my gifts all those centuries ago and has directed my path through all these ages."

"Who?" Igneus asks. "Who is it?"

Drake holds each of our gazes in turn.

"My brother," Drake says. "Abel."

All three are on their feet. Drake looks proud, even regal. Longinus looks confused and even a little frightened. Igneus looks like a used-up sponge.

Igneus collapses on the soft leather chair as if, for the first time, fully realizing the man's power. Cain knows—has seen all. Has lived through the flood and the plagues and the wars and the famines; has watched the rise and fall of Babylon and Rome; has seen the Jews driven from their homeland; has witnessed the rise of Alexander the Great, Napoleon, Hitler; has watched and learned, planning the day when he'll face God.

"Abel?" Igneus says. "That almost makes sense."

I realize what he means, can read it on his face. The realization Cain has guided them through centuries and fulfilled all that he's promised. An understanding that no one could do that without aid. After all, Cain's still a man, still human, born to mistakes. No man could manage the quagmire of world politics and finance, religion and society, so well for so long without some form of guidance.

All along Cain has been speaking to his brother. That explains how he'd known the meaning of the emerald aura and how to identify immortals. It explains Cain's gifts. It also explains the naked ambition of his quest to rule the Earth. All this talk about confronting God— instead, this man thinks he's going to meet God and then just become Him. I remember at one of our first meetings Cain talked about the first time he'd heard *the voice*. At the time, he wouldn't tell me who it was. Now I know. Abel, his brother, murdered by Cain, now his most trusted advisor.

"Why would the man you murdered help you?" Igneus says.

Drake grins. "He's my brother. My blood." He slides a cigarette in his mouth, then pats his pockets. I retrieve a lighter and light Drake's smoke. "He's forgiven me," he says around the butt. Then, "Thank you, dear Emery." I nod like an imbecile and slip the lighter in my pocket.

"Abel pleaded with God to end my sentence. When God refused, he came to me and offered his advice. He told me of God's plan— God's plan for me to take His place."

"And to replace Him you have to defeat Him?" I ask. "Couldn't He just clean out His office and show you where the coffee maker is?"

No one laughs.

"Yes, dear Emery, I must best Him. I must show I'm worthy of such a station. The only man in history to defeat God. My path's been ordained from the start. From the first field I sowed until now, God's plan for me has been clear. I've lived all these centuries training for what's to come. That's why I'm singled out and punished so severely."

The room is silent. I think about the implications of Cain as God, of Abel, of predestination, of omniscience, and of all Cain has revealed.

Then Igneus speaks. "If you fulfill the prophecy and bring about the end times of legend, what happens to the Earth?"

Drake looks at Igneus as a father looks at a child. "What do we care? They can all burn. I've acted with the sole purpose of rebuilding the Temple and confronting God. After that, my interest fades."

"Fades?" Igneus says. "Fades? Surely not the act of a God. Have you read John's Revelation? Earth becomes Hell. Billions suffer and die. Billions more will wish they can die. And your interest fades? What about Emery? Do you care nothing for him?"

Drake turns to me; his expression is not reassuring. "Dear Emery, if I could make you immortal I would. If I could take you to God, then I would. You must trust me. I will return *as God* and you'll be in my favor."

"As long as your interest doesn't fade?" I say. "As long as you don't forget?" I stand. "Jesus, you guys are full of shit. You can't accept each other and barely work together. You have a plan for mass genocide and talk about it as if it's the menu for Sunday dinner." I look at Drake. "Listen, asshole, I've nowhere to go and no one to trust— except for your sorry ass. The only thing that keeps me around is fear and pure curiosity. But the fear part is fading."

Drake's smile gleams. "Emery, the truth is, we'll be gone. We've *never* cared about these mortals, and sadly, that includes you. I gave you a choice when we met. Told you once you set your feet on this path, there's no turning back. You accepted. That was our bargain. For my part, if what I believe will happen is true, then you'll live a long and privileged life."

"And if you're wrong?"

"Then you can return to your pistol."

"Leave them to their fate at the hands of their God," I say.

"Aptly stated." Drake looks to Longinus as if seeking support. "Besides, it might not be that bad. I mean really, dear boy, what do you have to lose? When all this happens, you're going to die anyway."

The Roman moves to the bar and retrieves his glass. He picks up a telephone and speaks.

Drake continues. "This God will do as He will, if you don't know that by now, you haven't been paying attention."

I feel nauseated. Will God allow the world to end at the hands of the Earth's first murderer? The thought fills me with icicles.

I think of the prophecies, consider Igneus's role in this great plot. He's killed no one; neither has he prevented killing. He hasn't stolen; but neither has he stopped thievery. The same for exploitation, extortion, extermination.

The icicles melt under the fire of my own thoughts.

The elevator opens and three gorgeous women enter. They wear elegant evening gowns that are resplendent with sequins of white, violet and red. Their make-up is perfect, and they move with a fluid balance of sexuality and grace. They look at Longinus, await his command.

Longinus points to Igneus.

"Take him out and fuck the shit out of him."

Igneus leaps from the couch.

Their smells fill the room: vanilla and lilac and strawberry. Igneus stares and I see a different side of the little man. As if he's imagining the evening he can share with these women. Their skin, their curves, their red, full lips and heaving breasts. The sharp squeals of their passion.

Drake grins. Longinus refills his glass, then drains it in a single pull. He produces a cigar and lights it, puffing huge plumes into the air.

The ladies surround Igneus. Their hands explore as they breathe on his neck and caress his bald scalp. Their aroma intoxicates and Igneus appears to be fully hypnotized, all reason lost. I wonder if Cain cast some ancient spell on him.

A delicate hand slides down his chest and cups his crotch.

Igneus jumps, bolts to the elevator, mashes the button until the doors close.

The women's scent follows, mixed with the pungent bass of Longinus's laughter.

CHAPTER 33

JERUSALEM, AFTER THE CRUCIFIXION

He walks the land of his birth, enjoys the sounds of the plains, the earth, cool and soft, beneath his feet. Fields bloom with unnatural speed, present broad green stems and lush leaves that will bear much fruit. They run to the horizon in measured lines, toward detailed, jagged mountains beneath a sky that smiles pastel blue.

Cain inhales the sweet fragrance, hears the wind as it moves over the adjacent rows, then across his body. This is the sweetest field in a lifetime, in an age. He plucks an apricot and bites into it, savoring the sweetness. A drop of juice escapes the corner of his mouth and runs in a sticky trail down his chin.

He laughs out loud, cleanses his lungs with the field's moist aroma. The wind moves past and through the leafy trees beyond. The sun settles on his shoulders, calm and warm.

Cain steps through the tall harvest, eyes closed.

Now his mouth fills with ash and dust. The sun's heat, so soothing moments before, intensifies, burns his skin.

Fire surrounds him.

The soothing plain is a conflagration, slick emerald wavers dead brown, then turns ash gray and disintegrates before him. Surrounding trees are barren and broken as the arid fragrance of the desert smolders with the putrid horror of burnt flesh.

Cain stands among brown cinder and mud as men move past bearing the rough, gleaming implements of battle. Muscled, wearing strange splotchy uniforms of green and blue, their mud-caked leather boots tromp onto the field to face the enemy horde.

Savage screams rend the sky as they meet the enemy line, a raging river crashing against rocked dam. Weapons spit a harsh and clacking flame, expel both fury and death.

The enemy rank falls as large, oval blots appear on odd uniforms. Weapons spew, cause limbs to pop from enemy bodies, cause helmeted heads to explode in a rain of red-gray gelatin.

Cain's eyes fill with tears. Fear works his soul like a hoe through soft soil. Overhead great fleshless birds screech, fire spits from their wings to burn great holes in the earth. Dirt mixes with the partial corpses of men and explodes into the air. The sky rains blood, turns uniforms to spackled-crimson robes.

Trembling, blood-streaked hands reach toward his face and he jumps before realizing they're his own. He focuses on the carnage.

Those closest have reversed their weapons and use them as steely clubs, battling the enemy with any strength they can muster.

Enemy fire buckles his men, who fall twenty at a time. Their ranks thin; some, then all, turn and speed toward him, a torrent that breaks around him like a solitary rock.

Cain charges in with a cry of battle joined, the spurring wail of one man's hope, rooting the enemy in place as their eyes search for direction.

He meets the first and becomes liquid death, relieving the soldier of his steel spike then flowing into and through the others. The weapon is heavy and unbalanced, but Cain masters its movements in seconds.

He becomes a spinning dervish of glistening sweat and bulging muscle. His eyes two steps ahead of his body, his mind tuned to his surroundings and detached from the horrors. Hard-earned skills mastered on Persian, Muslim, Helen, Asian—on countless others—on a thousand battlefields through a thousand lifetimes.

Visions leap through his mind, quick flutters of other battles, other enemies, their awed, death-filled eyes, their open mouths, voiceless screams. Cain moves through them, threshes his fields, slices bone and tendon, then upends the weapon to smash with its angled, blunt end.

Twenty men rush him at a run. Cain spins into them, shredding, smashing until they lay dead at his feet.

Voices rise as his men race toward him. Their eyes sear the distance, focus on the next wave, emboldened by Cain's offensive.

Cain sprints to a nearby ridge and climbs. The vastness of battle stretches before him. Two armies amass, hundreds of thousands fight among the pocked, smoke-laden field. The great birds screech overhead, move faster than anything he's ever seen. Belching fire, they do little to stem the battle's tide.

The anguish of those below him meld into the greater cacophony creating a roar that sizzles like water on a white-hot pan. Explosions rattle the ground, send mud and rock inches from his face. Pillars of fire, miles-wide, leap into the air, miles-high.

Hundreds of thousands lay dead and become obstacles for those who still battle. Blood flows from fresh corpses to settle in the field's low spots. It pools, overflows, runs, searching for kin, then joins to rivers that stream across the landscape, thick enough to inspire wonder.

Entire legions are cut off, some swept away by the raging onslaught. The tide of the battle is turning. His troops need a leader.

Anger surges, he feels himself grow large. His voice booms as he barks orders to his battalions, scans the field, remembers the words of his old teacher, Sun Tzu: *The real battle is against the mind of the enemy commander.*

Eyes search through towering flame and clouded vapor, over howling soldiers, past gleaming firebirds.

Then, miles in the distance, a figure towers.

Glowing white, raining lightning over Cain's army, God Himself enters the fray and commands legions.

Cain calls more orders, tries to outmaneuver the enemy, but God's armies move like a gelatinous mass, all acting as one. They retreat with Cain's attacks—then assault his weakest, most hidden points.

The battle turns against him. His heart hammers as he spits commands as fast as his mouth can move.

In the distance, God's countenance grows bright, fully illuminates the carnage of war.

A man alights from the battlefield, soars into the sky on golden wings. Hovering above the din, he levels a flaming sword. His voice is rich, peels like thunder, causes all to stop, weapons half-cocked, eyes raised.

"Who threatens Heaven?"

Cain leaps in the air as leathery wings spread. He streaks toward the angel, the battle below a ghostly blur of tortured faces and eminent vapors.

The angel's lips part in an expectant smile.

They rocket toward each other. Cain braces for impact, sword ready, mind raging.

He cartwheels through deep snow, skids to a stop leaving a trail resembling the cleft of his buttocks.

Scrambling to his feet, clothing now changed to traditional, silk robes, he cranes his neck, searches for the angel.

He's surrounded by white-tipped mountains, rock-lined jaws set in temporal wonder and silence.

The angel is gone. Did he ever exist? A chill wind assaults his vantage point as snow strikes his face like fine gravel.

He raises his arms, peers between them. The Earth is miles distant and appears as a checkered tapestry of green, brown and dense gray. The sky rolls and spits lightning into the charged atmosphere.

Then all is silent.

"You are not helpless in your plight."

Cain leaps, wheels in a single motion. He sees nothing.

A man materializes from thin air. Well-dressed in maroon robes, he moves with a quiet elegance that punctuates his character.

Molten sky turns endless blue. Snowy peaks become a gentle, rolling plain. Birds chirp as the wind eases, becomes a mother's touch. Cain scans his form, unable to distinguish any feature. "Who's there?" he says.

The man's face becomes clear. His brother stands before him, smiling, arms stretched in front of him.

Cain races forward, embraces Abel, sword forgotten on the ground. Abel returns a warm smile.

"I'm sorry, my brother," Cain says, squeezing hard, hot tears streaming down his cheeks. "I'm so sorry for having wronged you, for having been so…petty."

Abel pushes him to arm's length. His eyes dart over Cain, take in the familiar face, years removed. Tears glisten as he speaks in a voice charged with emotion.

"I forgive you, brother, as I have from the first. I've often asked to come and ease your pain but have been denied."

Cain stands stunned in his brother's grasp, traces the centuries—all the guilty, sleepless nights.

Abel continues. "It is you who are wronged. For centuries I've pleaded with God to end your penance, but He denies me." His dark eyes dance between Cain's. He looks harried and hurried. "I come to you without His knowledge."

"O my brother," Cain says and moves again to embrace, "you tempt God to ease my pain?"

"Your pain causes me much grief," Abel whispers.

"It's as I deserve for the wrong I've committed. God has spoken."

Anger flares in Abel's eyes. "Why do you say such things?" He breaks the embrace, steps away. "Do you not understand? Your punishment is to forever walk the Earth, not to live in misery for all time."

Cain's taken off-guard. "Well, one rather flows into the other."

Abel steps close, holds Cain's eyes like a Persian mystic, riveting and hypnotic. "It need not," he says, "you can take dominion over this realm. You can subdue it, build a kingdom so vast that even if God never reconsiders your punishment, all your desires will come to pass by your own hand."

Cain blinks at the thought.

"God can't deny you because it fits the confines of your punishment."

Cain plops to the ground, wobbly knees refusing support. He's never considered this.

"If I'm to live for eternity, why not live as a king?" he asks in a whisper. Realization collides with possibility. A smile forms.

"Exactly," Abel says, running a hand through Cain's dark hair. Cain closes his eyes and absorbs the affection. It's good to feel his brother's touch once again, to know his brother's forgiveness.

Birds sing as a lavender-soaked breeze rolls over them. Cain feels nourished, feels clean.

"How shall I accomplish such a thing?" Cain asks.

"There are others like you."

"How do you know?"

"I saw it happen and so did you."

"I recall no other person," Cain says.

"Do you remember the emerald aura emitted by certain people?"

Cain sits up, recalls those people who affronted Christ, recalls his confusion at their odd, emerald luminescence. "I do."

"That's how you'll know them. You alone can see immortality. Find these men, raise an army, grow wealth, you'll need both in the times to come."

Cain thinks of the men, wonders how he'll ever find them, then scolds himself for not realizing the aura's true nature.

"Will I need this army for war?"

Abel strokes his hair, speaks in tones tuned with the breeze. "No, not for war, my brother, but to preserve peace, to ensure tranquility for all under your rule."

"A peaceable kingdom," Cain says, absorbing the idea.

"Yes, a peaceable kingdom," Abel says. He holds out his hands, in each is a package wrapped in dark linen. "I offer these to aid you."

"What are they?"

"Things you'll need. Things only God can give."

Cain opens the presents. One contains a dark fruit, fully ripe and succulent. Cain doesn't recognize it as anything familiar, but it looks delicious. The other contains a strip of meat, red and juicy; Cain's mouth waters at the sight of it.

"Eat," Abel says.

"What are they?"

"The fruit is charisma."

"And the meat?"

"The meat is diplomacy. Both will allow your kingdom to endure."

Cain raises the fruit to his lips, pauses. "You come to me without God's knowledge?"

"I do," Abel says.

"But you said these are gifts only God can give?"

"Yes. He gave them to me, and I give them to you."

His brother's eyes are dark, and Cain searches their depths for any hint of deception. Abel returns a small, pious smile, his face serene.

Satisfied, Cain consumes the fruit and flesh. Both are tasteless, but before he can say as much Abel speaks. "I must go, but you will see me again." His eyes twinkle as he takes a long, last look. "Be well, Cain."

Cain embraces his brother, squeezes with all his strength as tears flow in a hot surge. "Be well, my brother."

Abel evaporates like mist.

———————

Cain wakes in his bed, a bad taste in his mouth.

CHAPTER 34

OUTSKIRTS OF JERUSALEM, ISRAEL

The child glides through gleaming halls of steel. He seems glad to be rid of the heavy steel boots he's worn for the last few hours. The soft slap of bare feet echoes down the corridor, past high sun-filled windows, over floors shined to a mirror finish, and into the many rooms of the building.

We're separated by a thick, transparent wall. Laughter rolls down the halls from deep within the structure: other children. The child quickens his pace, anxious to be with his friends.

Drake grins. "This is Sebastian," he tells me.

I watch the boy, glance at Cain. "What is this place?"

"It's the home to the Children of the Rocks. I'm afraid, without them, all is lost."

"Do tell," I say.

Cain steps forward, motions at the transparent wall. "This building was designed more than a century ago. It's hermetically sealed and protected from *every* sort of impurity. A single speck of contaminant will set off alarms in the control room and seal down the compound."

I take in the steely structure, notice huge steel doors, at least three feet thick, the place where the child entered. It's been two days and Drake hasn't said a thing to me about our conversation at the Devil's

Needle. I suppose that's because he hasn't had to. He'd made his point, and I've made mine. I have serious questions about my own sanity, but follow the gloved man nonetheless.

"You have an entire biosphere here where you raise children?" The idea sounds ridiculous. There's no way Drake does this as some sort of philanthropy. "To what end? Don't their parents miss them? Is this even legal?"

Drake looks at me for a long moment, and I get the feeling he's judging my sanity as well. "They serve my ends, dear Emery, as does everyone. But this…" He steps forward and spreads his arms. "This is critical."

I watch the child wash his hands and face with slow deliberation.

"They're happy here," Drake says. "You'll see, just watch."

The setting sun casts broad rays through the long windows, and the surrounding steel corridor shimmers with light. Small spears reflect from the child's bare scalp and light his eyes a deep blue.

"Sebastian," Drake says.

The child lights up at Drake's presence. Drake gives a warm smile and smooths his dark suit.

"Good evening, sir," Sebastian says.

"Good evening, Sebastian. Did you have fun today?"

The child holds his hands cupped at his waist. He casts a suspicious look at me. "Who's this?"

"This is Mr. Emery, a dear friend. He's come to watch the ritual. He's writing a book for me."

The child stares me down. "I hate books."

"That's alright, dear boy, you're too young to read anything he writes anyway. How are you feeling today?"

"My feet hurt."

"Hmmm, that's a shame," Drake says. He juts out his lower lip. "Perhaps our lad is growing."

Sebastian looks down at himself. "Do you think so?"

Drake takes a long moment to look him over, then holds up one finger. He moves to a wooden desk and fumbles in a drawer.

He returns with a tape-measure. "Step close to the glass," he says, then waggles a finger, "and no cheating." Sebastian grins, steps forward, presses his nose against the cold surface, looks at me through the corners of his eyes.

Drake extends the tape and holds it against the glass. He takes a close look, dark eyes intent on the numbers. With a quick shake of his head, he steps back, rubs his eyes, then measures again. He shows it to me and I play along, both of us rubbing our chins and shaking our heads as if we can't believe the number on the measure.

"You've grown two inches since last time."

The child leaps into the air. "Woohoo! I'll be taller than you soon."

Drake kneels on one knee, his face close to the partition, inches from the boy's. "We simply *must* stop feeding you!"

Sebastian's laugh travels through the structure and is answered by other remote laughter. "Oh, I hope not," he says. "I'm starving."

Drake places his chin in his palm, index and middle covering his lips. "Starving, huh? And what would you like for dinner?"

"Fried chicken! With lots of gravy!"

Drake laughs, his eyebrows arch toward the ceiling. His entire face is gleeful. "Are you sure?"

"Oh, yes, Mr. Drake. That's my favorite!"

"Then it shall be yours—"

Sebastian leaps into the air, "Yippee!"

"—provided," Drake continues, "that you do exceptionally well at ritual practice today."

The smile remains on Sebastian's face. "Pshaw," he says waving a hand, "I can do *that* with my eyes closed."

"Then fried chitlins it is!" Drake says.

Sebastian's eyes grow wide, his smile disappears. He flicks me a glance. "Chitlins?" he says, stamps his foot. "I said chicken. *Fried chicken.*"

Drake twists up his face to a lemon-sucking expression. "Fried chicken! Why didn't you say so?" Then mumbling to me, "I thought chitlins a rather odd request for a child of twelve." I laugh out loud. Drake raises a hand to the air, an emperor making a grand proclamation. "Fried chicken for everyone!"

The child leaps again, his whoop resounds through the silver corridors. Then he stops, face subdued. "With extra gravy?" he asks, looks at us sideways.

Drake smiles and nods. "All the gravy you want. Now get to practice. Perform well, we'll be watching."

With a wave, the child sprints down the corridor then skids to a stop. He turns and races back, then bows his head, hands clasped in front of his nose. "God bless Mr. Drake, this day and every day." He shuffles a few more steps, then stops again. "And please bless Mr. Emery, too." He flashes a bright smile and is gone.

Drake watches him go, a large smile on his face. He looks at me and gauges my expression.

"What?" I say.

"You're looking at me in an odd way."

I adjust my gaze to the floor. "Uh, it's just weird," I say.

"What is?"

"Seeing you act so fatherly with this kid." I feel a little ashamed here because I haven't the balls to tell him what I'm really thinking. Fact is, I'm amazed this heartless, mass murderer can so easily slip on a mask of love and nurturing. I know Drake doesn't give a damn about this kid, or anyone for that matter. I'm reminded of the Greek masks of the theater, Comedy and Drama, and the way this man uses them.

Drake cares for no one.

We watch the child sprint into the complex. "These children are a masterpiece," he says, as he replaces the tape and moves toward the door. "Many years ago, I conceived the idea—the answer to the only mystery remaining in my quest—how to recreate the Children of the Rocks, the priest cleansers, the undefiled? These Children, reared through the centuries, are the only ones who can cleanse the Temple and allow me to enter. Without them, all will fail."

The corridor is well-lit as we pass rooms with labels over their doors—KITCHEN, THEATER, GYM, DINING—all on the opposite side of the thick glass partition. "I remember the day, a century and a half gone by now, I think. It was during the initial years of what is now called the Taiping Rebellion. I'd entered the Chinese city of Jintian on my way to see the rebel leader, Yunshan. I have to admit, I was intent on stoking the fires of war. Always profitable, war. Never forget that, Emery. A grand way to keep the money coming."

We approach a door, and he motions me through. "I stepped around a burnt-out hut to be confronted by a crying woman. She took a single look at my expensive clothes, then thrust a baby in my hands. I was dumbfounded and just stared at it, completely stunned. This little life with its chubby cheeks and dark eyes. I remember it had a head full of hair, which surprised me because I thought all babies were born bald." He waves a hand through the air, then waves at an adult on the other side of the partition.

"In any event," he says, "I was completely clueless and thought about just killing it then and there, but then it whimpered a bit. You understand? It…It actually mewed like a kitten or something."

I nod my head.

"This perplexed me, somehow humanized this kid." He trails off here, types a code into a panel beside the next door.

"What did you do?"

Drake tilts his head, a grand smile on his face. "I simply put it on the ground and walked away." The door opens, and we move through.

"In a war zone?"

"I was in a war zone, so yes. But the runt's mother must've been watching from concealment because I hadn't gone ten steps when she reappeared, cursed me like the devil, grabbed the child, and disappeared into the ruins."

"Then what? What happened to the child?"

Drake regards me here with a look I'll never forget. A look one gets when asking the stupidest of all questions.

"I've no idea, dear Emery. That isn't important at all." He holds my eyes for a second. "What's important is then and there, I realized what needed to be done. I'd had my breakthrough or epiphany or moment of clarity or whatever you'd like to call it. I set the plan in motion the following month. You see, even then, I hadn't realized the full profitability of war. I hadn't thought of those displaced by these conflicts, especially the orphans. Suddenly I had a purpose for them.

When a child was born to a mother who didn't want it, X'chasei doctors would arrange for it to be delivered, straight from the womb and under extreme sterile precautions, to a house like this.

"Of course, those days we didn't have much in the ways of hermetic sealing, steel buttresses, or super-computers to monitor the environment. We had only rock, mostly marble. But those had been enough to start.

"With a carefully trained staff and a team of the time's experts, I managed to give rise to the first Children of the Rocks—children whose feet can never touch dirt, even a single speck."

"Why can't they touch dirt?"

He gives me the same stupid-question look. "Because then they'll be unclean, dear Emery. The unclean can't perform the ritual."

I decide not to ask any more questions just to avoid that look.

"The first crop was raised in preparation for the ritual," Drake continues. "Raised in eternal practice so when the time came, all could perform it in accordance with the laws of Moses.

"As they grew and reached the age of puberty, they were no longer considered clean. But instead of being expelled into the streets, they became the mothers and fathers of the next generation, all assuming their roles in this small, but vital, galaxy—learning as the others have learned, then teaching as the others have taught.

"In time, the entire society consisted of children born of clean mothers and fathers, which made any sort of staff unnecessary. The commune was created.

"At first, I lost entire sects and had to return them to the streets, but as time passed and other building materials became available, sterility became easier to maintain—and the commune thrived. Soon enough, science delivered. Computers were able to carefully monitor the environment and erase any questions of sterility."

We stand on a balcony overlooking a glaring white room filled with bald heads of all ages. Drake motions. "The Children of the Rocks. Born from an abandoned baby in a godforsaken Chinese province, now through twelve generations and living happily within this structure and wanting for nothing." He raises his hand here, signals an addendum to his last sentence. "Provided the ritual is practiced and perfected as Moses commanded."

We ascend a long set of metal stairs and proceed through the door at the top.

Drake watches a group of children playing within the sterile confines on the glass's other side. Something here nags, but I can't quite get it to solidify. Is it that children are being used as pawns or the knowledge this entire ecosystem is of Drake's creation? Perhaps those within have no knowledge of free will or choice?

Then it hits me. War zone. Children from a war zone. I can't contain my gasp as the full force of the memory crashes down. My head spins, my stomach seizes. I feel like my entire body is numb and useless. Thoughts race, then collect to a terrifying point.

"Octavio," I whisper.

Drake holds my eyes, smiles calmly as I process all the word means.

"Yes, dear Emery, it's to me that you owe your second Pulitzer. And, as it seems, the third, which you'll receive after you report on these events."

The children have deserted the hall for other areas. In this silence, I stand before the gloved man, my fists trembling. He watches serenely, as if giving me time to decide on my next course of action.

I think of her, think of the uselessness of losing her to pursue a story that was just another machination in this madman's plan. I think of the fact that Drake cares little for me or for the loss of Rhyme and our son. He simply doesn't care, probably hasn't even noticed she's dead, or that our happy little life has been utterly destroyed. It dawns on me then. *He's* the kingpin for which I've searched. The missing link that ties everything together. All thought leaves me, all reason washes to oblivion. My mind flashes the memories. Rhyme turning white, popping me, the restraining order, the gunshot wound, the divorce, the call saying she's dead.

I leap straight for his throat.

Arms flail as I rain punches, try to clasp my fingers around his neck. I'll chop him to bits. I'll get these people to help, then free them all from this prison and expose them to the world. I'll destroy X'chasei, every part. Burn it down, raze it to the ground, and then piss on the ashes.

I land the first blow. See the sardonic grin and the pure molten evil tattooed on his face.

Then I'm on the ground, holding my throat, gasping for air. He'd hit me so fast I hadn't even seen it. He dropped me like a burning bag of shit. I cough, choke, larynx paralyzed, drool sliding from my mouth to drip on the cold, white floor.

The razor nails of impotent rage gouge a furrow through my heart.

Drake watches with an amused grin. "Dear Emery, do take a moment. Won't you?"

CHAPTER 35

OUTSKIRTS OF JERUSALEM, ISRAEL

Sebastian sprints through an immense, glass-covered alcove. One more right, and he slows to a walk, becomes solemn, hands cupped in front of spotless, white robes.

I rub my throat as the lad enters a circle of other children. They hold hands. A little girl, pigtails dusting her shoulders, looks at him and giggles.

Sebastian remains stoic, undistracted. His stomach gives an audible rumble, and all the children laugh. Sebastian smiles like a cherub, youthful innocence in full bloom.

Outside the circle, older children whisper amongst themselves, while farther out, adults— middle-aged to elderly—sit around the room's circumference, bald heads reflected in silver steel. The eldest among them doze as one of them chastises the group for their outburst.

They return to solemnity as Sebastian retrieves a silver scalpel from an ornamental tray.

He looks comfortable with the dangerous instrument, and with a well-practiced motion pierces the victim's taut flesh.

It jumps as scarlet freckles appear on Sebastian's face.

I'm impressed; the boy is nonplussed by the bloody mist, standing still and waiting for the struggle to cease.

The victim's chest moves in shallow flutters. Blood flows, soaks Sebastian's robes, drips on his bare feet.

He smooths the victim's hair, a gesture of comfort, as life slips away.

The children closest to him break into applause as Sebastian looks past them to the adults. Their faces say his skills require some additional refinement.

"Well done, Sebastian," Drake says, offers a radiant smile. All heads turn to the gloved man behind panes of spotless glass. They beam up as if looking at the world's savior.

The old ones think he's God; the young ones know it.

"Who's hungry?" he says.

CHAPTER 36

JERUSALEM, 1050 BC

C ain knows this place well, had toiled here for almost five years. He'd enjoyed the work; in the light of day, hoisting and carving stone, placing each one with keen precision.

Then the day King Solomon visited, had somehow known Cain for who he was and had ejected him without a word. Somehow, informed by God.

One year has elapsed since that time, and Cain passes the time working as a fisherman's hand; work he's done before, yet still despises. Hauling the catch, watching their smelly soon-to-be corpses wriggle within the net, open mouths gasping for air, slick oils congealed on speckled scales.

When the news comes that the Temple's complete, he's filled with gladness. Glad to bid farewell to the old fisherman's flapping lips and weathered face. Gladder, even joyous, to enter Jerusalem without incident and stroll unassaulted to the Temple Square.

Now he stands and stares as the Temple shimmers like a desert mirage, as wide rays of golden sunlight scatter through a crisp blue sky.

To his left is a fourteen-foot-high bronze cistern held aloft by a statue of twelve golden oxen gleaming in the day's sun. Brawny muscles bulge as etched eyes strain against a load that can only be the sins of the entire world. Cain knows the cistern to be water-filled, a place where Temple priests cleanse themselves before entering the holy place.

To his right, shining marble steps angle twenty feet in the air, open onto the sacrificial altar. Although he can't see it from where he stands, he knows it will be made of polished stone, square in shape, a place for sacrifice. He imagines the blood cooking in the hot sun on the altar's surface. The miserable stench as small insects gather for their blood meal. His stomach gives a subtle nudge, and he changes focus to the Temple itself.

The cistern and altar stand separated by forty feet or more, bisected precisely by the Temple's entrance. Sun glistens from the Temple's surface, reflects light across the square and onto his face. Clerestory windows line the top of the building's five stories, allows light to shine on those within. His breath catches as the Temple smiles down in hopeful golds and warming blues.

Today he will find his redemption.

In front of him, stairs lead to the Temple's entrance, perhaps fifteen feet across, each rise promising one step closer to God. Great bronze columns flank the stair's top, running the height of the building—the left, known as Joachim, representing northern Israel; the right, Boaz, representing the south. Cain traces their lines to the top where etched pomegranates mingle with water lilies done in intricate detail. He can almost smell the sweet nectar of his orchards of old.

Cain stares at the whole of the bright, looming building. Its rectangular shape expands its perfection and raises it into the heavens; offers a permanent foothold for God. He wonders why this particular tract of Earth is so special, then breathes off a rush of guilt, squeezing gloved hands to fists, gulping against the image in his mind.

On this very ground, he'd murdered Abel.

From the Temple's uppermost level, a small room juts like a large sapphire in the crown of a great king. The entire effect is brilliant, perfect in its symmetry, awesome in its design. Cain stands in awe, half-expecting God, in his pleasure, to reach forward and pluck up the structure and wear it as a favorite ornament.

He raises a gloved hand, strains against the brilliance to discern the quickest path to the stained and polished doors. He's tried to come at a time when the area won't be crowded, but it seems the place has become the city's focal point. People move about busying themselves with their individual tasks. Although not packed, the grounds certainly aren't desolate, and he considers for a moment to abandon his efforts. An impatient voice rings in his head. "Embrace hope!"

A priest in traditional robes of maroon and gold moves up the stairs and enters.

"My time has come," he whispers.

An odor of burnt flesh hangs stale in the air. The lingering smell from recent sacrifice assaults his gut and reminds him of the brand on his right hand. He moves forward, rubs his mark. Today I speak to God.

As if in response, a gentle breeze rises and pushes him forward. His smile grows as the wind carries the burnt-carcass scent into the surrounding plains.

He starts up the steps.

Before him, intricate carved flowers gild the great doors as spinning angels lift them from the Earth. Flowing around, through, and into one another, cherubic eyes see everything from their permanence; promising salvation, redemption, forgiveness. Watching, they speculate from their places among the buds and vines.

The door's darkness absorbs color from the surrounding land and fuses them into its depths. Cherubs, sliding on flowery vines, absorb these colors and hold the greedy vibrance for themselves, leaving only the reflection of gilded cedar. A richness that hypnotizes even as it beckons; enter and find salvation, all are welcome.

Cain flings the huge doors open and steps through.

Just inside the threshold, gooseflesh erupts. His fingers tingle and twitch. The expanse yawns before him, more beautiful than he ever imagined. A broad stone floor shines with the day's radiance beneath high walls gilded in gold. Massive angels stand on broad square pedestals, their golden wings raised above them, reaching toward the Temple's high-vaulted ceiling.

He's breathless.

Then, movement catches his eye. Across the great chamber, a heavy curtain flutters, lifts to waist level, then floats to its original position.

A rustle of wind begins. Then a howl through a distant chasm, starting small, then increasing in a sudden burst. The sound fills his head like cold water, shocks thought from his mind. A slight tingling sensation invades his right hand, a mild burning within his mark.

In the distance, a faint, abbreviated sound, like something being forced under pressure through a small opening. Pain ignites every pore and bathes it in fire. His right hand sizzles.

Then he flies.

He finds himself facedown fifty feet from the grinning cherubs on the Temple's door. Empty lungs strain for air. Fingers gouge furrows in the dirt. Pinpoints of light bloom in his vision, then burn away to reveal the Temple's entrance, serene and unmolested.

People approach from all sides. "What was that?" asks a man with a gnarled nose and vivid magenta robes.

Cain struggles to his feet, head spinning, chest thumping a painful rhythm.

The sky turns to smoke as wary clouds swirl like dancing gypsies. Foaming faces streak yellow as jagged lightning sizzles through ozone like flying scarves.

"Are you hurt?"

Cain pushes the gnarled-nosed man away, stumbles forward.

He climbs the steps once more, back aching, limbs lead-heavy, quivering and numb. Gleeful angels spin on the Temple's door, their fat, puckered faces contort in laughter.

A snarl crosses his lips. He steps through.

A siphon of air surrounds him. His head fills with a deafening crack. He is lifted, weightless, and then back on the ground, breathless. Once again, pain rings through his body, bathes each cell in molten agony. Rolling in the soil, he wrestles the pain as the whistling cackle of angelic glee assaults his ears.

The crowd becomes a mass with concerned eyes and open mouths. Angry gypsies dance through the black sky as fire rolls from their plumes then races toward the Earth.

A group of soldiers approach at a run. Cain turns to the hateful door, gathers his strength.

"I must enter!" he rages. "I must speak to God!"

He sprints. Thunder rolls. Sparks fly as lightning impacts around him.

Cain stumbles, arms flailing, then regains his balance and keeps on.

Hairs stand on end as static engulfs him. Flying shards cut his face as he pushes, as desperate gypsies rain fire. He pushes through the wind and up the stairs, dives headlong through the doors, arms stretched, body horizontal.

Then, the sound of a hollow God clearing His throat. The smell of burnt hair and flesh congealing into a miserable, burning soup and he, rocketing from the Temple's door, expelled like so much mucous.

The world explodes.

Cain's vision fills with fire; his brain, with a deafening hum; the feeling of weightlessness, the smell of his own burnt skin. He crashes into the lofted, bronze cistern, then to the ground fourteen feet below.

Waves of smoke clot the air, people rush toward him. He struggles to stand. Pain explodes in his soul, through his flesh, into every microscopic cell. Thick, white smoke rises from his right hand. His gloves burn to ash and fall away, revealing his mark. It glows furious and red, pulsing triangles and writhing Sun's rays.

"Ashem!"

An echo in his head.

"Ashem!"

Louder now.

Cain blinks through fogged vision, looks into the face of Carpte the Phoenician, the supervisor of construction for the Temple. This is the man who had hired, and fired, Cain. He's a kind man and a friend.

The Phoenician kneels, his hand on Cain's shoulder, eyes wide with fear and loyalty. "What are you doing?"

Blurs of color and flickering light turn Carpte's face to a kaleidoscope. Raising a hand, Cain says only, "Salvation."

Carpte's lips turn down at the corners, one eyebrow crinkles as tears glisten in his eyes.

Then, the soldiers are there, pulling him to his feet, their spears ready. The mass surrounds him, soldiers stare with fear-soaked eyes, bystanders with expressions of shock and disgust. Carpte holds his arm, tries to pry him from the soldiers.

"What's the meaning of this?" the captain of the guard speaks. Cain stares at the Temple doors, at cherubs who mock in children's tones, whose pursed lips reveal fanged, bloodthirsty smiles.

Enter and find salvation.

"You'll come with us," the captain says, pulling Cain's arm.

Snapping from the soldier's grip, Cain bolts toward the crowd, through the crowd, running, insane.

The crowd scrambles, then parts.

The entrance is in sight.

Cain, crazed, sprints forward.

"Cease and desist," cries the captain. "Stop him!"

Ten feet from the first step, a sharp pain sings through his abdomen.

The splintered wood of a spear protrudes from his gut.

Cain howls.

Onlookers widen their berth as Cain claws the pike. Blood flows from his gut, sizzles over the red-hot mark.

Cain masters his body, stands motionless, spear protruding like some cock-eyed weathervane.

The crowd gasps. The soldiers stand open-mouthed, unmoving.

He looks to the Temple's steps, toward the spear's master. A young soldier stands pale, face twisted in amazement and revulsion.

Cain grips the spear with both hands, begins to push it through himself, front to back.

The handle retreats, the shaft shortening with each agonizing effort.

He draws close to the soldier who stumbles backwards, then falls at the foot of the Temple's steps.

Cain forces the spear through. Agony rings through his spine as if the weapon's hooked a nerve and plucked it like a taut string.

Cain wills himself to stay erect as shaking legs threaten collapse.

He levels the spear at the soldier.

The young man quakes, eyes darting toward his comrades, lips mouthing apologies. None in the crowd, be they soldier or citizen, move to his aid. All stand dumbfounded.

Cain pushes the spear's blood-soaked tip toward the soldier's face.

"Seventy times seven," Cain spits. The young man stares at the spear. Seconds pass.

Cain drops the spear with a clatter.

Then a great crackling noise. Blisters appear on the soldier's skin, then spread across his face with great speed. His mouth freezes in a surprised O as pleading eyes bulge. Thin lines of vapor rise, then erupt to raging, white flame.

The youth's arms flap in an effort to douse himself, shrieks rising like the smoke from his body. Flames envelope, then consume, until all that remains is a jagged, charred circle upon the Temple's steps.

Cherubs watch with rueful gazes; disapproving faces solemn in darkened wood.

Gypsies dance furiously, spread their displeasure in flaming jolts.

Thunder shakes, lightning rails from soot-soaked thunderheads.

Soldiers stand shocked, their spears forgotten beside them. Onlookers back away, murmur prayers, create distance between themselves and this beast.

Cain moves forward, at first stumbling, then picking up his stride, peeling his ragged tunic and dropping it to the ground.

Gasps go up. There are no marks where the pike pierced, no sign he's been impaled.

The crowd breaks, scared sheep running toward the city.

Cain beholds their shock, their looks of disgust, fear, terror.

He sprints toward the city's gates, tears flowing over a soiled face, broken heart bleeding into his soul. Again, cast out.

CHAPTER 37

ISTANBUL, TURKEY

The city groans under a strong wind.

"Formerly Constantinople," Drake says with a grin. "Named by me, for me, long ago." He glances at me, beams at the thought. I rub my throat and glare. Drake continues without pause. "I love it here. The Turkish people have always been a delight—hard working, strong of heart and body, suffering no usurpers to their homes or thrones."

The building is huge, a third century fortress owned by X'chasei and used for these secret meetings away from the prying eyes of press and bystander. We walk up a long hallway flanked by walls of stone and torchlight. It seems Drake likes the old ways.

It's been three days since our tour of the Children of the Rocks, and I feel Drake's gifts working despite the simmering rage in my soul.

"It's been difficult to arrange the presence of these men; and, in the end, only the promise of money—*what these people won't do for that*—has secured their participation. Six months of planning," Drake says, "but now my plans reach their zenith."

Drake stands just inside the room, greets everyone as they enter. Various leaders from the Middle East are represented. Last night, Drake gave me a list of all expected attendees. I mark them mentally as they arrive.

Laslo Slabav is first. The Israeli Prime Minister scans the room. He looks uncomfortable, pointed features grazing over the others as if reckoning the distance from them to the door. He greets Drake with a politician's smile, nods at me, casts a nervous glance at Longinus, and enters.

Next comes Oshi Khalifa of the Muslim Brotherhood. He's dressed in rumpled olive drab like a common soldier, a keen switch from the suit he'd worn at the Devil's Needle. A three-day shadow makes his thin face appear thick and triangular. He nods at Drake and moves by without a word.

Behind Khalifa is Otho Usmani, the late Mr. Sundamir's lieutenant and now presumed head of the Palestine Liberation Organization. He nods at Drake, and Drake extends his hand. Usmani is reluctant to take it, then returns the gesture.

"My condolences for the loss of Mr. Sundamir," Drake says. "He was a good and gracious man."

Usmani's lower lip quivers, although from sadness or rage I can't tell. He shuffles his feet and flaps his robes. "I've lost many friends. What's important is that his death not be in vain. I am still here." Usmani releases Drake's hand and enters the room. Drake glances at Longinus and follows Usmani. I'm surprised by the man's presence; Longinus should've killed him with all other Sundamir associates. *Has X'chasei missed someone?* I think. By the subtle change in Drake's expression, I surmise he's thinking the same thing.

The room we occupy is more castle than high-rise. Dating back to the time of Constantine the Great, the fort has a deep history of repelling raiders, aiding crusaders, and serving as meeting place for various high-level talks. Drake had told me that through the centuries he's taken great pains to keep the place intact and maintained. The room is something from a gothic novel. A long rectangle with high, stone walls. I imagine what has occurred within. These walls have stood witness to war talks, peace talks, and decisions that have affected the history of the planet.

A cavernous table fills the hall. Made of heavy oak and polished to a brilliant sheen, it's weathered the centuries well. It stretches twenty-five feet. In the center, X'chasei's symbol, the Labarum, appears as a white octagon.

Suspended above the table are seven lamps, with the middle one shining directly on the Labarum. The symbol's white background glows like a halo, makes the lines appear thick and substantial, as if it hovers over the table's surface.

The room's stone floor is beaten with age. Each stone is worn smooth and probably not as level as they once were. Sconces light the walls at four-foot intervals. Flames dance within, flickering orange over strips of weathered iron bracing.

I scan the others in the room. Longinus grins through his thick beard. Igneus stares forward, says nothing. I move to a chair against a far wall to observe and record everything.

Longinus closes the heavy doors and turns, facing the room. Drake moves to the head of the table. The visitors assume their seats and focus their attention on him.

"It's a pleasure to have you all here, together," Drake starts.

"Where's the money?" Usmani demands.

Drake grins and raises a hand. Part of the reason for Mr. Usmani's success is his straightforwardness.

"Fifty million American dollars has been deposited into your account."

Usmani's crooked teeth peek past red lips, a ghoulish attempt to smile. He pulls a phone from somewhere within his robes and starts pressing buttons. Drake smiles and waits.

In a moment, he nods, content his money is secure.

Drake begins. "We gather on the brink of an historic day. I've arranged this meeting so we might iron out some differences away from the intrusion of cameras, and assistants, and lobbyists." Drake holds each man's eyes as he speaks. "Sometimes, privacy is the best diplomat."

I scribble on my note pad. I know this meeting's been called to accomplish two things. First, the release of press statements to inform the world that Thaddeus Drake has involved himself in the age-old

Arab-Israeli conflict. Second, to allow Mr. Usmani, the new PLO leader, a chance to decide upon his own course of action.

"Since the beginning of time, war and discontent have been bred by fear and misunderstanding," Drake says. "We have the opportunity to reverse those tides—" He looks at each man. "To sow the seeds of contentment and accord."

Usmani shuffles in his seat, the rest stay focused on Drake.

"We'll start by announcing the rebuilding of Solomon's Temple upon its original site."

Usmani leaps to his feet. "That's preposterous!" He looks to Khalifa, who remains as docile as a sheep.

Drake speaks to Usmani. "You'd be surprised to know most people at this table have already agreed to the terms for peace and the rebuilding of the Temple."

"Who would be such a traitor?" Usmani shouts, his cheeks growing heated from the effort.

Drake raises his hand. "No one is a traitor," he says, "but since you ask a reasonable question, you deserve a reasonable answer." He moves down the left side of the table and turns to face them. "Please be seated," he says, "and I'll explain."

The man sits and grumbles to those around him.

"Now," Drake says, "for Mr. Usmani's sake, if you are with me, please stand."

All stand but Usmani.

Longinus wears a broad grin. Igneus stares at Drake, burning eyes above a creased mouth.

"This is an outrage!" Usmani yells, his accent making the words thick and harsh. "There can be no agreement with them." He levels a finger at the Israeli Prime Minister. "We do not trust them because they are not trustworthy!"

"You're one to talk, when you enslave the populous with fear," Slabav says, standing.

Drake glares at the Israeli president who blinks twice, then sits. "Perhaps you're taking a long view of this," Drake addresses Usmani. "Perhaps these men have realized what's in the best interest of all involved. Now's the time to act, Mr. Usmani. Don't let your grief over the loss of your dear friend shade logical thought. Will his death mean nothing?"

Usmani looks stunned, then his face turns fire-red. He spits his thoughts at the Israeli. "And do you know who's responsible for the death of Sundamir? Them!" He points at Slabav.

Drake looks surprised. Slabav leaps again to his feet, stammers for words.

Usmani is shouting, turning his attention from Slabav to Drake. "Do you know the story? Not only was Sundamir murdered but so was his wife, his daughters, his cousins and brothers…his…his aunts and uncles, business associates. Dozens of security guards and household staff. All of his assets and deeds have disappeared. I've been in hiding this whole time." Spit forms at the corners of his mouth, his robes flap with his efforts. "Who has such far reaching power? Who can perform such an operation and leave no trace?" He points at Slabav. "It could only be the Jews!"

"That's a lie," Slabav says.

"Prove it!"

"How can I prove a falsehood?"

"Then deny it!"

"I do deny it…as well as condemn it! The accusation is preposterous."

Usmani's voice cracks. "Blood is on your hands Slabav!"

Slabav's face contorts, he looks as if he might leap for the Arab's throat. Longinus steps forward. Khalifa stands. Igneus inches his chair from the table.

"Enough!" Drake shouts. His normal graceful demeanor has been replaced by one of absolute power.

Both men stop, mouths open.

"That's enough," Drake hisses. "We'll have a calm proceeding, and you will *not* act like this in my presence. Mr. Slabav, please be seated. Mr. Usmani, will you at least hear us out?"

Usmani's mouth snaps shut. He stares at Drake, then glances at Slabav. "I will listen."

"We propose a sharing of the sacred site. Each party has been asked to give something. Mr. Longinus will supervise the dismantling of the Dome." Usmani opens his mouth but is stopped by Drake. "This has to be done in order to preserve the structure's integrity. We wouldn't want it collapsing with other construction so close." Usmani blinks, then nods. Drake continues. "Mr. Slabav has agreed to allow both your organization, and Mr. Khalifa's, full access during all aspects of the project. When the Temple is complete, the Dome will be rebuilt upon its exact spot. I can assure you that no expense will be spared to accommodate this. Mr. Slabav's government has agreed to bear the costs, which include the cost of reconditioning the Dome's materials."

Usmani's cheeks return to their normal color. He gnaws on his lip.

"During this project, the entire world will be watching. The entire planet will expect some catastrophe, some war or act of terrorism. What they will see is Arab and Jew cooperating. They'll witness peaceful, understanding leaders. When the project is complete, Muslim, Jew, and Christian will share the most holy spot on Earth —peacefully."

Usmani shakes his head as he stares at the table. "I'm no Jew, but I thought the new Temple had to be built upon the exact site of the old Temple—the exact spot the Dome now occupies. How can you build your Temple close to, but not on, the original spot?"

"Currently, the Dome doesn't sit on the Temple's original spot," Drake says.

Usmani's eyebrows crinkle, his lips purse. "But the Dome is built on the *exact* site of the original Temple."

Drake smiles. "No, it isn't. There's plenty of room for the Temple to be built on its *original* site. As a matter of fact, I was hoping to have the Mosque and Temple share a passageway. A kind of symbolic joining of religions for all the world's faithful."

"But the Dome *is* on the original site."

"No, it isn't."

Usmani looks at Khalifa who nods his head. Slabav smiles.

"How can you know?" Usmani says.

"How can you?"

Usmani blinks in response.

"Mr. Usmani, you're the only one who hasn't approved this plan. Even if I'm wrong about the Temple's original location, you can certainly see the benefit of rebuilding this structure. I mean, since September eleventh your organizations have been seen as bringers of terror, hate and violence, not as religious entities preaching love, truth, and brotherhood. Can't you see how a gesture of this magnitude would represent to the world the loving, tolerant, and charitable nature of Islam?"

Usmani leans forward, eyes bright and focused.

"God's big enough for all of us," Drake says, "and if we show a united front, the world will support us. Imagine the possibilities, in our lifetime we can end war—peace will reign upon the planet."

Usmani shakes his head, mouth open.

"Even now," Drake says, "the plans are in motion."

"What plans?"

"I'm sure you're aware of my abilities to bring peace to war-torn regions?"

"Yes? But I never took you for a braggart."

Drake's face flushes. "Well, as a condition for my...*assistance*, many nations have agreed to aid me in restoring peace to the holy land. The Israeli government supports this move." He nods to Mr. Slabav. "And fifteen other nations are ready to sign a treaty, including China and the United States."

Usmani stands. "What nations? What treaty?"

"The treaty that we'll propose. The Religious Tolerance Treaty," Drake says. "We will stand unified and explain to the world that the Earth is no longer a series of tribes and clans, but a nation in its own right—and that this *nation* will no longer tolerate the discord, intolerance, and terrorism of the past. All of us—Muslim, Jew, Christian—will announce this treaty and share our plans to rebuild the Temple. All we need is your support."

Usmani sits deep in thought. He doesn't look at the others and for some minutes contemplates the information.

I watch the man struggle between faith and logic.

Then Usmani's face turns red.

"Preposterous!" he shouts.

"No," Drake says, hurrying to speak. "A much-needed change."

"I will not honor Sundamir's memory by making deals with Jews!"

Drake leans in. Anger is evident in his eyes, his lips curl in a trembling snarl. "I will have my peace, Mr. Usmani," he whispers, "I *will* have my Temple."

Usmani leaps to his feet, slams his fist on the table. "Not in my lifetime, Drake!"

Drake looks down, shakes his head. His next words are soft.

"As you wish."

He produces a revolver and shoots the man twice in the chest.

Usmani slumps to the floor, eyes frozen with surprise. Two red blooms appear on his robe, his keffiyeh hangs askew on his head. I lean forward, hands over my ears from the gun's report.

Slabav leaps from the table, his face a mask of shock and fear. Khalifa looks at the dead man with a mixture of sorrow and glee. Longinus looks joyful. Igneus looks exhausted. I press myself against the wall, ears ringing, mouth agape.

Smoke rolls from the pistol as Drake places it on the table. He adjusts his gloves and buttons his suit jacket. "Longinus?"

"Aye?"

"Do remember to destroy Mr. Usmani's lineage."

"Aye."

Drake looks at Khalifa. "Igneus, see that Mr. Usmani's assets are transferred to Mr. Khalifa's accounts."

Igneus nods and says nothing.

Drake looks at Slabav, who's pressed himself against the wall closest the door. He looks as horrified as I feel, alternating his gaze between the pistol and the dead man.

"There, there, Laslo," Drake says. "Don't be afraid. Now you know the penalty for betrayal."

Slabav manages a shaky grin.

Drake moves to the exit, then turns to face us. The men remain seated, most wearing normal expressions. Two look terrorized. One lies on the floor in a growing pool of blood.

"Mr. Igneus has instructions for all of you."

"Instructions?" Slabav stammers.

"Oh, how terribly rude of me," Drake says. "Laslo, I do apologize for overlooking such an important detail. Mr. Igneus has been instructed to wire the sum of one hundred million dollars to the accounts of your choice."

Igneus nods at Slabav, although his expression shows contempt.

"Gentlemen, is there anything else?" Drake asks.

No one speaks.

Drake pushes the doors open and retrieves a Treasurer from his cigarette tin.

The hollow echo of his footsteps follow him from the building.

CHAPTER 38

ISTANBUL, TURKEY

"He's going to kill all the Jews. A final solution, he calls it. Sound familiar?" I speak into the Popephone, my speech rushed. Is Drake listening in? Coming to collect me soon? "You wouldn't believe what's going on around here. It's like complete chaos. Drake seems unphased but…" I trail off, realize I'm rambling. I take a cleansing breath, think to tell him about Octavio, to enlist his help in destroying Drake. "Have you spoken with the Pope?"

There's silence, and I imagine the Apostle's face, drawn tight, absorbing the news.

"I have, but I didn't know about these events," John says. "A final solution? Are you sure that's what you heard?"

"Yes, I'm sure. I was present when he explained his plan. He's fulfilling prophecies to end the world. Although I didn't know genocide was prophesied."

"It wasn't."

"Then why?" I ask.

"I'm not sure. I mean, if what you say concerning Hitler is true, then Drake's plan becomes a playbook he's drawn from before."

"Igneus told me he was trying to fulfill the prophecies even then.

Said the war ended because something happened whereby Drake couldn't attain his goals. That guy's nothing if not patient."

"Yes, a worthy adversary."

"He did offer an excuse. Said he wasn't planning to commit genocide but was using the Jews as bait to get the Arabs to agree to his terms. He also implied he'd warn the Israeli prime minister of the plan before he entered the Temple to confront God."

"Has he told you anything more about his brother?"

"No. Not much of anything really. I've had problems getting him alone for another interview."

"How about the cow? Did he find the one he was looking for?"

"No idea. He's flying out in the morning for a television interview."

"Do you know why?"

"Something about his peace summit. He's been spending a lot of time with Mideast leaders."

"That explains the corpses over there."

"Did I tell you I saw him murder Usmani?" The line is quiet, and I assume John is thinking these events over.

"So, will the Pope let you help? I mean, he just can't sit by while all the Jews get wiped out."

"I'm not sure. He's in bad health, and I think his mind is slipping a bit. Increasingly the other priests are looking to me for direction and vision, but I cannot act without the Pope's blessing."

"Even when millions are going to die?"

"Even then," John says, "the only thing that can make me forsake this tenet is if I know, absolutely, that the time of my task is at hand. I feel it isn't. Besides, rebuilding the Temple near the Dome of the Rock? I don't see it happening. Our Islamic brothers will never allow such a thing."

I think it over. "Drake seems pretty sure," I say. "I don't think he's worried about it. He's already got the Islamic and Jewish leaders in place and on the payroll. I think it's going to happen."

"I'll talk to His Holiness and ask if we may level the power of the Templars once more. Perhaps there's another way."

"What's that?"

"I'll let you know."

I toss the Popephone onto the hotel bed. As soon as it hits, it's ringing again.

I press the answer button, think it's John calling back. It turns out to be Drake. I'm certain he knows everything John and I discuss. He's always encouraged it, the pompous asshole. As each day passes, I feel more of a pawn on some grand chess board. A game that's been playing in my life for some time now.

All serve at the pleasure of the gloved man.

"Dear Emery, so sorry to interrupt, but I was wondering if you'd be kind enough to do me a favor. I have that TV interview in Los Angeles and was hoping you'd come."

Fuck you, I think.

"Of course," I say, "when do we leave?"

CHAPTER 39

LOS ANGELES, CALIFORNIA

"You're a hypocrite."

Drake stares at the little, bold man. "What in *the hell* are you talking about?"

"You preach peace, but mong war."

"*Mong?* Is that even a word?" Drake looks at me as if I'm the resident dictionary. I shrug my shoulders.

"It doesn't matter, you know what I mean." Igneus's hands shake, his left leg bounces like a scratching dog. His face is tight, his lips, a thin white line.

Jars and slim vials cover the desk in front of Drake. He faces a mirror fringed with soft white lights. The room is devoid of style. A cheap piece of art hangs on a wall, and by the door is an empty coat rack made of plastic.

There's a knock and a portly lady sticks her head in. "Five minutes, Mr. Drake."

He waves, puts on a grand smile. "Thanks, Tina."

It's been sixteen hours since I last spoke with Drake, and I'm tired from all the travel. Turkey to L.A., Igneus in tow. Not the grand vacation I'd expected as a world-traveler and the Dove's personal biographer.

Drake appears as fresh as ever, though. His hair trimmed, his suit impeccable.

Igneus glares, a look so sordid it casts the room in shadow.

"What's gotten into you?" Drake asks as he smooths make-up on his cheeks.

"You have! You and that braying ass we're imprisoned with." The small man is fully focused on Drake's back.

Drake drops his hand and looks at the man. "Thankfully, you won't have to deal with us much longer."

"You said that centuries ago, yet here we are." He spreads his hands in front of him with an angry jolt. "I don't think I can stand much more."

I'm not sure where the Jew is going with this or even what's gotten into him, but I keep my lips sealed.

Drake turns and leans toward him. "Again, what are you talking about?"

"I'm talking about the hypocrisy. I'm talking about the crimes committed: the murder, the blackmail, the prostitution, the gambling, drugs, weapons, *war.*"

"And?"

"And everything!" the little man shrieks. "First you convince me war is profitable—you sell weapons to both sides and keep the factions riled up. Then you tell me *after* war is profitable; you exploit the homeless, raise an army from the ruined lives of the out-of-work soldiers, arrange your own force of mercenaries, promise them X'chasei's protection and wealth—and when one of them changes their mind you wipe their entire lineage from the planet!"

Drake smiles. "Very true."

"Don't grin at me, you asshole!" Igneus is on his feet, eyes blazing, lips curled, teeth exposed like an enraged chihuahua.

"Please relax, my friend," Drake says.

"I won't! I can't! I have too much blood on my hands!"

"Perhaps, but that will soon end. Next week I'll speak at the peace summit, and I assure you, after that, the world will be at peace."

"You can promise that? What a glib bastard."

A brush of anger appears on Drake's face. He inhales, looks at the ceiling. "Yes, I can promise that. Have I yet failed?"

Igneus makes no response, just flops into his chair.

"Listen," Drake says, "you've come this far; please come a little farther. Your role is complete. Our global currency is complete. Don't you see? It's a vital step. It's a huge victory and all due to your efforts."

"How many have *died* due to my efforts?"

"How many have you killed?" Drake asks. "None as far as I know."

"Are you fucking crazy?" Igneus is on his feet again. "I've killed millions!"

"Really? When?"

Igneus looks at Drake, mouth open. "Seriously? Hmm? When?" He starts to pace, looks down at the carpet. "I can't seem to—Oh. I remember. Let's start with the Christians, then the Persians—where we kind of figured out how to exploit *everything*—then the, I don't know, *Ad Abolendam,* the Inquisition, as they call it now. That was a real record breaker, but not to be topped, we pressed on. More money to make, you know. And we got better…"

"I get your point."

Igneus is talking too fast to stop. "…the Holy Crusades, various assorted regional conflicts, warlords and the like, you remember. Then, having grown bored with purely continental conflict, you discovered world conflict. World War One was a beauty but still not good enough. So, on comes your crowning achievement: World War Two, where new records are set in industry, profit, and body count." Igneus is breathing hard, his face a bulging magenta.

"Then let's not forget— "

In a flash, Drake has him by the throat, his small body pinned against the wall. He speaks through gritted teeth. "Enough, you whining, scared, little whelp. Let us not forget that *you* are the cause of *your own* misery. *You* are the one who put yourself in this prison." A single vein swells in the middle of the Jew's forehead.

I leap from my seat and grab Drake's arm. It's like grabbing a steel bar. I remember Drake has only been made up to appear older, when in fact, he'd become immortal in his prime. A young, strong farm boy. Igneus's eyes are wide, the vein on his forehead turning blue.

"C'mon, Drake," I say in as calm a tone as I can muster. "Please. Let go."

Drake doesn't notice me, hisses into Igneus's face. "All you have is because of me. The only reason you've even survived is because of me." His voice changes as he talks, becomes coarse and guttural. "I will suffer you no longer. You've completed your tasks, but there are more. *Do not* forget you're still a member of X'chasei and as such, will fulfill your responsibilities to us when summoned. You *will* go to Iran with Longinus, and you *will not* return until the work is done."

Igneus stares at Drake, hatred evident in his green eyes.

"Drake. Please," I say.

Drake pulls the little man closer. "Do we understand each other?"

Igneus doesn't answer, only stares with the same blistering gaze.

"Answer me, you worm. For if you become unconscious before I have my answer, you will never again see the light of day."

I pull on Drake's arm without effect.

Igneus's answer comes in a rasp like a squeaking, rusty door hinge. "Yes. Yes."

Drake unhands him with a shove, then turns toward me, eyes full of rage. With a quick snap, he shakes me off and levels a finger in my face. "Don't ever touch me again."

He holds my gaze for a few seconds, his gleaming smile now twisted like a serpent about to strike. I hold my hands in front of me. "Sorry. Sorry. Just worried you were going a bit too far."

We match stares. My knees shake, and I can feel the sweat running down my back. As much as I hate him, I know now isn't the time. I'm no match for this immortal, and I'm certain if he kills me here and now, no one will ever know what's become of me.

He leans close. "You know nothing, dear Emery. Record and keep your mouth shut before you find yourself back in the hole I pulled you from." He holds my eyes for a second longer, then turns and moves to the make-up table. He smooths his suit with both hands, then adjusts his tie. He inhales, then looks down and exhales. I stand there like a dumb ass. Drake watches Igneus's defeated form through the mirror. "Please smile, my friend, your redemption is nigh."

Igneus smolders, says nothing.

The door cracks open. "One minute, Mr. Drake."

Drake smiles at the intruder. "Thanks, Tina." He turns and takes a final look in the mirror. "How do I look?" he says.

Igneus sighs. "Like my worst nightmare."

The red light atop the television camera remains unlit. Drake flips the *silent* button on his phone and slips it in his pocket.

He winks at me and enters the studio to take a seat beside the show's host, a sallow-looking old man known for his sneak attacks during interviews. The man smiles and nods. "Welcome."

Drake returns the smile and shakes the man's hand. "Thanks for having me, David."

An assistant moves close, dabs Drake's face with a small, makeup sponge.

David waves her away. "Nervous?"

"Should I be?" Drake asks.

The man smiles and adjusts his bow tie, then looks Drake up and down. "Maybe."

From behind the camera, a woman counts down from ten. The director steps into the light. "Five, four," she says, then uses her fingers for three, two and one. The red light blinks on, and she points to David.

"My guest tonight is Thaddeus Drake, one of the most recognized faces on the planet. A man revered around the world for his solutions to conflict. He's been associated with Mother Teresa, Archbishop Desmond Tutu, and the Reverend Billy Graham. He was also instrumental in the return of the Dali Lama to Tibet. He's been nominated for the Nobel Peace Prize four times and received the prize last year for ending conflicts in Africa and Korea." David nods to the camera, then turns to Drake. "People have been trying to do that for decades, how did you manage it?"

Drake smiles, spreads his hands before him, "I managed nothing. I merely gained an audience with opposing leaders and convinced them of their commonalities."

David exhales, lips pursed in a fake whistle. "Your results are remarkable, almost superhuman."

Drake laughs. "No, I just have a knack for bringing people together."

David nods, "Uh-huh, and is there ever money involved?"

"Excuse me?"

"It's rumored that you bribe officials with women and sports cars and secret bank accounts."

Drake flushes. "That's preposterous."

"Certainly, but there have been rumors tying you to organizations that, shall we say, deal in the unsavory?"

"I think rumors go with the territory of living in the public eye."

"So, you refute these rumors? You've never bribed heads of state? You've never participated in a military coup or set up a puppet government?"

Drake grins, perfectly at ease. "You're being naïve, David, if you think the leaders of some of the greatest nations on Earth can be blackmailed or extorted."

"Am I?" he asks, shuffling through his papers.

"You are. I've spent my entire life working only for peace. My accomplishments prove I've gained the world's trust and as such, these leaders listen to me."

"It seems the work pays extremely well. You live a nice life and want for nothing. How is it you manage to have such wealth? It's been said nations pay you a king's ransom to get certain results. Is this true?"

"It would be in a perfect world, David. What would be better than bringing peace to the world and getting paid to do it? Unfortunately though, that's not the world in which we live—not yet anyway. My personal finances are of no concern to the public, but I will say I'm blessed to be in a position to provide my services free of charge."

"You aren't involved in war-profiteering?"

A chuckle. "No."

"Trafficking in persons?"

"Never."

"Arms dealing?"

"Preposterous. Frankly, I'm offended by these accusations. The world is a miserable place, and my only motivation is to save lives. Which through God's grace, I've been able to do."

David looks at the camera. "We'll be back after this."

The red light fades, and David turns to Drake, smiles, offers his hand. "Sorry," he says, "ratings week."

Drake accepts the hand, then clamps down on the bony fingers.

David grimaces. Drake leans close, a broad smile on his face so that anyone looking will think the two are sharing some private, amicable conversation.

"Fuck your ratings," he says in a low voice. "How would you like to see your children murdered before your eyes? Or your wife raped by an endless line of soldiers?"

David's eyes grow big. "Are you threatening me?"

"I'm speaking about the atrocities of war," Drake says, "horrific scenes that could happen to any of us."

David's lips tremble, a thin line of sweat breaks through the heavy makeup on his face.

"That's why I work so hard for peace and I will not suffer you to make a mockery of me or my work." Drake still smiles, although his tone is a sharp hiss. "When we return to the air, you'd better be my biggest fucking fan."

Drake releases the man and turns toward the crowd of staff behind the cameras. "Then the bartender says, *I didn't say frog, I said bulldog.*" He says this as if it's the punchline of a joke.

Drake glances at David and starts to laugh. The man is old but quick on the uptake and starts to laugh as well. A few seconds later, the entire staff is laughing.

The director steps forward and does the same countdown as before. The red light flickers on and David begins to speak.

"Welcome back. Our guest tonight is Nobel Peace Prize recipient

Thaddeus Drake. A truly wondrous human who is expected to give the keynote address at the Mideast peace conference next week." He turns to Drake. "Mr. Drake, I must apologize for my line of questioning prior to the break. Your record as a humanitarian is unblemished and it should be noted for our viewers that you've *never* been accused of any of the things mentioned. I meant no disrespect."

Drake nods. "No problem, David. Thank you for setting the record straight."

David turns toward the camera. "Mr. Drake, can you share with us what you hope to accomplish at next week's peace conference?"

"It would be a pleasure."

CHAPTER 40

TEHRAN, IRAN

I gneus's face tells me he doesn't want to die again.

It's been four days since we left Drake, and we stand with our backs pressed against a rough stone wall on a no-name street deep in Tehran's heart. We'd been sent with Longinus to meet local clerics and leaders, X'chasei associates all. "Trips like these are necessary to cement the cooperation of certain groups, dear Emery," Drake had said. "An effort to secure their support and outline the uprise of the downtrodden. A visit from X'chasei leaders can do much to promote the organization's goals."

I duck more bullets, feel glass shower over me. More nonsense from the gloved man. It seems the populace doesn't need our help and has risen up to create large pockets of resistance within the city.

I can't help but wonder at X'chasei's involvement. I also can't wait to get out of here. Igneus cowers, his expression matching my emotion. "Where's Longinus?" he yells.

I shrug, stay low, scan the scene for the hulk. Longinus has been enjoying this, reveling in the chaos, eyes sparkling with bloodlust, taking an active role. He's even unleashed his sword a time or two over the last few hours.

Bullets hit the wall with a sharp thwack and send another shower of stones onto our heads. I cower lower than even Igneus. The reporters in front of us crouch but keep filming. Carson Cruze, the anchor of a popular prime-time news show, steps in front of the camera. Behind him civilians attack the army's front line. They're well-armed and rush in, shrieking as they go, as if their volume will repel the waiting force.

Beyond them, a line of soldiers and Iranian police inch closer to the crowd, riot shields raised, tear gas canisters flying.

I search for Longinus. The huge man had been at our side only moments before but has now disappeared into the debris-strewn streets.

Carson Cruze speaks to the camera, holds a microphone in one hand while balancing a khaki green helmet with the other. "As you can see, the street fighting continues. It appears the Iranian Army is being pushed back by civilian demonstrators." A Molotov cocktail arcs through the air to explode in a flash of flame. We all cringe as Cruze glances over his shoulder. "The militia is incredibly well-armed. Reports have circulated about the raid of an Iranian weapons cache somewhere close to here."

More bullets hit the wall above our heads, and my worry compounds. I flinch, then slide close to Igneus, behind Cruze's cameraman. I feel lucky. So far, the army has been firing over the heads of the demonstrators in an attempt to show force but do no harm.

But the civilians are undaunted, moving forward with momentum about fifty yards from the military line. I scan both sides and still see no sign of the Roman.

"We're receiving reports the Ayatollah has not left his home and that the Iranian President Rahstani has actually left the country," Cruze reports. "These are unconfirmed, but we're doing all we can to verify their accuracy." The newsman wears a khaki vest over a long-sleeve shirt rolled to his elbows. His pockets bulge with gear. Behind him the civilians are massed and moving.

Bullets tear into the line and mow down the forward rank of demonstrators.

Cruze glances at the cameraman. "Did you get that?"

The cameraman nods and steps to the side to film more of the carnage.

Around us, buildings are riddled with bullet holes. Small fires burn within smashed stores and mix dark smoke with the bright fog of tear gas.

Undaunted, the civilian line advances to take over a four-way intersection where they stop and huddle. Then all heads turn down a side street and out of my sight.

I hear a loud, clanking engine and move along the wall to look down the street.

The army advances, taking advantage of the distraction to fire another volley. Screams follow as six civilians fall to the littered street. A man bends to a fallen comrade, then starts to drag him to the rear.

A tank appears. It bears the markings of the Iranian Army. The soldiers cheer.

The civilians scatter, disappear into alcoves and side streets, leap into burnt out buildings or just race away.

Those closest to the tank clamber over it like so many ants on a praying mantis. Cruze chatters at high speed now. "An army tank just made an appearance and splintered the crowd," he says. "The civilians are attacking it."

Three more civilians climb metal treads and onto the tank's body.

The tank's turret turns, first left toward the fleeing civilians, then right toward the cheering army. It stops, shudders once in a quick left-right motion, then turns again toward the soldiers, who cheer and raise their rifles over their heads.

The crowd is all but broken. The street almost empty.

The tank fires into the army's front line.

The roar is deafening; the concussion, breath stealing. Cruze falls, the cameraman joining a second later, striving to get the camera in position.

Bodies cover the area where once the soldiers whooped. Those in the line of the shell were vaporized at the moment of impact. Howls rise from those who lie in the street, some missing limbs, riot shields splintered beside them.

I see Longinus behind the army's main line and can't fathom what the giant is doing in such a dangerous place. There's a clatter to my right. The fleeing civilians have changed course and now charge up the street, weapons raised, faces contorted in rage.

They flow past us to pour over the bewildered soldiers.

Cruze gains his feet, hoists the cameraman beside him. "Get this!" he yells and steps in front of the camera. "The civilians have a tank! We don't yet know if it's an army defector or perhaps a stolen vehicle, but they've punched a hole in the army's forward line." Behind him the scene is pure carnage. Civilians kill, then loot, the downed soldiers, peeling gear from the dead and covering themselves with helmets, flak vests and riot shields. Those without weapons have them now and raise them howling like tribal banshees.

The soldiers try to flee, routed, but are cut down by a riot of gunfire.

"The militia seems incredibly well-organized and have mounted an assault with military precision. There's speculation they may be supported by some other government, but again, as yet, the report is unconfirmed."

I look past the bloodthirsty mob, over the dead bodies and rolling smoke, past flaming walls and dancing militia.

Then Longinus appears, kneeling on the periphery, leveling a scoped rifle right at me.

I freeze, literally frozen by fear.

The Roman's head pops up and I'm certain I see him wink.

Then he's sighting again. A flame leaps from the rifle.

Cruze's head explodes in a rain of blood and brain.

CHAPTER 41

TEHRAN, IRAN

"We can turn this around, my friend. You have nothing to fear." Rafiz Rahstani, the Iranian president, tries to smile. Tension deflates his posture like a desert tent after a sandstorm. He nods, eyes filled with tears. "You are indeed a good friend, Oshi," he says to the man across from him, Oshi Khalifa, the leader of the PLO and Muslim Brotherhood. Rahstani looks to the ceiling, then flops in a chair. He exhales, his body trembling.

"Of course, concessions must be made," Khalifa says with a small shake of his head.

Rahstani turns his gaze from the ceiling. "What concessions?"

"Concessions to end this uprising. You must leave the country. I've arranged for Thaddeus Drake to visit and secure your good intentions." He says this with a wave of his hand as if it's a small matter. Rahstani's face flushes; he looks to the floor, leans forward in his chair, glares at Khalifa, then sighs again with a shake of his head.

"I understand your turmoil," Khalifa says. "But you must trust me. Drake will come, and he and the Ayatollah will present the necessary image for you to leave freely."

Rahstani's shoulders slump, he shakes his head. "And then what?"

Khalifa laughs. "And then you find a new place to live. I can promise you'll be well-provided for and will live out your days in peace and pursue those things that make you happy."

"Being president makes me happy."

Khalifa leans across the desk, looks deep in the man's eyes. "You've made a botch of it."

An instant of rage again flares on Rahstani's face. He moves to the window, looks over the thousands of demonstrators in the street below. They're well-armed, although, since the withdrawal of the army and police, they've been peaceful. "They'll kill me."

Khalifa moves to his side. "They'll forget about you." He places a hand on his friend's shoulder. "I've risen to power," he says. "I now control the PLO and the Brotherhood. I have powerful friends and can offer you sanctuary, but you must relinquish power and come with me."

A long pause ensues.

"I'd rather be dead," Rahstani whispers.

"Come now, it's not that bad."

Frantic voices fill the hall and bounce through the corridor. They grow loud as they grow close. The office door bursts open, and three large police officers pour through. They stand looking at the President, weapons readied at their sides.

Rahstani turns to Khalifa.

Khalifa frowns. "Did I mention you're under arrest?"

We move through crowded streets. It's late, and the starless sky sheds an ominous darkness on the revelers.

The populace is jubilant, dancing in the streets, within smashed storefronts, atop burnt-out cars. Gunshots crackle in the distance, and Igneus startles with each sharp pop.

"Jumpier'n a hot rock lizard," Longinus laughs. "Fightin's over, they'be jus' celebratin'."

Igneus shoots a wry look and quickens his step toward the safe house. I follow close, wish I could sprout eyes in the back of my head.

I haven't felt safe since we've arrived in this country and consider myself a genius for spotting the danger, which is everywhere. All the time. We don't exactly fit in.

We move through more revelers. The smell of burning tires mixes with that of fresh meat cooked on an open flame. Music blares, people dance in the darkness, in the streets. They cry out with excitement and hope. Cry out for finally attaining the hope to dream.

We round a corner and turn up a deserted alley. Bottles, papers and aluminum cans litter the ground as garbage cans sit upended at the alley's opposite end.

A faded red door appears, and Longinus produces a key. A few seconds later we're in, then up a flight of creaky, peeling stairs where another door is unlocked.

We enter the apartment and Longinus slumps onto a tired chair of faded brown. From a three-legged end table, he produces a remote control and clicks the TV to life. He speeds through the channels until he gets to a newscast.

I'm surprised any sort of local station is on-air but then remember the media had been the first thing X'chasei shut down, and the first thing it brought back up.

The room is small, perhaps twelve square feet, containing only the chair in which Longinus now sits and a couch that's caved-in as if someone has laid on it for years on end.

Igneus eases down on its arm, wears an expression as if he hopes the old thing will bear his slight weight.

The arm groans but holds and Igneus relaxes, then turns his attention to the television.

It's a live report on Carson Cruze's network, and I wonder if they know their star reporter is dead. Then Drake enters the frame, standing before the presidential office building. Oshi Khalifa is at his side, wearing his same strained expression and faded khakis.

Drake speaks, his charisma, even through the fuzzy screen of the small television, palpable. I find myself fighting the urge to go to him. "The people have spoken," Drake says. "The time for a free Iran has come!" People erupt with wild cheers as the camera pans across the square. There are probably eight thousand present, most holding guns provided by X'chasei. I gasp at the size of the crowd and draw a look from Igneus that says this is commonplace in his world.

Drake and Khalifa stand abreast, another man joins them. I recognize the Ayatollah Qasni, Iran's supreme religious ruler. They present a united front, smile, exchange words with one another, act as if the bodies around them haven't been noticed.

Drake speaks. "Today we've taken a vital step toward peace. Truly God has preserved us, has sanctioned our cause and delivered us from evil. Has brought us together and given us cause to celebrate, as one people, now free—!" A raucous cheer.

"—As brothers, unbound—!" More cheers.

"—As humans, united!" The crowd roars as Khalifa and the Ayatollah join hands and raise them overhead. Drake beams into the camera, waves at the crowd, then steps aside.

Khalifa and the Ayatollah move to the mic.

The television goes dark.

Igneus turns, a protest forming.

Longinus grins through his beard. "Are ye ready to non-be in this shite-hole?"

Igneus is at the door in a flat second.

CHAPTER 42

JERUSALEM, ISRAEL

The sleek, black limousine rolls to the curb as the mass around me surges forth.

"Ye may wanna get back," Longinus says, then moves toward the vehicle and blocks the rushing onlookers. The Roman opens the door, and I see Drake's Hollywood smile. Later today he's due to speak at the peace summit, his crowning achievement. The day he'll trick the entire world to do his bidding and become X'chasei *associates,* one and all.

I sidle close to Longinus as I think about Drake's grand plan. The great masquerade. His brilliant finale.

One week has passed since the fall of Iran and still no word from John on the Pope's answer. The Middle East is in shambles with small skirmishes occurring throughout the region. They're desperate and looking to Oshi Khalifa, the new leader of the PLO and Muslim Brotherhood, to unify them.

Peace is assured.

This little speech is just icing on the cake for the gloved man, a matinee of sorts. Tonight, when he speaks at the peace summit, he'll ensure his plan comes to fruition. Although Drake's gifts are powerful, I've noticed sometimes people who are enraged can overcome them.

Of course, Drake sees those are brought to a swift end. *All serve at the pleasure of the gloved man,* Igneus has said, and as I think of those *associates*—Slabav, Khalifa, myself—I realize the statement is true. Not a small circle of influence for Drake, but the entire world. I wonder if the U.S. and Russian presidents are counted among X'chasei associates. Drake said that X'chasei has the power to destroy the entire world. I can only assume that means he has the ability to launch nuclear weapons.

Let's hope it doesn't come to that, I think: *all us sheep roasted.*

Drake exits the limo to a flurry of cameras and reporters. He appears confident, *as if that's a surprise.* Abel's gifts have indeed served him well. He squints against the flash of blurted questions and news cameras, nudges past outstretched microphones. The crowd is massive, pushing and craning.

Longinus waves a hand, and a giant African man steps in front of the reporters to shield Drake from their onslaught.

Drake moves past without comment, and a cheer rises from the crowd as more people are able to see him. He smiles. He is loved. The Dove has alit on this place.

He walks fast, Longinus matching his stride; I, a step behind.

"Things are set," the Roman says.

A pretty blonde greets Drake and eases next to him. She hands him a stack of papers. "Your speech, sir." She's stunning like all X'chasei employees. Her flawless smile, an oasis in a dark place. Her plunging neckline is cat nip to the big Roman who stands with a goofy smile on his face.

"I thin' we should be gettin' to know each other," the Roman says to her.

She flicks her eyes, smiles, then speaks to Drake. "Mr. Drake, you have twenty minutes here, then off to the summit. You'll speak there in one hour."

Longinus grins, transfixed by the cleavage.

Drake snaps his fingers at the Roman. "Hey...hey!" More finger snaps. "Over here. Time for that later."

The blonde flushes as Drake continues forward, Longinus following. I stifle a laugh.

Drake rubs his right hand. Although gloved, it seems to bother him, and I wonder if his mark is up to its scaring-the-shit-out-of-everyone nonsense.

"You alright?" I ask as we stand at the bottom of the backstage steps.

He offers his gloved right hand. "Feel," he says.

The leather is hot. I see a flash of worry cross his face. "I think it's glowing," he says.

"Why?"

He shakes his head. "Too close to hallowed ground? I'm not really sure. But not far from here is where I killed my brother." His expression changes, as if he's going back those centuries to relive that day. I can only imagine what he's thinking.

"Maybe you should cancel?"

Dark eyes hold mine as he considers this, then his entire face changes, becomes brilliant and beautiful. "Nonsense," he says. "This is child's play. Besides, becoming God ain't easy."

The crowd surges forth and Longinus barks an order. In an instant a wall of security has them at bay.

Longinus grins. "Good luck."

Drake ascends the stage, pausing at the top to straighten his tie and button his jacket. He wears a Moschino suit, black, with a silky red tie and crisp white shirt. His shoes sparkle, his trademark gloves in place. He approaches the microphone, no traces of worry on his face.

CHAPTER 43

The tiller quivers in his grasp.

This sacrifice will find acceptance.

He crosses the orchard: the smell of dew and fruit rising in the darkness; the cold, dark soil pushing between his toes.

Overhead, birds screech and caw, skitter from branch to branch. The low of the herd wafts through the distance, carries a thick, fleshy stench through the precious glade.

How these things sicken him—their fur, their flesh, their blood, their dung— bags of putrid, pulsing purulence.

Bile rises in his throat, thick and stringy. Nausea rolls over his stomach and into his chest. He bends, heart pounding, hand gripping a small, rough sapling, nose searching for the sweet aroma of nearby dogwood and juniper, for the clean, lingering lavender. Jaw clenched, he waits for the sensation to pass.

Looking skyward, vines and branches stretch across the moon's pocked face. Swallows continue their skittering dance, bounding over bent branch, emitting excrement in dark, streaky blotches. Nausea grows as he steps forward.

A pair of squirrels bound into the underbrush as sinister eyes accuse, their matted fur a corpulent excess. The wind whispers encouragement with an aromatic hush as vines, ravaged by the sparrows, climb into the night.

Beyond, he hears the song. A little praise to God.

Crouched, caressing the fig tree's familiar skin, he peers through a tangle of branches into a clearing. Rock and desultory moonlight litter the gray smudge of soil before him.

His brother sits atop a fallen log close to a small fire. Light dances across his features, splays jagged blemishes over his face and tunic. He sings, head bobbing, inhaling quick, perfumed breaths into fetid, fleshy lungs. Geysers of mist expel with each syllable's exhale.

Cain creeps close. The night's jasmine tempts his nostrils. Muscles ripple as he tightens his grip.

His brother's back draws close, glows in shadow, unaware.

Sickness swells Cain's throat. Warm, gray beads of sweat break over his forehead, run down his nose and torso. The first shy marks of moisture bloom across his tunic in broad, dark smudges.

He stifles a gag, squeezes the tool, bile burning the back of his throat. His own acrid scent mixes with the smell of the nearby herd, overwhelms the orchard's aromas.

His revulsion doubles.

Blinking sweat, choking waves of panicked nausea, he forces his thoughts to a single, fine point.

And realizes all the meanings of his life.

God prefers blood.

He will attain favor.

He stands poised like a scorpion; tool cocked.

Abel's head bobs, black hair reflecting firelight.

"Cain?"

The tiller whistles through a sleek arc to lodge in Abel's skull.

His body goes stiff, eyes wide with surprise and terror. Limbs freeze in full extension, yet twitch with appended movement.

Dark liquid pours over the implement's handle, down Abel's shoulders, onto Cain's hands.

Abel's eyes pulse upward in their sockets, once, twice, then he collapses in the dirt. A ragged, gurgling staccato replaces normal breathing, then dwindles to nothing.

The moon's gray glow reflects a wound of hair and bone. Crimson liquid pours onto the ground. Cain's nausea swells in an angry torrent.

Then the Earth shrieks.

Visions fill his mind— the brutish countenance of nearby cattle, his brother's cackling laugh, his mother's angry face.

—His orchards brown and untended.

—His land defiled with bloody sacrifice.

—His world consumed by fire, tinted with crimson, consumed by an angry God.

Hands clamp over ears as tears squeeze through tightened eyelids. Hot vomit pours as legs kick aghast at the soil's agonized shriek.

The noise rises, becomes a furious avalanche, smashes every pore, abides in every cell, builds to a terrible crescendo. Visions flash— crimson fields; blood-drenched flowers; wilted trees; lifeless soil; animals roaming his grave; hands consumed in fire.

And always in the background, God's angry face.

Terror grows as amber flames dance, leap toward him, threaten to engulf. Demonic specters fill the orchard, looming, grinning. Their dappled faces form a canopy of horror—sly smiles hint dark secrets, twisted faces smolder with the haunted stare of those who have seen.

Cain writhes in the maelstrom, a whirling cesspool of terror and agony, and blood and earth. Vomit squeezes between his lips, through his nostrils, stealing breath, overcoming protest.

Cain wakes with a start and staggers to his feet. His brother lays motionless by the burnt-down fire. The implement's handle, blood-streaked and erect, juts from his skull.

The first rays of sunlight peer over the horizon. The trees, so ominous a few hours ago, take on the serenity of innocent watchers and silent judges.

Racing to his brother, he grips the implement's handle and twists.

Abel's head contorts in an odd way, but the tool doesn't budge. Cain pulls hard, shakes the handle. Chestnut eyes gaze with lifeless pity as the skull emits a muffled sound like a cracked nut.

The tool remains imbedded.

Panic tears his mind. He places a foot on Abel's head then pulls with all his strength. His arms, like pistons, jerking the tool in frantic spasms. Abel's head bucks, sends small, dirty plumes into the mists of dawn.

Sweat runs down Cain's dirt-caked face to mix with his tears.

Panic's claws dig deep, latch with barbs like fishhooks. He grinds Abel's head in the ground with his foot, then pulls with all his energy —a desperate effort to free the tool.

A final crack sends a spray of blood into the air. Each drop reflects his horrified image as they rise, arc, then fall to the Earth.

Cain drops to his knees, ears covered, awaiting the Earth's wail.

But no sound comes. Only a gentle wind and fragrant morning air.

He drops his hands, leans back on his haunches. The breeze feels good as he takes a deep breath and closes his eyes.

The sun nurtures, his thoughts begin to calm.

He extends a shaky hand, closes Abel's eyes, notices his own hands are covered and stained. He stares, hypnotized by maroon splotches.

For hours he can only sit and weep, staring at his brother's lifeless body. He remembers days spent in the fields. Days spent resting and talking until the Sun settled across the great valley. Days without care for the Earth had blessed them and they knew only joy.

Now, he's forever alone.

A dark bird floats across the sky, drifts lazy among sparse clouds. Cain watches it approach, then land beside his brother's body.

A large raven, black as his pain, hopping around the campsite, head twitching.

Then it scratches at the ground.

The creature toils, pecks the dirt, hops about on dark, thin legs as if admiring the efforts of its labors. This continues until a small hole appears, then, leaping from the dugout with a quick flutter, the raven retrieves something. Cain leans forward, squints through the murky shadows that cloud his mind.

The raven holds a blood-spattered stone. Two quick hops follow, and it drops the stone in the hole.

Black wings reflect the day as Abel's hair had cried to the night. The bird flutters, prances above the hole, dances with merriment at its own task. As Cain looks, he notices the motions aren't just joyous, but meaningful. The thought no sooner enters his mind when, with a final head twitch, the raven leaps into the sky and flies away.

Cain's thoughts crystallize. He leaps to his feet and grabs the tiller.

He strikes a furrow in the earth, then another, and still another, until the furrow becomes a hole, and the hole becomes a grave.

Chapter 44

Jerusalem, Israel

The assembled throng, about five thousand, goes quiet as Drake takes them in. Expectant faces turn upwards. The sheep mewing and jostling, knowing only their next urge, wanting a shepherd to lead them. Drake scans the crowd as a flash of something crosses his face. Something akin to recognition, followed by confusion, then instantly replaced by unshakeable confidence.

I try to see what the gloved man sees. Drake lifts his hands over his head and the crowd erupts. Then I see him, John the Apostle, standing deep in the crowd, barely noticeable. Could Drake have seen him? Does the emerald aura of which he speaks glow bright enough that Drake would've noticed?

Odd, I think, *he's left the Vatican to hear Drake's speech.*

Drake repositions the mic and begins.

"A common thread runs among us." At this single line, the crowd goes quiet and focuses all attention to the Dove.

Drake starts again but is interrupted, suddenly, surprisingly, by piercing shouts toward the back of the gathered crowd. I crane to see the source of the interruption, and when it comes into view, I'm a little stunned. A crowd, perhaps two hundred yards away, behind the crowd whom Drake now addresses.

This second crowd holds homemade signs. They chant slogans, demand retribution for some slight of which I'm unaware. It's clear, however, they wish to disrupt these proceedings, shouting insults into the day and pressing tight against the surrounding barricades.

Upraised fists pound the air as the tumult rises in pitch and fervor. I wonder if Drake's gifts have failed him, marvel that there's any group that escaped his lilting words and promises.

A single bottle lofts from them to arc over the barricade. It sprays glass in all directions.

Those closest scatter. The ripple effect spreads through the mass and splinters them. It looks like a human star bursting to panicked shards.

More bottles fly as people move in every direction. Then other projectiles, objects of stone and wood, and soon the air is filled with thrown debris.

The closest crowd panics, jostling, stumbling, frantic for shelter.

A man approaches from Drake's left. It's Stuart, the big African, Longinus's top choice for Drake's security detail. People scatter as he moves, almost as big as the Roman himself, hulking, bald, moving with powerful confidence.

He takes Drake's arm. "We should go."

Drake doesn't move, watching as people dodge hurled objects and search for safety.

The barricades are being overrun, a riot starting. Protestors stream toward the crowd as those closest flee in terror.

Drake pops the wireless mic from its holder on the podium. "Keep the PA system on," he says, shoving his speech at Stuart.

Stuart moves for the control panel as Drake zips by me and the herd of stunned reporters. I follow, think he's heading for his limo, which I intend to occupy as we get out of here.

But Drake has other plans, moving with a fluidity more athletic than his perceived, current age. He grabs a folding chair made of gray metal, then wades into the panicked fray.

I race after, pushing my way through the crazed mass. "We should go," I say. "Now."

His eyes hold a peculiar focus. "You go," he says, then rushes on without another word.

The riot grows. Those seeking peace have moved to the exits, wrestling with each other to get through the narrow gap. Fist fights break out and the angered mob hurls whatever objects come to hand. A man falls. A woman races past, blood running from a gash on her forehead.

The protestors are winning, getting close to the stage Drake just deserted.

Sirens wail in the distance as I look for any sort of police or military presence.

Drake dodges some blows, ducks a hammer that flies through the air missing his face by an inch. Another man approaches, levels a fist that Drake easily sidesteps.

I wonder why he doesn't subdue the man. I know how easily he can best whomever attempts assault.

I have a thought just then. A notion I know is true. Drake knows the press is heavily represented here today. It's hard to be seen as a peacemaker when you kick some poor protestor's ass up around his ears. He knows the press films everything. No, it won't serve his purpose to subdue anyone. Drake's ends can only be preserved through diplomacy, and he knows that better than anyone.

He moves into the panicked herd, places the chair with a clang and steps atop it.

Those closest to him stop, stunned by the Dove's appearance.

Drake holds the mic to his mouth, then stands rigid as a statue.

I move close, ready to intercept any who have a notion to harm him. It's like something else moves me. I can't imagine from where this protective instinct has sprung.

The rest of the crowd sense a change in the riot's flow and slow their motions. Some hold bottles, others hold their own countrymen by the shirtfront, fists leveled at cringing faces.

Drake waits moments longer, a true master of this medium, letting tension build, riding anticipation.

The single word he speaks echoes off the surrounding structures and rolls over the crowd at high volume.

"Why?"

The crowd becomes silent, glancing around for the speaker as the word bounds into the distance.

He has their attention, standing among them atop the chair.

I look for police, hear the sirens close but not close enough. I stand tall, ready for a fight I don't want and definitely won't win.

There's no way this pause lasts. No way this riot doesn't explode in the next few seconds.

Only Abel's gifts can save us. I swallow hard, look up at the gloved man.

"Why do you bloody the face of your brothers?" he asks, his voice just above a whisper.

"Why do you offer hatred instead of a warm embrace?"

Each word echoes, gains a life of its own. I look around, fists clenched, ready to try my hand at pugilism instead of journalism. The faces before me are hypnotized, standing like sheep, waiting on the Dove's next words.

"Today is a day of joy," he says.

"Today is the day that *you* people join hands with the *world*." He pauses, extends a hand to those closest to him. "Today, is *the day* that we abandon differences and embrace what is common." His voice drips with emotion, pleads, an altar call by a seasoned evangelist.

"Today we realize God is big enough for *all* of us and that today." Another pause. "He's living within us all." He scans the crowd.

They return his gaze with wide eyes and solemn faces.

"Today!" His voice rings across Jerusalem's face, we all startle at the sudden volume change.

"Today! We stop this nonsense!"

"Today!" he shouts, looking across the crowd. "We stop this killing!" Another pause.

"And violence!" A few voices rise in support.

"And destruction!

"Scars on God's very face. Scars that define us, *all of us*, as savages!" He sweeps an arm across the crowd, more voices join in support.

"Today! We, the human race, do not embrace because we are the same! We embrace because we are different!" Voices gain kin as the crowd starts to stir. It's like watching wind through tall grass. People drop their projectiles, turn his direction. I see some smiles, even a few expressions of serenity.

Drake picks up the pace.

"Today we *are* bigger than ourselves!" He watches them. "Yes!"

"Today we realize our differences make us strong!" His head bobs as he speaks, his voice rapturous, hypnotic, comforting, wise.

"Today we confront our struggles as one people!" With each sentence comes a dusting of cheers.

"And overcome them!" More cheers as people step close.

"Today we affirm that which ties us together in fate and destiny!"

"Today!" The word cascades over ancient stone and modern steel. "We embrace what God commands: to *love*, to *tolerate*, to *embrace*, to *rejoice*!"

The words flow like honey from a tapped hive.

"Today! We choose *our families* over ideology!

"Today! We choose *our countrymen* over dogma!

"Today! We find *shared blood* is stronger than spilled blood!

"Today! We accept God's promise of peace!"

More step forward, now feet from Drake.

"Today! We perform God's work—different people with a common purpose!"

The tension is thick, but the mass is his. The place hums with invisible energy, something subtle yet powerful, something palpable like a vibrant, living pulse.

His voice softens as his eyes move over them.

His whisper cracks with emotion.

"Today, *I beg you*, embrace your destiny. Today, be loyal to the many faces of our shared God."

He pauses again, holds the eyes of those he can see.

"Today, *I beg you*, embrace."

The silence is complete, the mass open-mouthed and awed.

Drake lowers the mic, stands regal atop a gray, metal throne.

Seconds pass as people process his words.

Then an old man steps forward.

TV cameras hum as the elder extends his hand to a fallen, younger man and helps him to his feet.

Then two young men approach a woman lying on the ground, the same woman with the bleeding forehead. They lift her as broad smiles fill their young faces.

The feeling spreads like falling rain.

Bottles and stones are discarded.

People begin to embrace.

Voices rise as those gathered start to speak, then to sing.

I'm the definition of awed.

Drake's gifts have prevailed, have calmed the savages and brought these people together. Truly, Abel's gifts are powerful.

Drake watches from atop the chair, perfect smile gleaming in sunshine, welcoming, comforting, assuring.

Thousands greet and embrace.

Cameras televise the scene throughout the world, and I notice Drake is careful not to look at them. Makes total sense because he can't afford the appearance of showmanship. It's vital to his aims that the media spread these scenes across the planet.

The mass abandons their violence, becomes the definition of kindness and compassion. Singing, dancing, lifting their voices together as Drake watches.

He's their king; they just don't know it.

Drake steps from the chair and offers his smile. I stare back, completely awed, a tumult of questions racing through my mind.

A young man steps between us. Dark with pleasant features, he smiles at Drake.

"Mr. Drake," the young man says, "you are very persuasive."

Stuart yells. I turn, see the big African split the crowd with his speed and size.

His face is harried. A gun appears in his right hand.

He stops, levels to fire.

I turn to Drake, see the young man holds a fat, silver revolver.

I notice his pin, two horsemen in tandem. The symbol of the Templars.

The hammer draws.

The cylinder turns by millimeters.

I yell, lunge for Drake.

There's no time.

The gun fires into his forehead.

CHAPTER 45

JERUSALEM, ISRAEL

"What have you done!" I shout into the Templar's face. "Some fucking Apostle, man. Jesus Christ—"

John holds up a finger. A warning not to use God's name as a curse.

"Really?" I say, "How about this?" I extend my middle finger the cool-guy way, with all my other fingers bent at the middle knuckle. I waggle it in his face. "You smug fuck. I thought you were all about holiness and Jesus and the lasting platitudes of the Sermon on the Mount. For Christ's sake, you just blew the guy's head wide open, live on international television. I mean... If you ever... Didn't you think about..." I'm flummoxed, stammering like an idiot, spitting my curses into the air for no one and everyone. I feel bad, talking to them like this, but can't help it. It's not so much I'm angry at them for shooting Drake, but more that I'm angry at them for stealing my opportunity. I'm angry I hadn't pulled the trigger myself. I'm angry at the loss of Rhyme, at the loss of our child, at my stinking life and this whole festering world.

I feel a hand on my shoulder, spin to see Igneus. His face strains over high cheek bones. He's never much liked confrontation or violence, but this seems to be weighing on him in particular.

"What?" I shout, jerking from his grasp. "What is it you're going to say that will calm me down? That you've seen much worse? That your centuries have shown you how to live with such savages? We may as well all go back to the stone age." I pace across the room and kick the garbage can with a clatter. Igneus jumps, John remains expressionless.

"Answer me, assholes, why on Earth was I dragged into all of this and what do I do now? Immortals? Hello? Can you explain it to me?"

My answer is their silence. Igneus raises a glass of liquor to his lips. John looks at his fingernails.

"So, I just crawl back into the sewer I crawled out of? Is that it? Slide back to the gutter, get piss drunk, nibble on a pistol?"

"Your money is secure." Igneus's words freeze me in place.

"Wh…What? My money? Are you fucking kidding?" The thought does nothing to relieve my anger. "Blatant murder!" I yell.

I wheel on John. "Didn't you say, 'I don't kill'? Didn't those words come out of your mouth? What was that? You're a goddamn Apostle of Christ and you sanctioned a hit? Care to explain that to me?"

John looks up from his hands. His face is—dare I say?—relaxed.

"It isn't murder. You know Drake can't die."

"Of course, I do. Then why kill him? What does that do to advance anyone's cause? He was on the verge of peace in the Middle East. Do you realize?" Then I laugh. Of all the people in the world, the two men in front of me realize more than anyone the impossibilities regarding peace in that region.

"He was going to eradicate the Jews," John says. "The Dove is a hawk. When I spoke to His Holiness, he granted me authority to handle it as I saw fit. I considered the alternatives and it seemed killing the persona, the Dove, would at least end all of his nonsense and set him back considerably. Now he'll have to lay low for a generation or two, re-emerge, possibly change his appearance and start anew with his plans to fulfill the prophecies. In the meantime, we—" he waves a hand around the room as if twenty people are here with us— "shall undo his other plans. We can alert the Israeli PM of the state of affairs and the truth of Cain. We can assure no Jews are called to Israel. Igneus has agreed to try and undo the one world currency. We will inflame tensions between Arab and Jew and nurture their hatred such that the Temple can never be rebuilt. Don't you see, Drake is alive somewhere, but his mission is hamstrung. All he can do now is go and crawl under a rock somewhere and regroup."

My mouth hangs open. I know it, can feel my tongue drying in the desert air. My lips feel tight and cracked. I pace to the bar and pour a glass of scotch whisky to the brim. It tastes good, its spirit matching my anger. Its burn matching my flame.

I'm out of things to say. At my rope's end, yet I don't know why. Had I been rooting for Drake all along and just playing at the concerned humanitarian bit? I do care about the man, even holding no malice against him for the events I've seen and can't unsee. It's as if he's become a valued mentor, opening my eyes to the wider realities all around me. Not to mention that he is, well, Cain. *The* Cain. Older than anyone on Earth. Did I feel a special privilege being part of his posse? Had he given me hope and vigor once more? I know the answer, and it's a resounding yes. The gloved man saved me, brought me into a special world. I realize my anger isn't so much for him being killed, but at my separation from him. The life he'd shown me, the plans he'd fulfilled, the way he moves and talks and ruminates and *lives*. Just not some guy you meet at a bowling alley. This was *the Man*, freed of time's constraints yet still striving to fulfill his destiny.

I move for the door, then stop and return to the bar where I collect the bottle of scotch. I consider apologizing but dismiss it. "Fuck you all and have a good life," I say.

I storm from the room into the thick air and stone streets of the Via Dolorosa.

CHAPTER 46

JERUSALEM, ISRAEL

The cell is small and smells of shit. My head aches, and my stomach threatens to empty its contents, mostly booze, onto the damp floor. I don't open my eyes. To what purpose? To see how far I've come? To fully bear witness to the place I now occupy with its beggars and thieves? My clothes are soiled with blood and vomit and each breath I take tastes like a morsel of bad fish. *Wouldn't Rhyme be proud?*

I remember being robbed, although it's pretty hazy. Remember some man speaking in some other language and then being struck from behind by a different, unseen criminal. It was over before I knew it because I was too drunk to put up much of a fight. *All the better*, I think. Had I fought they might've killed me. Of course, soaked with alcohol and freshly bonked on the head will go a long way to putting someone out of their right mind. What happened next, I don't remember, but when I'm booked into this shabby little dungeon, they advise me, in rough English, that I've resisted arrest and have, allegedly—they used that word a lot—allegedly, broken some poor police officer's nose.

They have me empty my pockets, which is easy because the thieves have already done that. I try to tell one of the guards the thieves are probably at my hotel right now stealing what little I have left. It's no use though. He doesn't understand English and I don't speak his language—Hebrew perhaps.

They strip me down and walk me into a room where, I think, they offer apologies and then another cop appears, a thick bandage over his nose. I try to explain, to apologize, but only say about two words before he clocks me square in the face.

To repay his kindness I vomit on his shoes. Which, by the way, they did not—none of them—care for.

There's a noise behind me but I'm too sick to move. They're probably coming to get one of the others anyway. I realize my journey is complete. I'm finally and officially a lowlife; too full of shit to be believed, too filthy to be credible. I've done it at long last and congratulate myself even as my bowels try to let loose. It turns out drinking oneself blind and then getting the shit kicked out of you is bad for the gastrointestinal system.

I can see only out of my right eye and can breathe only out of my left nostril. *Keeping it balanced*, I think, *big day for me.*

I press my face to the cool dampness of the stone floor. I've always been amazed how drunks will slap their face against any object—toilets, floors, bathroom stalls, urinals—to bask in the coldness it provides. I remember when I'd thought myself better than everyone I met; now I'm the worst of them, soaked in my own blood and piss, head pressed against a filthy, sticky floor. *Oh, how the mighty have fallen.*

And what now? Drake's gone to somewhere and even if he feels like finding me, I'm certain he'll reconsider when he sees just how far off the wagon this tomato has bounced.

I lean on my elbows and wretch.

I remember John saying, *The beatings will continue until morale improves.* Well, my morale is nowhere in sight, having run off with my dignity to Tahiti or some such place, leaving me alone with the herculean effort of trying not to shit myself.

The cell door clangs open, and the criminals who sit around me stop talking. Then I'm lifted in the air and carried out of the room.

"The beatings will continue until your moral improves!" I bellow. Then I hear it.

"Shud'up lad."

It's Longinus, the big Roman, my pal. I'm draped over his shoulder as he carries me down the corridor.

"I might vomit," I say. "Don't want to ruin your suit."

In response, he hefts me none-to-gently to the other shoulder. I wretch but manage to keep it down.

"Aye. Shud'up."

CHAPTER 47

JERUSALEM, ISRAEL

Thaddeus Drake is dead. *The Dove* is no more.

I catch my reflection in the glass of the morgue entrance; I look like an early check-in. The front desk attendant trades looks between us, and I imagine we make quite the pair. The big Roman hulks over the desk, doing his best, which is considerable, to intimidate the young man.

As for me, well, my nose is bruised from the right hook I suffered at the hands of the police officer. My clothes are torn, filthy. Black shiners shade my eyes like a pro baseball player early for the next game.

I waiver in place, fight nausea. The young man seems to feel the wave I ride. Repulsion and self-preservation battle for dominance in his expression. The ride on Longinus's shoulder was as pleasant as he was gentle, and I think I'd probably feel better if Longinus just checks me in, then stuffs me in a drawer to wait for the end.

I clutch a plastic water bottle. My dearest friend at this point, providing lukewarm hydration to better facilitate heaving. The fury of alcoholism kids. Avoid it if you can.

Despite Longinus's hulking countenance and bad attitude, the young man is cordial and polite, telling the Roman:

"The body of Thaddeus Drake can't be released. The autopsy hasn't been performed."

In the time it takes me to close my eyes and shake my head, the few seconds I need to battle the hot bile in my throat, Longinus has him by the shirt front and hauls him over the desk.

This motivates the lad to be a bit more cordial, and within seconds we're walking through a *Clockwork Orange* corridor checkered in green and white tiles. I keep my gaze on the floor. It's hard enough to maintain the erectness of my species without the lime green squares and cruddy grout spinning in an array before me.

Longinus leans in, whispers something to the man. "Ye get me?"

A bead of sweat runs down the youth's forehead. Fingering a green clip-on tie, he mutters his willingness to comply.

I can probably guess what the brute told him, but my mind isn't ready for such hijinks.

Longinus grasps my arm and propels me into a large room lined with silver cupboards. The steel is bright but better than the hallway's tiles, so I move in and protest my treatment in grunts and heaves.

"Aye. Shud'up," he says. "We need be gettin' the man, then beatin' feet."

The words take a second to process. "Why?" I ask, leaning my forehead against the cold steel of the temporary tombs.

"They do non exactly be giv'n up the dead to jus' any who enter,' he says. "Ye best be lookin'."

I'm sure these things have a better name than cupboards, but suffice it to say, there are about thirty set on each side in three rows of ten. The challenge here will be finding Drake's body.

"Let me guess," I say. "I get to do the honors."

Longinus smiles, eyes twinkling. "Aye."

I take a deep breath, steel my mind and stomach for the things I'm about to witness.

And then, as if angels have heard the prayers of my poor soul and ravaged body, I hear the noise.

A mild thumping at first, complete with muffled screams. I'm reminded of a Hollywood horror movie that takes place in a morgue and think for a second we've entered Hell's Funhouse.

Longinus perks up, steps close to the long line of cupboards. He holds his ear close, motions for me to do the same on the room's other side.

"I thin' ye did it," he says.

"Did what?"

"Shush," he says, "listen."

I wonder what I did to make the Roman treat me so today. Perhaps he hates a sloppy drunk. At least I didn't puke on him. In my estimation, he owes me some small courtesy just for keeping my stomach under control. In fact, he owes me a Fig Newton and a juice box.

I follow the muffled sounds like a gong in a pillow. The voice rises, although I can't understand what it's saying.

Then I'm close, can actually see the edges of the cupboard shake with the protests of the man inside.

Longinus appears beside me, wraps a big hand around the mirror of the door's handle. His image is curved and distorted in the metal as he throws the door open and slides the drawer out.

Drake's eyes are wide, panicked even. I take a frightened step back.

He leaps from the drawer, blood raining like a fine mist. Dandy hues of red splatter my already filthy duds.

One eye regards us cautiously.

The other points straight at the sky.

The middle of his head is missing. A giant U scooped from the space that used to be his forehead. It appears moist as I look at it, through it, see my own astonished reflection in the steel cupboard behind him.

"Are ye tryin' to wake the dead?" Longinus grins, somehow enjoys this.

Cain looks confused as he stares at me with his googly eye.

"I bet ye have a *splittin'* headache," Longinus says, still grinning.

Cain moves to a closed cupboard, peers at his own reflection. He moves a hand through the furrow in his head, stares as his brain mingles with what's left of his skull.

My legs go weak. My head swims, mouth suddenly parched. My stomach heaves and I find myself wrestling my old pal nausea.

I start to fall when a big hairy arm wraps around me and pulls me upright. I glance to Cain, see his good eye focused someplace far away. The lopsided U that is his head starts to sway and I hear Longinus say, "Oops," as Cain stumbles, then loses his footing in a shower of his own blood.

A hairy arm catches him, as well.

And that's us, the members of this secret society, one of our heads half gone, two of us waging war on Newtonian forces.

Longinus hefts me and I stumble across the room to grasp the handle of another drawer. I hold it for all I'm worth, try to avoid accidentally opening it to another horror show. Whatever's in there might be the final tipping point in my battle to stay upright and conscious.

"It's okay, lad," Longinus says. "Ye'll be fine." He speaks to Cain, his expression caring, loving even, fatherly. "Ye'll be fine, lad. Take a tick or two, then see what's anon and agin."

Cain pushes the arm away, forces himself upright. "I know that!" he yells, then starts for the exit. He's a sci-fi super monster at this point. Butt-naked with a googly eye, toe tag tied to his right foot. I'm amazed at the transformation, amazed he shook off the trauma so fast and is able to go on. How does his body even work with half his mind missing? Aren't there connections and such, nerves that need to operate in order to move and think and talk?

Cain storms across the room, bare ass flapping in the breeze, mirrored a hundred times by surrounding cupboards.

Longinus clears his throat, and Cain stops mid-stride.

The Roman offers a change of clothes, his face wears the same grin.

Cain snatches them like a cobra, then dresses while trying to avoid the relentless shower of blood.

This affects me too much and I rush to the end of the cupboards and empty my stomach near the wall.

"Come on!" Cain yells.

I push off the wall, manage to stay upright. My hangover is in full force, my nose fat and swollen, my stomach tight and rebellious, my clothes stained with blood, jail dirt and whatever I last ate. I notice my reflection, a wayward raccoon with a human face. I enter full-blown, feel-sorry-for-myself mode.

Longinus clears his throat again, a deep, snorting sound.

Cain is angry now, anxious to be gone. "What!"

The Roman offers a knit cap in black wool. "In case ye ears be gettin' cold," he says, a grin etched on his face.

Cain's expression is blank, as if it takes him a second to process words.

"Ye need be coverin' the bleedin' crevice through ye skull."

Cain snatches the cap, and we all turn to the door.

Just then the attendant returns, sees Cain, glances at us, goes pale, then drops in a dead faint.

I chuckle, shake my head. "Pussy."

CHAPTER 48

JERUSALEM, ISRAEL

Six weeks later, tens of thousands gather at the Temple to watch the final brick drop in place. As it drops, a roar rises from the mass. People of all races, all religions, embrace.

Loudspeakers blare The Police's, "One World (Not Three)." They dance to the hammering drumbeat. Some laugh, some cry, but all move.

The young leap, cry out, twirl and spin. The old clap their hands and tap their feet.

Children run through the throng, chasing, tagging, stopping only to try and dance like the grown-ups around them.

Cain looks in disbelief.

"What do ye thin'?" Longinus fingers the remote, a broad smile on his clean features.

"I think the Apostle made an error," Cain says, fingers the giant scab that's now his scalp. "Being shot was the best thing that could've happened for us."

Longinus moves to the bar and fills a glass with ice. He pours Macallan until the glass is full, then two more and brings them to Cain and me.

The Roman downs the liquid in a gulp, exhales with a snort. "Aye, that's good."

"What else?" Cain asks.

"The lad who shot ye was a Templar. It seems the Apostle has a thorn in his arse."

"Ahh," Cain says.

"By martyring ye, the Apostle lit an international movement. I could non believe it meself. Peace was *demanded*, ye death, a world symbol for tolerance."

"Amazing."

"Aye, amazin'." I say, doing my best Longinus impression. "The first stones were laid within a few days of your assassination."

"X'chasei members posin' as UN peacekeepers kept order," Longinus says. "I do non recall ever seein' such unity between nations. Israel had non choice but to act. The Rabbi counsel lifted the ban on Jews visitin' the Temple Mount, and Khalifa was the lad who assured support from Mid-East nations, the PLO, the Muslim Brotherhood, and Hamas."

Cain rubs his mark which glows a barely perceptible red. His gloves rest on the table beside him.

"Anon and agin, the buggers still be tryin' the usual suicide bombin's and a few riots, but after those were...*snuffed*...things became as calm as a sleepy whore, if ye be catchin' me drift." Cain downs his drink in a swallow. "It's amazin' what can be bought when jabbed with the right stick."

"The planet thinks you're dead," I say.

"That solves a problem," Cain says.

"Aye, ye be a martyr. Saint Drake."

Cain's laugh is foreign after so long. I hate how it makes me feel good.

Longinus retrieves the remote and points it at the wide LCD screen.

We watch endless news briefs. Since his death, Drake has become a media darling. Hailed as the greatest man since Dr. Martin Luther King, his image fills the screen again and again as Longinus changes channels. Reports speak of Drake's legacy and how history will remember him as the world's unifier. Media clips of his last speech play on a loop. I feel the presence of Abel's gifts even as I watch. It seems they're no less effective on video.

"It's been weeks, and this be still playin'." Longinus refills his own glass. "They also can non figure how the Templar lad burst into flame. They'be sayin' he had a bomb malfunction."

Cain rises, looks stronger than he did even this morning. "This speeds up the timeline in a wonderful way," he says. "Our time has come. Longinus, call a meeting of X'chasei."

Longinus looks surprised. "What fer?"

Cain raises his glass. "For the final stroke, my friends—our meeting with God. Call Igneus and tell him to meet us, we'll go there directly."

"What of the Apostle?" Longinus asks. "I be fit for tunin' his pipes, if ye have a mind."

"Nonsense," Cain waves a hand. "When the time comes, I'll take care of that pest myself. Currently, we have more important things to accomplish."

Longinus nods, "Aye. I'll be seein' to it then."

CHAPTER 49

JERUSALEM, ISRAEL

We sit around a long table as ancient stone drips candlelight. Longinus's chair strains at his huge frame. His sword is by his side and his fingers tap the pommel.

By contrast, the chair in which Igneus sits threatens to consume him. Frail wrists jut from expensive suit-sleeves and lead to fragile, matchstick fingers. He looks at Cain without expression.

Cain speaks. "How's the Apostle?"

Igneus squirms like a fish on a hook. "He's well. He's interested in what you're up to, but I suspect you already know that."

"You two have become fast friends. I do hope you're not angry with me when I attend to him. He ordered my execution, and that's something I can't abide." He massages one gloved hand with the other. "Bad manners, that. I'll have to repay him in kind."

He casts a glance at Igneus, who's stopped squirming but won't look him in the eye.

"Are you still with us, my dear friend?"

A few moments pass before Igneus nods. "I am."

Longinus leans forward, props his huge arms on the table. The Labarum glows from the surrounding light and reflects lines and swirls onto his face. "Our time is at hand. Eh, little one?" He leans forward more, looms over the table. "Do non fuck it up." Igneus opens his mouth but is interrupted by Cain.

"My friends, the time has come for us to reveal our true power and to leave this world and this miserable, endless life."

A large smile crosses Longinus's face.

Igneus's takes on the frozen image of fear.

"I've spent centuries preparing for this," Cain says. "Now we confront God."

He lights a Treasurer and continues. "Since God prefers blood, let's give it to Him. We'll use the Earth as our bargaining chip and see if He truly cares about His flock." He turns to Longinus. "Is the heifer ready?"

The Roman clenches his fists like grabbing a prize. "Aye."

Cain glances at the smoke curling from the cigarette's glowing eye. He speaks in a soft voice. "At last, I've fulfilled the prophecy. I've used you, my friends, to help me do this. Israel has been returned to its rightful heirs. One currency has been established throughout the entire world, the Temple has been rebuilt on its original spot, the world is at peace and the red heifer is ready."

He leans on the table, looks at each of us in turn. "Tonight, I'll cleanse myself in the heifer's ashes and finally…" He presses his fist to the table. "*Finally*, I will enter the Temple, where I'll stand in the face of God and embrace my destiny. Are you ready to finish the journey? Will you trust me once more? Travel with me a little farther? We hold the world in our palms and can crush it at will. God can't remain silent. He has no choice but to notice us."

I realize Cain's plan for genocide has as much to do with tempting God as it does for baiting the Muslims. The Jews, God's chosen people —what better way to get God's attention?

Igneus's chair scuttles back. "Wait!" He stands. "We can't!" He stammers some incomprehensible syllables, then his eyes widen over a tremulous mouth: "We— *we must vote!*"

His squeaky voice bounces off the chamber walls, eyes dart between Cain and Longinus.

Longinus crosses his arms over his chest. His next words surprise me. "Aye, we must."

Cain and Igneus stare dumbfounded at the Roman.

"In the ancient way, with the candles."

He's not joking. In fact, his face turns grim in the gloom of the candlelight as it laps at the walls and makes our faces appear sinister.

Cain breaks the pause. "Very well, let us vote." He strikes a match and lights the candle in front of him. "I vote yes."

Igneus scrambles for his own candle, frail arms fly as he slaps it from the table. It rockets past me to shatter on ancient stone.

"I vote no!" he exclaims, eyes wide, lips stretched and white.

The Roman strokes the pommel of his sword, looks far away. I wonder if he's considering the implications of his vote or just lost in some drug-induced fog.

Candlelight burns across his features as he tickles his blade.

He turns his candle upright and holds a match in his fist, focused on the phosphorous tip. The match sparks to life with a flick of his thumb, an orange flame sways on its tip. Longinus stares into it, appears unafraid.

Igneus leans close as if contemplating a desperate attempt to blow it out.

Cain draws on his cigarette.

Longinus stares at the Jew. A scowl turns his face a maze of shadows.

"I'been happy bein' a wolf among these sheep," he says, then looks directly at Igneus. "I cast me vote only hopin' to be rid of ye."

He lowers the match and the candle sparks to life. Longinus smiles, perfect teeth within thick lips.

Igneus lets out a groan and falls to his knees.

I hear a cry. All eyes fly to Cain.

Smoke pours from his right hand in clotted, black clouds. His glove disappears in a burst of flame. He leaps from his seat, whipping his hand back and forth, desperate to quench the fire.

Longinus grabs his sword.

Igneus cowers behind the table.

I slide from my seat, move as far away from Drake as possible.

Cain's eyes water, his teeth clench. Muscles strain as he leaps around the room, flaps his hand as flames grow high and smoke clots the air.

He stops suddenly, holds his hand before him, astonishment on his face.

The mark throbs in blinding red neon. The smoke thickens to blood hues and bathes us in its fog.

I shield my eyes.

The pulsing redness grows like a newborn star.

Cain looks cowed. He hasn't expected this. His pain seems to recede, but the light remains, overwhelming in its brightness, shocking in its intensity.

Icy claws of terror grip my heart. My knees shake beyond my control. This mark, this brand, this symbol of the forsaken, is total in its chaos. It is pure evil, pestilence, hopelessness. The totality of abandonment. An absolute separation from goodness. Something ethereal yet all powerful. I realize I can't escape. As the light washes over me, consumes me, I realize I'm outmatched, that there's no power as wicked, no thought as impure, no longing so bereft. I'm abandoned. Awash in the absence of hope, swirling, pulled into its depths, helpless. I try to stand but can't. Try to scream but remain silent. I collapse, shielding my eyes, tears streaming down my cheeks, head filled with terrible visions.

CHAPTER 50

JERUSALEM, ISRAEL

onsciousness fades as I struggle to stand, to flee the room, the mark, the terror. Igneus cowers, trembling fingers white as they grip the table's rough edge. He peers over the table, filled with terror, as if his soul is beset by purest evil. Tears stream down his face.

The room is drenched deep red, turning the gray stone a bristling maroon. The mark's beams permeate everything.

Cain's face takes on a demonic quality. His head has healed completely; his dark hair washes blood red, eyebrows draw to a wide, abrupt triangle. Bloodstained fangs appear in his mouth, and Igneus stares as if his nightmares have come without the benefit of sleep's shroud.

I'm crumpled at the base of the wall near the door, catatonic, paralyzed. Petrified.

Longinus sits shadowed on the table's opposite side, huge muscles bulging, dark lines tracing the raging redness that flows over him.

Igneus struggles, manages to move somewhat, turns to stare at the mark, as if confronting it will allay his terror. I watch as it beckons. Watch it take the Jew in a trance and draw him into its recesses. His eyes go dark, his face becomes serene. He's somewhere far off, his soul circling within the mark, speeding, spinning, a dizzying ride on some new-fangled contraption.

"Igneus," I manage the word, fight to stay conscious. He doesn't hear, is eons away, traveling in appended visions, floating within the mark's embrace, off to other places.

CHAPTER 51

JERUSALEM, DURING THE CRUCIFIXION

All strain for a better view, craning necks, on tiptoes, looking for the criminal. Igneus feels one with those assembled, watches with them, anxiety filling his heart as nausea creeps up his throat.

He's heard of the gruesome spectacle of the crucifixion, has never, until now, been to see one. This is to be his cleansing; a way to finally overcome that which his disposition lacks, a way to confront the fear that plagues him, making him not only small of stature, but small of heart.

Today he'll overcome. Today he'll find the courage other men possess: the courage to look upon this horrific act of justice and be unaffected. From this point forward, he'll master fear and thusly, himself.

When he first sees the Man, he turns away. The blood and putrescence of the body's inner workings hold no appeal for him. The Man labors up the hill. Blood pours down His face and across His chest, spittle dangles in strands from edematous lips. Strips of flesh gape on His torso, bleeding ribbons where the cat has scratched.

Goaded and prodded by the guard and various onlookers, He approaches, one shuffling step at a time. Igneus forces rebellious eyes open. He wants to flee, to be at his estate with its soft, fragrant breeze and among the distant sounds of forests and cattle.

He focuses on trembling legs, tries to overcome his horror as the criminal approaches.

The Man's face is a congealed clot of blood and bruise. His lips fat with inflammation. His cheeks purple and streaked maroon.

Pity rises. No man should endure such a fate, he thinks. His eyes snap shut, and he forces them open, chastises himself for his feelings.

To be like the others is to abandon pity.

He wonders what the Man has done. What atrocity He's performed to be punished so. He wonders if the Man Himself is remorseful. If He now thinks of those He's harmed. The Romans are brutal in their punishments, and this Man wears that brutality on his entire body.

He watches, struggles, realizes the Man stares back at him.

Their eyes meet. Igneus startles. Instead of remorse and agony, he sees love and compassion. Kind eyes take him in and hold him, search his soul, expose all the miniscule details of his life, then hold them out before the light.

In a vague way he moves. Somewhere outside himself he hears the protests of those he pushes past. In the distance, he feels hands grip and try to halt his progress.

He doubles his efforts, eyes fixed, struggling.

A voice comes calm and soothing. Speaks to him of mastery of will, of persistence and obedience, spurs him with a need to act, an all-encompassing purpose that courses through him like living breath.

He is strong, robust, confident. His frail shell stripped away, a courageous heart beating within his breast.

"You are not insignificant," the voice whispers.

"You are a tool of God."

Echoes fill his mind, visions of the man he dreams of being: a master of others, a leader, a hero.

Whispers intensify, overlap, coalesce into a strong wind that carries Igneus, fearless and proud, to heights he's never dreamed.

He feels himself lifted, soaring high above the Earth.

In the distance, far below his place atop the zephyr, his mouth moves. He hears the subtle rumble of his own voice.

The world sprawls below him; God waits above.

Then the zephyr disappears.

He falls, arms flailing, grasping, finding nothing.

He crashes onto the cobbled street, lands finally inside his own thoughts, inside his own body.

He blinks as he comes to himself, realizes he's face to face with the bloody criminal.

The Man's lacerated lips move, the effort causing blood to crawl anew through thick whiskers.

Igneus concentrates, knows he must hear.

"I shall rest, but you shall go on," the Messiah speaks.

Fear sizzles through his body awesome in its proportions.

His lips quiver as the Master looks upon him, kind eyes peering through purple sockets.

Fear rages, thickens, dense as a spring fog, chill as death.

Igneus tries to speak, to apologize, to beg redemption but his mouth won't move, his voice absent.

Panic embraces, holds him tight in its cold grasp, suffocates.

The Master's eyes command.

His legs gain life, burst into action. He runs, crazed, flees the bleeding Messiah as laughter and humiliation nip his heels and heart.

Bathed in raging red, Igneus goes numb with the realization.

Not condemned, but a worthy tool of almighty God.

Tears flow as evil surrounds him, as needles prick his skin and probe his body. His thoughts scream for movement, to desert this wretched place and those masters of its evil.

He forces his body to action, crawling at first, then rising strong and powerful to burst through the door and into Jerusalem's streets.

CHAPTER 52

JERUSALEM, ISRAEL

I feel it in the center of my chest, a scratch, like an abrasion in my esophagus. Like every swallow holds spiked bits of sand. It gnaws, interminable. Something's wrong. Since being bathed in the terrifying light of Cain's mark, this feeling has clung to me.

Perhaps it's conscience, I think. A feeling of doing the wrong thing, choosing the wrong side.

Cain stands regal as the Children of the Rocks perform their tasks.

The Temple's courtyard is awash in waning sunlight as the lead child steps forward. I recognize him, Sebastian, the boy with the penchant for fried chicken. He looks angelic, frocked in perfect white robes as he approaches the red heifer.

Cain is giddy, can't stop smiling. "This is the culmination of centuries of work, dear Emery. Today I'll be cleansed by the unblemished. Children selected and bred for this sole purpose." He motions at them, pauses to watch. "They fulfill their destiny, the one task for which they've been raised." The sun glitters from his teeth, makes his eyes bright and content. "There can be no greater calling."

I say nothing and swallow another mouthful of sand.

"Each child, bald from head to toe, has been trained in the exact performance of this ritual to the very letter of Moses' law."

The robes of these cherubs hang loose, glimmering and white.

"This is the Red Heifer, the perfect unblemished cow. Longinus took nearly a century to find it, and in the process, brought one-third of all the cows on the planet into X'chasei's possession."

The sun dips behind the Temple, a great halo appears over its sharp angles, every corner alight and brilliant.

"It's said the perfect calf is born only once every ten thousand years." He laughs, slaps me on the back. "Fortunately, I haven't had to wait quite that long. When this was born, it was examined on every level—microscopic, genetic, and visual. It can't possess even one bent hair or one hair of a different color." He speaks in awed tones, amazed such a thing can exist. "I employ a fleet of scientists, veterinarians, for the sole purpose of examining these cows." He exhales with feeling, looks to the sky, smile firmly in place.

"I've been encouraged many times over the years, but as the cows matured, flaws became apparent and I had to start the search again."

He comes back to himself here, takes in all that's happening before us. The Temple, huge, majestic, a singular jewel in Israel's tarnished crown. The Children, blessed, undefiled, moving about, performing their tasks, small hands in thick gloves, tiny forms in sparkling white linen.

"But now," he says, "*now* the Red Heifer of prophecy stands before a Temple rebuilt. A perfect specimen, another sign God wants me to take my rightful place."

Sebastian approaches with an iron box, aged and rusted. He kneels and places it on the ground, then from it produces an iron pot.

"The Kilal," Cain says, perfect teeth matching the Temple's brilliance. "What the Apostle wouldn't do to have this." He stops, smiles wider. "What *I* didn't do to have this. The age of miracles, dear Emery. An age of stupendous achievement if one has the will to pursue boldly."

The rounded bronze container glistens in the wavering sun, sits on a base held aloft by angel's wings. It's no bigger than a shoe box, and I wonder that something so small can be so important. Sebastian places it on the ground. Its lid has a ring on top as if made to hang from a pole. I see etchings but can't quite make out what they represent. A delicate hand, made thick by monstrous mittens, grasps the lid. Then Sebastian shakes the gloves off, reaches in to withdraw a handful of ash.

"The Temple can never be cleansed without this relic. All my plans would fail."

Sebastian walks about, sprinkling ash. Titanium boots click neatly with each footstep, as if he wears taps. He's meticulous, moving in ever-expanding circles to assure the altar site is completely covered.

He returns to the Kilal and waits, fingers clasped in front of him. Other children chant their prayers, some ancient language that I try to guess. Latin, Hebrew, Greek?

Three children lead the heifer into the altar's center. Sebastian strokes its nose as the cow lifts its head and absorbs the attention. The other children have removed their gloves as well and stand on either side stroking its perfect fur.

Sebastian feels down the side of the heifer's neck, probing, then pierces with the scalpel.

It starts, but quickly becomes docile as blood pours from a small incision. The Children continue their ministrations.

Sebastian dips his fingers in the stream of dark blood, then walks toward the Temple, his steps punctuated by that neat clicking sound.

I gulp, feel more sand, the gnaw in my chest relentless, rattling, scraping, impossible to ignore.

Sebastian snaps his arm down, splatters the heifer's blood on the Temple's wall. The child returns to the cow as hypnotic prayers float into the evening and cast us all in a sort of melancholy procrastination. He repeats the same act as before, to the Temple and back, until he's done it seven times.

He strokes the heifer's nose as blood continues to flow down a thick, perfect neck, splashing on the ground, over the children's shoes and robes.

As the sun dips ever lower, the Temple's brilliance starts to fade. Shadows appear in corner and clerestory as dark reflections stretch toward us.

The heifer waivers, then collapses.

After a few minutes, Sebastian confirms its death, then motions to a score of other children to finish the final stanza of their chanted ritual.

They approach, and I notice they've donned thick gloves that span to their elbows. Small arms struggle heavy wooden blocks, which they pile atop the dead heifer. Others approach, carry large cans of gasoline, some dragging the receptacles over the smooth stone.

They douse the heifer and the wood.

Sebastian, satisfied, motions them away. He bends and applies a lighter to the outermost corner of the altar.

The gas ignites, races greedy over the cobble to pounce on the feast of wood and beast.

Cain cackles, gives a little jump, punctuates his excitement with a single clap of his hands.

The heifer burns, its flames coating us in dark orange, chasing off the shadows that threaten to engulf the Temple. Smoke rises thick toward waning daylight as the flames crackle protest at their limited boundary.

Cain speaks, eyes focused on the altar. "Surely, this sort of spectacle would've caught the world's eye if we'd done it in public, but the area has been sealed and all air traffic diverted."

A fighter jet streaks overhead, its whine diminishing as it speeds toward the horizon. "X'chasei associates," he says. "Patrolling the sky with strict orders to destroy anything nearing the Temple. All anyone in the city will be able to see is some smoke in the air, and if that happens to arouse curiosity, X'chasei spokespeople stand ready to explain it away as a small fire. Certainly, nothing to worry about. By the time anyone knows the truth, it won't matter at all, I'll be God."

The sinister trappings of his gaze are not lost on me, and I wonder if I share the same features. Thick orange, flickering in shadow, darkening features that contrast with the brightness of his smile. Perhaps I'm a madman. Perhaps I've fully joined them, perhaps the symphony of blazing, flickering shadow serves as a sign that my journey has reached its conclusion.

I'm content with that. Without Rhyme, without a future, all I have to look forward to is my date with Sig somewhere down the road. But perhaps not. These men offer me things I couldn't imagine. Things that will assure my comfort and give me purpose. Sure, they're evil, but that's only a function of their predicament. In other times, with normal lives, I'm sure they would've been like the rest of us. Average, miniscule, brief.

It's as if Cain reads my thoughts. "Try and cheer up, dear Emery. I can't imagine how you can be so morose when all we've planned stands waiting before us. Soon I'll return, and you'll be in my favor. You've been loyal and for that you deserve a boon."

My face stretches to a smile. I'd be a fool to walk away. Call it fate or destiny or just the dreams of a broken man who happens upon good fortune.

Before me the ritual continues as the sun drops to the horizon.

I *can* be a madman.

The realization hits me full force. The scratch in my throat rises, and I gulp it down. Morals are folly; goodness, guile. Rhyme is dead, and without her, what's the point of the charade. Flames dance like savages on the heifer's carcass. My soul strips its shell and joins in, howling, nude, jubilant. A choice made, a freedom of purpose, a map with a destination. Around me, the children watch with solemn faces. The abrasion throbs in my chest, subtle, undermining my joy.

"I've some bad news."

Longinus stands beside us, frowning.

For the first time today, Cain's smile loses some brilliance. "Longinus, why oh why do you disrupt my joy?"

Exactly.

The Roman rubs his chin, shuffles his feet. "We've lost the Apostle."

Cain blinks. "So?"

"So, we can non find him."

"Where did he go?"

"We do non know. Our contact says he just vanished."

Cain considers this for a long moment, ponders the possibilities. "It doesn't matter," he says finally, waving his hand in irritation. "He can't possibly undo our plans. We'll finish this, then never again shall we concern ourselves with him. That's until it's time for me to pay him back." He beams here, eyes riding thoughts of revenge. "For now, keep up the perimeter's security and return here at nightfall."

The Roman nods, "Aye." He starts to walk away but Cain stops him.

"Have you seen Igneus?"

"Non since he run'd off."

"Try to reach him and convince him to enjoy this moment with us. It'd be such a shame not to share this with friends."

Longinus's face contorts, perturbed. "Aye."

Cain returns his attention to the burning heifer, stares hypnotized as the Children move, sallow ghosts, stoking the fire.

Flames leap as the fire grows. I swallow more sand as an easy smile crosses my face. I'm with them now. No other choice.

CHAPTER 53

JERUSALEM, ISRAEL

The phone rings in the distant recesses of the well-appointed apartment. Igneus ignores it.

He's been cleansed by Cain's mark, made whole by the vicious light. Turmoil has vanished. He knows now what the dreams mean and why he's been so punished for a slight he can't even remember.

His is to stop Cain, to conquer the beast. To be a hero yet.

In the end, it all comes down to choice, whether to help or to hinder. Personal choice, then swift action.

Relief washes over him. His suffering hasn't been without purpose. Not condemned by God, not cast aside like used-up refuse. He's an instrument of power, a sleek and shining sword forged to slay the beast.

The apartment resounds with his laughter. Igneus, the weakest and frailest of men; now a champion, rising to vanquish the vagabond.

Excitement, boldness, wash every fiber of his body. His resolve steels like wrought iron infinitely folded. He's never felt like this, so assured, so strong, so unafraid.

It's time to go. He pauses only to send a quick text, hoping as he types that Cain doesn't see it before the intended recipient.

With luck, the Dove is too occupied by the ritual to notice anything else, too occupied with his quest and vanity to notice a single short message.

The phone rings again as Igneus strides into the evening.

CHAPTER 54

JERUSALEM, ISRAEL

I stand with Cain and Longinus as the evening's buttery yellow gives way to shades of magenta and robust pink. We're under strict orders to maintain a five-foot separation from Cain as it won't do for him to become tainted.

After the fire consumed the heifer, the Children collected its ashes, then mixed them with the Kilal's original ashes, ashes from the time of Moses. They mixed those with water, creating, as Cain said, the waters of purification according to Moses' law.

They'd bathed him head to foot, then washed his silken robes in the same water and helped him dress. Now, according to law and prophecy, he's purified.

Cain's mark burns bright, gaining strength with the help of the waning sun and falling darkness. It seems his mark heralds certain things, and I make a mental note to record its presence more acutely. Feelings of fear and despair have disappeared since I'd cast my lot, since I'd made my choice to join these men. The mark knows somehow, can read my heart, can peer through intention as surely as lifting the lid on a Christmas box. It casts an odd light on the Temple's exterior, illuminates us all in more ways than just a magenta luster.

Cain stands poised to enter the Temple, his face resplendent with joy and anticipation.

The cool night air is refreshing, and it must feel good for him to be free at last of those miserable gloves. It dawns on me, I'll never see him again with his gloves in place.

Goosebumps are visible on his skin as his excitement grows. I think about the ocean of centuries he's endured. Remember him saying the first time he'd tried to enter the Temple: Ignorance of the rituals had been his mistake. Not knowing the prophecy had undone his plans, and by the time he figured it out, it'd been too late.

I marvel, try to appreciate the significance of this meaningless piece of Earth, so precious to God, so contemptable to Cain. For here had he slain his brother.

I imagine the scene, try to picture the lush trees and verdant earth. Try to picture Abel, alone, singing his praises, innocence snuffed. This is a special place, something magic, something mystic, its ground hallowed, drenched in that precious fluid which God prefers.

I hear Cain's whisper. "This time," he says. "This time I won't be cast out." In a hushed voice, he checks his thoughts. "I've followed God's commands to the letter, fulfilled each prophecy. Abel has forgiven me. I *will* enter."

He glides up the steps, spotless, bright robes trailing behind. The massive doors loom before him as he stares at their detail. Cherubs swirl amongst carved vines, angelic faces beaming and serene.

He takes a deep breath and holds it in. The smile remains, but he somehow looks like a man headed for the gallows.

Around us, the city is silent, void of distant car horns or squawking youngsters. I watch the man, feel the same sentiment, like the earth holds its breath, like the soil he once farmed senses the return of its master.

It's as if his brother's blood has mastered the soil in his favor, as if the earth rejoices in his victory.

He exhales and grips the door's wrought handles. Knuckles blanch as he squeezes. Beside me, Longinus shuffles and sighs.

Cain casts a glance at the giant, then pulls.

The doors slide silent on greased hinges. In the distance a moonlark calls.

I look into the beauty of the Temple, crane to see while keeping my distance. I wonder if it's how he remembers.

A vast hall looms over checkered marble. White pillars run its length, span the cubits to the ceiling. The roof is etched in white, gilded in gold, flying high over stone statues of angel and saint. Frescoes adorn the rafters, depict God's mercy, God's love, and, in some, His wrath.

He inhales once more in an attempt to master fear, and it occurs to me that a god shouldn't suffer such emotion.

He steps through.

CHAPTER 55

JERUSALEM, ISRAEL

"Well, that be that," Longinus says as we descend the Temple steps. Night is upon us now, and I find myself wanting to go to Cain, to offer my assistance in whatever fashion I can, to record the transformation of God for humanity to come. I glance at the grinning cherubs, wonder if Cain meets with God at this exact moment.

I'm humbled a bit by the thought that *the* God can be so near right now.

The moon casts a glow over the altar site, turns the ground to gray splotches as clouds race across its face. The night is fair and cool, a perfect night for something such as this.

From a distance, I hear someone yell. At first, I think it comes from the Temple. Then, I see a man running toward us.

Longinus reaches the bottom step, then recognizes the man.

John sprints forward.

I join Longinus as a great smile appears through his beard. "Speak of the devil and up he pops," he says.

John raises a hand, now three feet from us, out of breath. "I come in peace."

Longinus chuckles. "Shame," he says, "'cuz ye found a thin' entirely different."

The Roman moves like a jungle cat, faster than I can follow. A giant hand seizes John's throat, and his eyes pop as Longinus squeezes his larynx.

I move to defend the Apostle. My body comes to a quick, shuddering stop, then I stand watching. *Not my problem,* I think. *I've cast my lot.*

John kicks impotent, claws at the Roman's face.

A giant fist rises in silhouette against the night, then slams into John's nose.

He's thrown through the air to land hard on the stone-covered ground. Wind escapes him; he rasps, searches for breath.

Longinus moves after, heavy steps that menace and warn. John raises his head, tries to stand just as Longinus levels a kick to his ribs. More air escapes the Apostle, and I'm amazed he has even a molecule left. He rolls across the stone with the force.

John gasps, struggles for breath, tries to stand on legs that refuse support. Hands paw stone as Longinus hefts him from the ground.

The sight would be comic if this were at all funny. Like Longinus offering a struggling stick figure to the moon.

There's a sickening crunch as the Apostle slams to the stone.

The Roman laughs as he circles, misty vapor rolling from his mouth. "And ye was thinkin' this t'be a borin' night."

John tries to speak, looks like a fish out of water, gasping and gaping. He tries to move, but his muscles lack strength. He musters a sitting position, arms clenched around his torso, blood pouring from a bent and crooked nose.

Longinus laughs again, silhouetted by the moon like an enraged werewolf, fogged breath a pillar from his large mouth.

I feel the weight of my decision not to act. Sides have been chosen, and with that comes the loyalty of one's station. My mind fills with all the Apostle has endured in his centuries; all he's overcome to get to this point.

All that stands between him and his special task is a single man. A Roman.

I shake my head, take a tentative step forward, then stop again. His task will fail, and John must know that to his core. He can't best the Roman, I mean, who can?

He lifts his head toward the darkness as lips move without sound. He's praying, asking a bloodthirsty God for assistance.

The sand feels coarse in my throat as I watch the beaten Apostle lift up his eyes to the hills.

Then another man approaches, and a wall of liquid hits Longinus from behind. Droplets fly, glisten in moonbeams, drench the Roman.

Longinus turns.

My nostrils fill with an acrid, sharp scent.

The Roman faces his attacker, sees the emaciated silhouette, then breaks into laughter. "I see ye got me message!"

Igneus stands bold before the Roman, David and Goliath facing each other. The Jew raises a steady hand. "I do not fear you, centurion. Be gone from here!" I'm amazed at Igneus's tone: strong, clear and powerful.

The Roman bends double, mists his laughter through bearded nostrils. "Anon and agin," he says, "ye've grown some marbles."

He steps forward, but Igncus holds his ground. A discarded gas can lays lopsided at his feet, remnants of the ritual, left behind by the Children.

"You must be stopped," Igneus says.

Longinus stretches his arms to the night, a gladiator in the coliseum. "Ye can non stop me, lad. I'm immortal!" He moves toward Igneus. "I'm glad ye came tho. I'been waitin' centuries to beat ye arse."

A sword appears in Longinus's hand, a devil's grin on his face. "Killin' time," he says.

A deep, red slash appears on Igneus's chest and he stumbles back, falls to the stone. Longinus kicks him in the ribs, sends him rolling like a rag doll.

Sword raised high, Longinus moves for the killing stroke.

The sand in my throat becomes raging acid, burns to my core, through my innards, into my heart.

Igneus rolls, tries to keep his distance. Then, John is there, blood dripping from his face and onto the gray stone. He moves swift and silent, circling behind the Roman, seeking advantage.

He crouches, then springs in the air, displays an athleticism I don't expect. Arms reach for the Roman's throat, stretched long like a trapeze artist, body horizontal against the shadows and above the stone.

The Roman's speed is astounding. He spins a tight arc, catches John mid-air. A massive arm lifts the Apostle, uses his own momentum against him. He flies high, lands hard with a breathless grunt.

A rasped whisper reaches me. "Emery. Help us." It's Igneus, his eyes searching mine, his face confused by my inaction. A betrayed friend, measuring the depths of my abandonment.

I look at my palm, realize I'm holding the lighter I'd pocketed at the Devil's Needle. Igneus nods. I shake my head. *You're on your own.*

The giant, a roaring, dark mountain, stands over the Apostle. John cries out, raises his arms. The gleaming point of Longinus's sword is poised above his chest, held in both of the Roman's huge hands.

His face is gleeful, orgasmic.

John braces for the sword.

Two frail arms loop around the Roman's neck. Igneus has leapt upon him like some sort of death-wish lunatic. He fights like an alley cat, scratching and clawing, fingers wrapped in Longinus's thick hair.

Longinus is undistracted. The Jew is like an ant on an elephant, like a flee on a jetliner. He has no effect on the giant, who levels his sword at John's breast and starts to slam it home.

John tries to roll but runs into the centurion's huge foot.

Igneus rides the Roman, pulls his hair, gouges his eyes.

The sword plummets toward the Apostle's exposed breast.

The acid ignites my soul. I'm moving, unbidden, faster than I ever thought this body could go.

I slam into the Roman like a linebacker, feel my clavicle fracture as air spews from my lungs.

Yet, the Roman is hardly phased. Our eyes meet and he gives a you-shouldn't-have eye roll, then with a flourish and quick spin, the sword pierces my gut next to my belly button.

I crumple, all thoughts of betrayal now the rantings of a madman.

Longinus's teeth flash and glow in the moonlight. His eyes feral, wild. Blood blind.

I lay back, ready to die. Ready, at last, to go to Rhyme.

Longinus, turns to John, raises the sword and drives it down, a gleaming pike intent on John's heart. The Apostle gives a last desperate roll as Igneus doubles his efforts on the Roman's back.

I see it clearly. Sword moving, practiced and clean.

The wide-eyed Apostle, hands outstretched, struggling to roll past the giant foot that blocks him.

Igneus's mouth stretched in fury. One hand twisted in the Roman's hair, the other stretched around the Roman's head, a bony finger clawing at the Roman's eye.

Then the sword hits home.

All of our efforts have made only a sliver of difference.

But sometimes, a sliver is all you need.

The sword misses by a fraction, slices the Apostle's shirt then sparks yellow against the stone.

The Roman bursts into flames, wailing, spinning through the courtyard, his voice a howl in thundering bass. He leaps for Igneus, who side-steps him easily. The Jew holds a gas can and heaves it at the flaming hulk.

Longinus's cries reach deafening levels; he spins, slaps at the flames. He crashes to his knees, flames dancing over him like the witches of yore. Curses resound, threats to Igneus, threats to me.

Igneus retrieves another can and dumps it. Flames explode high and hot as Longinus's screams match the blistering heat.

Igneus continues until no more gas remains. Then he stands and watches the man burn until the cries cease and all that remains is a charred mass.

Longinus lays motionless, burnt like the red heifer and on the same spot.

Igneus moves to John, blood flowing from the large gash on his chest. "You okay?"

John nods.

He races to me. "Emery, you alright?"

My hands are covered in blood, my gut a white-hot branding iron.

"How's the Apostle?" I ask.

"He needs a hospital."

John tries to stand, can barely manage to his knees, let alone walk. "My task—" he moans.

I use Igneus as a crutch, manage to stand through the agony of movement.

I heft John, wrap his arm around my neck. "We'll get this done," I say, "even if it kills us."

I'm surprised by his laughter, then realize he's immortal. "Emery, you don't have to do this. If you betray Cain, he'll kill you."

I heft him forward, feel the sticky hot sensation of my own blood over my leg, into my shoe.

"Emery, you need an ambulance. I can't have you dying in there," Igneus says sharply, staring at my wound.

John glances at Igneus and then to the Temple's entrance.

I shake my head, heft John up each step, my broken clavicle crunching under my skin like a splintered tent pole.

"Someone needs to handle Longinus if he rises," I say.

"Emery, don't." Igneus's face is tortured. "Cain *will* kill you."

We take painful step after painful step, determined, each of us, to complete John's task.

"I'm told there's worse," I say.

The sand is gone, the nagging acid, the venom of betrayal, of bad choices, of conscience.

I *am not* a madman.

I glance over my shoulder at Igneus. He stands watching from the bottom of the steps. In the moonlight he looks robust, a knight in moon-laced armor, a feral alley cat, a hero.

The Apostle breathes a prayer, and we enter the Temple.

CHAPTER 56

JERUSALEM, ISRAEL

"You cannot enter!"

John stands on his own power, fists clenched, speaks in a voice that doesn't match his condition.

Cain turns, blinks twice, glances at the curtain still in his hand and looks at us again. His face becomes rage. "And who is to stop me? You? The reporter? You may want to reconsider, dear Emery." He spits my name like ejecting something distasteful.

"Mine is to stop you." John says, then leaps toward the curtain and slaps Cain's hand away.

Cain strikes like a viper, a palm into John's Adam's apple that ends any hope of fulfilling the Apostle's task.

The disciple's eyes bug out: his hands jerk to his throat. He backs away, sputtering and coughing. Cain takes a step forward, then stops and yanks the heavy curtain aside.

He steps in.

I kneel beside the Apostle. His neck is bruised and swollen, his breath a rasp over sheet metal. I glance to the curtain. "John, get up." I try to lift him, but he's dead weight. His eyes loll, his lips are crinkled and pursed. He tries to mouth something, then slips into unconsciousness.

What to do now? Follow Cain? Enter the lion's den? I'm no hero, not imbued with superpowers. Not immortal.

A fine rage fills me, Rhyme's voice through a distant fog. What would she think, seeing me here like this? I look around for something with which to battle Cain, see a ceremonial dagger gilded in silver, a subtle glint in the darkness.

I move past the curtain and into the room beyond.

It appears as a dark square, the shadowed form of Cain standing lonely in its center. This is the Holy of Holies, illuminated only by Cain's mark.

He blinks, frustrated eyebrows bent in concentration.

I share his surprise. I expected a bit more, something like Blake's *Vision* come to life in all its glory, God sitting on a throne surrounded by all of Heaven's hosts.

A great marble slab, waist high, is the room's only furniture, and Cain leans on it with both hands, shakes his head. "I don't understand," he says. Then he howls all his rage into the confined space. "Where are you!" His words echo to nothing, and I feel a bit of pity for him, even as I grasp the dagger tighter. His long life, his dashed hopes, his quest failed.

"What could I have done wrong? What detail has been overlooked?" He paces, ignores me completely as lifeless stone walls mock from the periphery.

But then he turns—truly looks at me, sees the dagger in my hand. Realization blooms on his face, and before I know it, he's on me.

I manage to block the first blow, which is aimed at my throat. The same blow he'd struck at the Children's compound. The second, third, and fourth blows catch me off guard, and I find myself on my back, blood pouring from my nose, my mouth, and down my side from the wound Longinus provided.

Cain leans over me. Holds the dagger close to my face. "God prefers blood, dear Emery. I've neglected to bring a suitable sacrifice. Let's have you up on the altar."

The young, strong farm boy hefts me like a bale of hay. Easily lifting, to throw me down on the cold marble slab. I struggle, try to stand, feel weak from loss of blood. Cain straddles me, eyes crazed, dagger lifted to plunge into my heart.

I refuse to close my eyes, refuse to look away. My thoughts fill with Rhyme. *Soon my love, very soon.*

In the outer chamber, the Apostle coughs and sputters. The sound sneaks through the curtain and Cain freezes. A sardonic grin crosses his face.

He leaps from the slab and rushes through the curtain, only to return a second later dragging a limp Apostle by the ankle.

In a quick motion, he pulls me from the table to land on the floor like a sack of shit.

He hefts the Apostle atop the slab.

Cain's skin glows in the shadowy redness of his mark. He removes his robe and uses the dagger to cut it to thin strips. The Apostle struggles a bit but is easily restrained as Cain loops the fabric under the table, wrist to wrist. He does the same with the Apostle's legs until the man is splayed, spread-eagle on the altar.

I hear the dagger slice as he cuts John's clothes away. "Oh, don't mind me, dear Emery," he says as he works. "Just preparing the sacrifice. Everyone knows God needs blood to keep up His strength." A quick swipe of his hand clears the altar of any leftover fabric.

He admires his work. "There now," he says, "the perfect sacrificial lamb. My destiny is at hand. Emery, care to say a few words?"

I try to rise, try to crawl, anything to get to the altar, to stop this madness. God isn't here, isn't coming, has abandoned us as He's abandoned the entire Earth. Just an ant farm, a toy for a God who, childlike, grows bored with the thing and goes in search of something new, better, more tantalizing.

"Cain, no. Please. Stop." I slip in my own blood, my vision wavers, blurs. I lose perspective, can't tell if I'm moving, crawling, standing. I know only that I spin, that I haven't much left, that I must stop the lunatic from completing his task and bringing doom down upon us. I can face Rhyme having done that. True amends for all I put her through.

Cain lifts the knife above his head.

It hangs above the Apostle's heart, waits to be driven home.

Cain sighs a prayer. "Bless us, O Lord, and these thy gifts."

The knife slams down. John's cry rends the sacristy, his body jolts. Arms jut out as his head falls back. Blood surges from the wound, splays across Cain's naked body, then runs over the altar, where it collects beside me in a crimson pool.

I collapse, tears flowing, exhausted.

The room fills with light, blinding, palpable, not sunlight or natural light but something effervescent, something more brilliant than a thousand suns.

I struggle to my haunches, watch the ceiling disappear. The walls become a clear tapestry of what can only be Heaven's endless landscape.

I will my eyes to focus as I squint into the brightness.

A figure approaches, shadowed and dark.

The light blinds, manifold suns in all directions, flooding the room and making the blood on the altar appear black by contrast.

Cain stands in awe, wears a perfect smile, fists curled, ready at last to confront his creator.

The figure sweeps in; its edges solidify, become clear. Dark hair, olive skin, sharp features akin to Cain.

"Abel?" Cain says.

Abel's face is hard as stone.

A roaring wind rushes, fills the room, howls over us with such force, it slides me a few inches on the slick stone.

I stand, use the altar as support, reach for the knife in John's chest.

Then it stands before us, an angel sizzling in golden light, wings wide and majestic, mesmerizing and opulent. A cherubic face without emotion.

Golden wings send a gale of such strength, I abandon my efforts and cling to the marble slab. Shimmering robes flow in his wake, his hair twists in golden curls that stream around his face.

His eyes are like fire. His sword, liquid gold, coursing in shimmering hues, flames dancing on its edge.

His voice fills the chamber, the entire world, like nothing I've ever heard, an endless, immense entity.

"I am Michael. Prepare to be judged."

Cain's lips twist to a snarl as a harsh battle cry flows from his mouth.

He leaps for the angel.

Michael's arm flashes, flings Cain headlong against the translucent stone of the chamber's walls.

He crashes, falls.

Then, gains his feet in an instant. Fists clenched, eyes wide with fury, he faces the blazing Archangel.

Michael raises his sword. Golden flames roil on its edge, dancing, hungry for battle. The angel hovers on shimmering golden wings. "Submit," he says.

"Who are you to judge me?" Cain spits, circling, buying time.

"Mine is not to judge, but to subdue." Michael's voice is the echo of centuries.

Cain's muscles contract as he launches himself again.

Michael deflects the attack, sends Cain hurtling again toward the wall. He smashes against it, slumps to the ground next to me.

I move between him and the angel. "Cain," I say. "You've lost, let's get out of here."

He gives me a look. "Never. I've come too far. I'll not be bested by a lowly birdman."

His gaze shifts from my face to somewhere past me.

I turn.

The angel floats above me. Dazzling wings move in great arcs, lifting, holding him aloft with effortless intent.

I'm awed, speechless, realize this isn't a man, nor a God, but a mystical creature, something mortals aren't supposed to see. Something most mortals don't believe exists. He holds my gaze, looks upon me as I do him. Both of us enamored, awed, curious.

"Step away," he says.

I use the marble to hoist myself. "I will not," I say. "Return from whence you came." I don't know where the words come from, maybe too many fantasy novels, but it just sounds like something one should say when confronted by an archangel.

Then I feel the dagger against my throat, Cain's hand coiled in my hair. "You cannot harm mortals without cause, Michael!" Cain screams. "Desert this place. Tell God I'm ready to make my bargain. His children for my release, nothing more. I care little for this mortal and will readily slay him if you don't comply."

I struggle, shocked, betrayed even as I betrayed.

Michael's face is still as stone. His blade, laced with dancing flame, held loosely in his right hand. I stare at his wings, trace the billions of feathers, each a miracle of sight and color, each with infinite detail, strength, elegance.

Then he disappears.

I feel myself fly, then bounce off the altar to skid across the slick stone floor.

By the time I stop, Michael has Cain pinned to the wall halfway between floor and ceiling.

A flaming sword protrudes from Cain's gut, a giant spike that holds him ten feet above the floor.

Michael's face is a hair's breadth from Cain's. His wings massive, unstoppable, fierce. Fire reflects in his eyes, a horrible, garish orange.

The angel floats backwards, lands lightly on the stone floor. Giant wings fold behind, tuck so neatly they seem to disappear.

He looks to me, his face serene.

Cain wails as molten fire ravages his body. He bucks and kicks, flailing wild, pinned ten feet above the floor, seeking escape from the conflagration.

He grasps the sword but pulls back burnt stubs as fingertips fall to the floor.

"Abel," he pleads, "my brother, my blood, save me."

Abel approaches, floating on air until they're face to face.

"Abel? Help me," Cain begs.

Abel's face shows neither anger nor deference, nor joy or recognition. He speaks with a voice of confident authority, dispassionate, easy.

"I am Abel, appointed by God to judge all men and mete their fate." His voice fills the chamber, impossible to ignore as it fills my head, bypassing my ears to enter my brain directly.

Something ghostly appears over Cain's body, like the shadow of a mimeograph, a photographer's double image. As Cain moves, this moves too but a second behind.

"You, who are marked by God to wander and be a vagabond, are a deceiver of men and the son of perdition. You are the lawless one. The profane and wicked prince of Israel, you are a shepherd of idols and a blasphemer before the Lord and, in so being, doomed to yet go on." Abel's voice booms, fills my brain. I cower in weakness, hold my gut, tremble with fear.

The ghostly image emerges, tears through the flesh and sinew of Cain's body. It's a replica of him, a doppelganger, but instead of confidence and elegance, it exudes only fear, only hopelessness.

Cain's shriek curdles my blood, makes me cower and cling to the floor, overwhelmed. Abel's voice grows until it drowns all else.

"You are judged!"

Cain's soul streaks from his body, the lines of his mark burst into flames that spread until they consume him entirely. He howls, pinned to the wall, arms flapping, head whipping side to side. Spit flies from his lips, is made instant vapor from the heat.

Before my eyes, he fades to nothing, leaving only a burning sword affixed to the wall.

CHAPTER 57

JERUSALEM, ISRAEL

A bove me, the vastness of Heaven. Silver clouds streaked with golden light, the sky opalescent, endless, shimmering like raindrops on glassed waters.

I look to the altar, feel my very essence oozing from my wound.

"John?" My voice sounds far away. I'm unsure if I've spoken or merely thought the word.

A pinpoint of glorious light floats in, hovers above him, solidifies to the form of a man.

A rush of wind makes me blink. Then Michael, scooping John in muscled arms as wings reflect beams in infinite color, in infinite streams. The Messiah reaches for the Apostle, and their hands clasp in an image worthy of Michelangelo and the Sistine Chapel. I see the wounds, the stigmata where iron nails pierced His flesh.

"Be well, my friend," I think, perhaps say, as a serenity floods, as fears ease.

The sky flickers, shimmers, a rock tossed in the water. Glorious clouds waver as gleaming beams congeal to a ceiling of inert stone in darkened alabaster.

"Emery, what happened? Where's Cain? You okay? What happened?" Igneus kneels beside me, pulls me close.

"I'm losing my vision," I say. "Think this might be it."

Tears fill his eyes. "Aw, Emery."

"It's okay. Just as well really, got a chance to go out in style. Now I get to be with Rhyme forever and ever." I chuckle. "With Rhyme, all the time. Someone should write a song." His eyes hold mine as he pulls, tries to coax me upright, force me to walk.

"It's worth it, I think. Completely worth it," I say. "Hope she recognizes me."

His hand is cool on my forehead. "An ambulance is coming," he says. "We have to get you up."

I look past him. The room is empty, barren, nothing amiss. "Did you see it?" I ask.

"What?"

"Michael? Abel? John?"

"Just walked in. Come on, try to get up. Let's get out of here."

It's hard to keep my eyes open. "Can't do it, amigo. Too far gone I fear."

"Emery," his voice sounds harried. "There's something I need to tell you, something about Rhyme." His voice is distant, far off.

I smile, fading. "I know everything about Rhyme. She's my life." The room blurs, feels dark and cold. Fear grips me and I can't feel my hands. My lips tingle.

I reach for his hand, can't tell if I'm holding it. "I'll be seeing you, Igneus. Cain's gone. You're free now. Do something amazing for me, eh?"

Igneus speaks through dense fog, a rattle in the depths of my mind. "Rhyme..." The words wander, lilt, trail off and disappear.

All is silent.

I hope Rhyme meets me.

EPILOGUE

"Rhyme? Is it you?"
　　　"Yes, love."

I feel her hand on my hair, the wetness of what can only be a tear drop. She is here, and my heart swells with love. I try to speak but can't tell if words are forming or if I'm just babbling. It's dark here and everything beeps and chirps. She dances in my dreams. When I close my eyes, she's there, smiling, beautiful, kind. She visits in shadow and attends with loving grace, a sip of water, a kind word. I see only silhouette, a dark outline, an angel's aura. Same old story, dark tears like falling pearls, seems they never stop. I smell vanilla and lilac; so clean, so vivid. Her scent, bound to my psyche.

I relax; give in, give up, fully commit to this new journey.

We are together.

I move to the light.

———

Fire and humanity surround him. Guttural wails flow through a timeless expanse.

In the distance, figures writhe, shriek with contorted voices.

Scaled creatures dart in to inflict some horror, then speed off, high-pitched laughter following. Wherever they alight, fresh anguish follows, then streaks of blood, of rent flesh. Despite the fire, all is black in this place, permeating all who stand within, drenching the vastness in misery and horror for as far as one can see.

To Cain it feels good.

The place has no end. His vision fills with endless, hopeless humanity. He moves toward them. Fire recedes with each step. Flames roar a thousand feet high as he passes.

Terror fills this place, and those wide-eyed supplicants surrounding him burst with it, every minute a new agony.

None of it affects him. He feels neither pain nor emotion as he moves through the wretched mass.

Through the blackness comes a man, slim and dressed in a modern suit and tie.

"I've been waiting for you."

"Who are you?"

"You choose."

The man smiles.

Then his face changes.

At first growing large, snarling through a mouth of razor-sharp teeth. Horns appear as skin turns a deep crimson, as a sharp tail sizzles behind with whistling light.

Then the face of a non-descript everyman, a man one could stare at for hours and not be able to recall a single detail; which gives way to the face of Pontius Pilate; then Hitler; then a priest; Caesar; a rapist; a pedophile; a drug-addict; a corporate executive.

The pace slows and Cain starts to recognize them one by one: Longinus; then his own face; then the face of Abel.

Cain jumps at Abel's image.

The man reassumes his first appearance, giggles into a clenched fist.

"Don't be alarmed," he says. "I show only what you need to see."

"You... But..." he stammers.

"Yes, me," the man says, adjusting his tie. "Or more aptly, I'm. I'm the one who has guided you all this time, and I'm the one who can show you how to achieve your destiny."

"I want no more of this," Cain says. "Let me die."

The man laughs, and millions of demons join. "You can't die." He says this as if speaking to a toddler. "You're a God. Your path was charted long ago."

His voice is sweet in Cain's ears. "Do you not wonder why God didn't destroy you? Why He only separated you from your soul?"

Cain says nothing, his mind spinning.

"It was the only part of you He *could* take."

The man adjusts a cufflink, then his lapels. "The rest He cannot touch. You've achieved equal footing. He knows His mistake but can't do anything about it. So, He's banished you here to Hell." The man smirks, nods a single time. "Except I'm the master here. Not Him. And I can help you return to Earth, where together we will overcome Him."

Cain listens, riveted. He makes perfect sense. His logic, undeniable.

Screams tickle his ears, the mass of humanity, shrieking, pleading.

The sounds are delightful.

The man continues. "Until now, I've been the only one who's ever sought to topple Him. But I've learned from watching you that, together, He cannot withstand us."

He's right, Cain realizes. God can't kill him at this point or He would have. In an instant, Cain realizes the errors of his actions, the limited scope of his thinking. He feels enraged, as if he could dismember every man, woman, and child on Earth and still have the energy to tear down each structure stone by stone. His anger grows like a summer gale on sizzling thunderheads, partly for not realizing sooner, and partly for all the centuries he's suffered. He remembers when he would've bowed before God, a time when a word from Him was all he craved.

His portion of malice grows a full measure.

He remembers being cast away, his sacrifice rejected as if trivial and unimportant. He realizes now, that from that day to this, hatred has burned within him. Always there, always growing, now reaching its zenith, pulsing within, filling him with power.

"What must I do?"

"You must return and continue your work. There's still more to be done, more prophecy to be fulfilled. I told you before when I came to you, you've been too limited in your thinking."

Hatred and rage fuse to replace the void that was Cain's soul. Evil washes over him like hot oil.

He is anointed.

Flames blast from his mark in all directions, streak thousands of leagues like a mushroom cloud. Blistering light reveals mountains of scorched stone and running lava, an unending landscape of horror. Fanged, red demons and wailing souls fill those spaces beyond what even he can see. The fire grows, leaps into each little crag, rolls over every crooked peak. Billions of souls shriek as flames cover and lay them low. Their misery builds to a sustained crescendo. Small demons race away, flames igniting on leathery wings, leaving thick, smoky tendrils in their wake.

To Cain, it's as soothing as a child's laughter. As sensuous as a lover's touch. He is one with the fire and misery and terror. A brilliant new entity, savage and fierce, born to bring judgment to a puny God and unending misery to His followers. He focuses and the flames grow to a pure supernova.

Hell's walls burst aflame, the souls within throb with white-hot energy.

He licks his lips, closes his eyes as fire pours from every pore. Sweet aromas bless his nostrils. Humanity's horror is a symphony, he a master composer. Bursting with blackest hate, he accepts it all into his being.

Lucifer stands behind him.

His whisper holds the full truth.

"*You* are the Antichrist."

END

DEAR READER

Thank you for reading *A Portion of Malice,* Book I of the epic series,
Ages of Malice.
Be sure to leave a review and spread the word!

CLICK HERE or SCAN BELOW TO LEAVE A QUICK REVIEW!

Join Lloyd's advanced reader circle, get news, and more at:
www.lloydjeffries.com

Turn the Page for an Excerpt

A MEASURE OF RHYME

AGES OF MALICE, BOOK II

LLOYD JEFFRIES

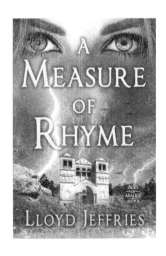

A Measure of Rhyme

Ages of Malice, Book II

Washington D.C.

The knock at the door is expected, room service. Rhyme checks her phone, ten am. She pulls the soft terry robe close to her body and ties the silk sash in a knot.

The suite at the D.C. St. Regis is comfortable and well accommodated. Done with expensive furniture in pastel blue over a thick carpet the color of the ocean after a storm. A gold chandelier hangs in the room's center but appears useless as a large, arced window sends plenty of sunlight through gold-checked curtains.

She exits the master bedroom, a room all its own, then passes pastel chairs, a beautiful Victorian desk, and a small, round dining table. She squeezes the robe closed at the neck and answers the door.

"Your order, ma'am," the man says. He wears black pants over matching shoes shined to a high gloss. Luxury shoes, expensive. His shirt is white, covered by a smart, tailored vest in deep maroon. A bow tie completes the appearance. Rhyme notices it isn't a clip-on, but one that requires the wearer to have a knowledge of the complexities of tying a bow tie.

She steps aside and the man enters pushing a small cart. "I hope you're enjoying your stay," he says, nearing the dining table. He arranges the dishes, a small white plate, fork and knife on either side, spotless cloth napkin. "Looks like it's going to be a lovely day."

Rhyme feels a tingle in the nape of her neck. An old feeling she'd thought disused and forgotten. A kind of sixth sense, intuition, a warning. Something isn't right.

Sunlight splays wide rays through the window and makes a bright square onto the room's lush carpet. The man busies himself arranging the modest breakfast: an oat muffin, some orange juice, coffee. He seems to be taking his time, not acting like normal waiters who enter with a sense of purpose, then speed through their task anxious to collect their tip.

This waiter is unassuming, even casual.

But the shoes don't fit. What waiter, even at a five-star place like this, can afford shoes this expensive? And the bow tie, the expert knot, what service staffer would be skilled at such a thing?

Painful experience has taught her to trust her instincts and she adjusts her position, noting the waiter's dominant hand.

Through the years Rhyme has learned most people prefer their dominant side. She's learned that when expecting the unexpected, preparation has no equal. She's been caught by surprise too many times, has suffered severe consequences as a result.

The waiter is right-handed, which tells her he'll prefer an assault that comes from his left. She moves behind him, in a direct line with his right shoulder. If he's up to something, he'll spin to his left in order to give his dominant hand the most room.

He seems unaware of her motion as he pours steaming black coffee into a small white cup. He snaps a napkin, folds it to a tight V, and places it atop a round, white plate.

Rhyme watches him work, examines every detail, looks for even a small advantage, anything out of place, any clue to reinforce her already enhanced sense of danger.

Then she sees it, a thin black strap jutting from the rear shoulder of his vest. It sticks out about an eighth of an inch, but Rhyme knows what it is and what it holds. She imagines the line of the strap, circling the man's left shoulder to join another strap in the center of his back, making an X.

A shoulder holster, which means he has a weapon just under his left armpit, possibly one under the right as well.

She knows she has only a few seconds, examines her options.

The man turns to his left just as she anticipates. She steps close, brings her right leg between his feet and reaches into his vest. She feels rusty, slow, hasn't needed these skills in some time.

The man's eyes widen, then narrow an instant later. A normal response here is to attack, she thinks. He'll try and push me back, to create distance with which to work.

He does just that, but with unexpected speed. His hands go for her throat, stabbing for her neck. She steps close, sliding between outstretched arms, an inch from his face, and slams her knee into his groin.

He gasps and doubles over.

He'll try to grab me now, she thinks. A giant bear hug. If he's a pro, he'll fight, ignoring the enormous pain in his testicles. Professionals never give up, ever, are willing to die to complete their mission.

His arms close around her even as his face changes to bulging purple. Rhyme moves, fluid and elegant, ducking the hug, taking two steps back.

She holds his black revolver. Its color mutes the window's natural light. It appears cold and deadly. She levels it, prepared to empty it into the man's chest if he continues.

He shuffles a step, then crumbles to a knee overcome by the pain in his groin.

Rhyme smiles, happy she doesn't have testicles, such an obvious target, such an immense weakness.

"Poor fella," she says. "I bet that hurt."

Dark eyes glimmer rage. The man steams from a purple face.

He lowers his head, seems to give up.

Rhyme knows better.

The man's weight is on his left knee. His head lags and gives the appearance of being subdued. She knows what's next. None of these guys are one-trick ponies, not the good ones anyway.

He doubles over, bending with his abdomen, trying to conceal what Rhyme knows is coming. He's trying to block her view, his hand tracing down his right leg to retrieve god knows what from his right ankle. Could be another gun, a poison dart, a dagger, pepper spray, a taser.

She sees through it all, thinks to shoot the man and end the conjecture. Such a beautiful carpet, seafoam blue, plush, lovely on the toes. It'd be a shame to stain it with blood. Besides, the man needs to answer some questions.

But first, he needs to accept defeat.

She racks the pistol. A cartridge ejects, spinning from the chamber to land on the thick carpet. The action serves two purposes. First, when acquiring the pistol, Rhyme hadn't known if there was a round in the chamber. That is, if the pistol is ready to fire. A distinct disadvantage as the man who carried it would've known its status and could use that knowledge to his advantage. If she assumes a round is ready to go and attempts to fire, she'll be surprised when it doesn't and lose precious seconds attempting to chamber a round. Seconds the man can use to his own advantage. She'd been taught better, taught by the best, won't repay such wisdom with simple mistakes.

Second, the pistol is a Glock, lightweight, made in Austria. A Glock 43, if she has to guess, Vickers tactical version, judging by the feel of the extended magazine and custom slide lock. The good thing about racking a round is the sound it makes. Anyone close knows immediately what the sound means, and she doubts this man expects to hear it. Not from a pretty woman in a hotel bathrobe ordering juice and muffins from room service.

The man freezes, raises his head. He looks like he's going to vomit although his color has improved a bit.

She nods. "I wouldn't," she says. "Take it out and drop it."

A second goes by. Rhyme knows he's considering a full rush, considering the distance between them, her stance, watching the gun to see if it trembles in her clutches. He's looking for weakness, seeking advantage. A prowling tiger sizing up his prey.

He produces another revolver, smaller, tactical, the Mossad version of a .22 caliber handgun. He's Israeli and she startles. The thought is unimaginable.

She's recently been appointed as the Israeli ambassador. Did they send a Mossad agent? She can't begin to guess why the man's here or what he could want. The questions tumble along, cascading through her mind like a waterfall. She forces them away, thinks about what she knows for certain. The man's highly trained. Deadly. Unpredictable. She can't lower her guard for a single instant.

"Toss it over," she nods, slightly squeezing the Glock's trigger safety.

He raises it, holds the grip loose between thumb and index finger. "Careful," she says, "don't try it."

She sees his anger, knows the calculations whirling through his mind. He's been overcome by a woman and isn't happy about it.

This, sometimes, is hard for men, especially tough guy commandos who kill for the government. Some can't take it, can't wrap their mind around the possibility of being bested by a female. When it happens, it throws them into a crazed, irrational state.

Certainly, Rhyme has seen this before, always caused by something as inane as outsmarting a male. Always made worse when she bested them physically. Most just can't see past their own inflamed ego. Their misguided perception that the part that makes them male has anything at all to do with ability.

Whatever the reason, Rhyme has learned not to underestimate the reaction and to always, always expect it. For them, women are weak, meant to be mother's and lovers, not capable on levels that include combat or intelligence.

His eyes dart back and forth as if he's reading something. She knows they don't miss anything. She also knows that she hasn't missed anything. He's subdued, a cornered lion to be gently defanged and treated in such a way as to not further damage his already bruised and childish ego.

A few seconds pass. Rhyme is steady, ready to end the man's life at the first sign of threat.

He tosses the gun, and it bounces across the carpet to land by her feet.

Her tension reduces a half measure. He still has tricks though, is no less dangerous. She knows he'll always be looking for an advantage, will be ready to seize it the moment it presents.

She'd be a fool to think there's nothing more concealed beneath his uniform. A knife perhaps, a mace, something deadly to be sure.

"Stay where you are," she says. She doesn't want him to rise, doesn't want him anywhere but on his knees where it will be harder for him to stand and either bolt for the door or at her.

She steps backwards, feels the Victorian desk at her hip. She reaches behind and slides the phone forward, keeping it in her line of vision as she watches the agent. She can't afford to divert her eyes for even a second. Can't afford to give him even that much time.

"Look at the floor," she says.

The man lowers his head and Rhyme glances at the numerous buttons on the clunky hotel phone. She keeps her gun trained as she pokes the 0 button with her left hand.

The man sighs, seems to deflate. She's been waiting for this, visible confirmation that he knows he's beat.

The phone buzzes twice before a voice comes on. "Yes, Miss Carter, how may we help you?"

"I'll need the pol..."

The door explodes in a shower of splintered wood and flying fragments, then hangs by a single hinge. Two men rush in, pistols drawn. The agent turns, startled, not expecting this. He leaps like a jungle cat, faster than Rhyme can believe, toward the intruders.

The shots are sharp, painful in the enclosed space, shrill pops from flaming pistols. The agent is almost on them, dashing through the small distance between. She hears more shots. Sees the agent stagger and fall.

He collapses on the carpet as two men stand just inside the door, pistols drawn, faces covered in tight, black neoprene masks.

They turn their weapons toward her.

She has to act. These are neither police nor Mossad. No, these are a different variety altogether.

The pistol jumps in her hand as she fires four shots. The first is aimed high center mass, the other three designed to send the men running for cover. She dives left, toward the suite's master bedroom.

She hears a gurgling sound, then a thud. She's hit one, has only one more with which to deal.

Unless there are others.

The remaining man enters the room and fires just as Rhyme dives over the bed, into the two-foot space between it and the wall beyond. Muffled shots enter the bed's mattress; wood and plaster shower down on her from the wall above.

This is bad.

She's trapped, pinned down, knows the man will continue to fire, will keep her pinned and cowering until he can close the distance and shoot her point blank. She doesn't have much of a chance cramped where she is, has only seconds to come up with something before she dies.

A thought forms, a longshot at best but better than no shot.

She lies flat, rolls on her left shoulder and slides her right arm from the robe. More shots strike the wall above, more debris falls. He's closing, peppering bullets to keep her pinned.

She rolls right, slides her left arm from the robe. She's nude now, completely disrobed.

Her attacker will expect something dramatic and clever. He'll expect her to either pop up and fire wild, or stay flat until the last possible second, then poke around the bed's end for a surprise attack.

Rhyme plans neither.

She rolls the robe into a loose ball and places it atop her lower legs. The Glock is ready in her right hand. She knows a round is chambered; the pistol ready to fire. She'll only get one chance and better not mess it up.

She lies motionless. Feels chilled, exposed as she is. She inhales, controls her breathing, focuses her eyes loosely above her.

Another shot hits the wall as splinters fly from a smoking hole. The attacker spaces his shots at random. She counts, sees seven holes. A couple went into the mattress, she thinks. A couple more to kill the first agent. She hadn't heard him reload. He probably has only one or two shots left unless he's using an extended clip, or something special-made.

She can't rely on the calculations, can't risk her life based on the number of shots fired. Too many variables, too little time. This guy is too well-trained to give a clue to his position, too well-trained to use all his bullets and force a reload.

She hears the smallest shuffle, a single foot pressing into the carpet. It could be anything really, that sound. Could just be her imagination or wishful thinking, but Rhyme has learned to trust her instincts above all. Has learned to act on the slightest hunch and her sense of intuition.

She guesses the man's centered at the foot of the bed.

She kicks with both legs, hard and fast.

The robe flies into the air.

As her legs drop, she uses the momentum to propel her body to a sitting position, minimizing exposure while maximizing sight lines. If the man isn't where she's guessed, she'll be dead.

Her head pops above the bed and she hears two shots. Sees the man closer to the bed's left, closer to her hiding spot than she'd thought.

He's facing left, gun leveled, firing at the robe as it floats back to the floor.

Rhyme aims, fires twice.

The bullets strike the man's temple, one behind the other. The impact, dull, as he hits the floor.

She pauses, gun ready, scanning for other attackers, seeing no one. Naked, she eases around the bed, poised, ready for anything; more agents at the door, more who've entered as she was pinned down.

Blood trickles from the man's temple. So much for the carpet. She steps over him and stalks across the room, alert to every sound, ready for other assailants.

The other men lie where they dropped, no longer a threat, dead.

She passes them, pokes her head into the hall and looks both ways. It's deserted.

The long, shrill sound of sirens demand her attention. Police have been summoned.

She moves to the first agent, searches his waiter uniform. She finds a hotel staff ID with someone else's picture on it, stolen. She checks his pockets, finds a small leather wallet with his identification. Daniel Peretz, from Washington, D.C. She searches further, finds a small set of lockpicks, a few American dollars. She palms the lockpicks, a slim silver rake and tensioner.

Sirens grow closer by the second. She does the calculation, guesses about three minutes until the room fills with police.

She moves to the other man, searches the body, finds his billfold. Mohammed Ashani of Arlington, Virginia. She stares at the ID, tries to connect the pieces, straining to make them fit as they spread farther apart.

She steps across the room, kneels by the man at the end of the bed. A search reveals him to be Bahri Boutros, also of Arlington.

The pieces spread farther. An agent and two Muslims from Arlington. Obviously fake IDs for them, but why had they come? And why had the Muslims killed the agent? Had they expected him or been surprised? Had they expected her? Obviously yes, they'd kicked the door down. She'd been their target. But why? What had she done to incite such attention? And why attack so brazenly, in broad daylight?

She moves to the window, looks down at the hotel driveway's wide arc. Three police cars arrive in single file. Five officers leap from the vehicles.

She has only a minute now, isn't prepared to answer questions for which she has no answers.

A shiver traces her spine as she realizes she's nude. She goes to the closet, puts on the extra robe. Then she ducks in the bathroom, pulls a band from her makeup case, and ties her hair in a tall bun atop her head.

She goes to the Victorian desk, grabs her purse. A tiny, sequined bag just large enough to hold a thin, rectangular pocketbook. The bag contains very little of importance and she dumps its contents onto the desk. Lipstick, a pack of Kleenex, a few coins. She replaces them with her pocketbook, the Glock and the lockpicks. Obviously, the first agent considered picking the lock to her room, probably while she slept. She wonders why he changed his plan. Shudders at the thought of him finding her asleep.

Down the hall, the elevator chimes. The police have arrived and will be rushing the room in just a second.

Screaming at the top of her lungs, she races into the hall, sprints toward the officers.

She sobs, flies toward them, panicked. They lower their weapons, motion her past, tell her to wait in the lobby. Then, guns drawn, they move toward the room with careful patience.

Rhyme sobs for effect as she enters the elevator and thumbs the button for the second floor...

Available Now

Click or scan below for your copy today!

A Measure of Rhyme, Book II, Ages of Malice

About the Author

 **Lloyd Jeffries** enjoys dark comedies, philosophy, clever turns of phrase, religious studies and thought experiments involving the esoteric and legendary. A decorated veteran of numerous conflicts, he served in the U.S. military and has practiced Emergency, Trauma and Wilderness medicine for more than twenty years. He hides out in Florida with his family and Buck the Wonder Dog.

A PORTION OF MALICE is the first in his award-winning epic series, *AGES OF MALICE*.

Join Lloyd's advanced reader circle, get news, and more at:

www.lloydjeffries.com

 twitter.com/LloydJeffries2

Made in the USA
Las Vegas, NV
11 December 2023

82569266R00203